Billionaire BOSSES

BEHIND THE BOARDROOM DOOR

ANNE McALLISTER
MICHELLE CELMER
AMY ANDREWS

MILLS & BOON

First Published in Great Britain 2016
By Mills & Boon, an imprint of HarperCollins*Publishers*
1 London Bridge Street, London, SE1 9GF

BEHIND THE BOARDROOM DOOR © 2016 Harlequin Books S.A.

Savas' Defiant Mistress © 2009 Barbara Schenck
Much More Than a Mistress © 2011 Michelle Celmer
Innocent 'til Proven Otherwise © 2012 Amy Andrews

ISBN: 978-0-263-91774-1

24-0116

Our policy is to use papers that are natural, renewable and recyclable products and made from wood grown in sustainable forests.
The logging and manufacturing processes conform to the legal environmental regulations of the country of origin.

Printed and bound in Spain
by CPI, Barcelona

SAVAS' DEFIANT
MISTRESS

ANNE McALLISTER

Best-selling two-time RITA® winner (with a further nine finalist titles) **Anne McAllister** has written nearly seventy books for Mills & Boon Modern, Desire, Special Edition and single titles, which means she basically follows the characters no matter where they take her. She loves to travel, but at home she and her husband divide their time between Montana and Iowa. Anne loves to hear from readers. Contact her at: www.annemcallister.com.

CHAPTER ONE

"I WAS thinking little square boxes with silver and rose jelly beans in them." Vangie was saying breathlessly into the phone.

Sebastian, who wasn't listening, had his attention on the computer screen in front of him. His sister had been rabbiting on in his ear for nearly twenty minutes. But truthfully, she hadn't said anything important in the last three weeks.

"You know what I mean, Seb? *Seb?*" Her voice rose impatiently when he didn't reply. "Are you there?"

God help him, yes, he was.

Sebastian Savas managed a perfunctory grunt, but his gaze stayed riveted on the specs for the Blake-Carmody project, and his mind was there, too. He glanced at his watch. He had a meeting with Max Grosvenor in less than ten minutes, and he wanted everything fresh in his mind.

He'd worked his tail off putting together ideas for this project, aware that it would be a terrific coup for Grosvenor Design to get the go-ahead.

And it would be an even bigger coup for him personally to be asked to head up the team. He'd done a lot of the work. Using Max's ideas and his own, Seb had spent the past two months putting together the structural plans and the public space layout for the Blake-Carmody high-rise office and condo building. And last week, while Seb had been in Reno working on another major project, Max had presented it to the owners.

Still he'd had a big hand in it, and if they'd won the project, it made sense that that was what today's meeting was about— Max asking him to run the show.

Seb smiled every time he thought about it.

"Well, I wondered," Vangie was saying, undeterred. "You're very quiet today. So…what do you think, Seb? Rose? Or silver? For the boxes, I mean. Or—" she paused "—maybe boxes are too fussy. Maybe we shouldn't even have jelly beans. They're sort of childish. Maybe we should have mints. What do you think of mints? *Seb?*"

Sebastian jerked his attention back at the impatient sound of his name in his ear. Sighing, he thrust a hand through his hair. "I don't know, Vangie," he said with just the slightest hint of impatience himself.

What's more, he didn't care.

This was Vangie's wedding, not his. She was the one tying the knot. And since he never intended to, he didn't even need to learn from the experience.

"Why not have both?" he said because he had to say something.

"Could we?" She sounded as if he'd suggested having the Seattle symphony play the music for the reception.

"Have what you want, Vange," he said. "It's your wedding."

It was, to Seb's mind, fast becoming The Wedding That Ate Seattle. But what the heck, if it made his sister happy—for the moment at least—who was he to argue with her?

"I know it's my wedding. But you're paying for it," Vangie said conscientiously.

"No problem."

Where family was concerned, Seb was the one they all turned to, the one who offered advice, a shoulder to lean on and a checkbook that paid the bills. It had been that way ever since he'd got his first architectural job.

"I suppose I could ask Daddy…"

Seb stifled a snort. Philip Savas begat children. He didn't raise them. And while the old man had plenty of money—the family's considerable hotel fortune residing in his pockets—he didn't part with it easily unless it was something he wanted. Like another wife.

"Don't go there, Vange," Sebastian advised his sister. "You know there's no point."

"I suppose not," she said glumly with the voice of experience. "I just wish…it would be so perfect if he'd remember to come and walk me down the aisle."

"Yeah." Good luck, Seb thought grimly. How many times did Vangie have to be disappointed before she learned?

Seb could pay the bills and offer support and see that his siblings had everything they needed, but he couldn't guarantee their father would ever act like one. In all of Sebastian's thirty-three years, Philip Savas never had.

"Has he called you?" Vangie asked hopefully.

"No."

Unless Philip wanted to foist a problem off on his responsible eldest son, he couldn't be bothered to make contact. And Seb was done trying to make overtures to him. Now he glanced at his watch again. "Listen, Vange, I've gotta run. I have a meeting—"

"Of course. I'm sorry. I shouldn't bother you. I'm sorry to bother you all the time, Seb. It's just you're the only one here and…" Her voice trailed off.

"Yes, well, you should have got married in New York. You'd have had all the help you could use then." When Seb had come out to Seattle after university, it had been expressly to put a continent between himself and his multitude of ex-stepmothers and half siblings. He didn't mind supporting them, but he didn't want them interfering in his life. Or his work. Which was the same thing.

His bad luck, he supposed, that when Vangie graduated from Princeton and got engaged, her fiancé, Garrett's, family was from Seattle, and they decided to move here.

"It will be wonderful. I can see you all the time. Like a real family!" Vangie had said at the time. She'd been over the moon at the prospect. "Isn't that great?"

Seb, who had given up any notion of "real family" by the time he'd reached puberty, hadn't seen anything to rejoice in. But he'd managed to cross his fingers and give her a hug. "Terrific."

In fact, it hadn't been as bad as he'd feared.

Vangie and Garrett both worked for a law firm in Bellevue. They spent time with each other and with their own set of friends and he rarely saw them.

He pleaded work whenever they did invite him to one of their parties. It wasn't an excuse; it was the truth.

Vangie said he worked far too hard, and Garrett thought his almost-brother-in-law was boring because he did nothing except design buildings.

That was fine with Seb. They had their lives and he had his.

But as the date for the wedding approached, things had changed. Wedding plans made months ago now required constant comment and consultation.

Vangie had begun calling him daily. Then twice a day. Recently it had increased to four and five times a day.

Sebastian wanted to say, "Get a grip. You're a big girl. You can make decisions on your own."

But he didn't. He knew Vangie. Loved her. And he understood all too well that her wedding plans were symbolic of her biggest fantasy.

She'd always dreamed of being part of a "real" family, of having that built-in support. It was what "normal" families did, she told him.

And Vangie, more than any of them, had always desperately wanted them to be "normal."

Seb was frankly surprised she even knew what "normal" was.

"Of course I know what a normal family is," she'd told him sharply when he'd said so. "And so do you."

He'd snorted at that. But she'd just come back with, "You have to try, Seb. And trust that it can happen."

There was no reply to that. If Vangie wanted to live in a Disney movie, he couldn't stop her. But whenever she called, he let her talk. At least, he did when he didn't have to get to a meeting sooner rather than later.

But Max had left a message on his mobile phone last night while Seb had been flying back from Reno to say they needed to talk this afternoon.

Which meant, Seb thought with a quickening excitement that owed nothing to jelly beans or mints or the color rose, that they'd won the Blake-Carmody bid.

He and Max had spent both many long hours working up a design for the forty-eight-story downtown building that would be a "complete village" with shops, office and living space. And even though Max had been the one who'd taken the main port-folio to meet with Steve Carmody and Roger Blake, Seb knew it was unspoken that he was being groomed for the head archi-tect's position. So he had kept on improving, revising, detailing the general plans.

"I just don't know," Vangie said now. "There are so many things to think about. The napkins, for instance—"

"Yeah, well, we can talk about it later," Seb said with all the diplomacy he could muster. "I really have to go, Vange. If I hear from Dad, I'll let you know," he added. "But he's more likely to ring you than me."

They both knew he wasn't likely to ring either of them. When last heard from, Philip was about to marry his latest personal assistant. She'd be the fourth who'd had her eye on his wealth. At least his old man knew how to do a decent pre-nup at this point.

"I hope so," Vangie said fervently. "Or maybe he's been in touch with one of the girls."

"What girls?" Philip was taking them on in pairs now?

Would it be harems next? Seb wondered, as he shut his portfolio and stood up.

"The girls," Vangie repeated impatiently, as if he should know which ones. "*Our* sisters," she clarified when he still didn't respond. "Our *family*. They'll be here this afternoon," she added, and all at once her voice sounded bright.

"Here? Why? The wedding's not till next month, isn't it?" God knew he was busy, but Seb didn't think he'd lost the whole month of May.

"They're coming to help." Seb could hear the smile of satisfaction in Vangie's voice. "It's what families do."

"For a month? All of them?" He could even remember how the hell many there were. But it didn't sound like anything to rejoice about.

"Just the triplets. And Jenna."

All the ones over eighteen, then. Dear God. How was Vangie going to put up with them all for a month? That ought to make her think twice about how much she wanted all of them to be a "normal" family.

"Well, good luck to you. So you want me to arrange for them to be picked up at the airport?"

"No. Don't worry. They're coming from all over and at different times, so I told them they should just take taxis."

"Did you? Good for you." Seb smiled and flexed his shoulders, glad Vangie was showing a bit of spunk, and grateful that she hadn't stuck him with all the logistics of shifting their sisters around as well as having to listen to the jelly bean monologues. He picked up his portfolio. "Where are they staying?"

He supposed he ought to know that. He might even drop by and take them to dinner on Sunday—in the interests of "normal" family relations.

"With you, of course."

The portfolio slammed down on his desk. "*What!*"

"Well, where else would they stay?" Vangie said reasonably.

"All those rooms just sitting there! You must have four bedrooms at least in that penthouse of yours! I have a studio. No bedroom at all. Three hundred square feet. Besides, where else would they stay but with their big brother? We're a family, aren't we?"

Seb was sputtering.

"It won't be a problem," Vangie went on blithely. "Don't worry about it, Seb. You'll hardly know they're there."

The hell he wouldn't! Visions of panty hose drying, fingernail polish spilling, clutter everywhere hit him between the eyes. "Vangie! They can't—"

"Of course they can take care of themselves," she said, completely misunderstanding. "Don't fret. Go to your meeting. I'll talk to you later. And be sure to let me know if you hear from Dad."

And, bang, she was gone before he could say a word.

Seb glared at the phone, then slammed it down furiously. Blast Evangeline and her "normal" family fantasy anyway!

There was no way on earth he was going to share his penthouse with four of his sisters for an entire month! They'd drive him insane. Three twenty-year-olds and an eighteen-year-old—giggly, silly girl who, he knew from experience, would take over every square inch. He'd never get any work done. He'd never have a moment's peace.

He didn't mind footing the bills, but he was *not* having his space invaded! It didn't bear thinking about.

He gave a quick shuddering shake of his head, then snatched up his portfolio and stalked off to Max's office, where he would at least find an oasis of calm, of focus, of sanity, of engaging discussion with Max.

Gladys, Max's secretary, looked up from her computer and gave him a bright smile. "He's not here."

"Not here?" Seb frowned. "Why not? We've got a meeting."

Besides, it didn't make sense. Max was always here, except when he was on a site. And he never double scheduled. He was far too organized.

"I'm sure he'll be along. He's probably stuck in traffic."
Gladys gave Seb a bright smile. "I'll ring you when he gets here
if you'd like."

"Is he…on-site?"

"No. He's on his way back from the harbor."

"The harbor?" Seb frowned. He didn't remember Max having
a project down there, and he knew Max's projects.

Max was—had been ever since Seb had come to work for
him—his role model. Max Grosvenor was utterly reliable. A
paragon, in fact. Hardworking, focused, brilliant. Max was the
man he wanted to become, the father figure he'd never had.

Philip couldn't be bothered to turn up when he said he would,
but if Max wasn't here at—Seb glanced at his watch again—five
past three in the afternoon when he was the one who'd scheduled
the meeting, something was wrong.

"Is he all right?"

"Couldn't be better, I'd say." Gladys said cheerfully. Though
only ten or so years older than her boss, she doted on him like a
mother hen—not that Max ever noticed. "He's just been on a bit
of an outing."

Seb's brows drew down. *Outing?* Max? Max didn't do "outings."
But maybe Gladys had said "meeting" and he had misheard.

"I'm sure he'll be along shortly." Even as she spoke, the phone
on her desk rang. Raising a finger as if to say, wait, Gladys
answered it. "Mr. Grosvenor's office." The smile that creased her
face told Seb who it was.

He tapped his portfolio against his palm, watching as Gladys
listened, then nodded. "Indeed he is," she said into the phone.
"Right here waiting. Oh—" she glanced at Seb's way, then smiled
"—I'm sure he'll live. Yes, Max. Yes, I'll tell him."

She hung up and, still smiling, looked up at Seb. "He's just come
into the parking garage. He says to go right in and wait if you want."

"Right. I'll do that." He must have misunderstood. She must
have said "meeting." Max must have had a new project come up.

"Thanks, Gladys." With a smile, Seb stepped past her and opened the door to Max's office.

It was always a jolt to walk into Max's office on a clear sunny day. Even when you were expecting it, the view was breathtaking.

Seb's own office, nearly as big and airy as Max's own, looked out to the north. He could sit at his desk and see up the coast. And if he shifted in his chair, he could watch the ferry crossing the water.

But Max could see paradise. Across the water, the Cascades spiked their way along the peninsula. A bevy of sailboats skimmed over the sound. And to the south the majesty of Mount Rainier loomed, looking almost close enough to touch.

The first time Seb had seen the view from Max's windows, he'd stopped dead, his eyes widening. "I don't see how you get any work done."

Max had shrugged. "You get used to it."

But now he stood and stared at the grandeur of Rainier for a long moment, Seb wasn't sure he ever would. And the memory of his first glimpse reminded him that when he'd first come out to the Pacific Northwest, he'd vowed to climb Rainier.

He never had. There hadn't been time.

Work had always been a bigger, more tempting mountain to climb. And there had always been more peaks, bigger peaks, tougher ones. And he'd relished the challenge, determined to prove himself. To make a name for himself. And make his own fortune to go with it.

The family had a fortune, of course. The hotel empire that Philip Savas oversaw guaranteed that. In another family, that fortune and those connections could have smoothed the way for a budding young architect. It hadn't. In fact, Seb doubted his father even knew what he did for a living, much less had ever wanted to encourage him.

Philip didn't even care. He owned buildings, he didn't create them. And he had no interest in Seb's desire to.

The one time they'd discussed his future, when Seb was eighteen, Philip had said, "We can start you out in Hong Kong, I think."

And Seb had said, "What?"

"You need to get a taste of the whole business from the ground up, for when you come to work for us," Philip had said, as if it were a given.

When Seb had said, "I'm not," Philip had raised his brows, given his eldest son a long disapproving stare, then turned on his heel and walked out of the room.

End of discussion.

Seb would have said it was the end of the relationship, except they hadn't had much of one before that, either.

At least Philip's indifference had provided a wonderful incentive to do things his way, to make his own mark.

And standing here, in Max's office, feeling the cool spare elegance of his surroundings and admiring his spectacular view—which also happened to include over thirty buildings Grosvenor Design had been responsible for creating—Seb felt that surge of determination all over again.

He opened his portfolio and began laying out further sketches he'd done so they could jump right into things, when the door burst open and Max strode in.

Seb glanced up—and stared. "Max?"

Well, it was Max, of course. There was no mistaking the tall, lithe, angular body, the lean hawkish face, salt-and-pepper hair and the broad grin.

But where was the tie? The long-sleeved button-down oxford cloth shirt? The shiny black dress shoes? Max's uniform, in other words. The clothes Seb had seen Max Grosvenor wear every workday for the past ten years.

"You'll be more professional if you look professional," Max had said to Seb when he'd hired him. "Remember that."

Seb had. He was wearing his own version of the Grosvenor

Design uniform—navy slacks, long-sleeved grey-and-white pin-stripe shirt and toning tie—right now.

Max, on the other hand, was clad in a pair of faded jeans and a dark-blue windbreaker over a much-washed formerly gold sweatshirt with University of Washington on its chest in flaky white letters. His hair was windblown and his sockless feet were stuffed into a pair of rather new deck shoes. "Sorry I'm late," he said briskly. "Went sailing."

Seb had to consciously shut his mouth. Sailing? *Max?*

Well, of course thousands of people did—even on weekdays—but not Max Grosvenor. Max Grosvenor was a workaholic.

Now Max shucked his jacket and took a large design portfolio out of the cabinet. "I would have gone home to change, but I'd told you three. So—" he shrugged cheerfully "—here I am."

Seb was still nonplussed. A little confused. He could understand it if it had been a meeting. Even a meeting on a sailboat. And admittedly stranger things had happened. But he didn't ask.

And Max was all business now, despite his apparel. He opened the portfolio to their design for Blake-Carmody. "We got it," he said with a grin and a thumbs-up.

And Seb grinned, too, delighted that all their hard work had paid off.

"We went over it all while you were down in Reno," Max went on. "I brought along a couple of project people as well. Hope you don't mind, but time was of the essence."

"No. Not at all." Seb understood completely. While he had done considerable work on the project, Max was the president of the company.

And no one else could have gone to Reno in Seb's place. That medical complex project there was all his.

Max nodded. "Of course not. Good man." Still smiling, he dropped into the leather chair behind his desk and folded his arms behind his head, then nodded at the other chair for Seb to take a seat, too. "I was sure you'd understand. And I told Carmody a lot of the work was yours."

Seb settled into the other chair. "Thanks." He was glad to hear it, particularly because then Carmody would understand that Max wasn't solely responsible for the work and he wouldn't feel as if they were being fobbed off on an inferior when Seb took over.

Max dropped his arms and leaned forward, resting his forearms on his thighs as he locked his fingers together and said earnestly. "So I hope you won't feel cut out if I see this through myself."

Seb blinked.

"I know we'd talked about you taking it over," Max went on. "But you've been in Reno a lot. And you've still got a finger or two in Fogerty's project and the Hayes Building. Right?"

"Right." But that didn't mean he wouldn't be willing to work even harder to do Carmody-Blake.

Max nodded happily. "Exactly. And you'll have more time to run the bid on the school in Kent this way," he went on. "They were really impressed with your ideas."

Seb made an inarticulate sound at that point, hoping it sounded as if he was pleased with the compliment. It *was* a compliment. It was just—he'd really wanted the Blake-Carmody project.

He had no right to be disappointed, really. Logically he knew that. Yes, he'd been invited to share his ideas for the project, and yes, Max had taken them seriously. They'd even discussed the possibility of him taking over as head architect on the job. But while it had been unspoken, it had never been official.

And he could understand why Max would enjoy overseeing a plum job like this one. It was just that over the past couple of months Max had been talking about "stepping back" and "taking it easy."

And hell, he'd just come in from *sailing,* hadn't he?

"I knew you'd understand. Rodriguez is going to boss the office space side of it. Chang's doing the shops," Max went on.

That made sense. Frank Rodriguez and Danny Chang had also contributed to the portfolio with ideas that reflected their specialities. Seb nodded.

"And I've asked Neely to take charge of the living spaces."

"*What!*" Seb sat up straight. "*Neely Robson?*"

All of a sudden it didn't sound simply like Max keeping the plum job for himself. It sounded like—

Seb shook his head as if he were hearing things. "You can't be serious."

At his tone, Max stiffened abruptly. "I'm perfectly serious."

"But she's not experienced enough! She's been here, what? Six months? She's green."

"She's won awards. She got the Balthus Grant."

"She draws pretty pictures." All warm cozy stuff. She might as well be an interior decorator, Seb thought.

He'd only worked with Neely Robson one time—and that had been merely at the discussion stage in the first month she was there. It hadn't gone well. He'd thought her ideas were fluff and had said so. She had been of the opinion that he only wanted to build skyscrapers that were phallic symbols and had said that.

To say they hadn't hit it off was an understatement.

"The clients like her."

You like her, Seb wanted to say. *You like her curve body and her long honey colored hair and her luscious lips that curved into dimpled smiles.* But fortunately he clamped his teeth together before any of those words got past his lips.

"She's good at what she does," Max said mildly. He leaned back in his chair and steepled his fingers in front of his mouth, a smile playing on his lips as if he were thinking about something very different than designing buildings.

And what exactly has she been doing with you? Seb wondered acidly. But he had the brains not to say that, either.

Still he had to say something. It wasn't as if he hadn't noticed Neely Robson's appeal to his boss over the past couple of months. She was an attractive woman. No question about it. A man would have to be dead not to notice.

But the firm was big enough that she hadn't really come to Max's notice until she'd won that damned award in February. Then he'd invited her to work on the hospital addition.

Since then Max had paid more and more attention to her.

Seb couldn't count the number of times he had noticed her coming out of Max's office or the multitude of times in the last couple of months he'd heard her name on Max's lips. And he'd certainly seen Max's gaze linger on her in staff meetings.

He hadn't worried. Max wasn't Philip Savas, he'd told himself. Max was single-minded, determined, professional. If anyone was the poster boy for workaholics, it was Max.

There was no way Max Grosvenor was going to let himself be seduced by a pretty face. He was fifty-two years old, and no woman had trapped him into matrimony yet, had she?

Seb supposed there was always a first time. And Max could be ripe for a midlife crisis. He'd gone *sailing,* for crying out loud!

"I just mean she doesn't have a lot of expertise with condos as a part of multi-use buildings and—"

"You don't have to worry about her expertise. I'll be working closely with her," Max said now. "And if she's green, well, she'll learn. I think I can help her out." He raised a brow. "Don't you agree?"

Seb gritted his teeth so hard his jaw ached. "Of course," he said stiffly.

Max grinned cheerfully. "She's got a lot on the ball, Seb. Very creative. You should get to know her."

"I know her," Seb said shortly.

Max laughed. "Not the way I do. Come sailing with us next time, why don't you?"

"Next— You went sailing with—" He didn't finish the sentence so appalled—and disbelieving—was he at the prospect. Max and Neely Robson had spent the afternoon sailing? Dear

God, yes, he must be having a midlife crisis. That was the sort of thing Philip Savas would do, but not Max Grosvenor.

"She's not a bad little sailor." Max grinned.

"Isn't she?" Seb hauled himself to his feet and picked up his portfolio. "I'm glad to hear it," he said flatly. "But I still think you're making a mistake."

Max's smile faded. He stared out the window at Mount Rainier for a long moment, though whether he saw it Seb had no idea. Finally he brought his eyes back to meet Seb's.

"It wouldn't be the first mistake I've ever made," he said quietly. "I appreciate your concern." He met Seb's gaze squarely. "But I don't think I'm making a mistake this time."

Their gazes locked. Seb wanted to tell him how wrong he was, how he'd seen it over and over and over from his own father.

He gave his head a little shake but then just nodded. "I'll just be getting back to work then, if you don't have anything else to discuss."

Max gave a wave of his hand. "No, nothing else. I just wanted to let you know about Blake-Carmody in person. Seemed tactless to leave it on your phone. And it's no disrespect to you, Seb, my taking this on. It's just—this is one I want to do."

With Neely Robson.

He didn't say it. He didn't have to.

"Of course," Seb said tightly.

He had the door open when Max's voice came from behind him. "You should take a little time off yourself, Seb. All work and no play—you know the saying."

Seb did. But he didn't want to hear it from Max Grosvenor. He shut the door wordlessly as he went out.

"There now, isn't it lovely?" Gladys looked up and sighed happily.

Seb frowned. "Sorry?"

"Max," she said with a sappy maternal smile. "It's lovely he's finally getting a life."

* * *

If Max was finally getting a life, Seb didn't envy him.

Life—the "relationship" sort—as Seb knew from a lifetime of experience, was messy, unpredictable and fraught with chaos. That Max, the most focused of men, should be tempted by it, simply meant he was deep in a midlife crisis.

And with Neely Robson—a woman half his age, for God's sake! It was a disaster waiting to happen.

Max had always had what Seb thought was an ideal life. Satisfaction through work, through creating magnificent buildings, a life of order, clear and controllable. Not messy, unpredictable and tangled.

If Max was getting a life, Seb pitied him. He was doomed to disappointment.

Seb shook his head, then shoved away the thought of Max's idiocy and tried to concentrate on the Kent school project.

It was after six. He could have quit. But why? There was work to do here and certainly no reason to go home.

Talking about messy and uncontrollable, by now he was sure his penthouse condo would be teeming with half sisters. There would be panty hose in all the bathrooms, cell phones ringing at every minute, toast crumbs and marmalade on the countertops, half-eaten yogurts in the refrigerator and bridal magazines littering every horizontal surface.

Even worse they would all be talking at once—about the wedding, about Evangeline and Garrett, about how perfect it all was, about how they were going to live happily ever after, about how everyone should live happily ever after. And then they would begin comparing their own love lives.

And speculating about his.

Ever since they'd been in junior high school his sisters had been pestering him about the women in his life. Who was he dating? Was it serious? Did he love her?

Love! Titter, titter. Giggle, giggle.

It made Seb's jaw muscles twitch every time he thought about it.

He didn't have a love life. Didn't intend to have one. Not one like they meant, anyway—not that he could get it through their romantic fluffy-brained heads.

He had needs, of course. Hormones. Testosterone, for God's sake. He was a red-blooded male with all the right instincts. But that didn't mean marriage or happily ever after.

And it certainly didn't mean he believed in fairy tales.

On the contrary, he believed in giving his hormones exactly what they wanted in a sane, sensible fashion. And he had done so over the years through a series of discreet liaisons with women who wanted exactly what he did. No more, no less.

And if his last discreet liaison had ended a few months ago because the pretty blonde software engineer with whom he'd been satisfying those hormones had taken a job in Philly just after the first of the year, that simply meant he needed to find another woman to take her place.

It didn't mean he had to get a love life or get serious.

But his sisters thought he should. And they were never hesitant to say so.

And since Evangeline had foisted them on him for the next month—and he knew he wasn't going to be able to turf them out—they would feel entitled to express their opinions. At length.

God help him.

He needed a bolt hole, a bachelor pad. A tiny hideaway of his own—just for the month—where none of them could find him. He could appear and be big brotherly when the mood suited him, but generally he could play "least in sight."

He toyed with the idea of moving into the empty studio apartment in the building he'd bought two years ago. It was tempting. But it was only three blocks from where he lived. And Vangie knew about it. They'd all know about it if he went there.

It wouldn't be a bolt hole for long.

He'd like to stick them there, but that would never work. One room plus one bathroom and the four of them? It didn't bear thinking about.

Maybe he could buy a futon for his office and sleep here. A few months ago Max would have applauded the idea. Now, in his new "isn't playing hooky wonderful?" mode, he would have a fit.

But damn it, Seb wasn't having a midlife crisis. And if he wanted to work 24-7 why shouldn't he? At least here at the office, he could still focus.

Deliberately Seb shoved the thought away and focused once more on the Kent school designs. Almost everyone else had gone home now. It was close to six-thirty. Max had breezed out half an hour ago.

He'd stuck his head in on his way to the elevator. "Still here? It's Friday night. No hot date?"

Seb just looked at him.

Max grinned and shook his head. "Learn from me, man. There's more to life than work."

Like hot dates with a woman half his age? Seb sucked in his cheeks. "I have some work to do for Reno, then I want to think a bit about the Kent project."

Max gave him a wry look that said he recognized the guilt being offered him, but then, pure Max, he shrugged it off. "Up to you." He started away, then returned to stick his head round the door again. "We're going sailing on Sunday. Come along?"

Oh, yes. That was exactly how Seb wanted to spend his Sunday—watching Max make a fool of himself over Neely Robson—and watching Neely Robson gloat. Seb gritted his teeth. "Thanks, but I'm busy. My sisters are in town."

If he was stuck with them, the least they could do was be useful.

Max nodded. "Right. You have a big family. I always forget that."

Seb wished he could.

"Lucky you. I'm glad you'll have some distraction," Max said. "You won't make the same mistake I did."

No, he wouldn't! There was no way on earth Seb was going to go all ga-ga over an unsuitable conniving woman. "Have fun," Seb said drily.

Max flashed him a grin. "I intend to."

And he sauntered away. Whistling, for God's sake!

Seb thrust his fingers through his hair and kneaded his scalp and tried to focus again.

He tried for another half an hour after Max left. But his stomach began growling, and he needed to get something to eat. At least he didn't have to go home for that. He could get takeaway, bring it back here, stay and work until it was time to go to bed.

Like the triplets *ever* went to bed.

He shoved back his chair and grabbed his suit jacket off the back of his chair, then stepped out into the common room.

There was only one other light still on. Four doors down in Frank Rodriguez's office. Frank, who was doing the Blake-Carmody office space, would be happily burning the midnight oil. And as he walked toward the office on his way to the elevator, he could hear Frank and Danny Chang in deep conversation.

Seb felt a prick of envy, then tamped it down. He didn't want Frank's job. Or Danny's. And it wasn't their fault he hadn't got the job he did want.

"Can't help you," he heard Danny Chang say. "Wish I could." He stepped out of Frank's office, then paused in the doorway and turned back. "I thought you had it sold."

"So did I," Frank's tone was glum. "Cath is going to freak when she finds out the deal fell through. We want this house. How the hell am I going to put the down payment on the house if I don't have it?"

Danny shrugged. "If I hear of anyone who wants one, I'll send 'em your way." He turned to go, then stopped and did a double take at the sight of Seb. "Hey, wanna buy a houseboat?"

Houseboat?

Did he want to buy a...*houseboat?*

Any other day Seb would have laughed. Today as the words registered, he found himself saying cautiously, curiously, "What sort of houseboat? Where?"

Danny and Frank exchanged glances.

Then Frank got up from behind his desk and came to the door of his office. "Not big. You probably wouldn't want it. Two bedrooms. One bath. Pretty small really. On the east side of Lake Union. Bought it after I'd been here a year. I love it. But Cath—we're getting married—and Cath doesn't. She says she's not into *Sleepless in Seattle*."

Seb had no idea what he meant. He wasn't into chick flicks. But a houseboat... "Tell me more."

Frank's eyes widened in surprise. And then, apparently deciding Seb was serious, he ticked off its virtues. "It's perfectly functional. Fifty-odd years old, but it's been well cared for. Pretty quiet place. Right at the end of the dock. Great views, obviously. My tenant was going to buy it, but the financing fell through. I just got the call."

"Tenant?"

Frank shrugged. "I rent out the other bedroom. Helps with the payments. But nothing's going to help with this," he said grimly. "We're not going to have the money for the down payment and we're going to lose the house."

And tenants could be moved. "How much do you want for it?"

Frank blinked. "Seriously?"

"I'm asking, aren't I?"

"Oh! Well, um..." Frank looked a bit dazed as he spit out a figure.

Not a bargain. But what price did you put on peace? Sanity. A lack of clutter and giggles and panty hose? Besides, he could always sell it.

Seb nodded. "I'll write you a check."

CHAPTER TWO

IT WAS perfect.

Seb could see the houseboat as he came down the hill. It sat at the end of the dock. Other houseboats were moored on either side, but his was right at the end—two stories high of weathered grey wood and very crisp white trim, it looked snug and welcoming, just as Frank had said it would be.

As it was backlit by the setting sun, Seb couldn't see all the details. But from what he could discern, it was the bolt hole of his dreams.

He couldn't have made a better decision, Seb thought as he parked his car, then grabbed two of the duffel bags he'd packed and headed down the dock. He felt alive somehow, energized, actually smiling in anticipation.

Sure, it was a lot of money to pay for a month's bolt hole. But what else was he doing with his money besides footing the wedding bill for his sister, paying college tuition for all of his sundry siblings and providing tummy tucks and face-lifts for his father's ex-wives?

Besides, Frank had assured him, a houseboat was an eminently resalable item. His urgency to sell only had to do with his impending marriage and baby. He was sure his tenant would buy it whenever Seb wanted out, presuming the financing worked out then. And if not, there would be plenty of other interested buyers.

So, when—*if*—Seb wanted to sell, he might even make a profit.

But it wasn't the profit that interested him now. It was the peace and quiet. The solitude.

If he'd needed any convincing that he'd done the right thing by his impulse down payment and promise to get the financing tomorrow, walking into his penthouse tonight had done it.

The panty hose were already everywhere. So were the crumbs and the sticky marmalade plates. The cell phones shrilled and his sisters giggled. There they were talking—all of them at once—and throwing their arms around him, hugging him, getting him sticky, too.

He had been prepared for that.

But he'd forgotten the music, the television, the shouting over each other to be heard. He'd forgotten the smells. The sickly sweet shampoos, conditioners, hair sprays, gels, mousses, not to mention umpteen kinds of perfume actually supposed to have fragrances.

His whole apartment had smelled like a bordello.

If he'd thought for one second he'd been wrong to jump at Frank's houseboat, those few minutes had convinced him he'd done exactly the right thing. He could hardly wait to escape.

His sisters had been appalled when he'd slipped out of their embraces and headed for his bedroom to pack.

"You've got a trip? Now?"

"Where are you going?"

"When are you coming back?"

They'd followed him into his room. He could see makeup bottles scattered on the countertop through the door to his bathroom.

"I'm just giving you some space," he said. "And trusting you with mine," he added with his best severe older brother glower. It went from them to the open door of the bathroom where there were also wet towels on the floor. Then it went back to them. They smiled contritely.

"Keep things clean," he said. "Pick up after yourselves. I've got work to do and I need to focus."

"We won't be any trouble," they vowed in unison, heads bobbing.

Seb had smiled at that. Then he'd gathered up the few things he was sure he would need or that he really didn't want them to break—like his grandfather's old violin—and patted their heads.

"I'll be back and take you to dinner on Sunday," he promised.

As he left, Jenna borrowed money to pay the pizza delivery man.

"Sure you won't change your mind, Seb?" she'd said, forgetting to give him the change.

Seb had shaken his head. "No."

But now, as his stomach rumbled on his way down the dock, he wished he'd at least thought to snatch one of the pizzas.

No matter. He'd grab something after he settled in—and dealt with Frank's tenant. A guy who rented a room on a houseboat ought to be delighted to be offered a studio apartment rent free. And maybe by the time Seb was ready to sell, he'd have his finances in order and could get a loan.

Seb found himself whistling just like Max as he stepped aboard his houseboat and turned the key in the front door lock.

"Home sweet home," he murmured, and pushed open the door and stepped into a small foyer with a staircase leading up to the second floor on one side and bookshelves and a door on the other. Straight ahead, down a hallway he glimpsed the setting sun through the window. It drew him on. So did the music he heard.

Unlike the cacophonous racket he'd left behind with his sisters, this was a Bach minuet, light and lilting, rhythmic, orderly.

The lingering tension in Seb's shoulders eased. He'd wondered how he would convince Frank's tenant that he needed to move. The Bach reassured him. A tenant who played Bach would see the logic and good sense in Seb's offer to put him up rent free.

He made his way down the hallway and into an open living area and stopped stock-still at the sight of a rabbit hutch—complete with two rabbits—on a window seat. There was an aquarium on the bar that separated the kitchen area from the rest of the room. There were three half-grown kittens wrestling on the floor and one attempting to clamber up a cardboard box that had been strategically placed to keep it inside while the door to the deck beyond could be left open.

But none of it was quite as astonishing as the sight of a pair of long bare very female legs halfway up a ladder out on the deck.

"You're back?" the female said, apparently having heard Seb shutting the door. "This is way too soon. Go away and come back in half an hour."

Seb didn't move. Just stared at the legs. Felt wholly masculine interest at the same time he felt stirrings of unease.

His tenant was *female?*

And Frank hadn't bothered to mention it?

Well, maybe to Frank it hadn't made any difference. He had been spending his time at his fiancée's afterall.

"Cody?" The woman's voice said when Seb didn't reply. "Did you hear me? I said, Go away."

Seb cleared his throat. "I'm not Cody," he said, grateful his voice didn't croak as his eyes were still glued to those amazing legs.

"Not…?" Bare feet moved down the ladder one rung at a time until the woman could hook her arm around one side of the ladder and swung her head down so that she could see him.

Seb stared, transfixed.

Neely Robson?

No. Impossible.

Seb shut his eyes. It was just that his irritating meeting with Max had had the effect of imprinting her on his brain.

When he opened them again he would, of course, see some other stunningly gorgeous woman with dark honey-colored hair and legs a mile long.

He opened them again.

It was Neely Robson.

They stared at each other.

And then, almost in slow motion, she straightened up again

so he could no longer see her face—only her legs—and for an instant he could tell himself that he'd imagined it.

Then slowly those amazing legs descended the ladder and she came to stare in the open doorway at him, the paintbrush in one hand as she swiped her hair away from her face with the other.

"Mr. Savas," she said politely in that slightly husky oh-so-provocative voice.

Did she call Max "Mr. Grosvenor"? Seb wondered acidly.

"Ms. Robson," he replied curtly, keeping his gaze resolutely away from her long bare legs, though seeing her blowsy and barely buttoned above the waist wasn't entirely settling.

"I'm sorry. I wasn't expecting—I thought you were Cody with Harm." There was a flush across her cheeks and she suddenly looked confused.

Seb shook his head, not sure what she was talking about and feeling confused himself.

"My dog. Harmony. That's his name. Well, not really. But it sounds better. His name is Harm. As in, 'he does more harm than good.'" Her words tumbled out quickly. "The boy down the dock took him for a walk. I thought you were them coming back and I'm not done painting yet."

Seb had never heard Neely Robson babble before and he would have found it entertaining under other circumstances. Now he raised a brow and she stopped abruptly.

"Never mind," she said. "You're looking for Frank."

"No."

She blinked. "No?" A pause. "Then…why are you—?" She looked him in the eyes, then her gaze traveled down and he saw when it lit on his bags. Her frown deepened.

Damn, he wished he could enjoy this more. Wished he had been prepared. Wished he were a lot less shocked than she was by the turn of events.

No matter. What was done was done. And Neely Robson was on her way out.

"Sorry to disappoint you, Ms. Robson," he drawled. "I've already seen Frank. Now I'm moving in."

"*What?*" The color drained from her face. Her tone was outraged.

Seb did enjoy that. He smiled thinly. "If you're the 'tenant,' Ms. Robson, you have a new landlord. Me."

She was hearing things.

Neely used to tell her mother that would happen.

"I'll go deaf if you keep playing that music so loud," she used to say all the time she was growing up with hard rock at a hundred decibels blaring in her ears while her mother made jewelry out of old seeds and twigs.

She was probably the only child in the history of the world who had a parent more likely to shatter her eardrums than to wait for Neely to do it herself.

Lara—her mother had never wanted to be called Mom or Mother. "Do I look like somebody's mother?" she would challenge anyone who dared—had always laughed at her.

But apparently, Neely thought now, staring in dismay at the man in her living room, she had been right.

It was appalling enough to have God's gift to long-sleeved dress shirts, Sebastian Savas, standing in her living room looking down his nose at her, but to think she heard him say he was moving in and that he was her landlord. Well, that simply didn't bear contemplating.

"I beg your pardon," she said, enunciating clearly so that he would, too, and she could figure out what he really said. "What did you say?"

"I bought the houseboat."

Neely felt her knees wobble. She braced a hand on the doorjamb to make sure she didn't topple right over.

"No."

"Oh, yes." And he bared his teeth in what she supposed was

intended to be smile. Or a smirk. "*This* houseboat," he clarified, just in case she thought he meant another one. "I'm moving in."

There was no consolation at all in discovering her hearing was just fine. Neely stared at him, aghast, disbelieving even in the face of evidence, then shook her head because it couldn't be true. "You're mistaken. *I'm* buying the houseboat. It's *mine*."

"Sadly…for you—" Sebastian stressed these last two words, because it was, quite apparently, not sad for him at all "—it's not. Not yours, I mean. Frank sold it to me a couple of hours ago."

"He can't! He wouldn't! We had a deal."

Sebastian shrugged. "It fell through."

She stared at him, feeling as if she'd just caught a lead basketball in the stomach, feeling exactly the way she always had whenever Lara had told her they were moving. Again. And again. And again.

"You don't know that," she said slowly, setting down the paintbrush and wrapping her arms across her chest. But even as she said the words, she felt an awful sense of foreboding.

"Personally, no, I don't," Sebastian said easily. "But Frank knew. He said someone called Gregory called him. A mortgage broker, I assume?"

The sense of foreboding wasn't a sense any longer. It was reality. Neely nodded. "A friend of Frank's." Her fingernails dug into the flesh of her upper arms. "He promised to find a loan for me."

"Yes, well, apparently it didn't work out."

"There are other places to look," Neely insisted urgently. "Other lenders."

Sebastian nodded. There wasn't a flicker of sympathy in his gaze. "No doubt. But Frank couldn't wait. Something about a down payment on a house? A wedding? A baby on the way? He was pretty stressed." Something else Mr. Coldhearted Savas couldn't possibly care about.

And why should he?

It had all worked out perfectly for him.

Now he set his duffel bag on the floor and his garment bag on the sofa, then turned toward the door.

"What are you doing?" she demanded shrilly, clambering over the big cardboard box and coming after him.

"Going back for more of my things. Want to help?" She couldn't see his face, but she had no trouble imagining the smirk on his lips.

He didn't wait for a reply. He left.

And she steamed. She grabbed her mobile phone off the table on the deck and punched in Frank's number.

He wasn't answering.

"Coward," she muttered.

"Are you talking to me?" Sebastian Savas came back in carrying two big boxes and set them on the coffee table. *Her* coffee table!

"That's mine," she snapped.

He followed her gaze to the table in question. "I beg your pardon. Frank said he was leaving some furniture."

"Not that table," Neely said, knowing she was being petty. Not caring.

"Right." He picked up the boxes and set them beside it on the floor. "It is my floor," he said, making her feel about two inches high—until he gave her another one of those smiles and walked out again.

Neely wanted to scream as she watched him return with another big box and deliberately set it beside the others on the floor. *His* floor.

"I can't believe you bought it," Neely muttered, still fuming.

"I can't, either," Sebastian said so cheerfully that she wanted to smack him. "But it's perfect."

That comment actually surprised her. She would never have thought Sebastian Savas would consider a rather battered half-century-old houseboat perfect at all. She'd never seen his place, but Max had said he lived in a penthouse somewhere. What had happened to that?

"I can't imagine why you think so," she said acidly.

"But then, you don't know my circumstances, do you?" he said, hands on his hips as he stood surveying his domain.

"Did you get evicted?" Neely asked sweetly.

He gave her a stare hard enough to make her back up a step. She would need to watch her mouth if he really intended to stick around.

But the next instant she found herself saying, "Or maybe you ran away from home."

"Maybe I did," he agreed.

She blinked. "Yeah, sure. Tell me, why did you do it?"

"Danny asked if I wanted to buy a houseboat."

"And you just thought, 'Sure why not?' and whipped out your checkbook and said, 'I'll take it'?"

"Something like that."

She didn't believe a word of it. "Get real."

He just shrugged.

She hated that about him—that superior cool detachment, that nothing-gets-to-me disdain. At work they called him The Iceman behind his back. They might have called him Iceman to his face for all he'd care.

She watched him open one of the boxes, remove some books and casually begin taking over the bookshelves. She sucked in her breath.

Sebastian turned and glanced her way. "What? No protest? Are the shelves mine, then?"

"As they're built in, it seems they are," Neely said through her teeth. "But as the renter I'm entitled to use some of the space."

"Ah, yes. Your rent."

"It's locked in—the amount," she said firmly, in case he decided to triple it. Or worse. "On my lease."

He didn't reply, just said, "Shall I measure and divide the space, then? To be sure you're getting your fair share?"

"I think we can work it out," Neely muttered, glowering at him as he straightened again, hating the six feet, two inches of hard, lean, dark masculinity taking over her space and scoring her with assessing looks from his piercing green eyes.

They were gorgeous eyes—such a pale green at contrast with his olive complexion and thick black hair. They made his strong, handsome, almost hawkish face even more memorable—and appealing.

"Who's he? He's hot," all the temp girls at the office said when they first caught a glimpse him. "I'll take him for *my* boss."

But once they'd worked for him, they changed their minds.

Sebastian Savas had a reputation for being exacting, demanding and unflappable. Absolutely businesslike. And completely cold.

To a woman, the fools flirted with him, batted their lashes at him, simpered and brought him endless cups of coffee in the hope that he would: speak to them, date them, marry them.

He barely noticed them.

As far as Neely could tell, he only noticed buildings—the taller and pointier the better.

A fact which she had once mentioned to him. Had wondered aloud if his fascination might be a means of overcompensation. But only because he'd dismissed her sketches saying they weren't building doll houses for Barbie!

No, they weren't. They were designing offices for a trendy women's magazine publisher whose signature color was hot pink. But Sebastian hadn't understood that. He'd just dismissed her attempt to get the color in the interior lines of the offices.

She hadn't had anything to do with him since.

Didn't want to.

He was Max's right-hand man and Max thought he was terrific. He'd sung Sebastian's praises often enough. But they were pretty much two of a kind, so why wouldn't Max think so?

"You'll like him when you get to know him," Max had promised.

Neely didn't think so. And she had no wish to get to know him at all.

She had no use for workaholic men. Twenty-six years ago, a

workaholic man hadn't married her pregnant mother. Not that her mother had been, at the time, the marrying kind.

But all of that was irrelevant at the moment.

What was relevant right now was finding out exactly what sort of game Mr. Iceman Savas was playing.

"So you're saying you just whipped out your checkbook to save Frank's bacon?" She pressed.

"I did us both a favor. He wanted to sell. I wanted to buy. We made a deal. Simple."

It wasn't simple at all. Not to her. Neely opened her mouth to argue further with him, but knew there was no point.

Arguing wasn't going to change anything. The loan had fallen through. And to be honest, she'd always known it might. Her bank balance was promising, but not substantial, certainly nowhere close to what Sebastian Savas's was.

She'd only been earning good money since her graduation from university two and a half years ago. And a good chunk of that every month went to repay her student loans and provide a bit more ready cash for her mother. Lara, who had married finally when Neely was twelve, was now a widow with a limited pension and a small jewelry business. She was self-sufficient, but there were no extras—unless Neely provided them.

Buying the houseboat had been her dream. She'd loved it from the moment she'd rented a room from Frank six months ago. And she'd dared to hope, when he decided to give in to Cath's wishes and sell the houseboat, that she would have enough saved to qualify to buy it.

Apparently she hadn't. Yet.

And with time of the essence, Frank had been unable to wait and had taken the easy way out.

The Sebastian Savas way out.

"Speaking of deals, I have a deal for you, Ms. Robson," Sebastian said now. He was standing there holding a stack of books in his hands, regarding her steadily with his green gaze.

"Deal?" Neely said, suddenly hopeful. "You'll sell to me?"

Would he really? After all the bad things she'd thought about him? After the less-than-pleasant things she'd *said* to him?

He shook his head. "No, but I've got a place you can go."

She felt punched in the gut again. So much for pipe dreams.

"There's a vacant studio apartment in a building I own." He looked at her expectantly, as if he thought she would jump for joy at the prospect. "You can have it rent-free for six months."

She shook her head. "I'm not going anywhere."

His brows drew down. "You have to. I'm moving in." He hefted the books to make his point.

"Bully for you."

He stared at her. The green gaze grew icier than ever. "So you're saying you want to share?" His voice was silky with innuendo and hard with challenge.

Neely shrugged with all the indifference she could muster. She hoped it was an Oscarworthy performance.

"Well, I don't want to, but if you're moving in, apparently we are." She jerked her head toward the stairs. "Your bedroom is the one to the right at the top. It's smaller than mine, but it has the better view. Enjoy it."

She didn't wait to hear his reply to that. She didn't want to know. Besides, she needed to get away from him before she threw her paintbrush at him—or something worse.

So she climbed back over the cardboard box, picked up the paintbrush, scaled the ladder and began slapping paint on the wall again. In her head—and heart—she was slapping Sebastian Savas.

If she expected him to turn and leave, she was out of luck.

No big surprise there.

He didn't head up the stairs, either. Instead he set the books on the shelf, then moved the box out of the doorway and came after her out onto the narrow deck and leaned against the railing to stare up at her.

"The kittens will get out," she warned.

He ignored her and the kittens. "I don't want a roommate, Ms. Robson." His tone was flat and uncompromising. She'd heard it before—at the office.

"Neither do I," Neely said in an equally clipped tone. She dipped the paintbrush into the can and continued slapping the wall, not looking down, though she knew exactly where he was behind her.

The paint was a soft grey called "silver linings." When she'd bought it, she'd thought how appropriate it was, having a paint color that would reflect her journey—the hard road and eventual joyous return that had brought her back to her birthplace, to a job she loved and a houseboat she was going to call her own.

Now she thought that if there was a god of paint cans, it was very likely having a good laugh at her expense.

"Then you'll have to move," Sebastian said. "Understand that I'm not tossing you into the street. My offer is very fair, and the apartment is in a good location."

"No doubt. Not interested." Slap, slap.

She heard his breath hiss between his teeth. "Look, Ms. Robson," he began again in what she was sure were determinedly measured tones, "you don't seem to understand. Your staying here is not an option. You can take my offer of a very nice studio apartment for the next six months or you can simply pack up and leave. You can't stay here."

Neely turned her body slightly so she could look down over her shoulder at him in the twilight. He looked big and imposing even below her, and she was grateful for the ladder's height. "On the contrary, Mr. Savas," she said in measured tones of her own. "I certainly can stay here. I have a lease. As in a legally binding contract. An agreement," she added with saccharine sweetness. "In writing. Frank's Cath is an attorney. She wanted to be sure he had all his legal i's dotted and t's crossed. Ironclad, she said. I believe her. Just try to weasel out of it." The smile she gave him would have challenged the Cheshire cat's.

His jaw tightened. "Then I'll buy you out of it."

Neely shrugged. "Sell me the houseboat. I offered Frank good money."

"And couldn't come up with it, apparently."

Neely bristled. "I'm good for it. I have a good job, good prospects."

He snorted. She'd never heard so much derision in a single sound. Now it was her turn to frown. "What's that for?"

"Your prospects." His tone was disparaging. "Is that what you're calling Max these days? I'm sure he'll be delighted to hear it."

"Max?" Neely's jaw dropped as his meaning became clear. He thought she was...using Max?

She stared, openmouthed. Then abruptly she snapped her mouth shut. She'd have liked to tip the paint can over on his arrogant head.

At her silence he shrugged. "And I see you're not denying it."

"I most certainly am denying it!"

"Well, don't bother. Just because he's too blind to see what you're after doesn't mean the rest of us are."

Neely's fingers strangled the paintbrush. She wished they were strangling Sebastian Savas's strong muscular neck. "The rest of you?" she forced the words past her lips. "Who exactly?"

"Me for one. Gladys."

"Max's secretary thinks I'm out to use him?"

"Oh, she's delighted you're humanizing him." Sebastian sneered at her. "I can think of another word for it."

"You don't know what you're talking about," she told him frostily.

A sardonic brow lifted. "Don't I?"

"No, Mr. Savas, you don't. And you shouldn't presume." So saying, she wrenched around and set to painting again. Slap, slap, slap. God, she was furious at him! She was positively steaming.

"So, what's it going to take to shift you, Ms. Robson?" he persisted. "What's your price?"

Neely ignored him. The sun had almost set. She needed to turn on the light if she were going to actually see that she was accomplishing something. But then again, who cared? If this was Sebastian Savas's houseboat now, not hers, why should she bother to paint at all?

Because it *was* hers, damn it!

She was the one who had painted it, who had coddled it, who had taken care of it when Frank was more interested in just moving in with Cath. He'd *promised* her!

Maybe she should have taken Max up on his offer.

When it had become clear to him that he was never going to talk her out of her independence and into his glass and stone and cedar palace overlooking the sound, he'd said he would help her finance it.

Neely had refused, too stubborn, too proud to let him.

"No," she'd said firmly. "I appreciate the offer. Thank you. But I want to do it myself."

And look what it got her—out on her ear.

If Mr. Jump-to-Conclusions, Look-Down-His-Nose-At-Her Savas only knew Max had already offered, he'd blow a gasket. But then, obviously Sebastian thought he did know—everything. Pompous jerk.

He didn't even *want* her houseboat. Not really. She was sure of it. He had a use for it now, though she had no idea what. But ultimately he'd move back to his penthouse.

She set down the brush and deliberately turned to look down at him once more. "What's *your* price, Mr. Savas?"

"*My* price?" He looked startled.

But then his insolent gaze started at her bare feet and took its time sliding up the length of her legs, making her supremely aware of exactly what he seemed to be assessing.

Neely felt her cheeks begin to burn and she wanted to kick his smug face even as she waited for what would certainly be an unpleasant suggestion. And she had only herself to blame because she'd asked for it.

But then slowly he shook his head. "You don't have anything I'd want to buy, Ms. Robson."

Oh, God, she wanted to kick him.

But before she could react at all, Cody and Harm burst into the room as only thirteen-year-old boys and one-year-old bloodhounds can do. "We're back! Harm got in the mud and I need a towel and—"

Cody wasn't reckoning on a stranger on the boat. Harm loved strangers. Actually he loved everyone. There was no accounting for taste.

Still, in this case, Neely couldn't complain. One look at a man on the deck and Harm broke loose from Cody's grasp. Sebastian had moved the box to pursue her onto the deck. It wasn't keeping the kittens in the living room. And it certainly didn't stop Harm as he shot straight through the living room.

"Oh, dear," she said. "Hang on."

Too late.

A ninety-seven-pound missile of canine enthusiasm launched his joyful muddy self at Sebastian Savas—and sent them both straight over the railing into the water!

As much as Neely would have loved to stand there and laugh, it would be just her luck for Sebastian to be a nonswimmer. Bad enough that he would probably sue her and her dog for everything she might ever own.

She scrambled down the ladder as he sputtered to the surface, water streaming down his face. "Are you all right?"

She wished he would yell or shout or even threaten her. She wouldn't even mind if he tried to strangle her dog.

He didn't. Jaw set, he took the two strokes necessary to reach the side of the houseboat, then began to haul himself out of the water. He didn't say a word.

Neely watched with wary fascination, expecting to see steam coming off him, and supposing he would be entitled if it did. Two of the kittens were peering over the railing, leaning perilously close to falling in. Harm was dog-paddling cheerfully and grinning at her.

Staying well out of Sebastian's way as he clambered over the railing, Neely scooped up the kittens, then stuck them back in the living room and dragged the box in front of the open doorway again.

"I told you not to move the box," she pointed out to Sebastian as he dripped. "I'm, um, sorry," she added. Though it would have been more convincing if she'd been able to wipe the smile off her face.

Sebastian, of course, didn't acknowledge it. He turned to watch Harm paddling around the side of the houseboat to clamber up onto the dock.

"I'll go get 'im," Cody volunteered quickly, and darted out the front door to do so before anyone could blame him.

But Neely certainly wasn't blaming him. And Sebastian still didn't say anything.

She found it amazing that even dripping wet he could still look unflappable. The man really was inhuman.

And then he murmured, "More harm than good?" in a quiet reflective tone that made her blink. And blink again.

Was that a sense of humor?

She wasn't sure. "Er, yes." She laughed nervously. Probably it wasn't.

Sebastian nodded gravely. "Does he do it often?"

Her lips twitched. "Knock people in the water? More often than I'd like, actually. Mostly it's me, though. I've learned not to stand by the railing when he's excited. He's still a puppy. Just a year old." Was that sufficient excuse? Probably not.

"I am sorry," she said again, finally managing not to smile. She snagged up the last escapee kitten and clutched it in front of her as if it were a shield.

Green eyes met hers. "No, you're not."

Their gazes met again. And Neely remembered the first time they had confronted each other—over her "fluffy ideas" and his "phallic skyscrapers." Something had sizzled then. And Neely, feeling it, had darted away, telling herself it was irritation.

Of course there was irritation now. In spades.

But there was more. If there had been steam before, there certainly was now, as well as something hot and electric and very very intense that seemed to snap between them.

Neely felt an unaccountable urge to fling herself into the cold Lake Union water.

Deliberately she took a deep breath, then strove for a calm she didn't feel as she met his gaze squarely and said, "You're right. I'm not."

And who knows how long they might have stood there, gazes dueling, heat and awareness crackling, if Cody hadn't returned with Harm just then?

"Got 'im. At least he's not muddy anymore." Cody looked hopefully at Neely, then his gaze went straight to Sebastian.

Neely went in and took the dog by the collar. "Thanks," she said to Cody. But he barely seemed to notice her. He was craning his neck to see past her toward the man still dripping on the deck.

"Who's he?" he asked.

"A man I work with."

"Your new neighbor," Sebastian said firmly, coming in the door.

Cody's eyes widened and he looked a bit worried as he turned for confirmation to Neely. "Really? Where d'you live?"

"Here."

That did make Cody's eyes bug. "With Neely?"

"No!" they both said in unison.

"I'm not moving," Neely said flatly.

Sebastian's jaw tightened.

Cody looked from one to the other nervously. "I got homework," he said. "Math. Lots of it. Gotta go." And he darted out the door before either of them could say a word.

In the silence that followed his departure, Harm shook himself vigorously, getting Neely almost as wet as Sebastian. She hauled the dog into the kitchen and began to dry him.

Sebastian came after her, loomed over her, still dripping. "I'm not leaving," he told her.

Neely looked up and met his stony gaze. "Neither am I."

"I own this boat."

She took a careful breath. "And I have a lease to rent a room on it for the next six months."

"I made you an offer of a better place to stay."

"Oh, sure. With a dog and five kittens, two rabbits and a guinea pig?"

His jaw tightened. He glared.

Neely shrugged. "I'm staying, Mr. Savas. And if you don't like it, that's tough."

CHAPTER THREE

"THAT," Neely said when Frank opened the door to Cath's apartment the next morning, "was low."

She had been fuming all night, pacing and prowling. But only in her room, because Sebastian Savas had taken over. He'd come down from his shower, all clean and pressed looking and set up his computer on the desk by the window.

"My desk?" he'd asked with one raised brow.

"Your desk," Neely had replied through her teeth.

And so he'd set to work in the living room. And she'd gone upstairs to fume because she certainly had no intention of betraying how upset she was to her new landlord.

She had no qualms about telling Frank exactly how she felt, though. "Really low. Sneaky, in fact," she said now.

The look on Frank's face said that he would have shut the door on her and bolted it fast if he thought he could get away with it.

He couldn't. She'd have ripped it off its hinges to tell him her opinion of what he'd done.

"Um, hi, Neely. I, er…good morning." He peered at her from behind the door as if it were a shield. As far as Neely was concerned, he needed one.

"Good, Frank?" She raised a brow. "Not exactly." And determinedly she strode straight past the door, backing him into the living room and flinging the door shut behind her.

"Just a minute. Hang on now—" Frank was backpedaling and glancing behind him, as if to see if the window was open and might provide an escape route, no matter that they were on the third floor.

"Don't even think it," Neely warned. "If I want you to go out the window, I'll push you."

Frank almost managed a grin at that—as if she were kidding. "Aw, come on, Neel', you know I wouldn't have done it if the loan hadn't fallen through."

Neely did know it, but it didn't make her any happier. She gritted her teeth.

Frank shrugged helplessly. "I know you're mad. I'm sorry. But I couldn't help it. It just…happened."

"You didn't tell me! You could at least have told me!"

"About Savas?" He looked appalled, as if doing that was more than his life was worth.

Neely shook her head. "About my financing falling through! I shouldn't have had to find it out from Sebastian Savas walking through my front door and telling me he'd bought my houseboat! Your dear friend Greg should have told me."

Frank cursed under his breath. Then he raked his fingers through his hair. "He tried to. Honest to God," he insisted. "He didn't call me until late. Said he couldn't get hold of you. He tried your cell phone. And he didn't want to leave it as a message. So when he couldn't get you, he called me. Thought you might be at the office. But—" Frank spread his hands "—you weren't."

No. She hadn't been.

Because she'd gone sailing with Max.

He'd called her the night before and said he was thinking of buying a sailboat, that he wanted to take it out on Friday, would she come along.

She'd been stunned—and torn. "Friday? It's a workday."

"Take it off."

"But—what would my boss say?" she'd asked him, only half-joking.

Max laughed. "Guess." But then the laughter died, and he said gravely, "He'd say you were doing him a favor, getting him out. Making up for lost time."

And there had been a ragged edge to his voice that spoke of a depth of feeling that she couldn't ignore. And as it was exactly the sort of "carpe diem" philosophy she'd preached at him more than once, how could she argue?

Still she hadn't given in at once. "You're sure?" she'd pressed him.

"Well, I'm going," he'd said firmly. "Whether you come or not—that's up to you. I'd like you to," he'd added. "The question is, can you spare the time?"

Which meant he was still Max. The leopard hadn't changed his spots entirely. He might not be Max Grosvenor, the 100-proof workaholic that he'd been when she'd first walked into his office seven months ago, but there was still a lot of the old Max Grosvenor inside him. And that was good, not bad.

He just needed balance in his life. By asking her if she had time, at least it showed he was learning how to weigh choices instead of always opting for work.

"I can spare a part of the day," Neely decided. "But I need to be back by three."

"Deal," Max had said.

So she'd met him at the boatyard at nine—and she had been sailing on the Sound with Max while her financing was falling through yesterday afternoon.

She swallowed and accepted it. "Right." she said to Frank now, squaring her shoulders. "My fault."

Frank patted her on the arm. "I'm sorry," he said again. "Really. And, um, I just…didn't know how to tell you about Savas."

This last he added quickly, stepping away from her as he did so, as if he were afraid she might do him bodily harm. "Sit down," he said, pacing the floor of the apartment, but jerking his head at a chair where he expected her to sit. But Neely shook her head and remained standing.

Frank shrugged. "Suit yourself." He took a breath, raked a hand through his hair, then turned to face her. "Savas was…a gift from the gods."

"Sebastian Savas?" Neely gaped at him. Greek gods bearing gifts, perhaps? Horrible thought. "I don't think so."

"You know what I mean. I was tearing my hair out in my office, telling Danny what had happened, and Savas came by—working late as usual—and Danny, joking, said, hey you want to buy a houseboat. And—" Frank shrugged, still looking dazed "—he did."

Neely felt just as dazed as Frank. She'd lain awake half the night denying it to herself, convincing herself it was a bad dream. But it was actually just very bad reality, because when she'd come downstairs she'd still found half a dozen boxes of gear and a computer in the living room this morning.

"So…what happened?" Frank ventured after Neely stood there in silence, remembering the sinking feeling she'd experienced.

"Before or after Harm knocked him over the railing into the lake?"

Frank's eyes bugged. "You're joking."

"I wouldn't be capable of making that up." The memory of it still made her smile, though very little else did. "He handled it with great aplomb," she added grimly. "Just as you would expect. Swam back to the boat, pulled himself on board, stood there dripping and acted like that sort of thing happened every day of the week."

Frank was shaking his head. "And…?" he prompted.

"And then he went upstairs, took a shower, changed his clothes, ordered a pizza, set up his computer and got to work. He was still working when I went up to bed."

"He actually…moved in?" Frank sounded as if he couldn't quite fathom it. "Without any warning?"

"He moved in," Neely said wearily. There were no other words for it.

"So…what about you?"

"What about me?"

"Well, you can't…I mean surely you're not…"

"I have a lease," Neely reminded him.

"But you'll be living with Sebastian Savas!" Frank sounded as if he doubted her sanity.

"Well, what did you think was going to happen?" she demanded, exasperated by his astonished look, by the sight of his mouth opening and closing like a fish.

"I thought—" Frank shook his head "—I guess I don't know what I thought. That maybe he wanted it as an investment?" It was more a hopeful question than a statement of fact.

"He'd have been far more careful if he were buying it for an investment. This was obviously a spur-of-the-moment decision."

"I guess," Frank scratched his head. "But why?"

"Maybe he wants to make Max jealous." Neely grinned.

Frank gaped.

"I'm kidding," Neely said quickly. "But he does think I'm sleeping with the boss. And he definitely doesn't approve."

"Oh, Lord." Frank laughed at that. "You haven't told him about Max."

"Of course not. He can think what he likes," Neely said righteously. "He hates me anyway. This is just one more reason."

"Hates you?" That surprised Frank. "The Iceman?" As if he couldn't be bothered to muster up enough emotion to hate anyone.

"He thinks I design fluff," Neely qualified. Maybe that wasn't hate. But it still rankled, his haughty dismissal of her work as "girly stuff."

"He just has a different vision."

Neely gave him a wry smile. "Oh, yes. A very pointed, vertical vison."

"Be kind," Frank grinned. "You'll have to be, now that you are living with him."

That wiped the smile off her face. "Thanks to you."

"I said I was sorry. Besides, I thought he was going to find you another place."

Neely's gaze narrowed. "You discussed it with him? He knew I lived there?"

"I said I had a tenant."

"But not who?"

"Your name wouldn't sell property to Mr. Savas."

"No joke."

"So didn't he find you a place? I thought he would before he moved in."

"Oh yes, he offered me a studio."

"Well—"

"Can you see me and Harm and the kittens and the rabbits and the guinea pig and the fish in a studio? Besides," she said, "I don't want anyplace else. I want the houseboat!"

And, of course, her vehemence made Frank wince. Too bad. It was true.

She had fallen in love with Frank's houseboat the minute she'd come to see the room he had for rent. She'd been there six of the seven months she'd lived in Seattle.

When he'd said he needed to sell it, she'd instantly offered to buy it.

She loved it and, having moved so much during her youth, she'd never really felt "at home" anywhere. Not the way she had on the houseboat. To be able to buy it and put down "roots"— albeit hydroponic ones—had been a cherished dream.

"Well, maybe he'll change his mind," Frank said hopefully. "You don't know—maybe he woke up this morning and regretted it. He might be ready to move out. Then he could sell to you," he added brightly.

Neely sighed. "And maybe tonight for dinner a roast duck will fly over and fall in my lap."

Frank blinked. "What?"

"It's a metaphor for incurable optimism, Frank," she said wearily. "Never mind. Unlike you, I'm not expecting miracles. But I'll simply have to convince him to sell to me. He's all about business. I'll just have to find his price. But I am *not* leaving."

She would leave.

Sebastian was sure of it.

He'd told her pointedly last night right before she went upstairs that she had to move.

"If you don't want to go to the apartment, that's fine. It wouldn't be a good place for your animals. But you've got to go somewhere."

She hadn't answered. She'd just given him a stony stare, then scooped up all her kittens and carried them upstairs.

But she hadn't been here this morning when he got up. Granted, it was after nine and she might be anywhere. But the fact that she wasn't here boded well as far as Seb was concerned.

It was a good day. The sun was shining, and he'd had—once he fell asleep—the best night's sleep he'd had in years. There was something about being close to the water that lulled his mind, soothed his brain and sent him out like a light.

He hadn't expected that. Ordinarily he didn't sleep well except in his own bed. But last night, even despite his uncharacteristic impulse purchase of the houseboat and discovery of its unexpected tenant, once he'd hit the bed it hadn't taken long for the lap of the water against the hull, and the ever so slight movement to carry him back to his childhood, to the summers spent at his grandparents' on Long Island.

Their house was by the shore, and his grandfather had a boat that he and Seb used to take out to sail. And every now and then he would cajole his grandfather into spending the night on the boat. It had been the treat of the summer.

Last night had reawakened that long-forgotten memory. And even this morning, that was what he was thinking of as he cradled a mug of coffee in his hands and stood in front of the wide glass window that looked out across Lake Union.

Just the sight, just the memory made him smile.

Neely Robson be damned, he'd done the right thing buying Frank's houseboat. It already felt more like home than his penthouse ever had.

He went out onto the deck and had a look at Robson's painting project. The ladder was still there. She'd cleaned up the paint and brushes and they sat in a neat row on one of the built-in benches around the edge of the deck.

He studied her choice of color in the light of the morning sun. She'd painted over a gunmetal grey with a softer more silvery shade of grey. It surprised him. He'd have expected her to go for pink. Or purple. Or some other gaudy touchy-feely color.

The grey wasn't bad. It would weather well, soften in the sun and it fit in well with the surroundings. He hefted the paint can to see that there was plenty left and was pleased that there was. She'd taken down the gutters and painted them. He'd hang them back up, then take up where she left off. But first he had to go to the grocery store and buy some food.

He went back inside and plucked a piece of cold pizza out of the fridge—left over from the one he'd finally ordered last night—and ate it while he reconnoitered, getting a feel for the rest of the boat.

With Robson glaring at him—and clearly upset—he hadn't spent a lot of time looking over his new purchase.

He'd gone upstairs, then stripped off his wet clothes, showered and changed—so he had a good idea what the bathroom was like, and was grimly pleased upon looking around to discover that she hadn't overrun it the way his sisters were doing to his at that very moment.

But he hadn't wasted time upstairs. Once he was cleaned up, he came back down, opened up his laptop and set up his printer on the desk in the living room and settled down to do some work.

Begin as you mean to go on, his grandfather had always advised.

It was cliché, of course, but it was true, as well. And Seb had long ago learned the wisdom of it. It had helped him cope with the bevy of new "mothers" his father brought home. It had stood him in good stead at work.

He never tried to please. He worked hard and he always kept his own counsel. It made life simpler that way.

If people didn't like him, too bad.

Neely Robson didn't like him.

As if he cared. He didn't like her much, either.

And it would be a damn good thing when she and her menagerie were out from underfoot.

With luck, by the time he got back from grocery shopping, she'd already be packing.

Neely had never been a Boy Scout.

She did, however, believe in the motto: Be Prepared.

So she was prepared, when she let herself in the front door that afternoon, to lay a proposal on the line to Sebastian Savas.

She'd thought it all out after she'd left Frank's. Maybe he was right. Maybe by now Sebastian had buyer's remorse. Maybe he woke up this morning seasick. Well, probably not. But she could hope.

In any event, she spent three hours at the public library— because she wasn't going home—reworking her finances, then calling her mother in Wisconsin to say that things would be a little tight for a few months. Lara wouldn't care. She never thought of money anyway.

And then Neely came back to the houseboat, prepared to make Mr. Cold-Blooded Businessman an offer he wouldn't refuse.

She wasn't prepared to walk into the living room and find

herself staring out through the plate glass window at a very different man entirely.

In the seven months she'd worked for Grosvenor Design she had never seen Sebastian in anything other than a suit. Sometimes he took his coat off and she saw his long-sleeved dress shirts. And once, on a job site, she'd seen his collar unbuttoned and his tie askew. Last night, of course, she'd seen him in a suit—dripping wet.

Even after Harm had knocked him in the water and he'd showered, Sebastian had come back downstairs wearing another dress shirt and a pair of pressed dark trousers. Okay, he hadn't worn a tie. But big deal.

She'd told Max once that she thought Sebastian had been born wearing cuff links.

It didn't seem far-fetched. He wore his cool, calm demeanor like a suit of well-fitting armor. And his well-pressed, totally-together look promised the icy aloofness and consummate unapproachability which was, with Sebastian Savas, exactly what you got.

So who was the guy with the bare tanned feet and faded blue-jean-clad muscular legs braced against the upper rungs of her ladder?

Neely stopped in her tracks. But even as her body stopped dead, her gaze kept right on moving up—until it was well and truly caught by the sight of several inches of hard flat masculine abs peeking out from beneath a sun-bleached red T-shirt.

There was even an arrow of dark hair visible until it disappeared into the waistband of the jeans as the man wearing them reached up and slapped paint on the wall above the window.

Neely wet her lips. She swallowed. Hard. And swallowed again.

Her heart seemed suddenly to be doing the Mexican Hat Dance in her chest. She forced herself to take a breath—and then another—as she tried to regain her equilibrium.

It was what came of being an architect, she told herself, still combating light-headedness. They just had extraordinarily well-developed senses of appreciation for physical beauty, for strength and economy and power all wrapped up in one neat, um, package.

Perhaps not best choice of words.

On the other hand, quite possibly the most accurate, she thought as her gaze fastened on the bulge beneath the soft denim right below his waistband and framed between the rungs of the ladder.

Her face flamed and, deliberately, Neely squeezed her eyes shut tight.

She didn't see the kittens tussling right in front of her. And of course, she stepped on them.

"*Mrrrrooowwwww!*"

"Oh, help!" Neely stumbled, shrieked, caught herself against the back of the sofa and jerked open her eyes just in time to hear the paintbrush clatter to the deck and see Sebastian—who else?—skim down the ladder like a fireman on his way to a four-alarm blaze.

His gaze locked on her even as he reached down to scoop the brush up off the deck and toss it in the paint tray.

"What the hell—?"

"It's n-nothing. N-nothing," Neely said hastily.

"If it was nothing, why'd you shriek? What happened?"

"Nothing happened!" Face still burning, Neely crouched down and snagged up the kittens, clutching them to her chest and gently kneading their small squirming bodies to make sure they weren't hurt.

Sebastian jerked open the door and glowered accusingly. "Don't tell me you were shocked to see me. I live here."

That wasn't what had shocked her. She cuddled the kittens closer. "I stumbled," she said. "I landed on the kittens."

He looked skeptical, but finally he shrugged. Why did his shoulders look even broader in a T-shirt than in a dress shirt? Unfair.

"You should watch where you're going," he told her.

"Obviously." And she wasn't about to tell him why she hadn't been. Instead she buried her face in their fur and took a few more deep breaths until finally she lifted her gaze again and said, "You don't have to paint."

He rolled his shoulders. "It's my boat. Or were you going to say it's your paint?"

Neely pressed her lips together. "It is, actually. But that's not the point. The point is—" she took a breath, then plunged on "—I want to buy the boat. Still. From you."

He opened his mouth, but she cut him off. "You can't really want it. You didn't have any idea it even existed twenty-four hours ago. It's some spur-of-the-moment mad purchase for you. Maybe you think you want it now, but you won't."

He started to say something again, but Neely knew she had to get it all out now without interruption, had to make it clear how very badly she wanted the houseboat. Maybe it was foolish. Maybe it would make him even less likely to sell to her.

But yesterday, when Harm knocked him in the water and he didn't take it out on her, when he actually sounded just slightly bemused. "More harm than good," he'd said. And it was so unexpected that she couldn't believe he was totally unfeeling.

"Hear me out," she insisted. "I know you think you want it now. But you'll get sick of it. You'll hate the way the dampness makes your computer keys stick. You'll get tired of the fog. You won't want birds pooping on the deck. You'll crave your penthouse again. I'm sure you will! So, I just want you to know that, when it happens—and it will happen—I'll take it off your hands for what I agreed to pay Frank—or even ten thousand more," she added recklessly. "And I will get financing."

She'd let Max help if she had to.

She stopped and looked at Sebastian, waiting for him to say something. He didn't say a word. Half a minute ticked by. Then he said, "Are you finished now?"

"Yes." Tick, tick.

"So tell me why. Why do you want it?"

She wished he hadn't asked that. Neely loved people and

made friends easily. She'd had to, given how often she was in a new place. But she usually took her time exposing the personal side of her life. And she really didn't want to do so to a man who formed judgments faster than the speed of light.

But he hadn't said no. And he stood there now, waiting expectantly, those green eyes assessing her from beneath hooded lids.

Right. So be it. "It felt like home the first time I walked in the door," she told him. "I don't know why." And she'd given it a lot of thought, too. "We lived all over the place. Here. In California. Montana. Minnesota. Wisconsin. To say we moved around is putting it mildly. We were always somewhere different and nothing was ever permanent…not until I was twelve, anyway."

"What happened when you were twelve?"

"My mother got married."

His eyes widened, as if she'd surprised him.

"My parents weren't," she said bluntly. "My father was a workaholic and my mother was a free spirit. Chalk and cheese. Worse," she said, "they split before I was born. We stayed in Seattle for a year. But then my mother joined a commune and we went to California. Like I said, we moved around a lot. And then she met John. And something clicked. They got married. It was wonderful."

Now he really did look shocked.

"It was," she insisted. "We had a home. I loved it. For six years it was the best. Then I went away to college and—" she shrugged "—you know what college is like—nothing is ever 'home.' Then, after I graduated I lived in first one apartment and then another. Even when I came out here, at first I rented another apartment for a month. When Frank said he was looking for a roommate, I came to see the houseboat—and I felt it right away. Home. Still is." She had been looking around at everything in the room as she spoke. But when she finished she looked straight at him. "That's why."

"All emotion," he said.

She bristled. "Something wrong with that?"

He didn't answer. "Are you going to paint it pink?"

"*What?*"

It was the accusation he'd thrown at her the one time they'd worked together—that she had wanted to paint everything pink. She had ignored the accusation because it was the client who had wanted pink, and in the particular funky magazine editorial offices she was designing, the color had worked.

Now she glared at him. And he looked back impassively, one brow lifted in that sardonic way he had of making you feel two feet high.

And then his cell phone rang.

Sebastian dug in his jeans' pocket, making her aware once again of the way they fit his body, of how they gave a whole new tough rugged look to the smooth cool consummate professional she was accustomed to.

Not, she reminded herself, that he behaved any differently.

Are you going to paint it pink? What kind of a smart-ass remark was that? He'd opened her cans of paint. He knew perfectly well none of them was pink.

She scowled at him as he flicked open his phone, glanced at the phone number coming in, made a slightly wry face, then said, "Excuse me. I have to take this."

Of course he did, Neely thought. "Go right ahead," she said. But he wasn't even listening. He'd already turned toward the door.

Neely was listening, however. And she was surprised he didn't say, "Savas here," in that steely businesslike tone she always heard at work.

On the contrary, his voice was totally different with a much softer edge. And he almost seemed to have a smile on his face when he said, "Hey, what's up."

So it was a girlfriend.

She didn't know why she should be surprised. He was certainly good-looking enough. And maybe there was another side to him than the one she saw at work. Maybe he was Mr. Charm after hours. Though according to Max, Sebastian worked as many hours in the day as he did.

What he said next she didn't know because he stepped out onto the deck. Not that she wanted to eavesdrop. She had no desire at all to hear Sebastian murmur sweet nothings to his girl-friend. She couldn't quite imagine that.

But she didn't have any trouble imagining, however, the sort of cool svelte ice goddess who would appeal to him. Tall and blond and minimally curvy. Expressionless. But she might have one of those slow smiles that never quite met her eyes.

Would they, between the two of them, generate enough heat to melt the ice?

But even as she had the thought, she realized that it seemed at odds with the flicker of emotions—gentleness and calm followed by impatience and what looked like eye-rolling irritation.

And then he spoke loudly enough that Neely had no trouble hearing him at all. "Don't cry, for God's sake," he said, exasper-ated. "I hate it when you cry."

He'd made his girlfriend cry?

Whatever she said in response, of course, Neely didn't know. But whatever it was, Sebastian grimaced, sighed mightily, punched the "end" button and tossed the phone onto the hammock on the deck. Then he jammed his hands in the pockets of his jeans and glowered at it.

At least, for once, he wasn't glowering at her.

"That's not very nice," Neely said loud enough for him to hear.

He turned to look at her. "What's not?"

"Making her cry. Then hanging up on her."

"She'll call back." He came back inside, leaving the phone on the deck.

Neely frowned. What sort of submissive wimp was this girl-friend that he could treat her so badly and she'd call him again.

"How do you know?" she demanded. "I wouldn't."

"Well, you're not my sister."

Sister? He had a *sister?*

It was hard to imagine Sebastian Savas having any family at all. She'd always imagined he'd been found under an ice floe somewhere.

"I wouldn't call you back if I were your sister," she told him.

"Yeah, well, you probably aren't expecting me to pay for your wedding."

Now that did shock her. He not only had a sister, but he was supporting her?

The phone rang again. He gave Neely an arch look. "See?"

"It might not be her."

A corner of his mouth twisted. "Want to bet?"

"No. Well, aren't you going to answer it?" she demanded when he made no move to go get it.

He sighed. "Might as well. She'll keep calling until I do."

He went out again and picked up the phone. Neely stayed inside, trying to pretend disinterest.

But she wasn't entirely disinterested.

It was hard to be disinterested in a man who filled out a pair of jeans that well.

Shallow, yes. But there it was.

And it wasn't only that. There was something about this Sebastian Savas that intrigued her. Maybe it was knowing he had a family. Maybe it was watching him deal with this sister. It wasn't a short conversation they were having. And Sebastian wasn't as perfunctory and dismissive as he was at work.

I hate it when you cry, he'd said.

The Sebastian from work wouldn't have cared if the whole design team had burst into tears.

Intriguing, yes. Not that she was actually *interested,* Neely told herself firmly. Just…curious. And appreciative—in a purely academic, architectural way.

He was still annoying. He owned her houseboat. He thought she'd paint it pink. *And* he believed she was sleeping with Max!

She narrowed her gaze at him. He ended the call and tossed the phone down again, then stood there a moment, staring in her direction. But somehow Neely didn't think he was even seeing her.

What he was seeing, she didn't know.

And then her own cell phone rang.

"Hey, what're you doing?" Max asked.

She smiled. "Trying to convince Sebastian Savas to sell me Frank's houseboat."

"What?" He sounded as shocked as she had been last night when Sebastian had walked in the door.

"Long story," Neely said. She saw Seb turn to come back into the living room. "I'll tell you later."

"Tell me at dinner," Max said.

Ordinarily she would have begged off. She had gone sailing with Max yesterday. They were going out again tomorrow. Of course she was glad he was getting a life after years of having his nose to the grindstone. But his entire life shouldn't revolve around her.

"I've heard of a great sushi bar," Max tempted her just as Sebastian walked through the door and gave her a narrow suspicious look.

On the other hand, why not?

"I'd love to, Max," she said delightedly.

Sebastian's jaw tightened.

"See you at seven," she trilled and hung up. "Max and I are going out for dinner," she told him, just in case he hadn't heard.

"Lucky you." His voice was flat.

"Yes, indeed," Neely said brightly. "We've had so much fun getting to know each other."

"I'll bet." A muscle ticked at his temple.

"He's found a new sushi bar he says we have to try. I have a bit of work to do, but I couldn't say no. He made me an offer I couldn't refuse." Was she laying it on too thick?

Sebastian's expression was stony. "Did he." It wasn't a question.

"Mmm." Neely gave him one more cheerful smile. "I think I'll take Harm for a run, then come back and get ready." She grabbed Harm's leash and started toward the door. "Bye-ee."

"Robson?" Seb's voice, hard and flat turned her right around again.

"Yes?"

"You want to buy the houseboat?"

Her heart quickened. "Yes. Of course. You know I do."

Sebastian's hard mouth twisted. "Make me an offer I can't refuse."

CHAPTER FOUR

MAKE him an offer?

Like what?

Like what he supposed she was offering Max?

She wanted to strangle him. Or punch him. Or do whatever was necessary to wipe that knowing look off his handsome face.

Instead she went out with Max and grilled him about the man who owned her houseboat.

"You're interested?" Max asked. "In Seb?"

"I am not 'interested' in Sebastian Savas," Neely said, still hot under the collar from Sebastian's remark. She picked at the spider roll on her plate, poked it with her chopstick the way she'd like to poke Sebastian. "Not the way you think. He just annoys me."

"Why? Are you still ticked because he thought you wanted everything pink?" Max grinned as he regarded her over his bottle of Japanese beer.

"Not 'thought.' Thinks! He thinks I'll paint the houseboat pink!"

"Oh, I doubt that," Max said easily. "He's just giving you a hard time. Maybe he's smitten."

"Hardly." Neely sniffed. "He thinks I'm sleeping with you!"

Max's laughter was so loud and sudden that half the diners in the small restaurant turned to look at their way.

"It's not funny!" Neely fumed. She did stab her spider roll then. And her *kappa maki* for good measure.

Max shrugged and lazed back in his chair, still regarding her with amusement. "You could tell him you're not."

"I did," she muttered.

He didn't say anything, just smiled and sipped his beer.

Neely glared at him. He grinned. "He has a dirty mind," she said after a moment.

"Probably. He's a man," Max said. "And he thinks I'm in danger of succumbing to your charms."

She blinked and stared. "You knew?"

Max lifted his shoulders. "He didn't think much of me bringing you on as the living-space designer for Carmody-Blake."

"You *asked* him?"

Max shook his head. "Didn't have to. He volunteered."

Sebastian was lucky he wasn't her *kappa maki* then. She'd poked it to smithereens. "How dare he?"

"He was looking out for my welfare," Max told him. "Thinks you're out to get your claws into me."

"How dare he?"

"He understands the appeal of a pretty woman."

"He doesn't think I'm pretty. He thinks I'm weird. And he doesn't like what I do."

"Maybe he wants you."

Neely looked at Max, horrified, at the same time she remembered that odd stab of awareness she'd felt this afternoon when she'd come into the living room and spied Sebastian up on the ladder. "Don't be ridiculous," she said now.

"Just saying." Max finished his beer.

"Well, don't," Neely retorted.

She didn't want to think about Sebastian that way. And she certainly didn't want to think about him thinking about her that way!

Not that he was, of course. It was all in Max's head.

But the awareness wasn't.

She felt it again later that night. She spent the evening at Max's discussing the Blake-Carmody project. It was the work she'd have done at home anyway, but it was actually better to do it with Max. It was nearly eleven when she got home. She took Harm out for a quick walk, then went upstairs to get ready for bed at the very moment Sebastian was coming out of the bathroom. His hair was wet and he was bare-chested this time, though he was wearing his jeans, thank God.

No matter, she still felt that unwelcome sizzle of awareness. And it seemed like every time she saw him now he was wearing less. Her cheeks warmed at the thought.

He raised a brow. "Have fun?" His tone was sardonic.

"I did," Neely said, keeping hers flat.

"But you didn't spend the night." The brow went even higher.

Neely, remembering the eviscerated *kappa maki,* wished she had a chopstick on her now. She gave him a brittle smile. "It's a work night."

His expression hardened. "Nice to know you have some standards."

"Indeed I do."

He stepped past her to go into his room. The hall was narrow and he was close enough that she felt the heat emanating from his bare flesh as he passed. The sensation was almost magnetic, drawing her toward him. Quickly Neely stepped back.

He paused, one hand on the frame, as he opened the door to his bedroom. "I'm leaving for Reno as soon as Frank and I close on the houseboat at the bank."

"Rubbing it in?"

"Just telling you. I won't be back until Friday."

"Good."

A corner of his mouth tipped. "I thought you might think that." He paused. "If you need anything—"

"I'll ask Max."

His knuckles tightened on the door frame. "Of course you will. Sweet dreams, Robson." Amazing how much disparagement a man could get into so few words.

Neely ran her tongue over her lips. "Same to you, Savas."

His bedroom door shut with a hard click.

Not until it had, did Neely breathe again. Even so her knees still wobbled. And for the first time she wondered if maybe she should spend the week looking for another place to live.

So what if she was sleeping with Max Grosvenor?

What did he care?

Well, he didn't, Seb assured himself as he tossed clothes into his suitcase preparatory to tomorrow's trip to Reno. Unless it interfered with the good of the company, it made no difference at all.

All the same, he was glad he was leaving. That way he didn't have to be around to watch.

It had been bad enough before—when he'd simply caught glimpses of Neely Robson waltzing into Max's office during the day. He'd been annoyed when they left together sometimes in the evening. And, yeah, he'd felt downright irritated Friday when Max had come late to their meeting because he was out sailing with a woman half his age!

But it had been worse over the weekend. At least when he was in Reno, Seb wouldn't have to watch her chatting to Max on the phone while she fed the kittens. He wouldn't see her razor on the shelf by the shower and wonder if she'd shaved her legs before she'd gone off with Max.

And he wouldn't have to see her run out the door and down the dock to meet him when he came to pick her up.

Not that he'd been watching…

He'd been minding his own business upstairs in his bedroom, putting some books on the shelves of the built-in bookcase, when he'd just happened to hear the front door shut and had glanced out to see her dance away down the dock, waving madly at Max who was coming to meet her.

Max hadn't been exactly reluctant, either. The grin Seb saw

on his face was one of pure joy. And when she reached him, damned if he hadn't wrapped his arms around her in a fierce hug.

Boss and employee?

Yeah, right.

Just good friends?

Not even close.

Not that they were claiming any such thing. They weren't claiming anything at all.

They didn't have to, Seb thought, banging his suitcase shut.

So it was far better that he was off to Reno for the week where he could focus on what was important—his work—rather than here where he would have to watch Robson work her wiles on Max and Max be no smarter than Seb's old man.

And that was another reason to be gone. No whining from Vangie about when their father was ever going to call. And no more endless phone calls from all the rest of the pack.

As if living with Neely Robson and watching her kiss up to Max over the weekend wasn't bad enough, the Savas sisters' invasion of Seattle was driving him mad.

Now instead of simply having Vangie's phone calls to contend with, he had the triplets and Jenna, as well.

Saturday night, while Neely was out having sushi with Max, he was listening to Ariadne whine about her boyfriend she'd left back in New York. Then Alexa moaned on about the three she had left behind in Paris. And just when he'd said, "Why do you need three boyfriends?" she'd turned the phone over to Anastasia who had rattled on about her fiancé who was heading to the Trobriand Islands to do field work for six months.

He didn't even know she had a fiancé. And all he could think was, *Not another wedding.*

Maybe three boyfriends was better than one serious one. He hoped the guy stayed gone five years.

The next day—while Neely was, naturally, out sailing with Max—they'd called again. Not once. Not twice. Half a dozen times or more. To ask where the blender was. Then where the vacuum was. Then where the broom was. Didn't he have a dustpan? Did he know if the recycler would take broken glass?

"What sort of glass?" Seb had demanded. "What'd you break?"

"Oh, don't worry," one of them said airily. He never had any idea which. "Nothing important."

Probably it wasn't, he'd lied to himself. But as he couldn't make himself believe it, he'd made sure he had time, before taking them out to dinner, to drop in and survey the damage himself.

There was clutter everywhere. But it wasn't much worse than he'd imagined—and he never did figure out what had broken. It hadn't been a bad evening. The food was good, his sisters had behaved well, and he would have enjoyed himself except for periodically wondering if, while he was eating salmon, Robson and Max were feasting on each other.

It had seemed all too likely when he got back to the houseboat at ten and only Harm, the rabbit and the guinea pigs were there to greet him.

Of course, she could have come home and gone to bed. Maybe she had, he'd told himself. But after an internal debate about whether he should or not, Seb decided that, as owner of the houseboat, he was allowed to check his tenant's room. So he cracked open the door, hoping to see her soundly sleeping.

He saw an empty bed. And all the kittens escaped.

Thank God he got them all back in and the door shut. But it was after eleven and he had just been coming out of the bathroom from taking a shower when she came up the stairs.

She looked tousled and tumbled and too damn beautiful.

And his shower had not been nearly cold enough.

"Savas here."

Ah, yes. The Voice of Authority. Clipped. Precise. Pure business. And with an unfortunate slightly rough, very masculine edge that sent a frisson right down Neely's spine even though she was determined to be immune.

"Your boat is sinking."

"*What!*"

So much for clipped precise authority.

Neely smiled. Perhaps it wasn't the nicest way to convey the news that there was a leak in the underbelly of Sebastian's new property, but as it could have been *her* houseboat, she wasn't very inclined to play nice.

"You heard me," she said. "There was water all over the floor this morning."

"*Robson?*" The voice was barking in her ear now. She supposed she ought to have identified herself. "Is that you?"

"Who else could it possibly be?"

"One of my sisters," he muttered. Then "What are you talking about?"

"Water water everywhere," she said. "It means there's a leak down under somewhere. I remember it happening once before. Frank had to call someone to come and pump something out, then get down under there and fix it. Sorry, I can't get more technical than that. I can find out who he called, if you want," she added helpfully. "Or maybe you have a better idea."

There was a moment's hesitation, long enough that she wondered if he might actually have a better idea. But then he said, "Get the guy's name. Call him if you can and ask him to do it. I can't get back until Friday."

It was Wednesday evening now. He'd left on Monday, so basically she'd enjoyed a Sebastian-free week so far. It had been quite blissful.

Or it would have been if Max hadn't taken to teasing her every day, asking her if she missed him.

"Right," she said now briskly. "I'll try to track Frank down. Sorry to trouble you."

"No trouble," he said. "It's my responsibility. It's my b—"

"Your boat. Yes, I know that. Okay. Bye." She was about to hang up when he spoke again.

"Robson?"

She put the phone back against her ear. "Yes?"

"How's Harm? Pushed anyone else in the water?"

"What?" The questions surprised her. "Um, no. But there hasn't been anyone else here, either."

"Good. I thought perhaps— Never mind. How's the weather?"

"The weather?" What on earth? She was talking to Sebastian Savas about the weather? "Well, it's raining," she said. "As usual. Imagine that."

He laughed. It was a low, intimate chuckling sound that sent a quick unexpected shiver of awareness down the back of her neck.

"Not here," he said. "It's hot in Reno."

"I should think it would make a nice change." She stared out the window at the rain bucketing down and tried to imagine a bit of sunshine.

"It does. But still I'll be glad to get back."

"So Harm can push you in the water again?"

"Not exactly." But there was the unexpected sound of a smile in his voice.

Neely was having a hard time believing this conversation was happening. She hadn't wanted to ring Sebastian in the first place. She'd imagined he would be abrupt, abrasive and think she was overstepping her bounds. When he was polite about the leak, that was as much as she'd hoped for. She certainly didn't expect casual conversation.

And while it was difficult to imagine it was Sebastian on the other end of the connection, at the same time she was having no trouble seeing him—in her mind's eye—at all.

It was evening. He was on the road. She'd been there often enough that she understood the scenario. There was no noise in the background, so he wasn't out in one of Reno's nightspots. He'd likely be in his hotel room, perhaps lying on his bed.

No. Don't go there.

But even as she warned herself, a vision of the last time she'd seen Sebastian—damp-haired and bare-chested—became all too vivid, and she had to swallow hard. But before she could say a word, he spoke again.

"I don't much like being on the road," he said quietly.

And what was she supposed to do? Say, *Too bad. Goodbye?* Her mother had raised her better than that.

She said, "I don't, either. I think it comes from moving so much when I was a kid."

"Tell me about it," he asked, sounding interested.

And the invitation to talk was somehow more than she could resist. She'd been trying to work ever since she got home. But she'd been restless—not to mention periodically mopping—and now she curled up on the sofa with Harm's head in her lap and watched the rain.

"Well, I was home schooled mostly. Or should I say, commune schooled?" she corrected herself. "My mother was a hippie of sorts."

"No joke?" He sounded surprised.

"Nothing funny about it," Neely assured him. "My mother is definitely an independent free spirit. But she was never quite able to be an independent free spirit on her own. She needed a base, a group of people. But she didn't like anyone telling her what to do. Mostly communes are live and let live. But they can have their idiosyncracies, and she always seemed to run up against them. And then we'd move on."

"Just you and your mother?"

"Until I was twelve," Neely said. "And then she met my stepdad. He was a policeman. We were living in Wisconsin at the time and he'd been sent to arrest her for selling her jewelry on the street without a business license. It's funny, really," she said, thinking about those days now, "they were so different. And yet they were just right for each other. They had a great marriage. It was awful when he died. But I knew good marriages exist because of theirs. I want a marriage like that someday."

"Do you." There was a sudden hard edge in Sebastian's tone and his statement wasn't a question. "Good luck." He couldn't have sounded less encouraging.

He was such a cynic. "You don't believe in marriages that last?" She asked, at the same time wondering why they were discussing it at all. It certainly wasn't the sort of conversation she ever expected to have with Sebastian Savas. But then, she'd never expected to be living with him, either!

"I wouldn't say they can't ever happen," he said. "But I'd bet against it."

"So did my mother. And then she found the right man. You won't say that when you find the right woman."

"There isn't a right woman."

"Well, maybe not yet, but—"

"Ever."

"Oh." She mulled that over, then said cautiously, "So…is there a right man?"

There was a moment's stunned silence. Then he laughed. "No, Robson. I'm not gay. I'm just not getting married."

Firm and final. The Voice of Authority was back now. This was the Sebastian Savas she knew.

"Act like that," she said lightly, "and it won't be a problem. No one will want to marry you."

"Good."

If there was ever an exit line, Neely decided, that was it.

"Right. Well, I won't be expecting to get an invitation to your wedding anytime soon then. Thanks for warning me. I'd better go make your phone call now about the leak. And Harm wants out. Don't you, Harm?" She patted the sleeping dog who never even opened an eye. "Bye." And she rang off before Sebastian could say anything else.

Not that there was anything else to say.

But she couldn't stop thinking about the conversation, even long after she'd hung up. It was as odd as it had been unexpected. But maybe he was just bored.

Still, when her cell phone rang the next evening and she saw Sebastian's name come up on her caller ID, Neely was amazed.

"What?" she demanded, the heightened awareness she always seemed to feel around Sebastian battling with her very real desire to hang up at once.

"And a very good evening to you, too, Robson." He sounded amused, and he'd lost the clipped tone he'd used when making his pronouncement on marriage the night before. Once again she heard the slightly sexy undertone beneath his sardonic response and she wondered if he was doing it on purpose. To bait her, perhaps?

She refused to succumb to its allure. "Good evening," she said politely. "To what do I owe the honor of this call?"

"Aren't we prim and proper, Robson? Wearing pink?"

"It's none of your business what I'm wearing!" The minute the words were out of her mouth, she felt as if she'd been had. Was she always going to jump at the bait he dangled?

"What do you want?" she muttered.

She had been enjoying a quiet evening on her own and allowing herself the pretense that the houseboat was hers and hers alone, refusing to think about Sebastian Savas who had, drat his hide, invaded her dreams last night. How perverse was that?

And now here he was again.

"I want an update," he said briskly, all business. "Did the guy come and fix the leak?"

Neely breathed easier. "Yes. Took him most of the afternoon, though. He's sending you the bill. A hefty one, I imagine."

"No doubt."

He wanted to know what was done, and Neely told him as best she could. She hadn't been there the whole time. "I had work to oversee," she told him now. "I let him in, and I came back later to check how things were going. But I can't give you a play-by-play. Sorry."

"It's okay. I appreciate your bothering at all. Thanks."

"You're welcome."

She expected him to end the conversation there, but he didn't say goodbye. He didn't say anything. Still, he hadn't hung up. She could hear him breathing.

There was no noise in the background of his call tonight, either. And Neely found herself with visions of Sebastian in his hotel room, lying on the bed flickering once more into her mind. She focused on a boat zipping across the lake, trying to get rid of the visions out of her head.

"Do you know where to buy little rose-colored boxes?" he asked suddenly.

Neely blinked. "What?"

"Not for me," he said hastily. "My sister's getting married. She's been rattling on about these damn boxes she wants on the table at the reception. For mints or something. She keeps calling me and bugging me."

Neely's mind boggled. Sebastian not only had a sister, but she called him and bugged him about tiny wedding favors?

"I said, try the Internet. But she wants to see them in person," he said wearily.

Neely almost laughed at the combination of fondness and frustration in his voice. "Oh, dear."

"So, do you?" he demanded when she didn't speak.

"Why on earth would I?"

"They're rose," he said. "That's almost pink. As far as I'm concerned, it *is* pink. But Vangie insists there's a difference."

"Of course there's a difference," Neely said. "But I don't know anyplace to get them. Some wedding place, I suppose. How many does she need?"

"Two hundred and fifty or so."

"Yikes. When's the wedding?"

"Three weeks."

"And she's just now starting to look for them?"

"No. She's just now decided for sure that's what she wants. Or thinks she wants. What difference does it make? How the hell long does she have to have them anyway?"

"Not long, I suppose. But…I should think she'd want things prepared."

"Oh, she does," Sebastian said grimly. "But she keeps changing her mind. Or having it changed for her. First they were silver. Then they were rose. Then they were silver and rose. Now they're rose again. For simplicity's sake," he quoted wryly. "And God knows how many more times it will change. Since the rest of them got here, it's four times worse."

"Rest of whom?"

"My sisters. Not all of them, but more than enough."

"All?" Neely said faintly. He'd mentioned one. That had been surprising enough. And now there were more? "How many sisters do you have?"

"Six."

"*Six?*" She gaped, unable to imagine it.

"And three brothers."

"Dear God."

"At last count."

"What!"

"My old man has a habit of getting married and having kids," Sebastian said grimly. "It's what he does."

"I see." She didn't, and she suspected Sebastian knew that. The whole notion of ten kids in a family astonished her. And then there was the "my old man has a habit of getting married…" part.

Did his "old man" have a habit of getting divorced as well?

Was that what was behind Sebastian's complete cynicism toward marriage? She could understand that. But somehow, even though he'd brought it up, she couldn't see herself asking him.

Still, that alongside the nine brothers and sisters would go a long way toward explaining Sebastian's standoffishness. When you were one of ten, you probably needed to draw pretty definite boundaries. But from where she stood, as an only child, there was a definite appeal to the sound of all those siblings.

"You're so lucky," she told him.

"Lucky? I don't think so."

"I would have given anything for a sibling or two."

"A sibling or two wouldn't necessarily have been bad," he said heavily. "It's nine of them that gets old."

"I suppose." But she wasn't sure. She thought it sounded like far more fun than being dragged around from commune to commune after her mother.

"It's why I bought the houseboat," he told her. "They were moving in on me."

That was why? She sat up straight on the sofa. "All of them?"

"Four of them. Four too many." She could hear the edginess in his voice.

"Just until the wedding?"

"God, I hope so. In fact, no question. After that, they're gone." There was certainly no doubt in his mind about that.

"So, when they're gone, will you sell to me?"

He laughed. "My God, you're persistent."

"When I want something, yes. Will you?"

"Like I said, Robson. Make me an offer I can't refuse."

"And what would that be?"

"You're a smart cookie. Max is always saying so. Figure it out."

The sight of the houseboat at the end of the dock made Seb smile.

He was always happy to get home. Like he'd told Neely on Wednesday, he didn't like being on the road. He didn't mind working all hours, but at the end of the day he liked his own place, his own space. Solitude. Peace and quiet. There had always been a sense of calm when he walked through his front door.

But there had never been a sense of anticipation before.

His heart had never kicked up a notch. On the contrary, it

usually settled and slowed. But today, all day long while he was still in Reno going over the building specs with the contractors, in the back of his mind Seb was already on his way home.

Ordinarily he would have stopped and picked up some take-away for dinner. But tonight he didn't. He thought he'd wait and see if Robson was hungry. If so, they could get something together.

It wasn't a date.

It was just a courtesy. They were sharing living space for a while. So, the way he saw it, they could share a meal.

Besides, he owed her. She'd called him about the leak. She'd arranged for the repair. She had been the one who'd had to come home and let the repairman in.

So he would buy her a meal. It was the least he could do. Simple.

But when he opened the door, she wasn't there.

"Robson?"

Silence. Except for the dog. He was there, stretching and yawning and thumping his tail madly as Seb came in and dumped his suitcase on the floor and briefcase on the table.

The kittens were there, too, purring and meowing, noticeably bigger and even friskier than they had been on Monday. They attacked his briefcase and his shoelaces with equal enthusiasm. One scaled his trouser leg, putting tiny claw holes in the fine summer wool.

"Hey, there!" Seb lifted it off and cradled it in his hands. "Robson? You here?"

The guinea pig whistled. The rabbit didn't even look up from crunching on its dinner. No noticeable change in them and, thank God, no more of them, either.

And no Neely anywhere.

He felt oddly deflated. Of course he had no right to expect her to be there. They hadn't discussed dinner. It would have seemed like a date if they'd discussed it.

Well, it wasn't a date, that was certain. It wasn't anything because she wasn't here.

It was only seven, though. Maybe she'd worked late. God knew he did often enough. So he took a shower and changed clothes and came back downstairs hungrier than ever.

Still no Neely.

There was however a blinking light on the desk phone. It wasn't his phone. But he wasn't sure it was Robson's either. If someone had left a message for Frank, he'd have to pass it on. Seb punched the message light.

"Neel'." It was Max's voice. "Couldn't reach you on your mobile. Left you a message, but thought I'd try you at your place. I'm running late. Just go on in. I'll be there."

Go on in?

Go on in *where?* His brain couldn't help asking the question even though, in his gut, he already knew the answer. But before he could follow the thought any further, his own mobile phone rang.

He answered without even glancing at the ID. "Savas."

"Oh, good. You're there!" Vangie's voice trilled in his ear. "Are you home? In Seattle, I mean?"

Seb slumped on the sofa. A kitten launched itself and landed in his lap. He winced. "Yeah. Just got back."

"Great! We thought you'd like to come have dinner with us." She was all bubbly and bright and eager. Seb could hear lots more bubbly bright female voices in the background. "See the progress we've made for the wedding!" Vangie went on. "Want to?"

No, actually he didn't. Dealing with five of his sisters was very close to the last thing Seb wanted to do tonight.

But he said, "I'll be there."

Because the absolute last thing he wanted to do was sit home and think about the implications of Neely Robson having a key to Max's house.

Neely was humming "Oh, What a Beautiful Morning" when she let herself in the front door at eleven the next day.

It was beautiful—sunny and bright with not much wind. Not

enough to go sailing, she'd told Max when she left his place, which was fine because she had other things to do.

"Hey, there," she said dropping her tote bag and kneeling as she threw her arms around Harm who launched himself at her. "Did you miss me?"

"He didn't, actually," a harsh male voice said, "because he had me to take him out last night and this morning."

Neely's gaze jerked up to see Sebastian standing at the entrance to the living room. He was backlit and she couldn't really see his features, but she had no doubt he was scowling. She gave Harm one last happy cuddle and stood up warily.

After their two phone conversations during the week, she'd dared hope they had reached some sort of friendly rapport. Obviously she was wrong.

"I didn't neglect him," she said firmly. "I arranged for Cody to come in last night and early this morning.

"Because you knew you were going to spend the night?" Sebastian demanded.

"Yes."

He didn't say anything, but she could hear his teeth grinding.

"Is there a problem? I called him this morning to make sure he'd come over and he said he did. Are you saying he didn't?"

Sebastian opened his mouth, then shut it again abruptly. He shrugged irritably and shoved his hands in the pockets of his jeans. "I never saw him." He turned away and stalked into the living room.

Neely tossed her tote bag onto the stairs to carry up later, then followed him. "Were you here?"

He turned back to face her. "I didn't spend the night elsewhere, if that's what you mean?"

"Unlike me?" Neely said, capable of filling in the blank.

"Yes. Unlike you." He bit out the words. "Was it worth it?"

"Oh, yes." She gave him a bright smile. "It was great. We had dinner and then we went upstairs and—"

"Spare me the details," Sebastian snapped. "How old are you?"

Neely blinked at the sudden shift in topic. "Twenty-six. Not that it's any of your business."

"He's fifty-two!" The words burst from his lips. He wasn't scowling now; he was glaring furiously.

It took Neely a second to make the leap. Then she narrowed her gaze. "You're talking about Max, I presume?"

"Damn right, I'm talking about Max! That's not to say he isn't well preserved. For his age, I guess he could be considered a stud—"

"A stud?" Neely's jaw dropped. "*A stud?*" She stared at him for three seconds, and then a giggle escaped her. It seemed to infuriate him.

"You know what I mean! But for God's sake, you've got skills, talent. You win prizes! You don't have to sleep with the boss to get ahead!"

She hesitated only a moment. Then she twirled a long curl around her finger as if considering the question.

"Oh, I don't know," she said. "I believe it's a tried-and-true method in some companies."

Sebastian's jaw locked. She thought she could see steam coming out of his ears. Served him right, she thought.

"And as you say, Max *is* very attractive…for his age." She giggled again, as if enjoying some private reflection.

"You're more attracted to me than you are to Max." He said the words flatly, yet there was a wealth of challenge in them, and he looked at her as if daring her to deny them.

She opened her mouth, then shut it again. She arched her eyebrows at him provocatively. "You think so?"

"You know you are," he insisted. "There's been a spark between us since day one."

This time she opened her mouth and didn't shut it, still trying to formulate the words. She gave a careless, dismissive shrug. "In your dreams, Savas."

But Sebastian didn't wait. "You want proof?" He closed the space between them so that she had to tip her head up to look at him. His mouth was bare inches away. She could see the whiskered roughness of his jaw, could feel the heat of his breath.

She swallowed. She blinked. She waited.

And the next thing she knew Sebastian's lips came down on hers.

Neely had certainly been kissed before. She'd known her share of masculine mouths, their hard warmth, their persuasive touch. She'd opened to them, dared to taste them in turn. And she'd always been able to keep her wits about her, to think, *hmm, kissing is interesting, but no big deal.*

All of a sudden, right now, with Sebastian Savas's mouth on hers, it became a very big deal indeed.

There was the hard warmth and the persuasion. But there was more—a hunger, a need, a seeking, a question looking for an answer.

And her mouth knew the answer even as it asked questions of its own.

It wasn't just a spark, either. Though she would have had to admit, had she been capable of rational thought, that yes, she'd sensed it, too.

This was far more than a spark. It was a fire, burning hot and fast, fanned to full flame. And the deeper the kiss, the less the fire was quenched. It raged and consumed, hungry and desperate and edging toward out of control.

His arms came around her, slid up her back, drew her closer so that their bodies leaned, touched, pressed. She had never felt like this, had never wanted a kiss to go on and on. Had never kissed without caring where her next breath came from because she knew—she was sharing his.

She lifted her hands and touched his back, his shoulders, the nape of his neck. Her fingers threaded through short crisp hair, then fell to clutch his shoulders as her need spiraled, her hunger grew.

And then, abruptly, Sebastian pulled away to stare down into her eyes, his own lambent with arousal, his breathing harsh. "Does Max kiss you like that?"

Stunned, shaken and absolutely furious—as much at herself as at him, Neely could barely find the words. "No one kisses me like that!"

Sebastian smiled a satisfied feral smile. "So dear Max isn't perfect after all? I'm not surprised. It's what you get, trying to get it on with a man old enough to be your father."

Neely's heart was still slamming in her chest as she wrapped her arms across it and hoped she didn't look as rattled as she felt. "I wasn't trying to 'get it on' with Max. We were working."

"All night?" Sebastian scoffed.

"No, but until two. And then I went to bed. Alone. In the guest room."

"Yeah, sure. So, you're saying you're just friends, is that it?" Sebastian mocked her.

And Neely slowly, firmly shook her head no. "We're not just friends." She lifted her eyes and met Sebastian's knowing look. "He's my father."

CHAPTER FIVE

"YOUR *father?*" Seb stared at her, poleaxed. His heart hammered, his body clamored, and he didn't believe a word of it. "He is not."

"He is. Max is my dad." Robson insisted, her chin jutting as if she was daring him to take a poke at it.

Seb was sorely tempted, especially after he dragged in a desperate breath and looked at that chin more closely, spying something familiar in the shape of it as he did so.

God Almighty, was she really Max's daughter? Was that the female version of Max's chin he was seeing? He stared at her, stunned, still disbelieving.

Robson glared right back, eyes flashing. And the longer and harder he stared the more Seb realized that the color of her eyes was the same stormy blue of the man he'd just accused her of sleeping with.

Oh, hell.

The boss's daughter. And he had just kissed her senseless.

Worse, it wasn't only Neely Robson who'd been senseless with desire. He'd been right there with her—wanting her.

And now…now he wanted to kill her.

Ordinarily Seb went to ice when his emotions were frayed. He was all steely coldness when he needed to be. But his emotions were beyond frayed at the moment. And he went beyond ice and straight into meltdown.

"What the hell were you playing at?" he demanded.

"*Me?*" She arched her eyebrows in a way that annoyed him. As if she had nothing to reproach herself with.

"Never mind." He cut her off before she could speak. "I know damn well what you were doing! You were baiting me, trying to get me to make a complete ass of myself!"

"You did that all by yourself," she informed him airily. "And I did not bait you."

"The hell you didn't! 'Max is very attractive…for his age'!" He flung her words back at her in a mocking tone. "That's not baiting?"

"I was agreeing with what you said. You're the one who called him a 'stud' first. You're the one who accused me of having an affair with him! You've been accusing me practically since the day you met me!"

"And you've been acting like he was your long-lost lover!"

"Or my long-lost father."

She said the words quietly, but Seb was too incensed to care. "You didn't have to lead me on. You could have said, 'He's my father,' anytime at all."

"I could have," Neely agreed. "But why should I?"

"Because it's the truth!" he shouted.

At the fury of his explosion, Harm put back his head and howled.

"Now see what you've done!" Neely dropped to the floor and wrapped her arms around the dog, shushing him. He stopped howling and happily licked her chin.

"I didn't do anything," Seb said gruffly. "He was just yelling at you, too."

"Was not." Neely's voice was muffled against the dog's fur. She hugged him tightly.

Seb scowled down at her, still infuriated. "Stop hiding behind that dog."

At the accusation her head jerked up, and she threw him a daggerlike glare. But when Seb just stood there staring at her implacably, she scrambled to her feet, threw her shoulders back. "I am not hiding behind anything—not my dog, nor my father. And I did tell you—just now."

"Thanks a lot," he said sarcastically. "Thoughtful of you. Got any more…revelations, Robson?" He arched a brow at her. "Is your mother the Queen of England maybe?"

"Who's baiting whom now? And my mother is exactly who I said she was."

"A hippie who just happened to have a fling with the most uptight workaholic in the western hemisphere?"

"She had a relationship with Max. They lived together."

Seb's eyes widened in surprise.

"They did," Neely insisted. "They were young," she said. "And in love."

"Sure they were."

"See?" Robson pretended to pout. Aiming those moist, luscious lips at him. "There you go again, making judgments, jumping to conclusions! That's exactly why I didn't say I was Max's daughter in the first place. If I had, you would automatically have assumed that he'd given me the job because he's my father."

"And he didn't?" Seb asked sceptically.

"No, he didn't. He didn't give me my job at all. He's not even the one who hired me. Gloria Westerman in personnel hired me."

"You never met with Max?"

She folded her arms across her chest now and leaned back against the bar between the kitchen area and the living room. "I never met with Max."

"But you knew he was your father." It wasn't a question.

Robson nodded. "Yes, I knew. But he didn't know who I was at all. I hadn't seen him in years. We moved to California when I was four."

"And you never saw him again?"

"Not until November when I came to work. And then I didn't want him to know who I was. I use my stepfather's last name.

Max didn't know it. I wanted to make it on my own before I told him."

Seb rubbed a hand against the taut cords at the back of his neck. He was still ticked by her having gulled him with her pretense, but he could appreciate the reason she had given for not telling Max or anyone else who she was. If he was honest, he knew that in her shoes, he'd have been tempted to do the same.

"You're not telling me he still doesn't know, are you?" Because there was no way on earth he'd believe that.

"No, of course not. After I won the Balthus Grant and he invited me to work on the Wortman project with him, I knew I had to. If we were going to be working together, I wanted him to know. Besides by then I'd won the grant, so I knew and he knew—and so did everyone else—that I could do the job. See?"

Seb grunted. He rocked back on his heels, muttering under his breath. Yeah, he saw. It made sense, what she'd said. But it still annoyed him.

"You could have told me."

"Like you told me you were buying the houseboat!"

"That's not the same thing at all!"

"No? Well, it sure felt like it. One minute I thought I knew what was going on—I was buying a houseboat from Frank—and the next minute you walked in and it was yours! My home belonged to you!" "

Her face flushed again, the heightened color making her more beautiful than ever, and Seb felt an overwhelming urge to stop arguing and kiss her again.

He took one step toward her and she said abruptly, "Stay away!"

He stopped, brows drawing down. "Stay away?"

"Yes." She wrapped her arms even more tightly across her breasts as if she were cloaking herself in body armor.

He gave her a sardonic look. "You're going to go all cool and detached and claim that I forced myself on you? Another prevarication, Robson?"

Her lips pressed in a tight line. "I'm not lying, Savas. And I'm not claiming any such thing. But—" and here she shook her head fiercely "—you're not doing it again."

"Why not? You liked it. You kissed me back."

Let her deny that if she dared.

For a moment he thought she might, but then she shrugged. "Yes, I did."

"So…why stop? Don't you like kissing? It felt as if you liked kissing," he told her with a knowing grin.

"Kissing's fine." Her voice rose, as if she were going to say more, but in the end, she didn't. She simply shook her head.

"But…?" Seb coaxed her.

Her eyes flashed. "But there's no point!"

He could definitely think of a point to a passion as hot as the one that had raged between them. "Seems like we could have come up with one." He grinned again.

Robson didn't. "Well, one point," she allowed. "I suppose we could tear each other's clothes off and make—have mad passionate sex. But we're not going to."

"You don't like sex?" He'd noticed how she cut herself off, changed what she'd been going to say. Make love.

"It's fine," she muttered.

"Ah, kissing's fine. Sex is fine, but…" he goaded her now. "But what, Robson? You're frigid? Can't convince me of that." His body was still humming from the heat generated by their passion.

"I'm not trying to convince you," she fired back. "I'm just saying it isn't happening again. Not with you."

Their gazes met, locked, battled. Dear God, he wanted to stop fighting with her and take her to bed!

"You wanted me," he argued.

"I already admitted to that. I'll say it if you want—my body wants yours." She flung the words at him. "But I don't do 'sex for sex's sake,' Savas. I don't do 'one-night stands.'"

"No one said anything about one night."

"I don't do 'affairs,' damn it."

"You're a virgin?"

The flush on her face deepened. "No. I'm not a virgin. But I've learned my lesson. And I want sex to matter. I want it to mean more than just making my body and yours feel good. I want it to be an expression of love, commitment, even marriage!"

He gaped at her. "*With me?*"

"Good God, no! With the man I fall in love with!"

Seb opened his mouth to argue—and shut it again.

The smile Neely gave him was both bitter and knowing. "Exactly," she said.

It could have been worse.

Neely told herself that over and over, like a mantra, as she huddled shivering in a perfectly warm shower. Right now it didn't seem like such a beautiful morning after all.

It wasn't telling him about Max that bothered her. That bit of information was long overdue and she knew it. She hadn't known how to work it into the conversation. Somehow "Oh, by the way, Max is my dad" just wouldn't fall easily from her lips.

Still didn't.

But he knew it now. And that was pretty much the least of her problems.

She could have been swept away by his damned kiss.

She could have slid her hands under the soft cotton of his T-shirt to caress the hard-muscled warmth of his back. Could have lain right down with him on the sofa and lost all her inhibitions.

Could have, let's be honest, done exactly what she'd said when she'd thrown the "we could tear our clothes off and have mad passionate sex" words at him.

No, not *could* have. *Might* have.

Or even more accurately, *would* have, had Sebastian not stopped when he had.

Neely was beyond mortification. It didn't bear thinking about.

And yet, she had to think about it—to come to terms with it.

You never got past things you didn't face. She'd learned that from all the years she'd spent watching her mother simply move on rather than confront her demons.

But after having come within a hair's breadth of making mad passionate lo—having mad passionate sex—with Sebastian Savas, God help her, a little retreat and regroup seemed in order.

So she had taken her tote bag and what was left of her shattered composure and climbed the stairs.

There she took a shower, washed her hair, scrubbed her body and, especially, her face, as if she could remove every vestige of Sebastian's kiss, and tried to get a grip on her life.

She should move out.

But if she did, he'd think she was running away from him.

"You *are* running away from him, idiot," she said aloud, wringing out a cold washcloth and pressing it to her face, tried to reduce the heat she still felt.

But even so, she resisted actually running. She wasn't a wimp. She was a strong intelligent capable woman.

"Reduced to putty by a single kiss." She said that aloud, too.

But she knew, even as she said the words that it wasn't being reduced to putty that bothered her. Perversely the feeling was one that she'd often hoped for.

It was the way her mother had said kissing John made her feel. It was also the way she'd felt with Max.

In all honesty, Neely had longed for that feeling. Had begun to wonder if she ever would. And now she had.

With Sebastian Savas!

Of all the unsuitable men—a man who didn't do love, who didn't do commitment, who didn't do marriage.

Not that she wanted any of those things with him. God forbid.

But why did she have to feel that way, *need* that way?

And why in heaven's name did it have to happen now? With him?

A part of her wished she hadn't admitted who her father was.

If she hadn't, she could have thrown herself into the charade of being Max's girl.

But even as she thought it, Neely remembered telling Sebastian that she wasn't hiding behind Max.

And she wasn't, damn it!

Still, she would have liked to spend the rest of the day—or the rest of her life—in her room. But that was just another hiding place. So she dried her hair and got dressed and went back downstairs, not sure what to say now. Not sure what to do.

Only sure she wasn't kissing Sebastian again.

No question about that.

He was sitting at his computer working with his CAD program as she entered the living room. He had his back to her, but she saw him stiffen at the sound of her footsteps. Harm padded over and nudged her hopefully, then ran to the door.

"Yes," she said, relieved for the suggestion. "We'll go for a run." But she had something to say to Sebastian first.

She waited impatiently until he finished whatever he was doing, then she cleared her throat. For a moment she didn't think he was even going to bother to turn around, but finally he spun his chair around her way.

"It's not going to happen again," she said.

He blinked. "What's not?"

Oh, great, he was going to pretend it hadn't happened?

"The kiss," Neely said. "Any kisses." She felt like an idiot saying it, expecting he would shrug and say, "Nobody asked you," but he didn't.

He scowled. "Because you think I'm coming on to you because you're the boss's daughter?"

That hadn't even occurred to her. But before she could say so, he went on fiercely. "Well, forget it. I don't do that sort of thing ever."

"Oh." She paused. "Um, good." Pause. "I guess."

He looked at her, apoplectic. "You guess?"

"Well, I wasn't thinking you were. I mean, you didn't know, did you? When you…kissed me?"

"No, I didn't know! Then. But now I do and—" his tone was measured, but his gaze was not. It was simmering and intense "—I just want it to be clear."

She nodded. "It's clear. But really, it doesn't matter."

He blinked, then looked quizzical.

"Because it isn't happening again. No kissing," she repeated.

"Why?"

Now it was her turn to be apoplectic. "I told you why! Because kissing has to lead to something!"

"It does."

"To love? To marriage?"

"To bed," he said. "What's wrong with that? Or do you never kiss without wanting a proposal first?"

"What I don't do is kiss without any kind of possibility of commitment!"

"Ever?" He sounded stunned.

"Well, I just did, obviously." And the truth was, she wasn't that stingy with her kisses when they didn't matter. It was when they did—when they threatened to make her lose all sense of propriety, when they could have her tumbling straight into bed without a thought for tomorrow or next month or next year—yes, then she was very stingy indeed. "No kisses," she said again and met his disbelieving gaze with unblinking ferocity.

"You are a dinosaur," he told her.

"I am a dinosaur," she agreed. Better he think that than think she was a complete pushover.

He stared at her, then shook his head. "You just expect us to live together completely platonically when we could burn the boat to the ground with a kiss?"

"Yes."

He barked a laugh, but it wasn't a joyful sound. "Sure you don't want to move out, Robson?"

"I'm sure," she lied. She thought perhaps she ought to be

running away as fast as she could. "We are, after all, adults," she reminded him.

"I'd say that's the problem, not the solution."

"We have self-control," she went on relentlessly. "Or I do," she added. "Don't you?"

His teeth came together. "I have self-control, Robson," he said flatly, just as she had hoped he would.

"So it won't be a problem, then. It will just be hands off," she said brightly.

For a long moment Sebastian didn't say anything. Then he agreed gruffly. "Hands off."

"And…mouths off?"

"What are you, a lawyer?"

"Just covering…all eventualities. So, no kissing?"

A muscle ticked in his temple. "I already said that."

"Just making sure." But at the same time she was extracting the promise, she was staring at him sprawled there in that chair. He was still wearing a pair of running shorts and a T-shirt that treated her to far too much visual stimulation. Sebastian Savas with his long bare legs splayed and his muscular arms flexing as he cracked his knuckles did disastrous and very unfair things to her libido.

It wasn't fair that such an unsuitable man should be able to make her heart kick over and her pulse quicken and other intimate parts of her body tingle with the mere awareness of him.

Their gazes met. And held. And held some more.

Sebastian swallowed. And even the sight of his Adam's apple moving in his throat was an enticement.

The discovery made Neely gulp. She moistened her lips with her tongue.

Sebastian shut his eyes. "Oh, for God's sake, just get the hell out of here."

There.

It was simple.

Mind over matter. Or libido. Or something.

It wasn't as if she wanted to want Sebastian Savas, after all. He was the last man she should be interested in.

She wasn't interested in him.

Much.

It would have been easy—or at least *easier*—if he'd had to go back to Reno. But he didn't. He was there—on the houseboat whenever she got up in the morning, coming out of his bedroom just as she was getting out of the bathroom. Coming abruptly face to breastbone with his bare chest was not conducive to pure innocent thoughts.

And then he would come downstairs looking all polished and professional—long-sleeved pale-blue starched dress shirts and dark trousers that should have looked like body armor but on Sebastian looked sexy as hell because she had no trouble imagining the hard-muscled man beneath them.

He was there at work, too. Not often. They didn't work together. She was working with Max on Blake-Carmody, and Sebastian was doing whatever it was Sebastian was doing—but every now and then she caught a glimpse of him, caught him looking at her.

And abruptly they would both look away.

And no matter what she was doing or saying or supposed to be doing or saying, in fact she was thinking instead about what it had been like to kiss him.

It wasn't just one day or two. It was the whole week. Day in, day out.

"What's the matter with you?" Max asked. "You don't have your eye on the ball."

No, she didn't.

She had it on Sebastian Savas.

It was the stupidest thing he'd ever heard.

No kissing!

What was she, a department store dummy? No feelings? No urges? No needs?

Of course he could control his libido—but why should he? It wasn't as if he was going to get emotionally involved.

Was she?

The thought brought him up short. He wasn't used to dealing with women who wanted more from him than he was inclined to give.

Did Robson want more? Was she in danger of falling in love with him? Was *that* what she was saying?

Of course she wasn't! She hated his guts for saying she designed doll houses. She was attracted, that's all.

And resisting.

So she'd come up with a silly rule.

Well, fine. He could abide by it. It wasn't as if he spent every day thinking about Neely Robson…imagining her lips under his…fantasizing about kissing her.

Well, he hadn't until the day he'd actually done it.

And now, damn it, he couldn't seem to forget.

It would have been easier if he'd got to go back to Reno this week. But no, he was stuck in Seattle the whole time, running into her first thing in the morning when she was still sleep-rumpled and soft-lipped.

"Oops, sorry!" she said, and skittered out of his way. But not before she'd brushed against him doing so. And how the hell was he supposed to just pretend his body didn't leap in response to that?

And then he came downstairs to find her playing with the kittens or sitting in her rocking chair cuddling the rabbit under her chin or nuzzling the blasted guinea pig—and his fingers itched to take the animal out of her hands and pull her into his arms and do a little nuzzling and cuddling of his own.

Ordinarily he got away from her at work, but it was uncanny the number of times he ran smack into her in the hallway and she licked her lips, startled, and he couldn't help staring straight at them.

Almost worse was going into the blueprint room to see her

leaning over the drafting table, her derriere so neatly outlined in her navy trousers as she'd sketched something in for Max. At the sight he'd slopped his coffee on his hand, making him curse.

Worst of all, though, was seeing her disappear into Max's office and knowing perfectly well that she wasn't in there coming on to Max at all.

She was perfectly free.

And—by her own decree—totally off-limits. Sebastian ground his teeth at the pointlessness of it.

But then he reminded himself that sex was simply a biological urge. Any appealing woman would do.

Only his father seemed to feel the need to marry them.

Sebastian didn't. Sebastian wouldn't. So he either had to put her out of his mind and find someone else to occupy his wayward thoughts. Or he needed to change her mind.

Soon.

The best defense might be a good offense in football and war and all those sweaty fierce masculine pursuits.

But as far as Neely could tell, the best defense for dealing with the effect Sebastian Savas was having on her was going out, keeping busy—and meeting other men.

"Running scared?" Max said when she told him she was playing intramural volleyball on Monday nights and going bowling on Wednesdays after work. She had gone to book discussion group at the library on Tuesday and she was giving serious thought to taking Harm to obedience class on Thursdays.

Any dog who knocked people into the water needed obedience, didn't he?

"Running scared?" Neely echoed Max's words and tried to invest them with as much scorn as possible. "Of what, pray tell?"

"Your roommate," Max said. He arched a speculative brow and regarded Neely with amusement.

She was beginning to wish she hadn't bothered to stop in his office on her way to the gym. "Why would you say that?" She couldn't be that obvious, could she?

"You never felt the need to get out every night when you were living with Frank." Max shrugged. "And you didn't last week when Seb was in Reno."

Neely glared at him. "Don't you have anything better to do than work out my motivations?"

A grin flashed across Max's face. "You're my daughter. I'm catching up on all the years I never got to be a father."

"If you want to practice all the things you missed, Mom's coming out this weekend."

Abruptly Max's smile vanished and he straightened up in his desk chair, put both feet on the floor and gave Neely a hard look. "Your mother and I are past history."

Neely gave an airy wave of her hand. "Just thought you'd like to know."

Max grunted. "Go bowl."

She did. She even went out for a beer with the group afterward. It was nearly nine when she got home. Sebastian was working at the computer. He didn't turn around when she came in, but kept working while she made a fuss over the kittens, then scratched Harm's ears and said, "Hang on. Let me put my stuff upstairs and I'll take you for a run."

"I already did."

She blinked as Sebastian spun his chair around and met her surprise with an unsmiling stare. "Oh. Well, um, thanks."

"And I fed the cats and the rabbits and the guinea pig. Maybe you shouldn't have animals if you're not going to take care of them, Robson."

Neely straightened, eye wide. "I beg your pardon? Who says I don't take care of them?"

"Well, you're gone all day and all night—"

"I came home at lunch and took Harm for a run. I came home before I went bowling and fed him and took him out. I fed the kittens. I played with them. I took the rabbits out on the deck. I *never* neglect my animals! And if you think I do, then you can—"

Sebastian raised his hands, palms out. "So, fine, you do take care of them, I didn't know. You weren't here. At least you're not here whenever I've been here. Which must take quite a lot of effort on your part." He paused and then repeated, "You aren't here. I wonder why…." He let his voice trail off.

Their gazes met and she knew Sebastian knew exactly why she wasn't here.

She waited for him to suggest, as Max had, that she was running scared, but he just said gruffly, "Anyway, I took him for a run."

"Thank you." Her tone was stiff. And she turned away to clip Harm's leash on his collar anyway.

"I'm leaving in the morning," he said to her back. "Back to Reno. So I won't be here to walk your dog. "

"I'm sure we'll manage," she said, still not looking at him, heading toward the door.

"Or kiss you senseless."

She spun around and stared at him.

He smiled. "Only saying."

It was far better that Sebastian was gone.

Really, it was. She didn't have to keep bumping into him in the hallway or on the stairs. There was no T-shirt hanging on the hook in the bathroom tempting her to pluck it off and breathe in the subtle scent of him. There was also no coffee container sitting on the countertop because he'd forgotten to put it away, and no running shoes by the door to trip over, and no pair of smoky-green eyes watching her every time she looked up.

It was a relief all the way around.

So why did the place seem so empty?

It wasn't empty, of course. Harm was here. The kittens were here. And the rabbits and the guinea pig.

It was exactly the way it would have been after Frank left.

Exactly the way it was when Seb had gone to Reno after the very first weekend he'd bought the houseboat. It hadn't been lonely then, had it?

Well, actually, now that you mentioned it…

No! Forget it. And it was true that she did breathe easier while he was gone—though she still felt his presence everywhere.

But she had to admit she was surprised and a little disconcerted when Friday came and Sebastian didn't.

She didn't go out on Friday night, actually sat home and worked and played with the kittens and, heaven help her, played the violin that Sebastian had brought with him.

Why not? She thought crossly. *He* never played it.

She was always careful to put it back where she found it. She didn't think he ever knew she'd touched it.

She shouldn't touch it. And yet she couldn't seem to keep her hands off.

She'd missed not playing, but she hadn't realized how much until she began again. It had nothing at all to do with it being Sebastian's violin.

Nothing!

Saturday her mother arrived and there was barely time to think about Sebastian, except to be grateful he wasn't there. Her mother wasn't going to stay with her; she'd arranged to stay with a friend on Vashon Island. But of course Neely was picking her up at the airport and would take her back to see the houseboat.

Still she hoped he hadn't come back while she was at the airport. She didn't think Sebastian needed to meet her mother, and she was quite sure Lara didn't need to meet Sebastian.

She hadn't seen her mother since going back to Wisconsin at Christmas, but Lara was the same as ever, rather like the weather—mostly sunny and with scattered clouds and the occasional rain shower whenever she teared up remembering "the good old days" with John.

"It's so empty without him," she told Neely in the car on their way from the airport to Lake Union. "Even after all this time."

"I know," Neely agreed, because it was—and because knocking around the houseboat the past two days had given her a glimmer of how empty life could seem—and how aware she was of a man who wasn't there.

"But he'd be glad I'm out visiting you instead of staying home," Lara went on as they drove north from the airport. "I can hardly wait to see your houseboat."

"Oh, er, about the houseboat…" Neely hadn't told her mother about what happened. Now she did, and watched Lara's consternation grow.

"You're sharing a houseboat with a man?"

"I've always been sharing a houseboat with a man. This is just a different man."

"What sort of man?"

"He's like Dad. A workaholic architect. Totally consumed by his job." Well, almost.

Lara looked appalled. "Like your father? You're not sleeping with him!"

"*What?*" Neely almost drove into the side of a fish seller's van.

"Of course you're not. You're far more sensible than I ever was." Lara shook her head at the memory. "But if he's really like your father you have to be careful."

Tell me something I don't know, Neely thought. "I am being careful, Mom," she said with more assurance than she felt. "You don't need to worry. We have an understanding."

Lara muffled a snort. "You might. Does he?" she asked sceptically.

"Of course he does."

"Mmm." Lara's doubts were evident. "If he's like your father he can be very persuasive."

"Mom!"

"I'm only saying," Lara said defensively. "Max was very determined."

Thank you for sharing, Neely thought, reasonably certain she could have done without the knowledge. "Speaking of whom, are you planning on seeing him while you're here?"

"Not likely," Lara said. "He wasn't pleased that I took you and scarpered."

Neely blinked. "You did?"

Lara made a noise that might have been agreement. "He was very bossy. And he expected me to just fall in with whatever he thought we should do. Or not do. And then, he worked all the time and I was just supposed to get the leftovers—a few minutes here and there, which there were damn few of," she said darkly. "He didn't even have time to get married." She shrugged. "So I left."

"Really?" The details had never been forthcoming before. It must have been coming back to Seattle that coaxed them out of her mother.

"Yes, really. What was I supposed to do? Just sit around and wait for him to come to his senses? Hardly likely. Max wasn't the type. So I thought I'd do something dramatic, like leave. And he'd wake up." She laughed a little bitterly. "The more fool I. He hated all that commune stuff so when I took off for the place near Berkeley, I was sure he'd come and grab us both back. But—" she shrugged "—he didn't. So it's good I left. He had a lousy sense of priorities."

Neely had been barely four at the time they'd decamped for the commune. She had few memories of her father from those days. Mostly she remembered waiting and waiting for him to come and pick her up—and then her mother saying, "I guess something really important happened. Let's you and I go to the park."

Now she gave her mother credit for not bad-mouthing her father when she easily could have.

"I think he might have changed a little," she said now. "He does go sailing with me."

"Hasn't stood you up?" Lara said with a wry look.

Neely shook her head. "I bet if we invited him to dinner, he'd even come." Though in truth she wasn't sure at all.

Lara just shook her head. "Don't play matchmaker. Your father and I had our chance. I came out here to see you and to get together with Serena." That was the friend she was staying with. "I've had a good marriage. I have no intention of trying to rekindle a fire that burned out a long time ago."

"You don't even want to see him while you're out here?"

Lara shook her head. "Only if he were tied down so I could tell him a thing or two without him running off to a meeting."

And given her father's less than enthusiastic response to the news of her mother's visit, Neely didn't think that was likely to happen. She kept her eyes on the road. But as she took the off ramp for Lake Union, she thought there was something almost ironic in discovering that her mother might be able to teach her something about dealing with men after all.

CHAPTER SIX

"IS SHE gone?"

The voice on the phone was Max's. It was midmorning on Sunday and Neely had just come back from taking Harm to the dog park to run with his buddies for an hour.

"From my place or from the state?" Neely replied, not having to ask who he was talking about.

"The state."

"Nope. Not for a couple of weeks. But she's not here if that's what you're worried about."

"I'm not worried," Max said gruffly. "Thought I'd drop off the specs for Blake-Carmody, but not if she was there. Want to go sailing after?"

"I can't. I'm meeting with Stephen Blake tomorrow morning. I need to get all the designs in order. Mom's out on Vashon staying with a friend. Why don't you take her sailing?"

"Don't make me laugh."

When Max showed up an hour later he still wasn't laughing. In fact he was edgy and kept glancing around, as if he expected a jack-in-the-box to pop out of a cupboard, rather like she was whenever Sebastian was around.

Only it was more amusing to witness someone else's agitation rather than feel her own.

"Why isn't she staying with you?" Max asked without preamble. Again Neely didn't have to ask who.

"Who would she sleep with? Sebastian?"

Max, who had been prowling the living room, jerked and spun to stare at her.

"Kidding," Neely said lightly.

Max's face cleared and he managed a grin. "Very funny." He gave himself a little shake. "Sure you don't want to come?" he nodded in the direction of the harbor where his new sailboat was moored.

Neely shook her head and picked up the portfolio she was working on. "Duty calls."

"Carry on, then," Max said, and left as quickly as he'd come.

In the silence he left behind, for the first time Neely actually did get some work done. Heaven knew there was plenty to do, and she'd been distracted all week. Now she didn't sit around waiting for the other shoe to drop—or Sebastian to walk in the front door.

So she was deep in a sketch of one of the condos' living spaces when the sound of the doorbell jolted her and sent her pencil skittering across the pad.

"Drat," she muttered under her breath, but got up to answer it, nudging Harm out of the way so he didn't launch himself enthusiastically at the kid selling cookie dough or magazine subscriptions or at Cody's mother, come to ask if she could borrow a cup of sugar.

Mentally she prepared to say no to the cookie dough and magazines and yes to the sugar, provided they had any. But when she opened the door there was a young woman standing there looking as surprised to see her as Neely was.

She was probably close to Neely's age, maybe a bit younger, certainly curvier, which her shorts and halter top all too clearly revealed. She was tall and tanned and had the most gorgeous honey-and-sunlight-colored windblown mass of hair Neely had ever seen.

They stared at each other in silence.

Then Harm, whom Neely held by the collar, said, "Woooof!" in his big deep bloodhound voice, and the other woman's gaze jerked down to see him and her eyes got even wider.

"I must have the wrong houseboat," she said, rapidly starting to back away. "I'm looking for Sebastian Savas. But I've obviously got it wrong. Excuse me. I—"

It took Neely this long to get her own tongue untangled. "No," she said, "you don't. This is…I mean, he lives here."

And obviously had enough time for at least one gorgeous woman.

"He does?" The woman's voice almost squeaked. "With you? I mean…I didn't know he…well, heavens."

Which was not quite what Neely was thinking, but close.

"He's not here now though," she went on, telling herself she was very glad to have met Sebastian's girlfriend. She could stop thinking about him at all now. Could stop wishing…

"Oh." The other woman managed a sort of smile.

"I don't know when he'll be back," Neely said. "He's out of town. But I can tell him you came by."

"Er, I'm not sure you should," the woman said. "He'll probably go ballistic."

As opposed to being The Iceman? Neely thought. Though it was quite some time since she'd considered him icy in the least. Rather she thought he smouldered. And that was conceivably worse.

"He didn't tell me where he lived," the woman confided. "And now I know why." This time she took her time as her gaze swept over Neely appraisingly.

Oh, dear. "I'm not—I mean, we're not—I think you're mis-understanding," she said quickly, not wanting Sebastian's girl-friend to get the wrong idea. The last thing she wanted was Sebastian blaming her for the bust-up of whatever sort of rela-tionship he had with this woman. "He's not my boyfriend," she assured the woman. "You don't have to worry."

The woman laughed. It was a real laugh, too. "I think you're mis-understanding, too. He's not my boyfriend, either. He's my brother."

Neely goggled. "Your—"

"Brother. Well, half brother, really. The best one in the world," she said firmly. "For all that he's a little, um, secretive, at times. He never mentioned *you*. Do you…live with him?"

"Yes, but—"

"That sod! He's living with a woman? After he told me *NEVER* to live with Garrett before we got married—"

"Oh, you're the bride?" Neely felt oddly as if a weight had been lifted from her shoulders.

Sebastian's sister nodded. "I'm Evangeline. Everybody calls me Vangie. Who are you?"

"Neely Robson. I work with your brother."

Vangie looked as if she was sure that wasn't all Neely did with her brother. But she didn't argue. She just knelt and put her arms around Harm. "And you two even have a dog! We never had pets."

"Er, well, Harm is mine, really," Neely said.

"But you share him," Vangie decided. "Seb always wanted a dog. But my mother didn't want to be bothered. And then Matt's mother didn't. Or the triplets' or—"

"What?" Neely stared at her.

Vangie shrugged. "I'm glad he has a dog now," she said simply. "He's finally getting what he deserves."

Neely wasn't sure at all about that. But then again, she wasn't sure what Sebastian Savas deserved.

His sister, however, gave Harm a fierce hug and looked up at Neely with her luminous green eyes suddenly awash with tears. "I just hope I do," she said, and the tears started rolling down her cheeks.

Good grief. Not given to drop-of-the-hat emotional displays herself, Neely stared, nonplussed for several seconds before she said, "Are you all right?" which was a stupid question because who burst into tears if she was?

Vangie gulped and blinking rapidly stood up again. "I'm f-fine. I just…wanted to talk to Seb. He gets me through everything. Always has. And I know he wouldn't expect me to show up here, but I thought he would understand…and help and…" She broke off and wiped her eyes on the back of her hand.

"Do you want to come in?" Neely asked because somehow she didn't feel she could just shut the door on Sebastian's sister, especially when she was crying.

Vangie gulped, then brightened visibly. "Would it…be okay? I mean, you don't know me. But you do know Seb," she added a bit more cheerfully. "You live with Seb, and—"

"Not the way you're using the term," Neely said again.

But Vangie had apparently decided that, yes, she did want to come in because she stepped past Neely into the hallway, then followed a tail-wagging Harm into the living area beyond.

"Ohhh," she exclaimed, looking around avidly. "I love it! It's so much nicer than Seb's penthouse."

"It is?" Neely blinked.

"Well, you know what I mean—friendlier, homier." Her eyes went straight to the guinea pig and the rabbits. Then one of the kittens who was on the back of the sofa launched himself at her and she gave a little shriek as she caught him in her hands.

Her gaze turned to meet Neely's, "It's a miracle."

"What's a miracle?"

"You…them—" she waved the kitten around as if encompassing the whole room "—this. And Seb. Unbelievable."

"The dog isn't his. Neither are the kittens. Or anything else—except the computer," Neely said stiffly.

"I'm sooo happy for you. And him."

Obviously his sister didn't listen any better than Sebastian did. For the moment Neely gave up.

"Can I get you some iced tea? A soda?"

"Iced tea would be lovely." She had better manners than her brother at least.

While Neely poured two glasses, she watched as Vangie explored, as politely as possible—definitely not like her brother—the downstairs living area. She ran appreciative fingers along the tops of the waist-high bookcases, studied the books on the bookshelves, all the while cuddling the kitten who'd leaped at her. Then scooping up another one, she went to kneel on the window seat and look out at the deck and the lake beyond.

"Here we are, then," Neely said, coming up behind her and holding out the glass.

"Oh, thank you." Vangie turned, blinking, and Neely could see more tear tracks on her face.

"Oh, dear," Neely said involuntarily. "You're not all right."

Vangie blinked rapidly and set down a kitten to take the glass. "I am," she said, managing a watery smile. "It's just…I don't know what to do! Seb always tells me and—"

"I can believe that."

Vangie looked startled. "Oh, I don't mean he's bossy," she said quickly.

"I do," Neely muttered, but then she smiled. "I'm sure he's not so bossy to you."

"Not often. He's so kind. And he listens!"

"Does he?" How unusual, Neely thought. Obviously there were bits to Sebastian that she had missed. Or that he had never allowed her to see.

"He's the only one who's been here for me through all the wedding preparations."

"Ah, yes. He mentioned your wedding." And the little colored boxes. But Neely didn't bring that up.

Vangie nodded and sipped her tea. "I know it's been hard for him, me calling him up at all hours, bothering him at work. It's not like he cares about any of it," she confided, which Neely found both astute and surprising.

"But he cares about me. He cares about all of us," Vangie went on. "And I know, if anyone can make Daddy come to my wedding, it's Sebastian!"

Her green eyes were wide and bright, an equal combination of eager and desperate.

"Are you sure?" Neely asked cautiously. Because while she didn't know much about Sebastian and his father, the one thing she did know was that, on Sebastian's side at least, there seemed to be no love lost at all. She didn't get the feeling he had much to do with his father.

Vangie bobbed her head. "Oh, yes. And he has to! Garrett's family think it's all a bit strange that Daddy hasn't turned up yet. And I keep saying he's a very busy man, that he'll be here for the wedding. But—" she gulped "—I don't know if he will!"

"Why don't *you* ask him?"

"He doesn't answer his phone. He doesn't answer e-mails. I don't even know if he gets them. He's in Hong Kong or Timbuktu or someplace like that. That's what I told Garrett. But well, it's a little odd—if you don't know Daddy. And Garrett's parents are—" the tears threatened again and Neely offered her a tissue "—wondering what sort of family he's marrying into."

"He's not marrying them," Neely said firmly. "He's marrying you."

"But they're asking!" Vangie wiped her eyes, then strangled the tissue. "And Garrett would like to meet him, too! He never has. And...and it's not *normal* to have a father who doesn't even show up at your wedding! For once in my life—just once—on my wedding day I'd like to be normal." Vangie said fiercely. "You understand, don't you?"

Actually, Neely did. All those years in the commune had made her long for a normal family life. It had mattered a lot to her when she didn't have a father to speak of. And the one she'd had once her mother married John was every bit what she'd thought it would be. And hadn't she come out to Seattle to try to establish a relationship with Max?

So who was she to say Vangie was wrong. She gave Sebastian's sister a gentle smile and patted her hand. "I understand."

Vangie swallowed and managed a smile. "I knew you would. You'll ask him for me, won't you?"

"What?" Neely started. "Me? Ask your father to come to your wedding?"

"No," Vangie gave a strangled laugh. "Not Daddy. Sebastian! To ask Daddy." She was nodding her head eagerly now.

"Don't be silly," Neely said. "Your brother doesn't listen to me."

"Of course he does," Vangie said. "He lives with you."

"Not the way you think."

"He cares about you."

Now it was Neely's turn to blink. "What?"

"Well, he must or he would have thrown you out. And he let you keep all your animals and—"

"It's a free country and I have a lease."

"That wouldn't matter to Sebastian," Vangie said confidently.

"He won't listen," Neely insisted.

Vangie set down her glass and reached out to grasp Neely's hands in hers, imploring her, "Try. Please just say you'll try."

"It won't help. It might hurt." *He doesn't like me,* she wanted to say. But she couldn't say that with confidence anymore. Truth be told, she didn't know how Sebastian felt about her. Only that he liked kissing her—and if she weren't careful he would do it again.

But saying that would not convince Vangie that Neely had no influence on her brother. Wordlessly she shook her head.

But Vangie didn't let go. She just clung to Neely's hands. "Please."

"I'll tell him you came by." Neely relented at last. "I'll tell him what you wanted. I can't promise any more than that."

Vangie looked at her with her heart in her eyes. Then, she pressed her lips together and her eyes shut. She squeezed Neely's hands between hers, and Neely got the worrisome sense that there was some praying going on and she was somehow involved in it.

Then Vangie opened her eyes again and smiled a beatific smile. "Thank you! You're a dear!" And she lunged forward to give Neely a fierce hug. Then almost before Neely could get a breath, Sebastian's sister bounced off the window seat, bent to give Harm a hug, too, then started for the door.

It opened just seconds before she reached it.

"Seb!" And she launched herself into his unsuspecting arms.

"What the—!" Sebastian dropped his suitcase and caught his sister with what were clearly the reflexes of long practice, hugging her to him with an obvious fierce affection at the same time glaring over her head at Neely.

"What's she doing here?" he demanded as if she had orchestrated the whole thing.

"You're asking *me?*"

He eased Vangie away from him to look down into her eyes. "What's going on?" he said, and Neely was once more caught by the mixture of love and exasperation in his voice.

"I need you to talk to Daddy," Vangie said plaintively. "Please!"

Sebastian's face hardened. He opened his mouth, but then his gaze went to Neely and grimly he shut it again.

"I think I'll just take Harm for a run," she said briskly, grabbing the leash. "You two have things to discuss."

"Oh, but you can stay and—" Vangie began.

But Neely was already brushing past them. "Lovely to meet you," she said to Sebastian's sister and, giving both Vangie and Sebastian a bright smile, she chivvied Harm out the door.

He was back.

Right when she least expected him, of course.

And maybe she was "running scared" as Max had accused her, because the very sight of him in the doorway sent her heart kicking over double time. And seeing him with his sister didn't help.

It was far easier to think of Sebastian as a coldhearted, cold-blooded iceman. And far harder to resist him when she knew how very hot-blooded he was—and how warmhearted his sister, at least, considered him.

"Which does not make him a good man to get involved with," she reminded herself more than once as she and Harm walked mile after mile, determined to stay away as long as possible. He was kind to his sister, yes. He was—though he might deny it—a family man.

But he didn't want a relationship. He was adamant about that.

And Neely didn't want anything less.

"Remember that," she said out loud, making Harm look back at her quizzically as if it were a command he didn't quite understand.

It was. But not for him.

She felt relieved, then, to open the front door and find the houseboat completely quiet. The only light was the one above the stove that she could see down the hall. Sebastian must have left again. Probably with his sister.

Despite the tears, Neely was sure that the two of them would have come to an agreement. And she had no doubt that Vangie had convinced him to contact their father.

Neely unclipped Harm's leash and shrugged out of her windbreaker, then padded out to the darkened living area. It was one big room, really, just carved into a living room space over by the deck, an office space, where she stood now, and a kitchen, where she should go feed her grumbling stomach.

But she wasn't hungry—or not for food. Her soul seemed restless still for something more sustaining. And so, almost automatically, she clambered up onto the cabinet where she could reach onto the top shelf of the bookcase. She'd done it so often now that she could take the violin and bow down in the dark.

The truth was, she'd played it a lot this week. The music soothed her restlessness, calmed her and focused her. And if Sebastian was going to come back tonight, she'd need to be calm and focused.

She resined the bow, tuned the violin and began to play.

She played her Mozart etudes and her Bach minuets. Harm never started to howl until she got to the Vivaldi. And she told herself he wasn't really protesting, he was moved and was singing along.

She could see him silhouetted against the lights from Queen Anne Hill that shone across the water, his head lifted as he warbled while she played, when all of a sudden a voice said, "Cut that out!"

The bow screeched across the strings and stopped abruptly. Harm's accompaniment lasted a couple of seconds longer.

Then another silhouette rose, this one from the far side of the sofa where he'd obviously been lying in the shadows. And Sebastian turned her way and said, "Not you. The dog."

Horrified, Neely stared at him, her fingers strangling the bow. They suddenly felt so clammy she was afraid she might drop it or, worse, the violin. "I thought you were gone!"

"Think again." Sebastian came around the sofa and crossed the room toward her. Neely set the violin down on the cabinet top as carefully as she could and backed toward the kitchen. A stupid move, if she'd thought about it, as there was only one way out.

"I'm sorry," she said quickly.

"Why?"

"I shouldn't have played it. I—"

"It was meant to be played. That's what it's for." He was much closer now. Practically looming over her, and there was nowhere to go.

"Yes, but you don't play it," she protested.

"Because I can't," he said simply.

"What?" She stared at him, astonished.

He shrugged. "I never learned. It's my grandfather's violin. He played it. Almost as well as you," he added after a moment, a corner of his mouth tipping up, his tone reflective.

Neely swallowed, still wary, but beginning to realize he wasn't angry. "Thank you. But I still…should have asked."

"When? You were never here when I was." He was sort of smiling now, teasing a little.

She didn't want to be teased, didn't want to smile back. Wanted to hang on to her sanity. Definitely needed to resist.

But Sebastian said, "You can play it whenever you want. However much you want. You're very good."

"Not very," Neely said. "You have low standards."

He shook his head. "I don't, you know." He was quite firm about it. And he was barely a foot from her now, definitely looming. Also smiling.

Neely, feeling the force of the smile, sensing the electricity that always seemed in danger of sizzling between them, felt herself melting. She raised her palms, then discovered that the only place to put them was on his shirtfront.

Quickly she let them fall to her sides again, cleared her throat, tried to look for a way to duck around him.

"If you think you ought to give me some recompense, though, I'd understand," Sebastian went on, his voice almost a soft purr.

"You mean pay for the privilege? I could do that," Neely said. "It's a terrific violin. I've never played one that good. How much do you want?"

"How about a kiss?"

She jerked back so hard she hit her elbow against the countertop edge behind her and winced. "Ow!"

"Or I could kiss it and make it better," Sebastian said, reaching for her arm and lifting it, then pressing his lips to her elbow before she even had time to think.

The tingle of the touch of his mouth against her skin sent a shiver all the way up her arm and her spine to the back of her neck.

"For heaven's sake!" she protested, trying—and failing—to tug her arm away.

But Seb hung on, bending his head over it, giving her more

tiny kisses, making her tremble as he worked his way up her arm to her shoulder, her neck, her ear, her jaw.

She made a helpless noise somewhere in the back of her throat—telling herself that she didn't want this. But every part of her, body and mind was telling her she wanted it very very much indeed. She just didn't want to pay the price. The price of having her heart broken.

Her body sank back against the line of cupboards below the countertop. And instinctively she braced her other elbow on it while trying to keep her knees from buckling from the effect he was having on her.

The kisses nibbled their way along her jawline as soft strands of his hair brushed against her cheeks, her lips. She breathed in the scent of him—woodsy shampoo with a hint of the sea mixing with something simply Sebastian. If she lived to be a hundred, Neely knew she would never forget it.

And then his lips reached her chin, touched her mouth. His tongue teased its way over her lips, parting them, tasting them— tasting her.

She sighed, reached for him. Clung. And kissed him back, because she was powerless not to. She kept remembering Vangie's desperation, her words of praise for her brother, her steadfast belief that no matter what the problem, Sebastian would make it right.

And she saw how much he cared for his family.

If he were, through and through, the blackguard she'd first imagined, if he were as icy and indifferent as he'd tried to be, she thought she might have been able to hold out.

But she couldn't. He even let her play his grandfather's violin.

She opened her lips to his and hung on and, for the moment at least, let herself enjoy the ride.

One thing Sebastian Savas was extremely good at, one thing at which he positively excelled, was kissing.

Neely couldn't imagine why she'd ever thought he was cold.

Certainly there was nothing cold in the feel of his mouth on hers, nothing icy in the touch of his hands as they slid around her waist and lifted her onto the countertop so he could step up between her knees. And there was absolutely nothing frigid about the way he made her feel.

It was a long kiss, a hungry desperate kiss, and it wreaked havoc with all her earlier determination to resist him.

He wasn't good for her. He didn't want what she wanted. But even knowing it, she couldn't seem to pull away. She could only hang on and savor what was happening between them.

It wasn't until his fingers slid up beneath her shirt and began to work on the clasp to her bra that she realized more was happening than the simply wonderful drugging taste of him. And she was torn, battling with herself first before she pulled her arms away from his back and pressed them against his shoulders.

"No," she said raggedly. "Don't. I don't want this."

His fingers stilled for a moment. He drew back enough to look down into her face, his own taut with desire.

"You do," he said, and his gaze dropped to watch the rise and fall of her breasts, then lifted to look at her lips before he met her eyes again. "You want me. Don't lie, Neely."

She swallowed and nodded jerkily. "All right, yes. I want it. But not what will come after. I don't want what you want!"

"What's that?"

"Sex."

"You don't want sex?" He looked incredulous.

Of course she wanted sex, wanted to make love with him. But his words said it all. Not making love—sex.

"You know what I mean! We already discussed this. It's why I said no kissing. No one-night stands!"

"I think I can guarantee it will be more than one night," Seb said with smile.

But Neely's eyes flashed fire. "Stop it. Stop willfully misunderstanding me. I want love. Maybe that sounds hokey to you.

But it's the way I think, the way I feel, the way I want to live my life. I don't want just sex. I want a future. I want a relationship that will last." To love and be loved.

"You know any of those?" Sebastian's tone was bitter. But he stepped back a bit, put some space between them. His breathing was still ragged. "Max some sort of poster boy for long-term relationships, is he?"

"No, of course not. But my mother and John were. Or they would have been if John hadn't died. What they had was deep and real and lasting."

"You don't know their relationship would've lasted."

"I do. I know it. Here." And she put her hand over her heart in a gesture that she supposed was corny to him, but it shut him up.

He grimaced, jaw tight, then shook his head and heaved a sigh. "You're going to be a pain in the ass about this, aren't you? You're really serious."

Neely nodded gravely. "I'm really serious." She managed a faint smile, thinking how hard it was to be sensible when she really wanted to finish what they'd started.

At least Sebastian had stepped back far enough that they weren't touching now. She pulled her knees together, sat up straighter on the countertop. "Why were you lying there in the dark?"

There was still barely enough lights from the moonlight and the lights on Queen Anne Hill for her to see his expression now that he'd moved away. He'd been staring out into the darkness, but now he looked back at her sharply. "What do you mean?"

"Just what I said. You don't usually do that. You're usually working."

"I've been working. I worked all weekend, damn it. I got home looking forward to a little respite and damned if Vangie wasn't here! No respite in that."

"She thinks the sun rises and sets on you."

He raked his fingers through his hair. "She's wrong."

"Obviously she knows she can depend on you."

"For sensible things she can. Not for this." And abruptly he turned and walked out of the kitchen.

Surprised, Neely jumped down off the counter and followed him. "You're not going to do it?"

"Hell, no! If she wants the old man at her wedding, she can invite him."

"I gather she tried."

"Exactly. And he ignored her. Just the way he'll ignore me."

"She didn't think so."

"She thinks what she wants to think!" He was pacing around the living room now, cracking his knuckles.

And Neely, watching, could feel the agitation rolling off him in waves. "Is she the first to get married?" she asked him. "Of all of your brothers and sisters, I mean?"

"Yes. But what difference does that make?"

"I don't know. I don't know him."

Sebastian snorted. "None of us knows him. He isn't around enough."

"I just thought, maybe he doesn't know how to be a father. Maybe he feels awkward and—"

"He ought to feel awkward!"

"But maybe if you invited him—" she put the emphasis on *you* "—as opposed to Vangie, who is emotionally involved, you could tell him how much it means to her."

"Like he'd listen," Sebastian scoffed.

Neely shrugged. "You don't know. He might. Even if he never did before, he might have changed. Max has changed," she reminded him.

"Max is not my father!"

"No. But he wasn't much good as mine, either, for a lot of years. Part of it was his fault. Part of it was my mother's. But I'm not sorry I got in touch with him again as an adult. I'm not sorry I tried."

Sebastian glowered at her across the darkened room. But it was true, what she'd said. She had been nervous when she'd applied to work for Max's firm. She'd been worried about meeting him again, apprehensive about who exactly this man was who had fathered her.

Maybe if she hadn't had such a wonderful stepfather in John she would have lacked the courage to try to become a part of Max's life. Because of John, she knew what a good father was like. Because of John, she knew a father's love.

She didn't need those things from Max. It hadn't mattered if he'd loved and accepted her or not because John already had.

That he did was her good fortune. And his, which she was sure he knew. But she didn't know anything about Sebastian's father.

Maybe it wasn't fair to suggest that he try again. Still, people didn't have to continue doing the same stupid things they'd always done.

"Maybe he's changed," Neely repeated quietly. "Only saying. Up to you."

And Sebastian's voice was flat when he replied, "Yes, it is."

CHAPTER SEVEN

HE WASN'T going to do it.

And Neely Robson had no right to act as if he was betraying his sister and his family and the rest of the free world just because he wouldn't.

His father wasn't Max. Never would be. And there was no point in tackling Philip Savas on this topic. If he wanted to come, he would. If he didn't…that was pretty much par for the course, in Seb's estimation.

But he couldn't stop thinking about it.

No, that wasn't true.

What he couldn't stop thinking about was Neely.

He'd been lying there on the sofa in the dark, thinking even darker thoughts about his miserable father and his needy sister and his whole wearisome demanding dysfunctional family, when he'd heard the door open and Neely and Harm had come in.

It was too late to get up and turn on a light and act like he was working, and the bleakness of his thoughts had made him uninclined to make an effort to sit up and act polite if she came into the room.

Besides, if she found him lying on the sofa in the dark she'd wonder what the hell was wrong with him. And he had no desire to discuss any of it.

So he'd stayed there, still and quiet, and hoped she would go straight upstairs.

Of course she hadn't. And if she'd turned on a light, he'd have feigned waking from a nap. He was tired enough.

But instead she'd got down his grandfather's violin and begun to play it. When he'd first heard her clambering up on the cabinet, he hadn't known what on earth she was doing. And the first squeaks and tunings were so unexpected that they'd startled him, making him lift his head enough so he could peer over the back of the sofa.

She was busy adjusting the pegs, tuning the strings and didn't see him at all. He opened his mouth to ask what she thought she was doing. But then she drew the bow across the strings and it became absolutely clear.

Stunned, bemused—and for the moment completely incapable of saying anything—he sank back onto the cushions.

And listened to her play.

It was a revelation. Of all the things he thought he knew about Neely Robson—even the things he'd been wrong about—he'd never once guessed she could play the violin. It hadn't entered his mind.

But the moment she touched the bow to the strings, music filled the room. Sound echoed and reverberated. Light and bright and airy, rhythmic, almost mathematical sounds. Spritely dancing sounds that made him think of spring and splashing in puddles. And then slower, broader, more soulful tones that wrapped him in a warmth that carried him back to his grandparents' home, that made him think of winter days in the house on Long Island wrapped in a blanket and sitting next to a fireplace, waiting for his grandfather to come home.

Nothing in his life had felt like that, nothing had reminded him of home—not since his grandparents had died.

She played sounds that made his throat ache, made his eyes fill, made his heart feel too large for his chest. She made him remember in a way he hadn't remembered for years all his childhood hopes and dreams and a future full of promise.

And heaven help him, he wanted it again.

No. Not just it. Not just a home, damn it.

He wanted a home with her.

He wasn't going to do it.

Neely had known it at once from the stubborn set of his jaw, the uncompromising tone, the fact that he had turned and walked out of the room right after he'd spoken.

She didn't chase after him. Didn't follow him up the stairs and into his bedroom.

Bearding Sebastian in his bedroom would not have been wise.

Going anywhere near a bed with Sebastian would have undermined all her best intentions. Her attraction to him was far too strong. She wanted him far too much.

Now she sat in her office and stared at her computer screen thinking through all the events of last night—of all the days since Sebastian had moved onto the houseboat—and she knew he was everything she wanted in a man. He was strong, caring, intelligent, honorable and sexy as hell.

But he didn't believe in love.

Not just the love of a man and a woman, but even the love of a father for his children.

Though why he should, given his experience, she could not have said.

Outside her window the rain was sheeting down and she knew she should get to work. But even though Blake had been enthusiastic over her designs this morning and had given her the go-ahead. She still felt unaccountably depressed.

It had nothing to do with work.

It had everything to do with Sebastian.

She hurt for him. She ached for him. But she couldn't change him.

So in the end she knew she had to leave him to his obduracy and his pain because she couldn't fight the one or deny the other.

The only thing she could do—and probably should do, she admitted for the first time—was find another place to live.

Her cell phone rang before she could argue with herself about it.

Just as well, she thought, punching the answer button, because there were no arguments, just the emotional tangle she couldn't get out of. And she really needed to get some work done.

"This is Neely Robson," she said doing her best business-like voice.

"Got a favor to ask." It was Max. His own voice sounded strained and a little tighter than normal.

"Name it."

"I'm at Swedish Hospital. Could you come by?"

"Sure. What's up? New project?" She thought she remembered Max mentioning something about a hospital addition bid at the last group meeting.

"Something like that." His tone was dry. "A load of pipe fell on me. I've got a broken leg."

She'd never been to Swedish Hospital. Well, truth told, she'd been born there. But she hadn't been back since.

So finding where she was supposed to go, especially feeling rattled, was tricky. And even once she'd arrived, she still had to find the emergency area and Max who had told her he was going to need surgery.

"Not till I get there!" she'd said at the end of his phone call.

"Well, I'll tell them to wait," Max said wryly. "But I don't suppose they'll pay much attention. Don't worry, kid. I'll still be here whenever you get here. I'm not going anywhere," he added wearily. "Damn it."

Neely had said the same two words several times over by the time she finally found herself in the emergency section at Swedish Hospital and hurried toward the reception area.

"I'm here to see Max Grosvenor," she said breathlessly. "I'm his daughter."

The receptionist smiled, consulted her list and said, "Yes, we've sent him to the Orthopedic Institute for surgery. If you'll just go out there and across the street." She pointed in the direction Neely should go. It was the direction she'd just come from.

Neely thanked her and hurried back the way she'd come. The multistory Orthopedic Institute was almost brand-new and definitely state-of-the-art. The receptionist there looked up Max's name and said, "He's in surgery, dear."

"But—" But of course Max was right. It wasn't up to him, and naturally they'd need to get on it as quickly as possible.

"We have a lovely area where you can wait," she said and gave Neely directions. "The doctor will come out and talk to you when he's finished."

"Thank you." Neely gave her a quick smile and, still worrying, followed the directions to the waiting area. The last time she'd been in a hospital was when John had suffered a heart attack. Swift and, ultimately, fatal. It wasn't the same thing at all.

But it had been as unexpected as Max's accident was, and somehow even though her mind told her to relax, her body was on adrenaline overload. She walked right past the waiting area without realizing it.

"Neely."

She spun around at the sound of the voice calling her name. *"Sebastian?"* She stared in consternation at the man standing in the doorway to the waiting room. "What are you doing here?"

"Max called me."

She let out a breath. Of course he had. She might be Max's daughter, but Sebastian was his second in command. Slowly she turned and walked back to the room. There were several other people sitting and waiting for other patients. They glanced up disinterestedly as Sebastian led her to a small conversational group and gestured for her to sit down.

She sat. Sebastian sat in a chair next to her. He looked calm and composed, the way he always did. The Iceman returns, Neely thought.

But looking at him more closely, she knew she was wrong. There was tell-tale strain on his face. His jaw was clenched. As she watched, he flexed his fingers, as if he would have cracked his knuckles if he'd been willing to display any feelings at all.

"Did you get here before they took him into surgery?"

"Just." Now he did crack his knuckles.

"Is he going to be all right? How bad is it?"

"I don't know a lot. Apparently they're talking about pins and plates. He didn't sound thrilled. But he didn't know too much yet. I suppose it depends on what they find when they get in to do it."

"Yes." Neely swallowed. "He's going to be livid that he won't be able to go climbing over things, that he'll have to oversee from the office."

"Yeah, well, he's not going to."

"Not going to what? Stay in the office? He'll have to!" Trust Max to not know his own limits. She shifted in her chair and gave a despairing shake of her head.

"No, not oversee," Seb said. "He's going to be laid up too long. There will be things he can do, certainly. But not the projects he has to be on the ground for. He can stay home and work on new designs. But as far as the other stuff goes, I'm overseeing or delegating."

His words took a minute to penetrate. The significance of them took even longer.

Finally Neely cocked her head. "What other stuff?" she asked.

And Sebastian ticked off several projects that she knew Max was involved in. "I'm delegating those," he said. "But I'll keep an eye on them."

"And Blake-Carmody?" she asked, because that had been Max's baby, the one he'd brought her in to work with him on. Was she going to get to do that one?

"That one," Sebastian said, "is mine."

* * *

If Neely thought Sebastian was a workaholic before Max's accident, it was nothing to what he became afterward.

"You don't have to do everything," she said. It was like a mantra, she said it so often over the next few days, because regardless of what he'd said about delegating, he didn't seem to be delegating at all.

He was up at the crack of dawn, working hour upon hour, going between the office, all the construction sites, the design meetings and the hospital where he kept Max updated but, by his own admission, "not very updated," because Max needed to rest.

Sebastian, apparently, needed no rest at all.

Or needed it less than he needed to prove something to himself.

He was gone before she even got up in the morning, and he rarely got home in time to grab a late meal before Neely went off to bed. One night he didn't come in before she went to bed and he wasn't there when she got up, so she wondered if he'd even been home at all.

"No," he said when she asked him later that morning when she stuck her head in his office at work.

"You can't go without sleep."

"I caught a nap on the sofa." He jerked his head toward the small one in his office. She couldn't imagine how anyone over the age of ten could have caught any sort of nap on it, without becoming a pretzel in the process. Sebastian was six feet two inches of solid muscle and bone. And stubbornness.

"Not good enough," she said.

He gave her a steely look. "I didn't have time, okay? I've got to get up to speed on Blake-Carmody. I have a meeting with the committee on Friday and Max said they still had some reservations about the lobby and atrium."

"Can I help? I just had a meeting with Blake. I know how he thinks."

Seb shook his head. "No. It's fine. Thanks. This is my end of things, not yours." He gave her a quick distant smile and bent over his work again.

Dismissed, and knowing it, Neely backed out of his office. But she was still concerned. And a bit peeved at his dismissal. Did he think she was only able to appreciate her own work?

Later that day she said as much to Max.

He was still in the hospital, his leg immobilized with seven pins and a plate, which he grumbled about continually. There was no way he could come to work and take some of the pressure off Sebastian. Neely knew that, but she thought he might tell Sebastian to ease up a little.

But Max just shrugged against his pillows. "He's conscientious. Doing what needs to be done."

"He's just like you," Neely countered.

"Somebody has to be," Max rejoined with a grin.

But Neely didn't smile in return. "Do you really think so?" she challenged him. "Is it really the way you'd advise him to live? After what it did to your life?"

And mine, she didn't add aloud.

Max's grin faded and he plucked at the sheet with his fingers. "I don't know," he admitted after a long moment. "I thought so when I was his age."

"And now?"

He shrugged and raked his fingers through his hair. "I can't tell him that," he said.

"Why not?"

"It's a guy thing," he said simply.

"Oh, and that means he should just work himself into the ground?"

"Not necessarily. It means he has to get his own priorities sorted out. I can't do it for him. He has to figure it out on his own."

"Like you did," Neely said, for the first time being just a bit sarcastic with her father.

Max's mouth tipped in a wry smile. "Exactly."

And Neely supposed he was right. But Sebastian didn't seem to be doing so. He kept up the dawn-till-well-past-dark schedule as the week wore on. He did turn some projects over to second in commands. But from Neely he refused all offers of help.

Wednesday, though, he was in the middle of working on the atrium proposal when Vangie had a meltdown right in his office.

Neely had been surprised to see Sebastian's sister appear in the office, but she'd been on the phone at the time and had only glimpsed Vangie through the glass window between her private space and the main room. So there had been no chance to go out and greet her, and when she'd got off the phone and looked up again, Vangie was gone.

Of course she was sure where Vangie was, but somehow turning up in Sebastian's office to say hi seemed not the smartest idea, given his current state of mind.

It didn't matter anyway, because ten minutes later her phone rang. "You said you wanted to help," Sebastian said without preamble.

"Yes," Neely began cautiously.

"Fine. Come and get her."

He hung up before she could say a word, and for a moment Neely considered simply ignoring the summons. But she had offered to help, and she hadn't put a limit on the offer. If Vangie was what he needed help with, so be it.

She hadn't expected tears. At least they were Vangie's tears, not Sebastian's, she thought wryly when she stepped into his office. Though truth be told he looked harried and harassed enough to shed a few himself.

"What's wrong?" Neely hurried to Vangie's side, shooting Sebastian a questioning look as she did so, silently querying what he'd said to her now.

"The boxes aren't silver," he said flatly, as if that explained everything. "They're grey."

"What?"

Vangie looked up, stricken, and said, "The mint boxes for the tables…a-at the reception," she gulped, "they're supposed to be rose a-and s-silver. And the rose are r-rose. But the silver are grey!" And she started sobbing again.

"End of the world," Sebastian said to Neely, "as you can see."

Neely patted Vangie's shoulder and glared at Sebastian. Professionally he'd rejected her every offer to help, but when it came to silver boxes…

But much as she felt like leaving him to deal with his sister, she couldn't. Help was help, and she'd offered.

"Come on." She urged Vangie to her feet. "Let's go see what we can do about it."

"We can't do anything about it!" Vangie wailed. "The reception will be ruined!"

"We'll see," Neely murmured. "We'll see." And she chivvied Vangie out of the office with barely a backward glance at Sebastian. He had already refocused on the atrium design.

It took a trip to the hobby shop for some silver paint and half a dozen small paint brushes to get Vangie's tears dried up. She still looked doubtful. "Are you sure it will work?"

"Of course I'm sure," Neely said because faintheartedness never won the day. "We can take care of this right now if your sisters will help."

Vangie sniffled and nodded. "They will," she said. "And my mom and my stepmothers, too."

So she got to meet the triplets and Jenna and ten-year-old Sarah, three of Sebastian's stepmothers and get a look at his penthouse digs, as well. It was enlightening.

The penthouse had probably been austere and minimalist before being overrun by the Savas women. One look around its cluttered surfaces and clothes-strewn rooms gave Neely greater understanding about exactly why Sebastian had been so desperate to move into the houseboat. Further reflection simply reinforced the notion that he was incredibly kind to all of them.

Not many men, she didn't imagine, would have allowed their siblings and stepmothers to simply move in and take over their home. But Sebastian had. And as she showed them how to add silver highlights to the boxes—which were in fact not quite as grey as Vangie had claimed—she heard plenty of stories about how many other things he'd done for them.

He was paying Jenna's college tuition. He'd footed the bill for a year's study in Paris for one of the triplets. He was helping Cassidy, a stepmother who couldn't have been much older than he was, go back to nursing school and get her degree.

"Does your father help, too?" she asked one of the triplets.

The girl looked blank. "Who? Oh, Dad? We hardly ever see him."

"We will at the wedding," Vangie said confidently. "Sebastian's organizing it."

Neely glanced at her, surprised and wondering if Sebastian had changed his mind or if Vangie was just making assumptions. It didn't seem wise to ask.

"There, now," she said. "I think that takes care of all of them." She stood up and surveyed the sea of tiny silver-highlighted boxes on Sebastian's dining room table.

Vangie beamed, then came to throw her arms around Neely. "Thanks to you," she said. She turned to her mother and stepmothers and sisters. "Didn't I tell you she was terrific? Seb is so lucky to have you."

"He doesn't have me," Neely said.

But Vangie and all the rest of them drowned her out, telling her how happy they were that she and Sebastian were together.

Arguing didn't do any good. Sebastian would sort it out, Neely decided. He would doubtless make it clear to them that they were merely roommates.

But as she drove home after sharing a dinner of pizza and salad with so many of Sebastian's relations, she envied him the joy of them and understood why, even though they exasperated him, he would move heaven and earth for them.

He loved them.

And Neely was stunned to find herself wishing that he loved her, too, the way that she, heaven help her, had fallen in love with him.

"No," Seb said into the phone. "I can't."

Which was an understatement and then some. He paced around the confines of his office and wanted to bang his head against the wall instead of sounding calm and rational on the phone. There was no way he could just pick up and fly off to Reno for a zoning commission meeting on Friday. "Sorry. But you'll have to reschedule."

"We have rescheduled," Lymond, the chairman of the medical group whose project he'd developed, reminded him. "This is the reschedule, Seb. And they aren't going to do it again."

"Then…" *you'll have to do it without me,* Seb wanted to say. But he couldn't. He'd asked them to put it off the day after Max's accident. They said they would, and now they had, and he'd promised to accommodate…

"I'll get back to you," he promised the chairman.

"The meeting's at twelve-thirty."

Seb cursed under his breath after hanging up the phone because he knew he couldn't ask them to change it again. It would be unprofessional. But he didn't see how he could be in two places at once. That wasn't unprofessional. It was flat-out impossible.

And he couldn't ask Roger Carmody and Stephen Blake to reschedule, either. Blake might be willing, but Carmody was already apprehensive about Max's having to leave the project. He'd raised a dozen questions about the public space and atrium when Sebastian had spoken with him on the phone.

It was insane. The plans were good ones. They were his, yes, not Max's. But Max had approved them. Max would argue for them if Max were able to be there.

Maybe Max would have to go after all. That would settle Carmody's nerves, they'd all be on the same page, and everything would go on according to the plans Seb had drawn up in the first place.

That's what would have to happen, he decided. There was no other way to handle it.

"Of course there is," Max said when he stopped by the hospital that night.

"Oh?" Seb raised an eyebrow. "Have you figured out how to clone me, then?"

"Don't need to. Send Neely."

Seb blanched. "You're joking."

Both of Max's brows went up. "Why should I joke? She knows the project better than anyone. She's worked with me on it since day one."

"I worked with you on it, too," Seb reminded him. "Until you phased me out."

"Yeah, and that was my mistake, " Max admitted. "But you had Reno to do, and I wanted to work with Neely. And now I've phased you back in, as you put it. Basically it's your plan we've used, and while you know it better than anyone, Neely's worked on the project the whole time. She knows it too."

"Not as well as I do."

"Which goes without saying. But she knows Blake and Carmody."

Exactly. She could undermine the whole damn thing. "She doesn't like what I do." That was the long and short of it right there.

"She's playing for our team," Max said flatly.

Seb remembered their encounter over her pink offices and his "pointy buildings"—in her term—and shook his head. Yeah, he knew Neely much better now. Certainly he liked her personally a lot better now. And that he would happily have taken her to bed went without saying.

But that had nothing to do with working with her, being on the same page with her in terms of the project. Bed was play, this was work. This was his career, his life.

"Have you talked to her about it?" Max asked.

Seb lifted his shoulders. "Haven't had time."

"You should take time."

Seb grunted. "Yeah."

Instead, after he left Max, he called back Lymond in Reno to see how things stood.

"Expecting you Friday morning. You need a ride from the airport?"

"No," Seb said grimly. "I'll be there."

He rang Roger Carmody to discuss the atrium. If he could answer the questions now on the phone, maybe the meeting would be a mere formality.

But Roger's secretary said he was out of town until Thursday evening.

"Ask him to call me no matter what time he gets in," Seb said.

But he had been tied up in another meeting when Roger had called. So all he got was Roger's voice message afterward saying, "I don't like it. We need to rethink. I'll discuss it with you tomorrow."

But tomorrow Seb wouldn't be there.

Neely Robson would.

He got back to the houseboat before ten for the first time since Max's accident. Neely was sitting in the rocker, holding one of the kittens. She looked up and smiled at him when he came in.

It was one of those Neely smiles that undermined his resolve and made him want to throw good sense to the winds and simply carry her off to bed. Not that she would let him.

All the more reason to be short and to the point now.

"I have to be in Reno tomorrow," he said without preamble. "It's unavoidable. They've rescheduled already. I can't ask them to do it again. And the Carmody-Blake meeting will have to go on, too."

"That's all right," she said quickly. "I can handle—"

"You don't need to handle anything. Just take care of your part and I'll take care of the rest next week."

Her smile faded. "I've already taken care of my part," she said a little stiffly. "The homespace is all approved."

A reminder he didn't need. "So it is," he said, aware that his tone was now even stiffer than hers. "And I wouldn't even ask you to show up, except this is supposed to be the final rundown, and since I can't be there, Max says you're the obvious choice."

"Max said that?" There was something in her tone he couldn't quite put his finger on, but Seb knew he didn't like it. It was both doubtful and challenging.

"That's right. He thinks you should be able to hold the fort." Seb met her gaze with an equally challenging one of his own. "So I'm counting on you to hold it."

Neely's didn't waver. "Consider it held."

The meeting in Reno was, for all of Lymond's hand wringing, far more of a formality than the Carmody-Blake meeting was back in Seattle.

Seb was determinedly attentive and made sure every *i* was dotted and every *t* was crossed. But in the back of his mind, he was in Seattle, mentally overseeing the meeting with Blake and Carmody and hoping to hell Neely didn't screw everything up.

He got out of the meeting at three. His fingers itched to punch in her number on his mobile phone and see what was happening. But of course, she would be in the meeting with Carmody and Blake right then and he wouldn't get an answer.

So he went to the airport and paced until it was time for his flight, telling himself she wouldn't mess things up, inadvertently, or even worse, deliberately, making clear her own dislike of Seb's designs. He didn't think she'd do him in deliberately, but how the hell did he know?

He glanced at his watch a dozen times or more, got halfway to stabbing out her number, then tucked the phone back in his pocket and kept pacing.

Right before the plane took off, though, he called Max.

"Reno's sorted," he said when Max answered.

"Of course it is." He could tell Max was smiling.

"Just thought you'd like to know."

"Sure. I'm going home this afternoon."

"Neely picking you up?" Seb asked, grabbing the chance to legitimately introduce her name into the conversation.

"Not sure."

"Haven't you heard from her?" Seb asked, not quite able to mask the worry in his tone.

"What? Oh, sure. She may be the one to do it. Said she might be busy, though."

"Busy?"

Max laughed. "I gather she has a life."

Seb didn't find it funny. "What'd she say about the Blake-Carmody meeting?"

"It went fine."

Seb ground his teeth. "What does that mean?"

"That it went fine, I guess." Max's tone was equable enough, but it didn't invite any further questions.

"Fine," Seb muttered. "I damned well hope so."

"Chill," Max advised.

"Right." Seb let out a long breath. They were calling his flight. "See you."

He tried to tell himself Max would have let him know if Neely had screwed things up for him. He tried to tell himself she'd keep her mouth shut and let him handle it when he got home. So it wasn't a good sign to find a voice mail from Roger Carmody when he landed in Seattle.

"Smart move," Carmody said jovially, "sending Neely. She and I have everything sorted. We're all on the same page now. Talk to you on Monday. Thanks."

Seb felt sick. Shafted. Was the atrium even in the design now? It was crucial to the whole design, damn it! Had his sweeping, open spaces been carved into dinky little "people-friendly" segments. Couldn't they see how the soaring planes of the atrium spoke to the human soul?

He supposed he had only himself to blame. He should have called Carmody and put off the meeting until Monday even if it looked as if he wasn't prepared. He should have insisted Carmody and Blake have the meeting in Max's hospital room if they wouldn't wait. At least Max believed in his designs.

He should have sent Danny or Frank or somebody—anybody!—but Neely Robson to meet with Carmody and Blake. God only knew what she had agreed to.

Seb was going to have her head on a plate when he found out.

He was in a cold fury by the time he reached the houseboat.

It was getting late, the sun was setting behind Queen Anne Hill. And on it streetlights were beginning to twinkle on the other side of the lake. The wind had died down and there was only a light breeze as Seb grabbed his suitcase, banged his car door shut and stalked up the dock to the houseboat.

The porch light was on, and when he opened the door, he was immediately treated to wonderful cooking smells, light classical music and Harm bounding to meet him. He dropped his suitcase, rubbed his fingers over the dog's ears and headed straight down the hall toward the open living area.

Neely was in the kitchen. She turned when he appeared, a bright smile on her face. "You're back."

"I'm back," Seb agreed flatly. He didn't smile in return.

Her own smile faltered a little. "Didn't it go well?"

"You tell me," he said.

"No, I mean Reno. You seem upset."

"Damned right I'm upset! You screwed me over. You went into that meeting and you didn't hold the fort at all."

Neely stiffened. "Who told you that?"

"Carmody! Who else?"

"You talked to him? What did he say?"

"He called while I was flying home. Left me a voice mail— all cheery and 'everything's swell.' So he got what he wanted apparently." Seb very nearly spat the words.

"Yes," Neely said slowly. "He got what he wanted." She picked up a towel and began slowly drying her hands.

Seb slammed one fist into the other palm. "I should have known better than to send you. I should have told them they had to wait and talk to me. I should have— Damn it!" He couldn't even speak he was so furious. He wanted to slam something, hit something, kick something. The kittens took one look at him and skittered for cover.

"What is it you imagine I've done?" Neely asked, her voice very even, very calm.

"I can't imagine, can I?" Seb flared at her. "I don't know what the hell you would do! You and I don't see eye to eye—"

"You and I are working on the same project. I was representing the whole project. Not just mine. Which, as you pointed out yesterday, has already been approved." She set the towel down and came around the bar to stand by the dining room table, facing him.

It was set for two. With candles already lit. Wineglasses. There was a bottle of champagne in a bucket of ice. He stared at it, then back at her.

"What did you do?" he asked her bluntly.

"You'd sent them the designs already. I met with them and asked if they had questions. Roger had a lot of them—especially about the public space, the atrium, the vastness of it."

"It sets a tone—" Seb began.

"It sets a tone," Neely said, cutting him off. "Of openness and space, but it doesn't dwarf the people because it leads them where they need to go. It provides a greenhouse sort of feel with warmth and foliage and curving lines not straight ones. It draws people in, and at the same time it gives them a break between the hustle and bustle of urban Seattle and the office they are seeking. It provides openness and the sense of shelter at the same time. It's people friendly. It's comfortable. It makes people feel welcome."

Seb stared at her.

Neely stared back. A powerful engine thrummed as the boat cut across the lake. Seb heard his own breathing more loudly.

She looked beyond him out the window. "It's all there in your plans," she went on. "We went through the drawings one by one. He asked questions because apparently he didn't have a feel for things. He needed more explanation. So I explained what your intentions were."

Seb digested that. "*My* intentions?"

Neely shrugged indifferently. "You're the one who drew up the plans."

"Max—"

"They were your plans. Max always said they were yours."

"You don't like my designs."

"I didn't like the design we tangled over. And some of your stuff is a little too austere for me. That's true. But this—" another shrug "—I could see where you were going with this. But Roger needed it spelled out, needed convincing. So…I convinced him."

She turned away abruptly then, didn't look at him at all.

"I—" She hadn't sabotaged him after all? "You actually convinced Carmody that my designs were what the project needed?"

"That's what I went to the meeting to do." Her voice was flat, hard. "It's my job."

He didn't know what to say. It came out as a hopelessly inadequate "Thanks."

"You're welcome." The words were carved in ice. She was angry, and who could blame her? He'd been an idiot.

"I mean it," he fumbled. "I thought—"

"It's quite clear what you thought. Someday, Sebastian, you're going to have to figure out that there are people you can trust."

He'd hurt her as well. Damn, damn, damn.

She still didn't look at him. Instead she reached over to snuff out the candles.

He watched as her fingers snapped out the flames. Belatedly he realized that she'd planned something special. The table was all decorated. Flowers. Wine. Candles, now lightly smoking, the acrid scent cutting across the rich smell of food.

"What are you doing?" he said, his voice hoarse. "Don't you want to eat?"

"Not anymore."

"But what about—" He gestured to the festive table.

"That? I'd thought we'd celebrate. I thought we actually had something to celebrate." Her voice was tight and she flicked a quick glance his way before taking off her apron and tossing it on the counter. She headed down the hall where she took Harm's leash and clipped it on his collar.

Only as she opened the door did she look back his way. "Obviously, I was wrong."

CHAPTER EIGHT

SHE wouldn't cry.

She *wouldn't!*

There was no way she would shed a tear over Sebastian Bloody Savas and his accusatory bullheaded idiocy!

But it didn't stop Neely's vision blurring as she hurried up the dock away from the houseboat, Harm bounding alongside, delighted at the sudden unexpected treat. She didn't know where they were going. It was very nearly dark. She was hungry and tired and she felt as if she'd been punched in the gut.

She'd been tired when she got home, but exhilarated, too. Absolutely thrilled that Roger Carmody had come around to understanding what Sebastian had intended in his designs. He certainly hadn't bothered to spell it out.

It was there in the soaring interior space and the gently meandering curves of the walks. It was there in the few rough trees he'd sketched in. But to a man like Roger, who liked every leaf drawn on every plant, it was too hazy a concept. And there wasn't enough focus on the people.

"I don't want 'em lost," he'd said to Neely over and over. "They can't be dwarfed by the damn place or they won't want to come back."

And Neely, who thought more like Roger did, but who understood Sebastian better now, had been able to take what he'd drawn and explain. "It's not going to dwarf them," she'd said. "It's going to give them a sense of spaciousness but with plan and direction. It's going to empower them."

It had taken a while, but with patience and word pictures, she'd made Roger understand.

"I see," he'd said at last and nodded. "Yes, I see completely. Why the hell didn't he say so?" he'd demanded.

"He did," Neely said. "In his drawings."

"Took you to explain 'em, though," Roger had pointed out.

"He's very good at what he does," Neely had said absolutely truthfully. "He just figured you'd trust him to get it right."

"Well, I do. Now," Roger said. "I trust you and your interpretation."

It was nice, Neely thought bitterly, that somebody did.

Before she thought anything else though, hard footsteps came pounding up behind her. A hand reached out and grabbed her arm.

"Stop!" And she did because Sebastian hauled her up short. He was as out of breath as she was. His tie was askew and his hair looked as if he'd thrust his fingers through it.

"What?" Neely said coldly.

"I'm sorry." The words seemed dragged up from the depths of his being.

But Neely just stared at him unspeaking, frankly doubting.

Even if Sebastian was sorry, she seriously doubted that he was sorry about what he ought to be sorry about.

"Look—" he dragged in a breath "—I was wrong. I apologize. I thought—" he stopped abruptly and dropped his hand from her arm, then just stood there staring down at her as he said heavily, "Well, you know what I thought."

"Yes, I do."

He raked fingers through his hair again. "You said…before…I never imagined—"

"No," Neely replied, her voice clipped. "You wouldn't." She turned away and began to walk again. She supposed that somewhere inside she was glad he at least acknowledged his mistake. But it still hurt.

In the past few weeks she had come to understand him—maybe not totally, but at least she didn't dismiss him out of hand anymore. She didn't assume he was The Iceman, the workaholic, the impersonal distant automaton she'd originally thought he was. She understood now that he was self-contained, that he didn't give of himself easily, but that he was loyal, dependable, and that he could—and did—love.

But he still apparently didn't understand—or trust—her at all.

He caught up with her and kept pace. "Forgive me?" It really was a question. It wasn't a demand. She had to give him that.

She kept walking, but raised a shoulder. "Sure. Fine."

"Come back and have dinner with me?"

She didn't reply. She continued up the pavement, but her pace slowed. "Why?" she demanded at last, stopping in her tracks and turning to face him. "So we can pretend that you understand? That you trust me? That everything is hunky-dory?"

A corner of his mouth lifted just a little. "How about because I'm starving, you probably are, too. I'm embarrassed to have misjudged you, and I wish you'd come back so I can say again how sorry I am. So we don't miss a good meal. And so you can tell me how you convinced Roger of what I couldn't seem to make him understand?"

Neely shifted from one foot to the other. She gnawed on her bottom lip. It was a far handsomer apology than she'd imagined Sebastian Savas would make her. Maybe she, too, had a ways to go in learning about him.

"All right," she said, and started back toward the houseboat. "Come on."

"Have you got a minute?"

Neely looked up from her sketch book to see Vangie poking her head around the corner of the door. "Oh, hi. Sure. Come on in. How're things going?"

It was a dangerous question, to be sure, even early on the Tuesday afternoon before the wedding because the big event was now only four days away.

Sebastian had stopped calling it "the wedding that ate Seattle" and had begun calling it "the wedding that ended the world."

Judging from some of the things he'd reported over the past three days, Neely thought he wasn't exaggerating much.

Over the weekend Vangie had called him in tears half a dozen times at least.

He'd forbidden her to come by and cry in person. He was still annoyed that she'd managed to track him down in the first place.

"If you have to cry, you can cry on the phone," he'd told her Saturday morning. Neely had actually heard his end of the conversation, so she knew that much was true.

The rest he reported as it came to pass—one bridesmaid dress was too long, one was too short. One wasn't silver—"it's grey," he'd said with a flash of an exasperated grin. And the other wasn't the right shade of pink.

"Rose," Neely had corrected, because she knew all about the color scheme now.

Sebastian had mimed banging his head on the wall. "Don't worry about it," he'd advised. "No one will be looking at the bridesmaids, Vange. You're the bride. They'll all be looking at you."

It was an inspired comment as far as Neely could tell. Vangie had rung off. But she'd called back again later. And Sebastian shared the details of those conversations, too.

After the wary, tentative meal they'd shared on Friday evening, he seemed to be making an effort to communicate with her. He'd made her tell him exactly how she'd explained his designs to Roger Carmody, and he'd stared at her in amazement when she'd told him.

"He couldn't see that?" he'd demanded.

"Not everyone can read your mind," she'd told him with some asperity.

He'd grinned. "I don't need everyone to as long as you can."

It shouldn't have made her quite as happy as it had. She was asking for it, Neely warned herself. Sebastian might be making an effort, but it was only because she'd made a difference to him at work. It had nothing to do with the rest of their lives.

Except now Vangie came in and shut the door and said, "He's done it!"

Neely finished the last few strokes to the bit she was working on in her sketchbook and looked up. "Who's done it? Done what?"

"Sebastian! He's seeing Daddy."

Neely felt her breath catch in her throat. "Is he?" she asked cautiously.

Vangie plopped down into the chair opposite Neely's and nodded eagerly. "This evening."

"You're sure?"

"Of course I'm sure. He told me. Said they were going out for a drink. I always knew he would," she confided. "I know he said he wouldn't, but you can count on him. We always have," she added simply.

"That's—" Neely took a shaky breath "—wonderful." She managed a smile. It felt fake because she was too stunned to muster up a real one. But as she kept it pasted on her mouth, she processed the notion and found that the smile came more easily.

"He's doing it for you," Vangie said.

"What?" That brought Neely up short. "What on earth are you talking about? Did he say that?"

"Oh, no. Of course not. But I know you're the one who talked him into it."

"I didn't! I never said a word."

"Really?" Vangie looked astonished. "I was sure you must have."

Oh, dear. Oh dear oh dear oh dear.

Because of course Neely realized that she had said something.

That day after Vangie had first come to see Seb they had discussed it, and she had told Sebastian he shouldn't resist trying to speak with his father. He should make the effort, she'd said, because his father, like hers, might have changed.

That would have been bad enough, but she remembered now an exchange they'd had over their tense dinner last Friday night. When she'd been explaining how she'd laid things out for Roger, she'd said, "I can communicate with him. You know that. You should have trusted me."

Sebastian had said, "I do trust you." But then he'd had the grace to look guilty and say, "Well, maybe I haven't always. But I will. I will trust you, Neel'."

It was, she thought, the first time he'd actually called her anything but "Robson." It touched her heart, and yet she'd forced herself to look him straight in the eye and challenge him. "Yeah, right. Prove it."

Now her guilty face must have betrayed her because Vangie gave a little bounce in her chair and said, "I knew it! I was sure you were the reason he came through."

"What Sebastian did or didn't do was entirely his own doing," Neely insisted.

"Sure. Of course. Whatever you say," Vangie agreed, all smiles. She stood up, beaming, and when Neely stood, too, Sebastian's sister threw her arms around her. "Thank you. Thank you so much!"

"I didn't do anything," Neely protested.

Vangie just shrugged happily. "You'll come to the rehearsal dinner with Seb, won't you?"

"I—"

"Of course you will." Vangie overrode any objections before she could even make them.

Truth be told, Neely didn't want to object. She wanted to go to the wedding. And anyway, Vangie was looking very much like a steamroller en route to getting exactly what she wanted.

Besides if, when he discovered the invitation, Sebastian decreed that she shouldn't go, well, she wouldn't.

But she dared to hope he would want her there.

"Of course it's what I want," Vangie said airily. "And what the bride wants, the bride gets." Waggling her fingers in farewell, she sailed out of the office.

And Neely stood watching her, wondering if she should be worrying or rejoicing that Sebastian had, against all odds, taken her advice.

He didn't say a word about seeing his father that evening.

They had a late-afternoon meeting with Danny and Frank and the rest of the project leaders for Blake-Carmody, to make sure that everyone was on the same timetable and all the pieces were in place.

While they were all together, Sebastian told them about her meeting with Roger and Steve on Friday. He congratulated her publically for having so successfully promoted the entire design package. His smile was as warm as she'd ever seen it at work. She tried not to think about the way he looked at her when he wanted her. It wasn't the best means of keeping her mind on the job.

She acknowledged everyone's congratulations and good wishes as they were leaving the room. She hung back, thinking he might say something to her then. But Danny stopped him with a question, and she couldn't really just stand there obtrusively and wait.

So she went back to her own office and rang Max as she had promised she would. Sebastian could come and tell her, she decided. He knew where her office was.

Max answered the phone on the first ring. He was home, but not in a walking cast, and not especially good with his crutches. He was going crazy, he told her. But not entirely because he couldn't get out. Mostly because of who was in his house with him.

"Your mother is driving me nuts," he complained now.

"Is she." Neely didn't make a question. She was staying out of the Max and Lara drama. She'd been doubtful when Lara had insisted on picking Max up at the hospital and taking him home. But no one else had volunteered.

So Lara stepped in. Or rather, showed up.

What happened after that wasn't precisely clear. She may have told Max a few of the home truths she'd threatened to tell him if she could ever get him tied down. He wasn't precisely tied down, but he was on crutches and that seemed to suffice.

Whatever had happened after that, they were still speaking— or yelling—and that was fine with Neely. She had problems enough of her own. The biggest one never came to say he was going out with his father at all. But when she drifted past his office at a little after five, it was to find the door shut and the lights off.

"He already left," Gladys told her.

"Did he say where he was going?"

The older woman shook her head. "He was total Iceman." She cocked her head. "I really thought he was getting over that."

"Not…entirely," Neely said. Under some circumstances she suspected he could be very much The Iceman still.

But he'd made the effort. He'd contacted his father. They were meeting for a drink. She smiled and crossed her fingers. Please God, let it be all right.

She went straight home, wanting to be there when he arrived. Lara called and invited her to come have a meal with her and Max.

"You can referee," her mother said.

"Thank you, no." Neely was adamant about that. She stripped off her work clothes and pulled out a pair of jeans. "I have other things to do."

"I thought you wanted your father and me to get together."

"I never said that!" Next thing you knew she'd be being

blamed for everything in the world. "I simply said I was coming to work out here so I could meet him. I never said you had to take up with him again."

"I wouldn't call what we're doing 'taking up with,'" Lara said tartly.

"What would you call it?"

"Discussing."

"Arguing," she heard Max correct loudly in the background.

"Going over past history," Lara went on as if he hadn't spoken.

"Throwing plates," Max's voice echoed through the phone. He didn't sound too upset, almost…amused.

"You didn't!" Neely said, aghast.

"Only one," Lara said guilelessly. "And not at him. Sure you won't come for a meal?"

"Quite sure, thanks."

Though it might have been entertaining to watch her parents coming to terms with each other—or not—after all these years, Neely wasn't leaving. She even resisted taking Harm for his usual nightly run, instead sticking close to home, where she could see Sebastian's car the minute he pulled in.

But he didn't come.

And didn't come.

Six-thirty turned into seven and seven into eight, and still he didn't appear. At first she worried, but then she told herself not to be silly. Sebastian's not appearing immediately was actually a good thing.

Certainly one drink together would have been enough for him and his father to have discussed Philip's appearance at Vangie's wedding if things were tense. But if they weren't—if father and son had actually hit it off—then one drink could have led to more than one. It could have led to dinner.

Which was probably exactly what it had done, Neely realized when it turned nine and still Sebastian hadn't appeared.

They'd probably decided to have dinner together catching

up, and right this very minute they could be chatting over cups of coffee doing some long-delayed father-son bonding.

Maybe Sebastian had even taken his father over to his penthouse so Philip could spend the evening with the entire family.

All of his brothers and sisters had arrived in Seattle for the wedding. The last of the brothers, a university student called Milos, had come in yesterday afternoon. They'd all been eager to spend time with him. She smiled, thinking how wonderful it would be if his father got to be there with all of them, too.

She wished she could be there to witness it. Unlike her own parents' reunion, she doubted anyone at Sebastian's place would be throwing plates. They were all on their best behavior for the wedding, and judging from what she'd seen of Vangie this afternoon, Sebastian's sister simply wouldn't allow it.

She took a shower a little past ten and came back downstairs eagerly, hoping that he would be home. But only the kittens and Harm were there to greet her. She paced. She prowled. And finally, in desperation, she got down the violin and began to play. And the music, as it always did, settled her, calmed her, reinforced her belief that all would be well.

And when the door finally opened at very nearly midnight, she set it down abruptly and spun around to smile at him when he came in.

He looked like hell.

Actually she didn't suppose he looked a lot different than he looked to most people most days. Stony, silent, serious, supremely self-contained—that was Sebastian ordinarily. That was Sebastian now.

But lately, as Gladys had noticed, the ordinary Iceman Sebastian had thawed a bit. Not just at home, but at work, he'd smiled more. He'd relaxed. He'd been more talkative. He'd even laughed.

Not tonight.

"What happened?"

He stared at her blankly. "Nothing." His voice was toneless.

He shut the door, came into the living room, shrugged off his jacket and sat down. He didn't look her way. One of the kittens started playing with his shoelace. He looked down at it, expression remote. Almost on auto-pilot he reached down and plucked it off, setting it on the back of the sofa.

No chiding it. No smiling. Nothing.

"Seb," she said urgently. "What happened? You saw your father…" she ventured.

There was the faintest stiffening in his demeanor. "Did I?" he said. His tone was conversational, light. But in it she heard the opposite.

"You didn't?"

He gave a quick almost imperceptible shake of his head. "No." He got up and went into the kitchen and with quick almost jerky movements, he poured himself a glass of water and drank it.

Neely watched his Adam's apple work as he swallowed. Tried to read his face. There were lines of strain, a little white bracketing his mouth. When he set the glass down, he shut his eyes, flattened his palms against the countertop and bent his head, dragging in a long harsh breath.

"Seb," she began again. "Tell me—"

He opened his eyes. They were dark, unfathomable. "Tell you what? There's nothing to say." Again that light, almost dismissive tone. A tone that said, it doesn't matter, when his entire being screamed the opposite.

What was she going to do? Was she just going to stand there and let him get away with it? Was she going to pretend to believe his words because he expected her to.

"Yes, there is," she said. "There's plenty to say."

And she came around the bar so that there was no longer a barrier between them. She walked straight up to him, and saw him, for once, retreat a step so that his back was against the cabinet.

He put his hands out as if to ward her off, but she kept coming until she was toe-to-toe with him, until her eyes were on a level with his chin and close enough that her lashes could brush against it.

"Neel'." Her name was a warning, a protest. "You don't want—"

"Yes," she said, "I do." And she was conscious even as she said the words that the vow was there within their meaning.

She put her arms around him, wrapping him tight and felt the hard strength of him when his own arms came around her. He buried his face into her hair, drew in a harsh breath and held it even as he held her. She felt a shudder run through him.

She kissed his neck, his jaw, ran her hands up the solid breadth of his back, and pressed herself even closer, needing the connection, knowing that Sebastian needed it, too.

She didn't know how long they stood there just holding each other in silent communion. And then slowly she become aware of another need—his and hers—a need that had been building for as long as they had been aware of each other.

It was a need she'd rejected, a desire she'd denied—because she hadn't dared believe that anything would come of it.

She'd been afraid to risk. But she had challenged Sebastian to risk. She had been adamant in her insistence that it was worth it. And she knew he had taken that risk tonight, whatever the outcome had been.

And she dared to believe he'd done it for her.

It seemed only fair—only right—to take a risk of her own.

Now she lifted her face to press her lips along his jawline, to find his mouth, to taste his lips with hers.

His fingers curled against her waist. "Neel'—" The warning was there again in his tone.

"Shh," she said. "It's all right."

He drew back to look down at her, his eyes alight with yearning and yet in them she saw still a hint of caution. "Is it?" he asked her. His hands spanned her waist, held her so that their bodies barely brushed. His mouth tightened. His face was taut. A muscle ticked in his jaw.

"Yes," she whispered going up on her toes to brush her lips once more against his, touching them with the tip of her tongue. "Yes, it is."

He believed her then. Took her at her word. Trusted that she knew what she was doing.

She did.

It was a risk. Loving was always a risk. Until Sebastian she hadn't dared.

But she couldn't ask him for a risk she wasn't willing to take.

"I love you," she whispered.

He stiffened, looked down into her eyes. "You don't. You can't." His tone wasn't dismissive any longer. It was as intense as hers.

"Too late." Neely smiled and once more pressed her mouth to his.

"Neel'," Seb protested as she once more wrapped her arms around him and kissed him. But his heart wasn't in it.

Whose would be?

What man in possession of all the proper instincts could possibly be noble enough to walk away from such an offer— such a woman.

He'd craved her, it seemed, forever. Even when he'd believed she was Max's lover, he'd wanted her. And since he had discovered she wasn't, the wanting had, if anything, grown stronger. Learning that she was Max's *daughter* might have tempered it a bit, given him a scruple or two that he wouldn't have had otherwise—but even that had not been enough to turn away from her.

He wanted her. Desperately. Intensely. With every fiber of his being. And he'd give her this one last chance to come to her senses, and if she didn't, she was his.

She didn't.

On the contrary, she was practically climbing inside his shirt.

And Seb almost laughed. "Not here," he murmured. "We're going to do this right."

So saying, he reached down and scooped her up into his arms, then carried her straight down the hall and up the stairs.

"Seb!" She flailed in his arms for a moment, but when he hung on doggedly, she stopped and laughed, shaking her head. "You'll have a heart attack carrying me up the stairs."

"I won't," Seb assured her—and proved it by making it to the top without even breathing hard. "Whose room?"

"Yours," she said without hesitation.

He raised a quizzical brow.

"There're photos of Max and my mother on my dresser. This isn't any business of theirs."

There were no photos on Seb's dresser at all. The room was as austere as his life. It made him a little self-conscious, actually, to let her see it.

He'd never had a woman in his bedroom before. Whenever he'd shared physical intimacies with a woman, it had always been elsewhere, always impersonal. Not especially intimate at all.

With Neely everything was personal, everything was intimate. She wasn't like any other woman he'd ever known. She terrified him. She mesmerized him. She drew him into that intimate world as no one and nothing in his life had ever been able to.

He carried her in and laid her gently on the bed, then turned and pushed the door shut so the dog and cats wouldn't be scandalized. Neely gave him a look of complete understanding, then smiled at him and held out her arms to him.

Seb came down into them. Nothing had ever before felt so right in his life.

He was a good lover. Women he'd been to bed with said so. He took his time, he learned what they liked, gauged their responses, gave them what they wanted. He took his pleasure, too. It was enjoyable. It was first intense and then, in the aftermath, relaxing. It was a shared experience of physical release.

With Neely it was something else entirely.

With Neely it wasn't just about getting her naked, it was about learning the texture of her skin. It was about lifting her shirt and stroking his fingers across her abdomen, thinking he'd never felt anything as soft. It was about tugging that shirt over her head and then cupping his hands around her breasts in their lacy bra and molding them, then with his thumbs bringing her nipples to a peak. It was about bending his head and pressing kisses along the edge of her bra, drawing a line there with his tongue, reveling in the sound of the sharp intake of her breath.

He drew her up so he could release the clasp of her bra and then he stripped it off. Holding the silken mounds in his palms, he pressed kisses to the tips, nuzzled them, savoring the taste, the texture, the soft sounds she made in response.

"My turn," she said, and made quick work of the buttons of his dress shirt. She fumbled with the cuff links—"trust you to make it difficult," she muttered—but she got them in the end. Then she dragged his shirt off him and slid her hands up, cool palms against hot flesh, making him shudder.

He reached up and grasped her hands and put them back on his chest. All the while he was kissing her, nibbling her jawline, tasting her ear, then slipping his fingers beneath her waistband, unfastening her jeans, brushing his hand against her, making her tremble.

"Seb!"

"Mmm." He smiled and eased her jeans down, doing his best to maintain his usual careful control, to make her happy, to see to her needs.

But Neely wouldn't just lie back and let him have his way with her. She had his belt undone, his zip down. Then she scrambled around to pry his shoes and socks off.

"What're you—?"

"You can't make love in your shoes and socks!"

"Can't I?" He laughed.

But she shook her head quite seriously. "No. I want all of you."

He thought she meant she wanted to see all of him—and that was fair enough—he didn't mind being naked with her. She had all that wonderful skin to rub against, to feast on, and to press against his.

But it wasn't just his body she wanted naked.

She gave herself to him—opened her body and her arms and her heart and her soul as she drew him down into the most wonderful warmth he'd ever felt—and as she moved beneath him, he lost all control, all ability to hold back, to give and take on his own terms.

He surged into her as she wrapped herself around him, meeting him thrust for thrust, heartbeat for heartbeat, cry for cry.

And when he shattered, as she did, too, he knew that Neely Robson had got more of him than anyone else ever had.

She got everything he had to give.

That, Neely decided, was the difference between sex and love.

The first was only about the body. The last had no limits. It involved the body, of course. But it was far more than simply taking physical pleasure with another person. It was becoming a part of that person—and of letting them become a part of you.

Scary. Risky. Absolutely wonderful.

And as she lay there savoring the weight of the man she loved as he rested on top of her, she felt a pricking of tears for all the people who were afraid to risk—and for those who risked and lost.

She understood a bit better now the edgy exchanges her parents were having. They had risked. They had loved—and lost. And now they were together for the moment—and very likely terrified of it happening again.

Would they risk? She didn't know.

But she knew she was glad she had. Glad she loved Sebastian. Glad she'd dared to say so and to show him.

Now she ran her fingers lightly over his back, traced the ridge of his spine, then curved her hand against the back of his neck and brushed her fingers against his hairline, learning him physically, loving him totally.

He made a soft sound against her ear, shifted slightly. "'M I too heavy?"

"No." She shook her head. "Never."

He turned his head and she could see the curve of his smile in the moonlight that spilled through the window. "I think I am," he said, and effortlessly rolled them over so that now she lay atop him, though still wrapped in his arms.

"Seb?" She lifted her head to look down at him. Their eyes were bare inches apart. "Will you...tell me...what happened?"

His jaw tightened, and she thought that, if he had stayed on top, he would have pulled away and tried to leave her. But now she stayed right where she was. She leaned forward and lay her cheek next to his.

"Vangie said you were going out for a drink with your father," she prompted.

She didn't think he was going to reply. But then, after what seemed like an eternity, Sebastian said, "Was going." He shifted as if he would have shrugged his shoulders. "He never came."

Once again she heard the tone of light indifference, the one he always used when it was safer and smarter not to acknowledge that it mattered, not to admit the pain.

Neely lifted her gaze and met his again. "His loss," she said.

Sebastian snorted.

But Neely wouldn't dismiss it. "He's a fool," she said as she kissed him again, loving him for the man he'd become without a father's love. "He doesn't deserve you."

It was only the truth.

CHAPTER NINE

It was a perfect day for a wedding.

A storybook sort of day, warm but not sweltering, breezy but not gusting. And there wasn't a cloud in the sky, which, for the Pacific Northwest, was nothing short of amazing.

And one look told Neely that Vangie was going to be a beautiful bride. She was a pretty girl to begin with, but today, with her honey colored hair pulled up into a sophisticated knot, her long white dress elegant and simple and her eyes absolutely sparkling, she looked exquisite and every bit the radiantly happy bride she was.

But she wasn't only happy, she was generous and kind.

Neely had been so proud of her this morning while she was getting ready and Sebastian came in. Despite her mother and stepmothers wringing their hands and trying to make her stay right where she was so they could get her train arranged just so, Vangie had dashed across the room to throw her arms around her brother.

"Thank you," she said. "I didn't say it the other day, but I should have. Thank you for trying…for trying to talk to Daddy and—" she stepped back and, still clasping his hands in hers, looked up at him with a tremulous smile "—for everything. You are the best."

He was the best. Neely knew that. And she loved him for the smile he had managed for Vangie.

"Anything I can do for you," he'd said. And Neely knew—they all knew—it was nothing more than the truth. Even though he hadn't been able to produce their father, he'd done everything else.

While he'd obviously been the one his sister had turned to for months, this week it became crystal clear that he was the one the whole family turned to as well.

He was always willing to talk to them and listen to them—whether it was about Vangie's silver and rose mint boxes or which medical schools Milos should apply to. He listened to his stepmother Gina fret about his brother Gabriel's umpteen girl-friends and he spent a morning taking his youngest sister to the office and to a couple of his job sites so she could learn what being an architect entailed.

He managed to defuse half a dozen wedding-related crises as well. He was the one who stepped in and arranged for the limo when the one Garrett had contacted had a conflict. He was the one who saw to it that all his stepmothers had corsages when nobody else had. This morning he was the one who tied all his brothers' ties.

And right after they got out of the car, he'd said to Neely, "Stand still." And he used masking tape to go over her dress and make sure there was no lingering rabbit or kitten or dog hair on Neely's dress.

"A master of details," she'd teased him, grinning.

He'd smiled that crooked half smile of his and said, "Someone's got to do it."

Neely understood now that that someone was always Sebastian.

And now she sat with the wedding guests in rows of white chairs on the lawn overlooking the sound, waiting to watch him do yet another task—this one a task he had every right to—walking his sister down the aisle and giving her to her groom.

She hoped he would smile when he did so. He had the most beautiful smile. She wasn't treated to it often. But he'd smiled at her the night they'd made love. He'd smiled that smile the next morning when he'd awakened with his arms around her.

And she dared to hope that she would see that same amazing smile someday soon at their wedding when he watched her walk down an aisle toward him.

Still, it was too soon to think about that.

The string quintet—one of the few things Sebastian had not had a hand in arranging—began at that moment to play the processional. Neely stood and turned with everyone else to watch as the bridesmaids proceeded in measured steps across the grass to where a handsome nervous Garrett and his grinning best man waited with the minister.

Little Sarah came first, her head high, her eyes straight ahead, her expression solemn, but every now and then Neely saw a flicker of a smile very like Sebastian's on her face. Then came Jenna, her ash-blonde hair a striking contrast to the rest of the girls. The triplets—Ariadne, Alexa and Anastasia—followed. Neely still had no idea which was which, but Sebastian never seemed to have trouble telling them apart.

"Not now I don't," he'd said when she'd marveled at his ability. "But when they were little it was like three little indistinguishable dark-haired devils. Seriously scary."

There was a pause in the music after the last of the triplets had reached the halfway mark of the procession, and then the quintet picked up the volume and plunged into the bridal music once more.

Everyone turned and twisted their heads and craned their necks to get their first glimpse of the bride.

Everyone except Neely. She was twisting her head and craning her neck to catch a first glimpse of Sebastian resplendent in black tie, white shirt and tuxedo jacket.

So she was poleaxed to see an older, craggier tuxedo-clad Savas male walking with Vangie up the path instead!

The bride was absolutely radiant, beaming at everyone, looking from side to side as she walked slowly toward her waiting groom. And the man was smiling happily and looking at her dotingly—as if he had a right to be there.

In one way, she supposed he did. She knew exactly who he was—Phillip Savas, the man who had given her life. He was her father in name. But who had been there for her every single day?

She looked around desperately for Sebastian. *Where was he?*

Not with his sister, that was certain. She had her father to give her away just as she'd wanted.

The way it should be.

Neely could hear the words echoing in her brain. They were the words Vangie had used. And Sebastian had reiterated them even as he'd refused at first to make the effort.

"She wants a normal wedding. A normal family," he'd said. "That's all she's ever wanted."

And this was what she wanted? A father who showed up for a few brief moments and stepped in at the last minute to give her away? As if it were his right when in fact he'd really given her away years ago!

It wasn't his right! Neely was outraged. How dared he? Where had he come from?

And most important of all, *Where was Sebastian*?

She should have been watching the ceremony. But she barely noticed that Philip had handed his daughter off to Garrett and had gone to stand by his string of ex-wives. She was craning her neck trying to find Sebastian.

Ah, there. At the very back she spotted his dark head. He was perfectly composed, though she was sure she wouldn't have been. He stood ramrod straight, looking for all the world like one of the ushers and not the man who had every right to have walked his sister up the aisle.

The wedding was short and sweet—at least Neely supposed it was. She barely noticed. Her mind was consumed with indignation for Sebastian, with annoyance toward his father. No one else seemed to notice.

The Savases looked like a normal family on the eldest daughter's wedding day: mother with a tear-streaked smiling face, father beaming as he bestowed her hand on her groom, the bride joyful, the groom solemn.

And where the eldest brother was no one cared.

Except her.

Neely cared. And she barely waited until after the ceremony to slip away and go to him. But when she looked around, he wasn't there. Vangie and Garrett, his parents and hers were in a reception line and everyone was lined up to go past and congratulate them.

Sebastian should have been there, too. If anyone deserved congratulations for getting Vangie married it was him. But she didn't see him anywhere. She could have waited in the reception line and asked Vangie, but judging from the happily dazed expression on Vangie's face, she wouldn't have known.

She did ask Gabriel, "Where's your brother?"

But Gabriel just shrugged and looked blank. So did Milos and the triplets. "He's around somewhere," Jenna said, waving her hand toward the hundreds of people milling about on the lawn.

It was Sarah who pointed. "He's over there."

Following her pointing finger, Neely spied Sebastian on the far side of the gathering. He was standing with a couple she'd never seen before. They were talking and he was listening. He had his hands tucked into the pockets of his black trousers. His dark head was bent.

He didn't look shattered. He looked perfectly fine. But Neely couldn't help cutting through the crowds of people to get to him.

"Ah, there you are!" She smiled brilliantly as she came up to him, and he lifted his gaze and smiled. It wasn't the best Sebastian Savas smile, the one that could curl her toes. But it was warm and welcoming and he reached out a hand and drew her to him, looping an arm over her shoulders.

"This is Neely Robson," he told the other couple, and to Neely he said, "My cousin Theo and his wife, Martha."

He introduced her to more cousins and aunts and uncles, and was completely affable and pleasant. He never once mentioned his father, never said a word about the switch. Of course she knew Sebastian well enough that she didn't expect him to make a fuss about it, but she thought he might say something to her in the few moments they were alone.

But when they were alone he stole a kiss, and while it was a perfectly discreet kiss in public, it meant she didn't get to find out what happened.

"Are you all right?" she asked him briefly.

He blinked, surprised. "I'm fine."

"Your father—"

But Sebastian simply turned away. "Let's get something to eat."

They got something to eat. They talked to a myriad Savas aunts, uncles, cousins and friends. Sebastian was perfectly polite, completely composed. He didn't seem like an Iceman on the surface—not the way he used to appear at work sometimes—but beneath the surface charm, Neely began to suspect that the ice was there.

She caught a sense of it in his tone of voice. It was that easy, polite and on-the-surface-pleasant tone, yet there was in it, too, a distance, a determined emotional detachment.

Yes, Sebastian agreed with everyone who said so, Vangie was a beautiful bride and Garrett was a lucky man. He allowed that it was terrific that their whole family could be here. And he even nodded and said, yes, wasn't it nice that they all—even the ex-wives—got on so well.

"Philip always did know how to pick 'em," his father's older brother, Socrates, said cheerfully. Socrates's son, Theo, winced at the comment, but Sebastian didn't bat an eye.

But he wasn't, Neely started to understand as time went on, quite as sanguine as he seemed. It was unobtrusive but apparent, to her at least—though she was sure she was the only one who noticed—that he was careful to keep a couple hundred people between himself and his father at all times.

Not that it was difficult. Philip Savas was clearly a charming, gregarious man. He was every bit as handsome as his son with a more affable outgoing manner. In situations like this Sebastian was pleasant but quiet. He didn't have the innate ease his father did with social settings. Wherever Philip went, people were smiling and laughing, beaming at him, shaking his hand, clapping him on the back.

His children—except for Sebastian—flocked around him, eager for fatherly attention. Even his ex-wives seemed to preen under his benevolent eye.

Philip was in his element. He paid attention to them all, charmed them all—his oft-neglected family, the multitude of wedding guests and, of course, Garrett's family as well. Her father's presence and his behavior was everything Vangie had wanted.

Neely found it interesting, though, that even as he conversed with all of them, his gaze kept shifting toward Sebastian. At first she thought she might have imagined it. But the more she watched, the more often she saw Philip's glance move their way. As he chatted his way from group to group, he seemed to be edging closer and closer to his eldest son.

Sebastian never looked his way. He kept a possessive hand on Neely's arm or looped his over her shoulders, but his focus was on whichever friend, relative or guest was talking with him.

And yet, somehow, without Neely quite realizing how, Sebastian managed to move them further away. It was a dance of pursuit and avoidance. Never directly acknowledged by father or son.

Once Philip caught her eye and smiled at her. She supposed it was even a genuine smile, but it couldn't hold a candle to his son's. She didn't smile back, but she did say to Sebastian, "I think your father wants to talk to you."

But Sebastian acted like he didn't hear, instead spinning her onto the small dance floor and taking her in his arms. "Let's dance."

Oh, yes. It was a slow dance, one that allowed Neely to loop her arms around his neck while his held her close to his chest. They moved together, swayed, shifted, shuffled.

Neely closed her eyes and rested her head on his shoulder, breathing in the scent of him—the piney aftershave, the starch of his shirt, a hint of the sea, something uniquely Sebastian. She felt the touch of his lips to her hair, felt his arms tighten around her. And she savored it, stored away the moment and knew she would always remember this.

"May I cut in?"

Neely's head jerked up as Sebastian's arms went stiff around her. They both looked around to see Philip just behind Sebastian, his hand raised from apparently having tapped his son's shoulder, a hopeful smile on his handsome face.

Sebastian seemed to turn to stone. He had certainly stopped breathing. Neely breathed, but what she was breathing was righteous anger at the same time she realized that there was no way she could make a scene in the middle of Vangie's wedding.

Everything had been picture perfect so far. She couldn't ruin it by telling Sebastian's father exactly what she thought of him. And even more clearly she couldn't allow Sebastian to do what she suspected he itched to do. Not that she blamed him.

But punching out his father's lights in the middle of his sister's wedding was not the "normal" family behavior that would endear him to Vangie—or anyone else.

She unclasped her fingers and stroked the back of his neck. He didn't speak, didn't even move—except for the tick of a muscle in his jaw and a sort of vibrato tremor that ran through his limbs.

Neely ran her hand down his arm and smiled her best well-brought-up smile. "How do you do?" she said. "I'm Neely Robson. And you must be Mr. Savas." She did not say, *You must be Sebastian's father.*

"Call me Philip," the older man said. He glanced at Sebastian. "I'm sure you don't mind if I make the acquaintance of your lovely friend."

"Sebastian and I are living together," Neely said firmly. So maybe not in the traditional sense, but she wanted it clear they were not merely friends. As if anyone could think so given the way they'd been dancing.

"Of course," Philip said genially. "My son doesn't believe in marriage."

"I wonder why," Sebastian said through his teeth. They were the first words he'd spoken since Philip had cut in.

Philip only laughed. "Well, I promise not to propose to Miss Robson. How about that?" His tone was light and jokey but what was going on between them was no laughing matter.

"Don't worry. I'd say no," Neely said in an equally light tone. But just as she did so, the music ended, and she breathed a sigh of relief, thinking the whole problem might have been avoided.

But the quintet immediately went into the next number and Philip held out a hand to her. "This one will be mine, then, I think."

Sebastian didn't move. His fingers curled into a fist. Neely pressed her hand down on his arm. "One dance, Mr. Savas," she said evenly. And she gave Sebastian's forearm a squeeze.

He looked at her hand on his arm, then he raised his gaze to hers, his eyes as hard as green granite, his mouth flat and uncompromising.

Neely pressed her own lips together and raised her eyebrows, then suggested gently. "Why don't you dance with Vangie? I'll bet she'd like that."

Sebastian's jaw seemed locked. Only his eyes moved—from her to his father, then back again.

But finally he gave a curt nod and released her. "Enjoy yourself."

He should have known.

It was just like Philip to breeze in at the last minute and act like he'd meant to be there all along.

"Got delayed in Japan," was all he'd said.

"For *four* days?" Sebastian couldn't mask his disbelief.

But of course it didn't matter. Daddy was here now, and that was what mattered to Vangie. To his brothers and sisters. To all the stupid stepmothers. To everyone.

Except him.

And he frankly didn't give a damn.

Now he stalked across the dance floor to the table where his sister sat with Garrett. "Dance with me."

She had danced with her husband, her father (of course) and Garrett's father. But then she had sat down, preferring to simply watch and share the day with her husband. But now she looked up, startled, then smiled up at Seb, delighted. "Of course. We didn't get to before, did we?"

Before—when they'd been supposed to follow Vangie and Garret's bridal waltz, Philip had danced with her instead.

"No," Seb said shortly and held out a hand to her. Beaming, she took the floor with him.

Over her head he could see his father smiling and talking to Neely. He was going all out to charm her. Sebastian recognized all the moves, the flatteringly intent expression, the easy flirtatiousness.

Neely's back was to him, so Seb wasn't able to gauge her reaction. But his father had never failed to win a woman over yet.

He hadn't expected Philip to cut in on them. He should have, he supposed. It was the sort of blatant, flagrant attention-seeking thing his father would do. Seb knew he should have seen it coming when Philip kept trying to catch his eye, as if they had something to say to each other.

He'd ignored it because he had nothing to say to Philip. And whatever his father might have to say, Sebastian had no desire to listen.

Now he didn't have to talk to Sebastian. He had a more malleable captive audience. And clearly he was making the most of it. He was a better dancer than his son and he twirled Neely in his arms and spun her around and she laughed.

Sebastian stepped on Vangie's foot. "Sorry."

"It's all right." Vangie was in a mood to be pleased by everything. "It's been a gorgeous wonderful day, hasn't it?"

"Mm." He could see Neely talking now. Philip's brows lifted, he opened his mouth, then shut it again. Neely kept talking.

"I couldn't believe it when Daddy showed up. Thank you for that."

"Me? I didn't do it." God forbid.

"You tried," Vangie said. "He told me he got your message. Told me you said he should be here."

"He never responded."

"Yes, he did," Vangie said happily. "He came."

And as always, just like bloody Caesar, Philip saw and then he conquered.

Seb's jaw grew tight. He tensed as he watched Philip spin Neely round again, then start talking while Neely cocked her head and listened.

Was this song never going to end?

Then he heard Neely's laughter. He turned his head to see her smiling up into his father's eyes. He stopped dead.

Vangie tripped over his feet. "Sorry," she said. "My fault."

"No." But he couldn't do this anymore. "Let me take you back so you can sit down before I walk all over you."

He took her arm and steered her back to Garrett before the music even ended. She sat down and looked up at him to smile again. "Thanks, Seb. For everything."

"For stepping on your feet." He smiled wryly as the music finally came to an end and Neely still stood with his father on the far side of the dance floor deep in conversation. Then she smiled, nodded and Philip leaned in and kissed her on the cheek.

Vangie squeezed his hands, drawing his attention back to her. "No. Thanks for making my dreams come true."

"You're welcome," he said because it was the right thing to do.

Some people's dreams did come true, he supposed as he walked away.

Frankly Seb found it hard to imagine.

"It was the most beautiful wedding I've ever been to," Neely said on their way home.

"Uh-huh."

She slanted him a glance. His gaze was, of course, on the road. It was late—past eleven—and they were exhausted, but fortunately they were nearly home. She'd been carrying the conversation all the way. Sebastian's contributions had, like the last one, been delivered in single syllables and a monotone.

Of course he'd done so much to make it a great day for his sister that she didn't expect him to talk a lot. But he'd been increasingly quiet, not just since they'd left the reception but since the dance his father had cut in on.

Now, as he turned down the hill to the parking area by the dock, she said quietly, "It's actually hard to hate him."

She didn't say whom. She knew she didn't have to.

Sebastian's fingers tightened on the steering wheel. "I wouldn't know." His tone was cold.

At least, Neely thought, it wasn't that light dismissive tone that made her crazy.

"You don't hate him," she said with more confidence than she felt.

"I don't give a damn about him," Sebastian said roughly. He turned into a parking space and cut the engine.

"Not true."

His jaw worked. In the streetlight she could see his knuckles whiten as his fingers clenched.

"He wanted to talk to you, not me," Neely said quietly.

He didn't look at her, just stared straight ahead. "He could have talked to me four days ago."

"He really did get delayed in Japan."

Sebastian slapped his hands on the steering wheel. "Don't make excuses for him!"

"I'm *not* making excuses!"

"No?" He turned to glare at her. "What do you call it?"

"Sanity?" she suggested. "Common sense?"

"To believe everything he tells you? To let yourself be conned?"

"I'm *not* letting myself be conned! He said he wanted to apologize. You wouldn't let him get close." That was more or less what he had said. Plus he'd said he wanted to get to know the woman who seemed to have captured his oldest son's heart.

Of course she didn't say that now.

Sebastian was already snorting his disbelief at what she did say. He jerked open the car door and came around to open hers, but Neely got out by herself and stalked down the dock toward the houseboat.

Sebastian caught up with her. "I don't want him close," he said flatly.

"I think you made that perfectly clear. Look," she said, rounding on him by their front door, "I'm not condoning your father's behavior. I think it stinks, but—"

"Did you tell him that? You didn't, did you?" he demanded furiously. "Of course you didn't! You're just like all the rest!"

He stuck his key in the lock and shoved the door open. Harm bounded up to meet them. Kittens tumbled sleepily down the stairs. Sebastian ignored them all, just held the door and simultaneously glowered accusingly at her.

Disregarding her dress and everything but the pain in her heart and the tears that stung her eyes, Neely marched past him and knelt to wrap her arms around the dog. She hugged him hard, pressed her face into his short soft fur. Drew a breath. Drew strength.

Then she stood again and turned to face Sebastian. "I did, you know,"

He stared. "Did what?"

"Told him it stunk, what he'd done. Told him he hurt you. Told him what a jerk he was." She glared at him defiantly.

Sebastian looked stunned. And then he shook his head in disbelief. "Sure you did. That's why he was laughing. Why you were! Why he danced you around and kissed your cheek!"

There was a short silence and then she said, "You don't believe me."

He hunched his shoulder. "I saw what I saw."

She slowly shook her head. "No, you saw what you wanted to see."

He didn't say anything, just stared stonily at her.

"You don't believe me. You don't trust me." Neely felt cold. She felt gutted. She felt as if her determined and furious attack on Sebastian's father, which he had certainly not been expecting when he'd asked for a dance, had all been for naught.

She'd had to give Philip credit. He'd first looked as stunned as Sebastian when she'd told him what she thought of him. But he'd listened. He'd shut his mouth and heard her out. And then he'd talked.

Of course she hadn't believed every word he said. Of course she knew a sound byte when she heard one. But she also heard some truth in the desperation Philip Savas had expressed. She'd heard a man who had made a mess of most of the relationships in his life, a man who'd lost the respect of his eldest son and knew it. She heard a man who could be both self-aware and self-deprecating, a man who understood his own weaknesses but who hadn't yet figured out how to compensate for them.

By the end of the dance yes, they'd laughed. But it had been equally tempting to cry—for him and for his son.

"Don't tell me my father didn't try to bring you around to his way of thinking," Sebastian said grimly.

"Of course he did. In his ham-handed way, he wants you in his life. He wants us to design a hotel for him."

"Oh, for God's sake! As if I would ever—"

"You could," Neely said stubbornly. "We could."

Sebastian shook his head. "I'll never! And you won't either if you want whatever we've got between us to work."

"What do we have between us, Seb?" she asked. She was almost afraid to, not really wanting to face the answer. "Do we have love? Commitment? Forever?"

His jaw tightened. "We have a good thing. You know that."

"I thought so," Neely agreed slowly. "Now I'm not so sure."

He raked a hand through his hair. "Why not? Because I won't knuckle under to my perennially absent father's demand?"

Neely shook her head. "This isn't about your father."

"No? Then what is it about?"

"It's about whether you're ever going to trust me to be on your side. Even when I challenge you, I'm still on your side. But you didn't believe I'd be there for you with Carmody, either."

"This isn't about Carmody!"

"No, it isn't. It's about trust, Sebastian."

He shook his head. "If that's the way you feel, we don't have anything else to say. I'm giving you everything I've got," he said flatly. "I can't give you any more."

"Can't?" Neely said quietly, looking at him and feeling her heart breaking. "Or won't?"

CHAPTER TEN

HE LEFT.

Neely heard him go.

She had run up to her bedroom and shut the door and prayed that he would come after her. But there were no footsteps on the stairs. There was no light knock on her door. There was no sound of her name.

There was only silence—and then the front door opening and closing.

She ran to the window and looked out to see him walking up the dock. He looked weary and exhausted and alone, and she wanted nothing so much as to call to him, to tell him to come back and to wrap her arms around him and tell him she loved him.

But if she did, he wouldn't believe her. He didn't trust her, didn't trust her word.

So he couldn't—or wouldn't—believe she loved him.

He kept walking until he disappeared into the darkness. Moments later an engine started, headlights came on. A car backed out and turned to go up the hill.

He drove away.

She was mad. She'd get over it.

Neely wasn't silly. She had to see that they were good together. And she had to know it wasn't worth throwing away over nothing.

He gave her the weekend to come to her senses. In the meantime, he made his sisters double up, his brothers take the sofas, and he moved back into his penthouse. It was a madhouse. Noise, clutter, commotion. It should have taken his mind off her.

It might have if they hadn't all asked, "Where's Neely?" and "What are you doing here?"

"I live here," he said shortly.

But as he took them one by one to the airport over the next day and a half and got his penthouse back, he didn't feel as if he lived there anymore. The penthouse didn't feel like home at all.

Home was where Neely was.

Tuesday evening he spent the day listening to Roger Carmody sing Neely's praises once again—"Makes complete sense, that girl. Got a feel for what makes people tick. Made sense of all that soaring space you like so much. Good thing you sent her to talk to me."

"She's very astute," Seb said in his best politic manner.

Now he hoped she was astute enough to have come to her senses. He'd missed her. He was ready to let bygones be bygones. So he went home.

And when he parked his car and went down the steps to the dock, despite his earlier anger, he felt that increasingly familiar sense of anticipation, of the eagerness he always felt when he was coming home to the houseboat.

To Neely.

Of course she wouldn't be home yet. He'd left Carmody early and she'd still be at work. But that would give him a chance to be there first, to surprise her.

He opened the door, prepared now for Harm's immediate dash and skid around the corner from the living room. He was already grinning in anticipation.

But the entry was silent and empty.

"Harm! Hey, buddy! Where are you?"

Seb supposed the dog could be out on the deck. It was a sunny day. He liked to lie in the sun's warmth. Or maybe Cody had come to take him running if Neely knew she was going to be late. A glance toward the hook told him that Harm's leash was gone.

But so was his food dish. And his water bowl.

Seb's stomach did a slow awful somersault and ended feeling as if it had lodged in his throat.

"Harm?" He called the dog's name louder now, an edge to his voice. A new unwelcome feeling settled in his chest.

Apprehension? Worry? Panic?

No, he thought. *No!*

But all the same, he strode quickly down the hall into the living area. The sofa was there, and the armchair, the lamps, the desk with his computer, the bookshelves.

But only half the books were there. His half.

The rocker Max had made Neely was gone. So was the afghan he knew her mother had knitted her.

And the coffee table that had been in front of the sofa—the one with the drawers for architectural drawings, the one that Neely had talked Max out of, her pride and joy, the one she wouldn't let him set his boxes on when he'd first moved in—that was gone, too.

Max could have taken it back, Seb told himself. Neely had said she was "trying it out" to see if it was the one she wanted or if she wanted Max to make her something else.

"Anything I want, he said," she'd told Seb. "But that's silly. He knows very well I want this one."

And Seb knew it hadn't gone back to Max.

It had simply gone.

Like Harm. And the kittens. And—he looked around desperately, hardly able to breathe—the rabbits and the guinea pig.

Gone. All gone. With Neely.

"The Iceman is back."

Seb heard Gladys mutter the words under her breath to Danny when Seb snapped at one of her questions. He stiffened, but ignored it, just as he had ignored every curious look and leading question the past five days.

It wasn't any of their business. He worked with them. He didn't owe them explanations.

If they wanted explanations, damn it, they could ask Neely.

But Neely wasn't here.

"She's out of town. She's taken on another project," Max had reported when Seb had rang him, demanding to know where the hell she was.

"And she took all her books and her furniture?" Seb said before he could stop himself.

"Did she?" Max said. "Mmm. Interesting."

That wasn't the term Seb would have used.

He had given up being gutted about personal relationships gone awry about the time his father had split with his third wife.

It didn't do to get close. It didn't do to try to make something more out of what was clearly going to be no more than a brief encounter.

Oh, sure, his new stepmothers might have promised "forever" but it hadn't taken Seb long to learn that it never lasted. They grew weary of Philip's absences, his distractions, his inability to get involved. And they left.

They took their children with them and made new lives for themselves. But they never took Sebastian because Sebastian wasn't theirs.

He only belonged to Philip—and Philip didn't care.

No one cared.

Three stark words that cut to the core of his soul.

For years Seb hadn't let it matter. Though at times the knowledge pressed against the inside of his head, making it throb, had clogged his throat, making it ache, he'd ignored it, put it aside, soldiered on.

He'd been wounded by his father's neglect, but he'd survived because he'd refused to care enough—to love enough—to let it hurt.

But all the resolve in the world was no proof against this pain. This emptiness.

This was different. This wasn't his childhood. This wasn't his past. He was an adult. He was over all that. This was now.

This was Neely. And there was no way to fight against her leaving him. No way to turn his back, to say it didn't matter.

Because it did.

Because, God help him, he was in love with her.

Fiercely Seb shook his head. Fought it off, lied to himself, told himself he didn't love her. Couldn't. Wouldn't.

"Can't, Seb?" she'd said coolly. "Or won't?"

He hated the challenge that echoed in his mind. He fought it off. Denied it.

He *wouldn't* love her. Or if he already did, damn it, he'd stop.

It would be all right. He would get by. There was nothing wrong with being an iceman. It was a hell of a lot safer. Saner. Less painful.

He'd cope.

He threw himself into his work. He spent hours overseeing every single detail of the Blake-Carmody project. If Neely wasn't going to be there to do her part, so be it. He'd do it himself.

He wondered what other project could possibly be more important, that Max would have sent her off now, but he didn't ask.

He didn't want to know. Max worked from home and Seb worked in the office and in the field. When he had questions on Blake-Carmody, he asked Danny or Frank or he got Gladys to call her.

"Don't you have her number?" Gladys asked.

"I don't have time. Just get the answers and put it in a memo," Seb said.

He didn't want to talk to her. It still hurt too much.

He left the houseboat and moved back to his penthouse. It was what he'd intended all along, wasn't it? The houseboat had been a stopgap, just until the wedding was over. Now he had his place back—all to himself.

The pizza boxes were gone. So were the panty hose. The bathroom countertops had been swept clean of nail polish, hair spray bottles, foundation, powder, lipstick and mascara.

He didn't step on plastic soda bottles or tortilla chips. He didn't see any remnants of his sisters' occupation after his cleaner blitzed her way through the place. And if there was a lingering odor of overly cloying cologne in the rooms, he could leave the windows open and it would vanish within days.

Everything went back to being exactly the way he'd left it.

Only he had changed.

Now he stood in his spare austere living room with its view across the skyline to the sound and didn't relish the view anymore. Or not as much as he had in the past.

It seemed too remote. Too far above things. Too impersonal.

It made him long for the little houseboat on the water. It made him want a kitten leaping out at his shoelaces when he walked into the kitchen. It made him want a dog smiling a doggy smile and thumping its tail when he walked in the door. He wouldn't even mind if it shed on his navy suit coat.

He had no one to talk to. No one to share a meal with.

He had no one at all.

Jenna was the first of his sisters to call him.

"How are you?" she asked, which surprised him. Usually she only called when she wanted something and it was the first thing she said. But while he waited, the expected request never came.

"I had such a good time with you," she said. "It was fun being a family, being together. I thought I might come back," she said. "To go to the university. If that's okay with you?"

"If you want," Seb said, wondering where this had come from and waited again for the request for money or advice. But Jenna only said, "Can you have cats in the dorms, I wonder."

"I doubt it," Seb said. "Who cares? You don't have a cat."

"I do. Her name is Chloe. Neely gave her to me."

Seb felt as if he'd been punched in the gut. "*Neely* gave you a cat?"

One of *their* kittens?

"Mmm-hmm." Jenna sounded thrilled. "She said she needed to find homes for them. They were getting big enough. We all have them."

"*What?*"

"She gave us each one."

She, the triplets and Sarah each had one of Neely's cats?

"And Marisa took the guinea pig," Jenna told him gaily. That was Sarah's mother.

"Yeah?" Seb wondered who got the rabbits. And Harm. He didn't ask.

"She said she wanted us to have a part of her," Jenna reported.

But she hadn't wanted him to have a part of her.

Or did she think he wouldn't want one?

The next day he bought a fish. Neely had once said she had started with a fish. They'd been sitting on the deck one evening and she'd told him about her first pet.

"I had a fish because fish are portable. Easier to take when we moved. And they don't run away back to where they've been. They're there for you."

Like Neely had been.

He knew that now. There was no way to deny it. And as time passed he didn't want to. He fed his fish and cared for his fish.

But frankly he thought the fish looked lonely. So two days later he bought another fish.

Maybe they'd have little fish. Or one would eat the other.

He wondered which.

Would Neely know?

"It's nearly midnight!" Max, hair ruffled and wearing what looked like hastily pulled-on shorts over his cast, leaned on his crutches and scowled furiously at Seb when he opened the door. "You might work at all hours, but some of us like a little time off now and then."

"I'm taking time off," Seb said gruffly, brushing past Max heading straight into the living room without waiting for an invitation. "But first I need to know where Neely is."

He turned and waited while Max crutched his way into the living room, sputtering and looking indignant. "What do you care where she is?"

"I need to talk to her. And don't ask me about what. That's between your daughter and me!"

Max's brows shot up, but he didn't answer at once, just looked Seb over sceptically.

Seb waited. He'd wait till kingdom come if necessary.

"She's with your old man," Max told him.

It was a blow. Seb felt his teeth come together, but he forced himself to simply nod. "Her choice," he said evenly.

Max's brows lifted. "One you didn't agree with."

"No." No use arguing that. "I didn't." He took a breath. "I've changed my mind."

Now Max's eyes really did go wide. But before he could reply, a husky female voice spoke up. "About time."

Seb looked up to see Neely's mother standing on the landing clad in what had to be Max's bathrobe and little else. Obviously there was more going on here than simple nursing care.

"Give him the address, Max," she said. "He looks ghastly."

"Maybe she won't want to see him," Max said.

"Up to her. At least he's going after her," Neely's mother said pointedly. "Which is more than you ever did."

Max grimaced and rubbed a hand against the back of his neck. "Well, you know how it is. Some of us take longer to wise up." He copied an address down and handed it to Seb. "Good luck."

"You'll need it," Lara added.

Seb had no doubt about that.

* * *

The cabin was in the middle of nowhere. Admittedly it was the most beautiful bit of nowhere that Neely had ever been in—a balm to the most troubled soul—and good thing because she needed all the balm she could get.

She stopped now to stare out the window at the expanse of Lake Chelan through the trees. She drew on the view for inspiration as she tried to bring the outside in—to capture the grandeur that Sebastian did so well in his soaring spaces and expanses of glass, while at the same time trying to create the sense of safe harbor, of peaceful retreat that her own heart sought.

Finding the balance between the two was the hardest work she'd ever done. Particularly because half the time she wasn't even sure she should be here.

Neely knew perfectly well that Philip had only asked her because he really wanted his son to do it. He'd been perfectly polite and welcoming when she'd shown up instead.

He'd been a little wary of course. "Does Sebastian know you're here?" he'd asked her the afternoon she'd come to discuss the idea.

Neely had had to admit he didn't. "We didn't exactly see eye to eye on things."

Philip wasn't clueless. "He doesn't want anything to do with me."

Neely rather thought that Sebastian felt Philip had never wanted anything to do with him. But she only said that she had discussed it with Max, and if Philip was interested in having her work on a design, she would be happy to do it.

She'd brought him a portfolio of her other work, and he'd been impressed enough to agree. Over the past two and a half weeks, she had worked with him almost every day, exploring the site, listening to his ideas, creating sketches and working out plans.

It was intense and creative and energizing—exactly the sort of time that would have gone a long way toward healing the rift between Philip and his son—if his son had deigned to come.

She hadn't seen Seb or heard from him since he'd stalked out of the houseboat the night of Vangie's wedding.

She'd waited. And waited. Had wanted to talk, to discuss, to explain. But when he hadn't come back she realized he didn't intend to.

No doubt he'd simply moved back to the penthouse and taken up his old life right where he'd left off. Without her.

Still, when she'd packed up her furniture, her books and her animals, Neely had dared to hope he would come after her.

She knew she loved him.

And despite his resistence, despite his reluctance to trust, she believed, deep down, that he loved her.

She stared at the boat cruising up the lake and wondered if Philip would be here soon. He came most afternoons and they reworked the sketches she came up with the day before. He was easy to talk to, warm and engaging, yet always edgy and on the move. There wasn't the peace in him that she saw in his son.

Peace? In Sebastian?

Maybe not always. But she dared to believe that he'd found a little with her.

Would that peace have been enough? Certainly she could have stayed—could have simply shared his bed and his house-boat and taken what he thought he could give.

And they would have had great sex and also a certain degree of contentment.

But it wasn't enough. Just as her mother had never been able to accept the little Max had been willing to give years ago, Neely knew she wanted more than great sex, a bit of peace and contentment with Sebastian.

She wanted everything. She wanted the love and connection that her parents finally seemed to be finding with each other now. Max and Lara together at last. Who'd have thought it?

It just proved, Neely supposed, that it was never too late.

But she couldn't imagine waiting another twenty-seven years

or so for Seb. After three weeks and not a word, not a sign—nothing at all—she didn't expect there was any point.

She reached her toe out and nudged her sleeping dog. "You're here for me, aren't you?"

Harm opened one eye and closed it again. So much for that.

She forced her attention back to the sketch she was working on. It was for the lobby area of what would be a fifteen-room inn. "Small and intimate, yes," Philip had said, "but with light and space. Bring the outside in."

He sounded just like his son.

Neely chewed on her pencil and tried to think how to convey exactly that when Harm jumped up and went barking to the door.

"It's just Philip," she said. "Don't fuss."

Usually Harm didn't. But he was barking his head off today. "Stop it, you stupid dog!" Neely got up and jerked open the door. "See! It's just—"

Sebastian.

She stared. Not Philip at all. His son. Lean and dark and as serious looking as ever Neely had seen him. Every bit as gorgeous, too, in a pair of faded blue jeans and a long-sleeved grey shirt.

The Iceman? Or not?

Harm flung himself onto Sebastian who scratched his ears and rubbed his fur and grinned broadly at him, making Neely want to fling herself at him as well.

She didn't because she didn't know why he was there.

For all she knew Max had sent him up here on some wild-goose chase. That would be just like Max—he was turning into an unrelenting romantic.

"Harm, get down!" she said, trying to tug the dog back.

But Sebastian just said, "It's all right. I've missed him." And then his grin faded and their eyes met and Neely thought she might drown in the depths of them before he said, "I've missed you."

There was a ragged edge to his voice she hadn't heard before.

This wasn't The Iceman, then. She wet her lips. Her fingers gripped the handle of the door.

"Can I come in?"

She nodded and stepped back, waiting until he came in, and she shut the door to ask, "Is something wrong? Are Max and Lara—?"

"They're fine. Together, apparently." He sounded a little dazed at that.

"Yes," Neely said. "They might make it this time. They have a ways to go, though."

"But they're taking a chance."

She nodded again. He was so close. She could see the pulse beat in his throat and wanted to reach out a finger and touch it. She could see whiskers on his jaw and wanted to rub her cheek against them, feeling them rough one way and smooth the other. She wanted—

"Will you take a chance on me?"

Sometimes in the forest all sound stopped. The birds hushed. The wind dropped. Nothing sounded. No one moved. It was like that now.

"Your father—"

"This is not about my father," Seb said firmly just as she had said it to him. But as he spoke there was a ghost of a smile on his lips. "But if you must know, he says you have to make up your own mind."

"He—" Neely stared. "You talked to him?"

Sebastian shrugged. "How do you think I found you?"

Abruptly Neely sat down. Her mind spun. He had come after her? He had talked to his father?

"He says you do wonderful warm and cozy," Sebastian told her, "but that you're struggling a bit with the light and space."

"He said that?" She didn't know whether to be delighted or outraged. "You've discussed this, have you?"

"I got to Chelan last night," Seb said. "I couldn't get a boat and come up the lake until this morning. We had a lot of time to talk."

Neely opened her mouth and closed it again. "I don't know what to say," she murmured.

A corner of Seb's mouth lifted. "How about yes?"

"What would I be saying yes to, exactly?" She held her breath, daring to hope, but wondering if she was actually dreaming. Perhaps she'd been in the woods alone far too long.

"Yes to taking a chance on me for starters," Sebastian said. He dropped down on one knee next to the chair where she sat and took her hands in his. "Yes to letting me contribute a little light and space to those hotel plans you're working on—"

She caught her breath and blinked in surprise.

"—but mostly yes that you'll marry me because you are the woman I love, the one who gives light to my life and joy to my heart and—" he swallowed and went on, his voice ragged "—because wherever you are is home."

She leaned toward him, his arms came around her and as their lips touched she answered him. "Yes and yes and yes."

When Philip came later that afternoon, Seb told him to go away.

"Don't be rude," Neely protested.

Seb shrugged. "It shouldn't be any hardship. He goes away all the time."

Father's and son's eyes met in challenge, acknowledgment and acceptance. Philip nodded. "I'll see you tomorrow," he said to them. "It's a workday."

"We'll be there," Neely promised, even as Sebastian scooped her up in his arms and carried her back to bed.

They'd already been there once. And now once again they shared their bodies as well as their hopes and their dreams and their hearts. Only after, when they were lying wrapped in each other's arms, did Sebastian sit up and say, "I brought you something."

"What's that?"

"Well, a few things, actually," he confessed. "I'll be right back."

He yanked on his jeans and disappeared out the door. Bemused and baffled, Neely waited while he went down to the boat—twice—and then came back.

"This is for you," he said, holding out a package that had a shape she recognized at once.

With reverent hands, Neely took it and unwrapped it. "Your grandfather's violin?"

Seb nodded. "Yours now." And she knew the depth of his love from the gift of the one thing of enduring love he'd carried with him all his life.

"Play for me?"

"Here? Now? Naked on the bed?"

He nodded. "Please."

And so she sat up straight and tuned the strings and, after a moment, she began to play. She played a minuet. She played an étude. She played a favorite from her commune childhood, the simple folk hymn, "Morning Has Broken," because in fact, it had.

And when she was done, she handed him the violin and he set it on the dresser, then came down on the bed beside her and loved her again, with a tenderness and a warmth that showed her once again that Sebastian Savas wasn't an iceman at all.

And after she kissed him, then asked, "What else did you bring? You said you had two things."

He smiled. "Fish."

She sat up. "What? For dinner?"

He folded his arms behind his head, grinning now. "No. For the menagerie. They're what got me here. You gave my sisters the cats."

"Well, yes. But I didn't think you'd want them."

"And my stepmother the guinea pig," he went on. "And I was alone. And I remembered about the fish. You started with fish. So I did, too. But I don't have a clue about fish. So I thought you might be able to help me raise them."

Neely laughed. "I might be able to do that."

"And kids?" Sebastian said.

"As many as you want," she promised, her heart full to overflowing.

He rolled her beneath him and began to love her again. "What'd you do with the rabbits?"

She grinned. "I gave them to Max and Lara."

MUCH MORE THAN
A MISTRESS
MICHELLE CELMER

Michelle Celmer is a bestselling author of more than thirty books. When she's not writing, she likes to spend time with her husband, kids, grandchildren and a menagerie of animals.

Michelle loves to hear from readers. Visit her website, www.michellecelmer.com, like her on Facebook or write her at P.O. Box 300, Clawson, MI 48017, USA.

To my Pumpkin Cookies

One

You can do this.
Jane Monroe walked from the parking lot to the front entrance of Western Oil's corporate headquarters, a legion of mutant butterflies doing the conga on her insides. She stopped just shy of the double glass doors and sucked in a breath of cool January air, flexing the jitters from her fingers.

In her first six months at Edwin Associates Investigation Services, she had logged hundreds of computer hours conducting background checks, tracking down deadbeat dads and finding assets hidden by cheating ex-husbands. When anyone needed legal advice, she was the woman to ask. And it had all been leading up to this very moment.

Her first undercover assignment.

Shivering from a combination of nerves and the brisk wind against her sheer nylons, she huddled down into her coat collar and wobbled into the lobby on four-inch heels.

She passed through the metal detectors, flashing the ID badge that would allow her to move freely throughout the building, even in areas reserved for the highest ranking employees.

She passed a bustling coffee shop on her way to the elevator, joining the flow of bodies as she stepped on, pressing the button for the third floor where she would report to Human Resources.

Some people, her parents and siblings in particular, would have considered her position at Edwin Associates a waste of her law degree. Which was why she hadn't exactly been honest about where she was working. They thought she was employed in the law department of a local corporation. It saved her a whole lot of headache that way. But when she cracked this case, and was made a full-fledged investigator, she could finally come clean.

How could they be anything but impressed to learn that she had been working undercover in the office of billionaire Jordan Everette, Chief Operations Officer of Western Oil, a man suspected of taking bribes and sabotage.

She won this case by default. The secretary she was replacing went into labor early, and the investigator who was supposed to be assigned to the case was stuck in another undercover position. It was her one and only chance to prove herself. She simply *could not* screw this up.

The agency was putting together a profile on Jane's target, but it wouldn't be messaged to her apartment until that evening. Until then, she would be flying blind. She'd never even seen a photo of her new "boss," much less met the man, but considering his position in the company she had already formed a mental picture. Late forties to early fifties, probably balding and thick around the middle from too many rich foods and malt scotch. A golf playing, cigar smoking man's man.

Jane tugged at the hem of the body-hugging, thigh-high skirt that was a complete departure from the conservative suits she normally wore. It had been assumed that a man like Mr. Everette, a confirmed bachelor who supposedly subscribed to the girl-of-the-month club, would be much more receptive to short skirts and spike heels than trousers and leather loafers. So she, the socially challenged geek who hadn't gone on her first real date until her second year of college, would be playing the role of the sexy temp secretary.

Even she hadn't been sure if she could pull it off, but after a weekend makeover that included a day in the stylist's chair, a crash course with a makeup artist, trading her glasses for contact lenses, and a trip to Macy's for a new work wardrobe, she was a little stunned to realize that she actually looked…sexy. When she'd stopped into work on her way to Western Oil to pick up her security badge, the girl at the front desk hadn't even recognized her, and heads had literally turned as she'd walked through the building to her boss's office.

She had driven to Western Oil feeling a confidence that was completely foreign to her. Right up until the second she stepped out of the car and let herself consider just how important this assignment could be.

Cracking this case would finally make her superiors take her seriously, and hopefully bring her that much closer to a corner office and an eventual partnership in what was a primarily male-dominated firm. Not only did she intend to be the first woman ever to make partner, but the youngest associate to climb the ranks as well.

More like *claw* her way up, she thought wryly, which

would be so much easier now with her new, siren-red acrylic nails.

The elevator stopped at the third floor and Jane walked down the hall to the HR office. She checked in at the desk and was told to take a seat. She took off her coat and sat in one of the hard plastic chairs. Only a few minutes passed before a sharply dressed, stern-looking older woman stepped into the waiting room. "Miss Monroe?"

Jane shot to her feet. Though undercover work often meant using an assumed name, for this particular position it was decided that she would stick as closely as possible to the actual details of her life. Not that she anticipated having deep and meaningful conversations with her new boss. But the fewer fabrications, the fewer she had to remember.

The woman gave Jane a quick once-over, one brow slightly raised, then shook her hand. "Welcome to Western Oil. I'm Mrs. Brown. I'll be showing you around. Would you follow me, please?"

Jane grabbed her coat and followed Mrs. Brown back down the hall to the elevator, her shoes pinching her toes to within an inch of their lives, making her long for a pair of her comfortable, low-heeled pumps.

"I'm assuming the temp agency gave you a copy of the office policies."

"Of course." In fact, she had memorized it. Other than Edwin Associates, Jane had never had a job outside of the family law practice. She'd worked there summers and after school since she was fourteen, and for five miserable years after getting her law degree before she'd had the guts to quit and follow her dream of being a P.I.

They stepped on the elevator and Mr. Brown hit the button for the top floor—the executive level—and Jane's heart climbed up into her throat. She was so nervous she could barely breathe. Or maybe the lack of oxygen was due to the underwire push-up bra digging into her rib cage.

The elevator opened to another security station.

"This is Miss Monroe," Mrs. Brown told the guard sitting there. "She'll be temping for Mr. Everette."

His badge said his name was Michael Weiss. He was twenty-something with military-short blond hair, built like a tank, and armed to the teeth.

"Welcome, Miss Monroe," he said with a nod, glancing subtly at her legs, which in the spiked heels looked miles longer than they actually were. At five feet seven inches no one could accuse her of being short, but now she felt like an Amazon. "Can I see your badge, please?"

She unclipped it from her lapel and handed it to him. He inspected it, jotted something on his clipboard, then handed it back. "Keep this clearly displayed at all times. You won't be allowed on the floor without it."

Security sure was tight. Understandably so, considering the combined net worth of the men working on that floor.

"This way," Mrs. Brown said, and as they walked through the double glass doors to the executive offices Jane could swear she felt the guard's gaze settle on her behind. She wasn't used to men looking at her butt, or any other part of her for that matter. Most men didn't give her so much as a passing glance. It was as if she was invisible— so drab and boring she faded into the woodwork. In high school the other kids called her "Plain Jane."

Not very original, but hurtful just the same. To finally be noticed was a little...exciting. Even if the woman people were noticing wasn't really her. Out of this costume she was the same old uninteresting Jane Monroe.

They entered another lobby area and stopped at the reception desk.

"This is Miss Monroe, Mr. Everette's temp," Mrs.

Brown told the woman sitting there, then she shot Jane a dismissive, borderline-hostile glance, and walked back out the door.

The woman behind the desk rolled her eyes and shook her head at Mrs. Brown's retreating form and mumbled in a thick Texas drawl, "Thank you, Miss Congeniality." She rose from her chair and smiled at Jane. She was short and cute, and on the plump side. "I'm Jen Walters. Welcome to the top floor, Miss Monroe."

"Hi Jen." Jane shook the hand she offered. "You can call me Jane."

She looked Jane up and down, shook her head and said, "Oh honey, the other girls are going to hate you."

Hate her? Her heart sank. "They hate all temps?"

"All temps who are as pretty as you are."

She opened her mouth to reply, but nothing came out. She didn't have a clue what to say. It was the first time in her life anyone accused her of being too pretty. And she had no idea why they would hate her for that.

Jen laughed and patted her arm. "I'm jokin', hon! They won't hate you. We're a friendly bunch up here."

That was a relief. She wasn't here to make friends, but it wouldn't be much fun working in a place where no one liked her.

"I'm really not that pretty," she told Jen.

Jen laughed again. "Do you not own a mirror? You're gorgeous. And I would kill for your figure. I'll bet you're one of those naturally skinny girls."

"If by naturally skinny you mean no bust or hips." And what breasts she did have hadn't come in until her senior year of high school.

She lowered her voice and said, "Take it from me, big boobs are not all they're cracked up to be."

Jane smiled, and realized that although she had walked

onto the floor trembling with nerves, Jen had put her completely at ease.

"Why don't I show you around and get you settled. Mr. Everette is in a meeting, but he should be out soon."

Jen showed her where the break room and restrooms were located, introduced her to the other secretaries on the floor—all of whom seemed very nice and did not seem to hate her—then showed her to her desk.

"Tiffany left you detailed instructions of your duties and how Mr. Everette likes things done," Jen told her, gesturing to the typed pages on the blotter next to a top-of-the-line flat-panel computer monitor. "She was hoping to be here to break in the temp, but her water broke at work two days ago. She wasn't due for another two weeks."

Jane looked at the chair, then back up at Jen. "Her water broke *here?*"

Jen laughed. "Not here in the office. She was walking from her car to the building."

Well, that was good. "I guess babies can be unpredictable like that," she said, not that she had any experience with them. Though both her brothers were married they hadn't started families yet, and like Jane, her sister was too career-oriented to even think about marriage, much less a baby. And being the baby of the family, Jane had no younger siblings.

"Mr. Everette's calls have been rerouted to my desk. I'll give you a couple of hours to get settled then have them sent to you."

"Thanks for showing me around," she said.

"Sure thing, honey. Call me if you have any questions. My number is in the office directory."

When she was gone, Jane peeked into her boss's office. Floor-to-ceiling windows lined two of the four sides, and overlooked the skyline of El Paso.

A corner office. Nice.

She hung her purse and coat in the closet then sat at her desk, setting her cell phone in the top drawer. She booted up the computer and unclipped the list Tiffany had typed up. It was pretty basic stuff—how Mr. Everette liked the phone answered, what he took in his coffee, who he took calls from on the spot and who was an auto callback—one being his mother, she noticed. Nothing she couldn't handle easily. There was also a list of numbers that included his housecleaning service, his laundry service and reservation lines for a dozen of the finest restaurants in the greater El Paso area. Clearly she would be handling some of the personal aspects of his life as well as the professional, which could only work in her favor.

She considered going through the files on the computer, on the very rare possibility that there might be something there to incriminate him, but as she ran her tongue across her upper lip, she realized that in her nervousness, she'd chewed off all of her lipstick. It probably wouldn't be a bad idea to freshen up before her boss came in.

She grabbed her purse and headed down the hall to the ladies' room. As she suspected, her lipstick was pretty much gone, so she drew on a fresh layer then gave her face a light dusting with the mineral powder the makeup artist swore by. It did give her skin a smooth, almost ethereal look. Although at twenty-eight—make that twenty-nine tomorrow—she wasn't exactly covered in wrinkles. But it did cover the freckles that had been the bane of her existence since middle school. It had been hard enough being two years younger than her classmates, and even worse looking it. She never imagined makeup could make such a difference in the way she looked. She had tried it once before. She was an awkward and geeky twelve-year-old, and had gotten into the makeup case her sister had left in the bathroom that they shared. Thinking she had done a pretty good job, she showed her sister, who had dissolved into hysterics at how ridiculous she looked. Then she had dragged Jane in front of their brothers who also laughed at her. She ran sobbing to her mother, who, instead of offering comfort, told Jane she had to toughen up, and face the fact that some girls just didn't look good wearing makeup. And as a former Miss Texas, her mother knew a thing or two about fashion and beauty.

It was the first and last time Jane ever tried that.

She didn't doubt that she'd probably looked a bit like a clown, but instead of pulling her aside and trying to teach her the right way, her sister had felt the need to boost her own ego—which was as overinflated then as it was today—and ridicule Jane instead.

She finished her face, studied her reflection, and smiled. She did look really nice. But she wouldn't get much work done if she spent the day gazing at her reflection in the bathroom mirror.

She stopped in the break room to grab a cup of coffee, then headed back to her desk. When she walked through the door and realized someone was already sitting there, she stopped so abruptly she sloshed coffee onto her fingers.

Thinking she must have walked into the wrong office by mistake, she shot a quick glance to the the name on the door, but this was definitely the right place. So who was the man sitting at her desk?

He was lounging back in her chair, his designer shoe–clad feet propped on the desk surface, reading the list Tiffany had left. He wore typical office attire, sans the jacket, and the sleeves of his dress shirt were rolled to his elbows. His hair was dark blond and stylishly short, and he had the sort of boyish good looks that made a girl swoon. Which was exactly what she felt like doing.

The question was, who was he and why he was in her office?

"Can I help you?" she asked.

The man looked up at her with a pair of deep-set, soul-warming hazel eyes and a grin that could stop traffic, and her heart actually flipped over in her chest. Who *was* this guy and where could she get one?

"I certainly hope so," he said, dropping his feet to the carpet and rising from the chair. She was at least 5'11" in her heels and she had to look up to meet his eyes. He was tall and lean and work-out-in-the-gym-every-morning fit.

"You must be the new temp," he said, reaching across the desk to shake her hand, which was still gripping the cup of coffee and damp from the sloshing. She quickly switched the cup to the opposite hand, wiped the damp one on her skirt and took his hand. It was big and warm and surprisingly rough for such a polished-looking guy.

His grip was firm and confident and she could swear she felt the effects all the way to her knees. She also didn't miss the way he gave her a quick once-over, one brow slightly raised.

"I'm Jane Monroe," she said.

"It's a pleasure to meet you, Jane Monroe."

No, the pleasure was definitely hers, though she still didn't have clue who he was.

"By the way," he said. "Someone named Mary called."

Her heart stalled. Her *sister* Mary? How could she possibly have known where Jane was working? Her family didn't even know she was working for Edwin Associates. "She called *here?*"

"Your cell," he said, opening the top drawer and holding up her cell phone.

"You answered my phone?" Who the hell did this guy

think he was? And how could she be so stupid as to leave it unattended in her desk with the ringer on?

"Actually, it went to voice mail before I found it in the drawer. But the display said it was Mary."

Whoever this guy was, he had a lot of nerve. "Do you make it a habit of snooping through people's private property?"

He shrugged. "Only if I think I'll find something interesting."

That was not the answer she expected. "Who *are* you?"

"You don't know?"

"Should I?"

The smile went from curious to amused. "I'm Jordan Everette, Miss Monroe. Your new boss."

Two

"M-Mr. Everette," Miss Monroe stammered, the color draining from her flawlessly painted face. "I'm so sorry. I didn't realize—"

"Not quite what you expected, I guess," Jordan said.

She shook her head, pulling her full bottom lip between her teeth.

Well, neither was she. In fact, he was surprised that anyone had shown up at all.

"So, the temp agency sent you?" he asked.

"That's right."

Funny, he had called the agency Friday afternoon to see what was taking so long—usually they had a temp to his office within hours of the request—but they had no record of a request ever being submitted. Yet here she was, bright and early Monday morning, standing in his office.

For a couple of weeks now there had been a strange vibe in the office. Something was just...*off.* He could only assume that the focus of the investigation into the explosion at the refinery had now moved from his employees to him.

After six years of loyal service, and three as Chief Operations Officer, he would have thought Adam Blair, Western Oil's current CEO, would trust him by now. And if they had concerns, why not just ask him? Why this elaborate charade?

Because if they mistrusted him enough to think he could do this sort of thing—put his workers' lives in jeopardy—they probably didn't think he would tell the truth if confronted. So instead they hired someone to do what? Seduce it out of him? He couldn't imagine another reason they would send a woman who looked as though she moonlighted as a runway model.

Did they really think he was that shallow?

They obviously thought a lot less of him than he did of them. He would have at least hoped that his brother Nathan, the Chief Brand Officer, would come clean and tell him the truth. If he even knew, that is. Hell, for all Jordan knew Adam could be investigating him too. Maybe even Emilio Suarez, the CFO.

The weight of the betrayal sat like a stone in his gut, but his options were limited. He could confront Adam and put an end to the investigation, but that might only make him appear as if he had something to hide. He couldn't let anything, not even his pride, interfere with his chance at the coveted CEO position Adam would be vacating soon. His only choice was to cooperate with their investigation.

Of course, that didn't mean he was going to make it easy for his new "secretary." Knowing who she was and why she was there, he could manipulate the situation, control the information she obtained. Let her see only what he wanted her to see. Not that they were going to find anything incriminating, because he hadn't done anything wrong. But there were certain aspects of his life—financial ones in particular—that he preferred to keep private.

"Here," Jordan said, backing away from her chair. "Have a seat."

Smiling nervously, Miss Monroe rounded the desk. "Can I get you a cup of coff—" The toe of one spike-heeled "do-me" shoe caught on the desk leg and she lurched forward. She grabbed the corner of the desk in her attempt to catch her fall, but the foam cup she was holding in the opposite hand went airborne. And hit him square in the chest.

Miss Monroe gasped in horror, slapping a hand over her crimson-painted mouth as coffee soaked not only his shirt, but the carpet where he was standing. "Oh my God. I can't believe I just did that."

She looked frantically around for something to clean up the mess and spotted a box of tissues on the desk. She lunged for it, ripping out a handful and shoving them at him. "Mr. Everette, I am *so* sorry."

"It's okay," he said, wiping up the coffee dripping from his chin. Not the most graceful runway model, was she?

She gestured helplessly at his damp shirt. "Is there anything I can do?"

"I keep an extra shirt in the closet for emergencies. You could grab it for me while I clean up."

"Of course," she said, scrambling for the closet.

Jordan walked to the bathroom in his office, unbuttoning his shirt. Some of the coffee had hit his pants too, but as luck would have it, he'd worn his brown suit that morning.

He dropped his shirt on the bathroom floor, and peeled his coffee-soaked undershirt over his head. Maybe she wasn't an agency operative after all. Or was this just all part of a clever disguise? A ruse to throw him off the trail?

"Mr. Everette?" she called from his office.

"In here." He wet a washcloth in the sink and wiped the coffee from his face and chest.

"Here's your…"

Jordan turned to see Miss Monroe in the bathroom doorway, eyes wide and fixed somewhere between his neck and his belt. She blinked and quickly looked away, a red hue creeping up from the neckline of her blouse. Why would an above-average-looking woman who practically oozed sexuality blush at the sight of a shirtless man?

Interesting.

Eyes averted, she held out the hanger with his clean shirt. "Here you go."

He took it, brushing his fingers against hers as he did, and she jerked her hand away.

Very interesting.

"Are you going to fire me?" she asked.

Why bother? They would just send a new agency person in.

"Did you do it on purpose?" he asked.

She blinked in surprise and cut her eyes to him. "Of course not!"

He hooked the hanger on the towel rack, tugged the clean undershirt free and pulled it over his head. "Then why would I fire you?"

She pulled her lip between her teeth again, and it brought to mind nibbling on a plump red cherry. He wondered if she had the slightest clue how sexy she looked when she did that. The coy bit had to be an act.

He pulled on his shirt and buttoned it. "In answer to your question, yes."

"My question?"

"I would love a cup of coffee. Although this time I'd rather not wear it."

Her lips tilted into an embarrassed smile. "Of course."

"My cup is on my desk." He unfastened his belt and the button on his pants so he could tuck in his shirt, stifling a grin when she quickly looked away again.

"I—I'll go get it now," she said, tripping over her own foot in her haste to get away.

He had the feeling that, until she discovered that the evidence she was hoping to find didn't exist and gave up, he could have an awful lot of fun at her expense.

The spike heels had been a really bad idea, Jane decided as she grabbed Mr. Everette's *World's Best Boss* cup from his desk and hurried to the break room, heart pounding from a combination of her own horrifying ineptitude and supreme lack of grace, and the sight of her new boss standing shamelessly bare-chested in her presence.

Not that he had *anything* to be ashamed of. His body—what she could see of it anyway—was a work of art. And she was betting that the bottom half was no less awe-inspiring. So much for her theory that he was middle-aged and fat. That's what she got for drawing hasty conclusions.

Some vampy, sex goddess secretary she'd turned out to be. She couldn't have made more of an ass out of herself if she'd dressed like a clown and donned a squeaky red nose. Proof that despite her physical transformation, deep down she was just as geeky and awkward as ever. Had she been completely fooling herself to believe that she could handle an undercover position?

She poured the coffee and added a teaspoon of creamer, mentally shaking away those negative thoughts. She could do this, damn it. She *was* good enough. She had been working up to this for months. Failure was not an option.

Squaring her shoulders, she carried the coffee back to Mr. Everette's office. She rapped lightly on the door before stepping inside, grateful to see that he was fully clothed and sitting at his desk. He was also on the phone, meaning she didn't have to talk to him. It was both a disappointment and a relief. If she was going to glean the information necessary for the investigation, she was going to have to talk to the man. Get to know him. Earn his trust.

He gestured her over, telling the caller, "I'm sure it was just an oversight."

She crossed the room, the cup cradled gingerly in both palms, and set it on his desk. She started to turn, but he held up a hand, signaling her to wait. "Yes, Mother, I promise I'll talk to him today." He paused, looking exasperated, then said, "Well, in all fairness, you ditched us on Christmas. Can you blame Nathan if he's feeling bitter?"

She could only assume he was talking about his brother Nathan, who was the CBO of Western Oil. Having worked closely with her own siblings for years, she knew how complicated the family dynamic could be. Especially when one broke tradition and made the decision to leave the fold to pursue their own aspirations. Not that she had a clue how the Everette family got along. Although most men in a decent relationship with their mother wouldn't have them on an auto callback list.

"The fact that he was a baron doesn't make it okay," he said, holding up a finger to indicate that it would be just one more minute. "I have to go, Mother, I—" He rolled his eyes. "Yes, I *will* talk to him. I promise." Another short pause then, "Okay, Mother. *Goodbye.*" He hung up the phone, blew out an exasperated breath and looked up at Jane. "Do you get along with your mother, Miss Monroe?"

The question threw her, and it took her a second to regroup. It wasn't that she didn't get along with her parents. They just refused to accept that they didn't know what was better for her than she did. And she couldn't help wondering why he cared about her relationship with her mother. "It's…complicated."

"Well, mine is a gigantic pain in the ass. She's a master manipulator and will browbeat you to within an inch of your life to get what she wants. You have to be firm and direct or she will walk all over you."

"I understand," she said, although firm and direct were never two of her strong suits. Her own family had been walking all over her for years. But she had broken the cycle, hadn't she? Well, for the most part anyway. She tended to just avoid them now. And, yes, bent the truth when it made her life easier.

"Would you mind pouring that coffee into a travel mug?" he asked. "There should be one in the cabinet over by the wet bar."

"Of course." She carried his cup to the bar across the room, asking casually, "Are you leaving?"

"I have a meeting at the refinery."

That would give her time to snoop in his office. Her heart surged with nervous energy. She found the cup where he'd indicated and as she poured the coffee in, her hands were shaking.

Relax, she told herself, taking a deep breath.

She could just imagine how impressed her superiors would be if she were able to bring them valuable information on her very first day. Then they would *have* to take her seriously.

It took a couple of tries but she secured the top on the cup and turned, jerking with surprise when she almost ran face-first into Mr. Everette. He was so close, she could smell the soapy-fresh scent of his skin. If the cup hadn't had a lid, they would probably both be wearing coffee this time.

"Sorry, didn't mean to startle you," he said, but the

grin he wore said otherwise. Was he *teasing* her? Were the makeup and the clothes actually working?

He took the cup from her, the tips of his fingers brushing against hers as he did and she tried not to flinch. He set it on the counter beside the sink. "I think we'd all be safer if you didn't carry that around."

She felt herself blushing. "Sorry."

With a grin that was nothing short of adorable, he stepped past her to the closet next to the bathroom and pulled out his coat.

"Is there anything you need me to do while you're gone?" she asked as he shrugged into it.

"Just man the phones and take the day to get settled in. Familiarize yourself with the computer. I have a lunch meeting at twelve-thirty so I should be back sometime before two."

Which would give her lots of time to snoop. No, not snoop…*investigate*. She had to start thinking like a pro, using the appropriate lingo. She had to play the part, even in her own mind. If she didn't take herself seriously, no one would.

"I should take you out sometime," he said.

She blinked. Did he seriously just ask her on a date? And how was she supposed to respond to that? What would a sophisticated woman of the world say?

All she could manage was a befuddled, "Um…"

"I'm assuming you've never been to a refinery."

Oh, he wanted to take her to the *refinery*. That made a lot more sense. "No, never."

"It's an impressive operation," he said, and she must have looked wary, because he added, "and contrary to what you've probably seen on the news, it's completely safe."

She had heard negative press about the incident at the refinery, but the agency had several employees working undercover directly on the line, and as far as she was aware, none of them had ever reported being in any danger. Sure, this was a high-profile case, but the other agents would never be sent into a situation that could cause them physical harm.

"I'd love to see it," she said.

"I'm there several days a week, so maybe the next time I go." He glanced at the platinum Rolex on his left wrist. "I'm late. If there's anything pressing while I'm gone, or something you aren't sure about, feel free to call my cell."

"I will." She handed him his cup, careful to avoid his fingers this time because frankly, she was nervous enough without all the intimate contact.

Cup in hand, he headed for the door. She followed him, stopping at her desk.

"By the way," he said, stopping in the doorway and gesturing the coffee stain on the carpet. "Call janitorial to take care of that."

"I will." Later.

He flashed her one last knee-melting smile, then left.

Here we go.

She stood there and counted to sixty, gauging the amount of time it would take him to get to the elevator and get inside, then she walked down the hall. The elevator doors were just closing as she stepped into the reception area.

"Did Mr. Everette leave yet?" she asked Jen.

"You just missed him, hon."

"Well, darn," she said, pretending to be discouraged.

"Did he forget something?" She put her hand on the phone. "Should I call down to the guard post in the lobby?"

"That's okay. It's nothing urgent. I just had a question, but it can wait until he gets back." It was a lie, of course. She just needed to be sure that he was really gone.

Jen smiled. "How's the first day going so far?"

With the exception of dumping hot coffee on her new boss and making a complete ass out of herself? "Pretty good."

"If you're interested, the secretaries are all going out for lunch today. You're welcome to join us."

She was inclined to say no, since she wanted to take as much time as possible in Mr. Everette's office, but she didn't want the other secretaries to think she was a snob either. She might learn something valuable from any one of them. Things that they may not even realize were important to the investigation.

She smiled and said, "I'd love to go. What time?"

"Noon. There's a café across the street. Just a few minutes' walk. The temperature is supposed to climb to forty, so it shouldn't be too cold."

"Sounds great," she said, cringing inwardly. It wasn't the cold she was worried about, but her aching feet. She should have brought a pair of flat shoes as a backup.

Jen smiled. "Great, see you at noon."

Jane walked back to the desk and kicked off her shoes. She wanted to be able to move quickly, in case someone happened to come by. If someone did, and they asked what she was doing in Mr. Everette's office, she would simply say that she'd spilled coffee on her jacket and was using the fabric stain remover she had seen on his bathroom shelf.

She opened the closet and rifled through her purse for the jump drive that Kenneth in Tech had given her at her briefing that morning. She was just hoping Mr. Everette's computer wasn't password protected. She doubted he would have any personal financial files at work, but she could at least get a look at his email. People sent personal emails from work all the time.

She slipped the jump drive in her pocket, heart pounding

with both fear and excitement, and turned toward Mr. Everette's office, but before she could take a step, the phone started to ring.

Damn it!

She picked it up. "Good morning, Mr. Everette's office."

"Miss Monroe, this is Bren, in Mr. Blair's office. He'd like a word with you."

Her heart jumped. Why would the CEO want to see her? Had she done something wrong?

Of course she hadn't. Other than the coffee fiasco, that is, and unless they had a surveillance camera in her office, there was no way he could have found out about that. Maybe he just wanted to talk to her about the case. "I'll be right down."

She took the jump drive from her pocket and slipped it in the top drawer of her desk, crammed her feet back into her shoes and walked down to Mr Blair's office at the opposite end of the hall.

"Go on in," Mr. Blair's secretary said. "They're waiting for you."

Jane stopped so abruptly she wobbled on her heels. *"They?"*

"Mr. Blair, Mr. Suarez and Mr. Everette." She paused and said, "The *other* Mr. Everette."

Suddenly Jane was having a tough time pulling in a full breath.

She thought she was just meeting with the CEO, which was intimidating enough. But to be in the same room with the CEO, CFO and CBO all at the same time? No wonder she felt faint. Meeting clients as a lawyer had never been a big deal, but then, she knew the law so well she could practice it in her sleep. The investigation business...not so much. She was still learning, and there was nothing she hated more than looking as though she didn't know what she was talking about.

Bren must have sensed that she was on the verge of a panic attack because she flashed Jane a reassuring smile and said, "Don't worry, they don't bite."

Jane tried to smile, when what she wanted to do was turn and run in the opposite direction.

"I'm sure they just want to ask you about the investigation."

Jane blinked. "The what?"

"It's okay, Miss Monroe. What Mr. Blair knows, I know."

Mr. Blair obviously trusted his secretary implicitly, which could definitely work in Jane's favor.

"You know," Bren said, lowering her voice, "we all like and respect Mr. Everette, and no one wants to believe he could have anything to with the sabotage. The sooner this investigation is over with, the better. If there's anything I can do to help, just say the word."

"Thanks. And we'll get to the bottom of this," she told Bren, hoping to convey a competence she was nowhere close to feeling.

Jane turned to the door, pulled back her shoulders, and took a deep breath. "Well, I guess I'd better get in there."

Bren smiled and said, "Good luck."

Considering that her knees were actually knocking, she had the feeling she was probably going to need it.

Three

Like Mr. Everette, Mr. Blair had a corner office, but it was nearly twice the size and much more luxurious. Mr. Blair, whom she recognized from the television news stories that had run after the refinery explosion, sat behind his desk. He was dark-haired, conservatively handsome, and the touch of gray at his temples said he was probably in his early forties.

"Miss Monroe," he said, rising from his chair, as did the man seated across from his desk. A third man stood by the window. "Come in. Close the door behind you."

She did as he asked and crossed the room, hands trembling, palms sweaty, praying she didn't trip and make a total fool of herself. Her toes were pinched so tight in her shoes that each step was torture.

Good lord, she was a wreck. She could only hope she didn't look half as terrified as she felt.

"Miss Monroe, I'm Adam Blair, and this is Nathan

Everette, our Chief Brand Officer." Mr. Blair indicated the man by his desk, then he turned to the one by the window and said, "And this is Emilio Suarez, our Chief Financial Officer."

She nodded to both men, who each gave her a very subtle once-over. Nathan Everette was darker than his brother, and a little larger in stature, but there was a strong family resemblance. Mr. Suarez was the utter epitome of tall, dark and handsome and of Hispanic descent. All three men were above-average in the looks department and she nearly felt faint from the ridiculously high level of testosterone in the room. She wondered if looking like a *GQ* cover model was prerequisite to their positions.

"Please, have a seat," Mr. Blair said, indicating the chair next to Mr. Everette.

She sat primly on the edge. Mr. Blair and Mr. Everette both took their seats while Mr. Suarez remained standing, arms crossed, his expression dark. As an attorney, she had gotten pretty good at reading people and situations, and there was a definite negative vibe in the room.

"First off, I'd like to make it clear that none of us are happy about the need to investigate our colleague," Mr. Blair said. "Your boss has assured me that this will be handled with the utmost care."

"Absolutely," she said, hoping they didn't hear the quiver in her voice.

Mr. Blair leaned forward in his seat, folding his hands atop his desk. "He told me that the plan is for you to get to know Mr. Everette on a more...*personal* level. To be honest, I'm not sure I'm comfortable with that."

Okay. Well, that was very...direct. She had barely begun the investigation and already they were unhappy.

She was so completely screwed.

She squared her shoulders and tried to sound as if

she knew what she was talking about. "If Mr. Everette is involved in a conspiracy, chances are slim he would be foolish enough to keep any incriminating evidence at work. More than likely I'll need access to his home."

"And you'll do that how?" Mr. Suarez asked. He didn't outwardly suggest impropriety, but the implication was there. She tried not to take it personally. Actually, she felt sort of sorry for them. They were clearly distressed by what they had to do.

"It's against agency policy to engage in activity that is illegal or unethical," she told him.

Mr. Everette rubbed his forehead, looking pained. "I don't like it."

"Two weeks ago you and Jordan weren't on speaking terms," Mr. Suarez said.

Mr. Everette shot him a look. "It just seems so… underhanded. That doesn't bother you?"

"Of course it bothers me. And if it were one of my brothers being investigated I would probably be just as hesitant. But, Nathan, we don't have a choice. We *need* to know, and we agreed this was the best way to handle the situation."

"You all seem to respect Mr. Everette," she said. "Why is it that you think he could have been the saboteur?"

"As you probably already know, a week before the explosion someone wired two hundred thousand dollars into Jordan's account, and a few days later he wired thirty thousand dollars out. But we don't know where the money came from, or who it went to."

"So you think that someone paid him, and he paid someone else to tamper with the equipment."

"That's one possibility," Adam said.

"Why? I've seen his financials. He's not hurting for money."

"Jordan is ambitious," Adam said. "This happened before everyone learned the CEO position was opening up. Maybe he felt he'd hit a ceiling. Maybe someone made him an offer he couldn't refuse, but expected something in return first."

"And you believe he would put people's lives in danger to further his career?" she asked.

"Maybe no one was meant to get hurt, but something went wrong," Emilio suggested.

"If you're right, and he got a better offer, why is he still here?"

"To avoid suspicion? Or maybe now that the CEO position is opening up, he has a reason to stay."

"Or maybe," Emilio offered, "since there were injuries, it killed the deal."

All plausible scenarios. Especially if he was as ambitious as they all seemed to believe.

"That's what we need you to find out," Mr. Blair said, looking to Mr Everette. "And either we're all in, or this stops today."

Jane held her breath. Would her first undercover assignment be over before it started? If she blew this on the very first day, would her boss blame her? They might never give her another chance to work undercover. She needed to take the bull by the horns.

"Mr. Everette," she said, reaching out to touch his arm, hoping he couldn't sense her desperation. "I have three siblings myself, so I understand how difficult this must be for you. I'll take whatever steps necessary to ensure that no one is hurt. You have my word."

Mr. Everette glanced from her to his partners, looking conflicted. For a second she thought for sure he would refuse to cooperate, but he finally sighed and said, "Okay, lets do it."

Jane breathed a silent sigh of relief. That was a close one.

Mr. Blair stood, which she took to mean that the meeting was over. She rose from her seat, her achy feet screaming in protest.

"If you need anything from us, don't hesitate to ask," he said. "We would like this resolved as soon as possible."

Nodding to each man, she said, "It was a pleasure to meet you, gentlemen," then she turned and walked to the door, praying she didn't trip on anything, and let herself out of the office, limp with relief. That had gone *way* better than she expected.

"Well?" Bren asked as Jane snapped the door shut behind her. She held up her thumb in an "okay" gesture, startled when the door opened behind her and Mr. Everette stepped out.

"My office, *now*," he told Jane, and her heart immediately sank. Oh hell. Maybe the worst of it wasn't over after all.

She followed him across the hall, knees knocking again. At this rate she was going to need a straightjacket before the day was over.

"Lynn, hold my calls," he told his secretary, who looked surprised to see him with his brother's secretary. Jane wondered if he realized that a move like this could very well blow her cover.

He gestured her into his office and stepped in behind her, closing the door. She actually flinched as it snapped shut. Was it possible that despite what he'd told his partners, he still wasn't okay with the investigation? Did he intend on giving her a hard time?

He crossed the room to his desk and sat down. "Have a seat, Miss Monroe."

She did as he asked, sitting on the edge of the chair across from his desk.

"In the interest of getting this investigation resolved as quickly as possible, there are a few things I should tell you about my brother."

He wanted to *help* her? "Yes, please. Anything you think would be helpful."

"I can only assume the agency is aware of my brother's reputation as a womanizer, and that's why they sent you."

"That was the idea."

"Well, I'm sure you've caught his attention. You're a very beautiful woman Miss Monroe, and please don't take this the wrong way, but it's going to take more than a pretty face and a tight skirt to *keep* him interested."

Take it the wrong way? A gorgeous billionaire just called her beautiful and he thought she would be *offended*? If her feet weren't so darned sore she might be turning cartwheels across his office.

"Do you have any advice as to what *will* keep him interested?"

"My brother loves a challenge, so don't make it too easy for him. If you're too aggressive, he'll lose interest. Make him work for it. Play hard to get."

Considering her pathetic lack of experience chasing the opposite sex, she liked the idea of letting Mr. Everette come to her.

"Also, he'll find you measurably more appealing if you make it clear that you have no interest in any sort of commitment."

She could definitely do that.

"But probably the most important thing to keep in mind is that my brother has a short attention span when it comes to the opposite sex. He'll have expectations, and if they aren't met, he'll get bored pretty fast."

Then she would have to work quickly. Because if he was talking about what she thought he was talking about, meeting *those* expectations was not even an option. She wanted to crack this case, but even she had limits. And even if she was that desperate, if her boss learned that she had slept with the subject of an investigation to get information, her career would be over.

"I'll be honest, Miss Monroe. My brother and I don't exactly see eye to eye on most things. The truth is, he can be an arrogant ass, but he's not a bad person."

"You protect him."

He sighed and leaned back in his chair. "For the life of me I don't know why."

"Because that's what big brothers do. I know, I have two of them." Although in her case, they didn't just protect. They domineered.

Mr. Everette smiled. He wasn't nearly as intimidating as she'd first thought. At first glance he seemed so dark and intense, but he definitely had a softer side. "With a sister as pretty as you, I'm sure it was a full-time job."

Wow, she really liked this guy.

"Well," he said, rising from his chair. "I'm glad we had this talk. But I should let you get back to work."

She stood and smoothed her skirt back into place. "Thank you for the advice."

He reached across the desk to shake her hand. His grip was firm and confident. "Good luck, Miss Monroe."

She left Nathan Everette's office feeling a lot less unsure of herself than when she'd walked into work that morning. The first day of her first undercover assignment may have had a bit of a bumpy start, but things were definitely looking up.

She hobbled back to her desk on her poor tortured feet, yet she felt a renewed confidence. If she could maintain her cool in a meeting with the CEO, CBO and CFO of a multibillion dollar corporation, she could handle just about anything.

When she got there she kicked off her shoes and opened her top drawer, fishing out the flash drive. It was time to go get some information.

"Is it my imagination or were you a lot taller the last time I saw you?"

At the sound of Mr. Everette's voice she gasped in surprise and dropped the flash drive back in the drawer. She whipped around, slamming it shut with her backside. He stood in his office doorway, arms folded, leaning against the jamb. And he must have been back for some time because not only was his coat off, he'd removed his suit jacket as well. "You're back early."

"I made it as far as the lobby and got a call that the meeting was cancelled."

If she hadn't been called away, he would have without a doubt walked in on her "investigating." The thought made her knees go weak. Next time she would have to make sure that he'd actually left the building before she set foot in his office.

"Imagine my surprise when I returned to find that my new secretary was already playing hooky."

"N-no...I wasn't..." She stopped and took a deep breath. What was the point of making excuses. "I'm sorry, it won't happen again."

"Where were you?"

Okay, she could handle this. It was all about thinking on her feet, and being prepared. So of course her mind went instantly blank. "The, um...HR office."

"Human resources?"

"Yes."

"For...?"

"Paperwork. There was a form they forgot to have me sign."

"And they stole your shoes while you were there?" he said, nodding to her stocking feet.

"No, of course not. They're under my desk. They're new and they were pinching my toes." At least that much was the truth. "I can put them back on——"

"Oh no. I wouldn't want to be responsible for your sore feet. Although maybe they would hurt less if you sat down."

She lowered herself into her chair.

"I need to go talk to my brother," he said, and before she could stop herself she sucked in a breath. Did he know she'd just been there?

No, of course he didn't. How could he?

He gave her an odd look. "Problem?"

She gestured to her feet. "Sorry, sore toes."

"As I was saying, I have to talk to my brother before my mother blows a gasket. But if anyone calls, I'm in a meeting."

"Of course."

With one last curious look her way, he walked out.

The man must have thought she was a loon.

Her cell phone started to ring and she pulled it out of the desk drawer, where she had left it again.

And it was her sister, Mary. Again. She pressed the talk button. "Hey Mary, what's up?"

"You sure are tough to get ahold of," Mary snapped in lieu of a hello.

Jane sighed. She had half a mind to just hang up on her. She wished she had the guts to do it, but things had been so strained lately already, she didn't want to make it worse. Mary was just pissy because Jane was no longer around the office to do her grunt work. Despite having graduated with higher honors than every one of her siblings, and passing the bar with flying colors, up until the day Jane had left, they had continued to treat her like an intern.

"I'm at work. I haven't had a chance to call you back."

"Whatever," she said, sounding like a spoiled adolescent. Though she was the older sister, she didn't always act like it. "I'm just calling to remind you about this Friday."

"What about it?"

She sighed dramatically. "Monthly dinner with the family, stupid."

Jane ignored the "stupid" remark, because although Mary may have been prettier, and more outgoing and popular, they both knew Jane was smarter. Though sometimes that was more of a liability than a asset. Being the "smart and practical" sibling didn't leave a lot of room for error.

"But we usually do that the last Friday of the month," she told her sister. "That's not until next week."

"Don't you remember, we decided to do it a week early because Will has a business trip the following week."

"That's news to me," she said.

"I could swear we talked about it."

"Nope." But then, since she'd left the practice, there were a lot of things she didn't hear about until the last minute because no one bothered to call her. She figured it was probably her punishment for deviating from their master plan.

"I'm sure I told you, but whatever. Mom booked our regular table at Via Penna. Seven o'clock."

"I'll try to be there."

"You'll *try?* What is your problem? You can't even make time for your family anymore?"

"Jeez, Mary, don't have a cow. I'll definitely be there, okay?"

"I'll see you Friday," she said, then hung up without saying goodbye.

Jane grumbled to herself and tossed her phone back into the drawer, then pulled it back out, walked to the closet and dropped it into her purse. It didn't occur to her until several minutes later that since her birthday was the following day, they were probably planning a party. That was probably the reason they were doing it a week early. No wonder Mary had been so insistent on her being there.

It didn't excuse the curt conversation, or Mary's bitchy attitude, but it made Jane feel a little better. And a little less like punching her sister in the nose the next time she saw her.

Four

Grinning to himself, Jordan walked down the hall to his brother's office. He had to hand it to Miss Monroe, she was quick on her feet.

He had figured there was a good chance when he came back early from the meeting, that he himself had cancelled, he would catch Miss Monroe snooping around. He was curious to see what sort of excuse she could come up with, and he was disappointed to not find her in his office. She wasn't at her desk either. It had taken one call down to his brother's secretary Lynn to learn that Miss Monroe had first been in Adam's office, then Nathan's. Until that moment Jordan had held out the hope that maybe his brother didn't know Adam was having him investigated. Not much chance of that now.

"I just need a minute," Jordan told Lynn when he reached Nathan's office. Then, as usual, instead of waiting to be announced, he walked right in. Mostly because he knew it would irritate the hell out of Nathan.

And it did. He jerked with surprise and said, "Jesus, Jordan, don't you ever knock?"

He had been reading something in a manila file and shut it quickly as Jordan approached his desk. Making Jordan instantly suspicious.

"Tell me you didn't deliberately forget to send our mother an invitation to your wedding."

Nathan sighed. "I take it she called you."

"Of course she called me. She's very upset."

He shrugged. "And I'm supposed to care *why?*"

Sometimes Jordan got so sick of being the go-between with Nathan and their parents. "Nathan, come on."

"To be honest, I didn't think she would care if she was invited or not."

"Well, apparently she does. She said she hasn't even seen Max yet." Max was the infant son Nathan hadn't even known he had until recently. He was the result of an affair Nathan had with the daughter of the owner of a rival oil company. If there was one thing Jordan could say about his brother, he liked to live on the edge, although lately he'd begun to act like a full-fledged family man.

"Did she happen to mention that I invited her over to meet Ana and Max last week, but something more important came up and she called it off at the last minute?"

"No, she left that part out." That was typical of their mother. Both the calling off and the leaving out part. She would say pretty much anything to make herself the victim.

"She had her chance," Nathan said. "I'm through catering to her whims. And for the life of me, I don't know why you still put up with it."

Neither did he. He wasn't going to deny that their mother was self-absorbed and narcissistic. That said, she was the only mother they had. And there was still a tiny part of him, a shadow of the awkward little boy who would do practically anything to win her attention.

"She sounded genuinely upset," he said.

Nathan's expression was deadpan. "My heart bleeds for her."

"Maybe she realizes that if she ever wants to see one of her sons get married, this might be her only chance. And possibly her only chance for grandchildren."

"She doesn't care about Max. She's already warned me that when he starts talking he is forbidden from calling her grandma. She said it would make her feel too old."

Jordan winced. "I'm sure she'll feel differently when she gets closer to him," he said, although honestly, he didn't know if even he believed that. Their mother hadn't had much of an interest in her own sons when they were small. They interfered too much with her social life. He and Nathan were raised primarily by the nanny.

But sometimes people were more open to the idea of children when it was someone else's child. Jordan was in no way, shape or form ready to have children of his own, and probably never would be, but he liked to tussle with little Max. He could have the fun without the responsibility.

"This has nothing to do with me getting married, or Max. She's just pissed off because she knows I invited Dad."

Jordan's jaw actually dropped. Until a few weeks ago, Nathan and their father hadn't spoken a word to each other in almost ten years, and Jordan had been on both their backs for ages, trying to persuade them to reconnect. Jordan understood why Nathan was hesitant. He and their father had a pretty volatile relationship, one that had often turned physically violent. But that was a long time ago and their father had mellowed since then. He also felt a lot of guilt and regret for the way that he'd treated Nathan. And though Jordan would never admit it, especially to Nathan, he felt his own share of guilt.

When they were kids, Jordan had been a late bloomer and Nathan had taken it upon himself to act as Jordan's protector. Instead of teaching Jordan to defend himself, Nathan took the knocks for him. It left Jordan feeling weak, small and resentful of his older brother. In rebellion he began getting Nathan in trouble on purpose, setting him up, knowing their father would take it out of his hide. It had, for a time, left Nathan with some serious anger management issues. Only recently, when Nathan nearly gave up his son because of it, did Jordan realize how deeply his manipulating had affected his brother.

Actually inviting their father to the wedding was a huge step for Nathan. Jordan had begun to think that maybe it was time he and Nathan began to repair their own relationship, time that they let go of the resentment. But now with the sabotage, and the accusations...well, it could be a while before they resolved anything.

"I think it's great that you invited him," Jordan said.

Nathan shrugged, like it wasn't a big deal. "Ana insisted."

Ana could insist until she was blue, but Nathan wouldn't have done it unless he wanted to. "And would it really be so terrible to invite Mom, too?"

"I put up with her crap for years because besides you, she was the only family I had. Well, I have my own family now, and I don't need her any longer."

Jordan propped his hands on Nathan's desk and leaned in. "All I'm asking is that you give her one more chance. If she blows it this time I swear I won't ever nag you about her again."

"Give me one good reason why I should."

"Because you're a good person, Nathan. Better than her, better than Dad. And I'll deny it if you repeat this, but at times even better than me. And though Mom will never admit it, not inviting her hurt her feelings, and you aren't the kind of guy who hurts people's feelings. And the guilt you're going to feel isn't worth the view from that moral high horse you're on."

"Wow." Nathan shook his head. "And here I thought you were just as shallow and self-absorbed as she is."

"It'll be our secret."

Nathan was quiet for a minute, then he blew out a breath and said, "All right, fine. One more chance. But if she blows it this time, that's it."

"Fair enough. Are you going to call and tell her?"

Nathan glared at him.

"Or I could do it," Jordan said. He hoped his mom came through this time, because he was tired of making excuses for her. In fact, if she let them down again, it might be enough to push him over the edge as well. And who knows, maybe it would snap some sense into her if both her sons shut her out.

"That reminds me, we haven't gotten your RSVP yet," Nathan said.

"It's on my to-do list. But you know I'll be there."

"I assume you'll be bringing a date."

"At least one. No more than three."

Nathan shot him a "get real" look.

"What? I'm in pretty high demand."

"So," Nathan said, leaning back in his chair. "Getting back to what you were saying earlier, since I'm the *better* man, I guess that means you don't plan to fight me for the CEO position."

Jordan laughed. "I've got to get back to work."

He turned and crossed the room, and as he was walking out the door his brother called after him, "You know, you're not as smart as you think you are."

Yes, he was.

There was nothing to fight over because the CEO spot was already his. Though no one had come right out and said it, Nathan's engagement to Ana Birch—whose father owned Birch Energy, their direct competitor—had killed his chances at the big chair. Even worse, Walter Birch was suspected of conspiring in the sabotage. Even if Jordan did back out, Nathan didn't have a shot in hell.

Emilio Suarez, who was also in the running, married a woman whose ex-husband was responsible for one of the largest Ponzi schemes in a decade, and had dragged her name through the mud with his own. Though the charges against her had been dropped, there were a lot of people who still held her partially responsible for the millions they lost. The CFO of a billion-dollar corporation did not marry a woman linked to financial fraud without serious repercussions.

On top of that, Jordan had played an important role in Western Oil's recent success. He firmly believed that happy workers were productive workers. He appreciated and respected each and every man in that refinery, and that respect was returned unconditionally. Since he took over as COO, productivity had jumped by nearly fifteen percent.

As far as he was concerned, he had the position in the bag. It was just a matter of waiting for the announcement to make it official.

When he got back to his office, Jane was studying something on her computer monitor.

"Any problems with using the system," he asked.

"I'm familiar with this operating system and most of the programs. What I don't know, I'll figure out."

"Great, because starting this afternoon I have a mountain of work that needs catching up."

"That's why I'm here."

Or so he was supposed to believe. He just hoped that while she dug into his personal life—or at least tried to—she also was competent enough to get some *real* work done. And after hours, when the work was finished, the fun would begin.

Sometime before lunch it started to rain, so instead of walking to the restaurant, the secretaries decided to order in and ate lunch together in the break room. It was a huge relief for Jane, as she began to doubt if she would have even been able to make it to the lobby in the torture devices they had the nerve to call shoes. And though Jordan left for lunch, and she could have spent that hour in his office trying to get into his email and files, she was glad that she'd taken the opportunity to get to know the other secretaries in the office. Not that she'd gleaned any new information, but she'd begun to build a base of trust that might come in handy later.

There was a sense of camaraderie between the women that was completely foreign to her. At Edwin Associates she worked mostly with men who barely gave her the time of day, and in her parents' practice…well, her siblings had to be the most competitive people on the planet. Sometimes she felt smothered under the weight of their enormous egos. Here, everyone seemed to like and respect one another. It was a nice change.

Jane returned to her desk at one, and Jordan walked in fifteen minutes later. After that, he didn't leave the office for the rest of the day, so she didn't get another chance to investigate. But she did make a good-size dent in that pile of work he'd warned her about. In fact, she was so engrossed in what she was doing, Jordan had to remind her at seven-thirty to leave.

"Sorry, I guess I lost track of time."

"No need to apologize," he said, leaning in his office doorway, tie loosened, looking slightly rumpled and attractive as hell. He was the sort of guy that no matter what he wore—be it a tailored suit or a pair of sweatpants and a T-shirt—he would make a girl's heart beat a little faster. "Most temps are out the door at five on the nose. If you're trying to impress me, it's working."

Honestly, she really had just lost track of time. When she got her head in the zone, the rest of the world ceased to exist, and hours passed like minutes. Besides, it wasn't as if she had anything to go home to.

"I can stay if you need me," she told him, realizing right after she said it how terribly pathetic it was that her social life was so barren, she would rather stay at work. She could tell herself that she simply wanted to stay until after he left, so she could have unlimited access to his office, but it would be a lie.

Even more pathetic was the disappointment she felt when he said, "Go home, Jane." Then it occurred to her that all day he had referred to her as Miss Monroe, and now he had used her first name. She'd never been too crazy about her name, but the way he said it, in that smooth-as-velvet voice, made her feel warm all over.

She shut down her computer, slipped her shoes back on, and stood. Following a full afternoon off her feet, they had stopped hurting, but she knew that by the time she made it to her car she would probably be in agony again.

"So," he said, as she got her coat and purse out of the closet. "How would you rate your first day?"

"Besides spilling coffee on my new boss, I'd say it was all right." She dropped her purse on the desk to put on her coat, but before she could, he took it from her and helped her into it. It was very gentlemanly of him, and she couldn't help wondering if he did it for his regular secretary.

"Thank you," she said, turning back to him and grabbing her purse. "I'll see you tomorrow."

"I'll walk you down."

To the lobby? "Oh…you don't have to—"

"I won't be out of here for a couple of hours. I could use a few minutes' break." He gestured to the open door. "After you."

For some reason the thought of being in the elevator alone with him so late in the evening gave her a serious case of the jitters. She wasn't used to being around men who were so blatantly sexy. Not to mention flirty. What if he came on to her? What would she do?

Of course he wouldn't come on to her. She barely knew him. Besides, if he were some sort of sexual deviant, she was sure she would have heard about it at lunch, but the other women had nothing but good things to say about him.

Jen had left for the night, and there was a different guard posted by the elevator. He was older than Michael but no less intimidating.

"Jane, this is George Henderson, the night guard. George, this is Miss Monroe. She'll be temping for me until Tiffany comes back from her maternity leave."

"Ma'am," George said, nodding stiffly, and he didn't even crack a smile.

Jordan hit the button for the elevator and it opened almost immediately. She stepped in first, leaning against the back wall to take some of the pressure off her feet because, surprise, they had already begun to throb again. Jordan settled beside her, his arm grazing the sleeve of her jacket. Did he have to stand so close?

As the doors slid closed she experienced the oddest sensation of anticipation, as if any second he was going to do something drastic, like…oh, yank her into his arms and kiss her senseless. And wow, wouldn't that be awful, because she was sure he was probably a terrible kisser.

She gave her head an exasperated shake. How he kissed was of no consequence to her, because she wouldn't be kissing him.

"Everything all right?" Jordan asked, and she realized he was watching her with a curious look.

She smiled. "Yes, fine."

"Something on your mind?"

She shook her head. "No."

"How are your feet?"

"Starting to hurt again."

"You might want to rethink the shoes tomorrow. Besides, I like you better when you're shorter."

She must have looked confused because he added with a grin, "I'm intimidated by tall women."

Somehow she doubted that. He struck her as the kind of man who wasn't intimidated by *anyone*.

"So, do you live close by?" he asked.

"Not too far. About fifteen minutes."

"Well, be careful driving. Even if the rain stopped it's cold, so it might be slick out there."

"I will."

The doors opened to the main lobby. She figured that would be it. He would say goodbye and ride back up, but he stepped out with her. He walked her all the way through the lobby, past the coffee shop, which was now closed, and past the guard station to the front door.

"Well, thanks for walking me down," she said, as he reached past her to open the door.

"I've come this far," he said with a shrug. "I may as well walk you to your car."

Five

He wanted to walk her all the way to her *car?* "But it's freezing out there and you don't have a coat," Jane said.

Jordan shrugged, as if it was no big deal. "I could use the fresh air."

Okay, this was getting a little weird. It was unlikely that he was worried about her safety, since the employee lot was monitored by security cameras. And even if that were the case, wouldn't he send a guard out with her instead? At Edwin Associates no one had ever bothered to open a door for her, much less escort her to her car. Was it possible that he suspected something, and he was going to spring it on her once they were out of the building? What if he knew she wasn't who she said she was?

Her pulse jumping, she stepped outside and he followed her into the chilly night. The wind had died down, but it felt as if the temperature had dropped. "I'm parked in the back."

"Lead the way," he said.

He walked beside her, and the farther from the building they went, the more nervous she began to feel. It must have shown, because after a minute he looked over at her and asked, "Is there a reason you're so edgy?"

"Is there a reason I should be?"

He grinned. "Because I'm walking you to your car?"

"Do you always walk your secretary out?"

"Would you be surprised if I said yes?"

"Would you be surprised if I were surprised?"

He laughed. "Do you always answer a question with a question?"

Only when she was nervous, and worried she would say the wrong thing. "Correct me if I'm wrong, but aren't you doing the same thing?"

"Touché. Maybe I think you're a really great secretary, and I'm worried you might slip in those behemoth heels and break a limb, in which case I would have to break in someone new."

"So what you're saying is, your motivation is purely selfish."

"Pretty much. My motto is, if there's nothing in it for me, what's the point?"

She couldn't tell if he was joking or serious.

As they approached her car she used her key fob to unlock it.

"Wow," he said, as they got closer and he saw the make. "That was not what I pictured you driving."

Her either. "It was a graduation present."

"College?"

"Yeah." Although actually it was law school. Her parents got a new car for each one of their kids when they passed the bar exam. Her oldest brother Richard got a fully restored muscle car, and for Will—the status monger—they bought a BMW. For her trendy sister, Mary, they purchased a cute and zippy red Miata, and for Jane, the "practical" child, they picked out a conservative, boxy white Volvo sedan.

Yeah, Mom and Dad.

He looked confused. "Did you actually request this? I mean, don't get me wrong, it's a really nice car...for a forty-something mother of two. I imagined you in something a little less..."

"Yeah." Her too. "It's not exactly my style, but it was a gift, so I'm sort of stuck with it." At least until she could afford something new. She'd taken a pretty hefty pay cut when she left her parents' firm and since then her savings had been slowly dwindling away.

She opened the driver's-side door and stood behind it, using it as barrier between them, not that she was afraid he was going to try something. Or maybe she was a little. Truthfully, she didn't know *what* to think. He was being so friendly and...flirty. She was definitely not the sort of woman whom people flirted with. And even if someone had, it probably would have had her retreating back into her shell.

He didn't need to know that.

She tossed her purse onto the passenger seat and clutched the top of the door to take some of the weight off her feet. "Well, I guess I'll see you tomorrow."

"You never did answer my question," he said.

"Which one?"

"Why are you so edgy?"

Oh, *that* one. She sort of hoped he'd forgotten about that. "Who says I am?"

He grinned and her knees went squishy again. Even with the door between them he was too close. He had a way of invading her space, even if he was standing five feet away.

"You're very good at that," he said.

"What?"

"Not answering questions."

As a lawyer, she'd had a lot of practice.

"And I know you are," he said.

"I am what?"

"Edgy." He leaned in a little closer, and—*Oh my God*—rested his hands on the top of the door beside hers, boxing them in, so that his thumbs were resting on her pinkies. She had to fight not to jerk away, and her heart started hammering about a million miles a second. She was alone, in the dark, in a deserted parking lot with a man she barely knew, her heart racing with a combination of fear and anticipation. And she *liked* it. What happened to practical, play-it-safe Plain Jane?

"You don't have to be afraid of me," he said, his face so close she could count the individual hairs on his chin. "I'm harmless."

Oh, she seriously doubted that.

"I'm not afraid," she said. More like *petrified.*

"Then why are you hiding behind your car door?"

Couldn't put anything past him, could she?

"Maybe I just don't like you," she said, hoping he didn't hear the quiver in her voice, or feel her hands trembling.

He shook his head. "Nah, that can't be it. I mean, look at me. I'm handsome, and rich."

"And modest."

He grinned. "Exactly. What's not to like?"

She had the feeling he wasn't nearly as arrogant and shallow as he wanted her to believe, that maybe it was some sort of…defense mechanism. And boy did she know about those. She had practically invented the concept. Keep a safe distance, don't let anyone too close, and no one could hurt her.

"Admit it," he said. "You like me."

She wasn't supposed to like him. Not like this. Not at *all*. But he was right, she did. And it seemed as though, the harder she pushed him away, the harder he pushed back.

"You're my boss," she said, but it came out all soft and breathy.

His eyes locked on hers. His pupils were dilated so wide his irises had all but disappeared. "Not after we walked out of the building."

She tried to look away but she was riveted. Then his thumbs brushed across the tops of her fingers, sending a ripple of sensation up her hands and into her arms. If the car door wasn't there between them she would...well, she wasn't sure what she would do. But she would definitely do something.

"I—I really need to get home," she said.

"You don't want to go home."

He was right. She didn't want to leave. She could stand there all night just looking into his eyes. Listening to the deep hum of his voice. Feeling the brush of his thumbs over her fingers. Back and forth. And then he was closer, and she realized he was leaning in. Oh my God, he was going to kiss her. He was actually going to kiss her, right there, in the parking lot. And she *wanted* him to. In that instant she didn't care about the investigation or her career.

She should have pushed him away, or run like hell, but instead she felt herself leaning in, her chin lifting, her eyes drifting closed. His face was so close she could feel the warmth of his breath against her lips and she held her own breath in anticipation...then she felt his breath shifting the hair over her ear and he whispered, "Yeah, you like me."

She felt him let go of the car door and by the time she

dragged her eyes open he was already walking away. She stood there, stunned and confused, wondering what the hell had just happened.

Whoa.

Jordan walked briskly back to the building, his pulse jumping, sweating despite the cold, wondering what the hell had just happened.

He hadn't meant to do more than tease Jane a little, yet he had come within a millimeter of pressing his lips to hers. He couldn't remember a time when the idea of doing nothing more that kissing a woman had gotten him so hot and bothered.

He shook his head and laughed in spite of himself. He was supposed to be toying with Jane, and here he was in even worse shape than her.

One thing was clear, though. The coy routine was no act. He could feel her unease as they rode the elevator down to the lobby, and when they got to the car. When he touched her hands, she was actually trembling. For the life of him he couldn't understand why a woman as beautiful and sexy as her could be nervous around anyone. She was a total contradiction. Confident and capable one minute, shy and awkward the next. If he didn't know any better he might have thought that he had two different women working for him. Or that this was some sort of twisted practical joke.

As he reached the building he heard Jane's car start, then pull out of the lot, but he resisted the urge to turn around and watch her drive away. Instead he pushed his way through the door and back into the lobby, asking the guard on duty, "Hey, Joe, you got a pen?"

"Sure thing, Mr. Everette." He grabbed a pen from his

station and handed it to him. "I take it it's going to be another late one."

"You know it." He jotted Jane's license plate number on the palm of his hand and handed the pen back. "Thanks."

He rode the elevator up to his office. He'd wondered all day if Jane Monroe was really her name, and he was about to find out.

He logged onto his computer and pulled up the website he'd registered for earlier that day—a service that accessed personal information through license plates. He punched in her number and the information popped up on the screen almost instantly.

Huh. Her name really was Jane Monroe. It listed her address, which he jotted down for future reference, and as she'd claimed, it was about fifteen minutes away. It also listed her birthday, which he was surprised to find was tomorrow.

Well, that had been almost too easy. He thought for sure they would have sent her in under an assumed name.

He pulled up a new page and logged onto a search engine, typing in her name. It came back with a couple hundred thousand hits. He scrolled the first couple of pages, finding an artist, a photographer, a professor at a university in Boston. There was even an actress who played bit parts on several popular television dramas. But no Jane Monroe investigator anywhere.

He started a new page but this time he typed in Jane Monroe, Texas. He got a hit for a website called *Linked Up,* a place to look up professional profiles. A Jane Monroe in El Paso, Texas, was the first on the list, but under profession it was listed as lawyer. That couldn't be right.

He typed in Jane Monroe, Lawyer, this time, and got a hit for a family-owned El Paso practice called Monroe Law Group. There was a small photo of the family on the info page. There was an older couple who were clearly the parents, two sons, and two daughters. One of the daughters had dark hair and was very attractive, but looked nothing like Jane. The other was borderline mousy with unremarkable brown hair worn in a long, straight style, wire-rimmed glasses that were a little too large for her face and a shapeless gray suit that made her look as though she was slouching. She wasn't unattractive, but compared to the rest of the family, she seemed to almost fade into the background. But there was something familiar about her. Something about the shape of her face, and the tilt of her mouth…

No way.

He looked closer, expanding the page to make the photo larger. Damn. Even bare he would recognize that plump bottom lip anywhere. The woman in the photo was *Jane*.

He sat back in his chair, shaking his head, having a tough time reconciling the image on his screen with the blonde beauty working as his secretary. And if she was an attorney in her family practice, what the hell was she doing working at Edwin Associates?

He checked the individual profiles, but hers was missing. Maybe she had left and they hadn't gotten around to changing the photo.

He tried a few more searches with different key words, but he'd reached a dead end. He could only assume that her career as a lawyer was an unremarkable one. Which might explain why she'd left it.

He blew out a frustrated breath. Honestly, he didn't even know why he cared. She was a toy to him. A way to amuse himself until she was finished here. Not to mention a way to take out his frustration against the people who should have trusted him. She was nothing to him, yet there was something about her that just…fascinated him. It was rare that any woman had that sort of effect on him, and frankly, he didn't like it.

Jordan went into his browser history and erased all evidence of his searches and any activity on the license plate site, then he erased the link for the site from his favorites, just in case. For all he knew Jane could be some sort of computer whiz and just waiting for the opportunity to get into his computer. And since he would be at the refinery most of tomorrow morning, she would certainly get her chance. He wasn't exactly thrilled with the idea of someone snooping around in his office, going through his things, but the sooner she found what she was looking for, or better yet, didn't find it, the sooner she would be out of his hair.

Walking into work the next morning after that almost-kiss in the parking lot was one of the hardest things Jane ever had to do. Though no one had seen what had happened, she couldn't shake the feeling that everyone would look at her and just *know*. And she could swear the guards posted at the security station snickered as she passed through.

She knew it was silly, and probably a figment of her imagination, but after a long sleepless night, she wasn't exactly functioning with all cylinders. And she was still no closer to understanding what had happened. Why he had come so close to kissing her then just...walked away. Was it some sort of game to him?

Of course it was. He was toying with her, pushing her buttons. The question was why? Because he could?

She joined the group of people waiting by the elevator then followed them inside when the doors opened, standing against the back wall. The spot where she'd stood last night with Jordan.

The worst part of last night was the realization that if he really *had* kissed her, she would have let him. She was not the kind of woman to let men she barely knew kiss her. Nor did she base her self-worth on looks, or the attention she got from the opposite sex. But when Jordan stroked her fingers and gazed into her eyes, she'd never felt so attractive, so *wanted* in her entire life. Or so confused and dejected when he turned away.

He'd made a complete fool of her, and she had made it all too easy. Her only consolation, upon arriving home and reading the file that had been faxed over from Edwin Associates, was learning that Jordan Everette hadn't always been the charming, handsome, confident man that he was now.

Though she would have pegged him for a jock, and probably class president, she couldn't have been more wrong. According to his file he used to be a scrawny, awkward, socially inept intellectual with an IQ in the genius range. He had graduated top of his class in prep school and attended an Ivy League college, where he not only grew several inches in height and took up weight lifting, he completed the business program a full year and a half early.

At the age of twenty-one he'd inherited a trust fund that he immediately invested and multiplied exponentially within only a few years. He could have lived in luxury and never lifted a finger for the rest of his life, but he chose instead to embark on a career with Western Oil, where he climbed the ranks with record speed. To meet him, one might suspect he'd made it where he was on personality and charm alone, but that wasn't the case at all. He'd worked damned hard.

The current CEO had plans to step down soon and if she believed what Jen told her at lunch yesterday, Jordan had a decent shot at his position. If he wasn't guilty of sabotage, that is.

The doors opened at the top floor and she stepped out. She showed her badge to Michael Weiss, who smiled and waved her past, and said hello to Jen on her way through the lobby.

"Aren't those just the cutest shoes!" she said, admiring Jane's peep-toe Dior pumps.

"Thanks." She didn't usually spend a week's pay on shoes, but they were really cute, and though the heel was a whopping four inches, they didn't pinch her toes. "Is Mr. Everette in yet?"

"Eight on the nose."

She forced a smile. "Great!"

"Oh, and happy birthday."

She blinked. "How did you know it's my birthday."

She smiled cryptically. "You'll see."

Adding curiosity to the nervous knots in her stomach, Jane walked down the hall. She had already decided that if Jordan—make that Mr. Everette—said anything about last night she was going to act like it was no big deal. She stepped into her office, jerking to a stop before she reached her desk. Sitting on the corner, with a mylar balloon stuck in the center, was an enormous arrangement of butter yellow roses. At least two dozen.

She dropped her purse in her chair and leaned down to inhale the delicate scent. There was no card, and nothing lying on her desk. Who in the world—

"I wasn't sure what kind to get," Jordan said from behind her and she whipped around.

He stood in his office doorway, and her heart dropped so hard and fast at the sight of him, it sucked the breath right out of her.

She had tried to convince herself last night that he wasn't

as amazingly handsome and devastatingly charming as she first thought, but he really was. And despite last night, if he were to walk up to her, take her in his arms and plant a kiss on her right then and there, she probably wouldn't do a damned thing to stop him.

Where was *Practical Jane* when she needed her?

"You did this?"

"Guilty."

If he was trying to butter her up, it was *so* working. "They're beautiful. How did you know it was my birthday?"

"I could tell you, but then I would have to kill you."

And he obviously *wasn't* going to tell her. "Well, thank you. They're lovely."

"Don't take your coat off," he said.

"Why not?"

"Because we're leaving."

Six

We? As in the two of them. *Together?*

"Um, where are we going?" Jane asked.

"To the refinery. I told you I would bring you along the next time I went."

She looked at the inbox on her desk, piled high with work that still needed catching up on. "But I have so much work—"

"It'll keep."

"But—"

"I'll go get my coat. The limo will be waiting."

He disappeared into his office. He clearly wasn't taking no for an answer. And the idea of being stuck in a car with him after last night made her knees go squishy.

He was back a minute later with his coat on. "Let's go."

Having no choice in the matter, she snagged her purse off the chair and followed him to the elevator.

"Can you take my calls?" he asked Jen as they passed

her desk. "I'm taking Jane on a tour of the refinery. We'll be back later this afternoon."

"Of course, Mr. Everette," she said.

Later this *afternoon?* How long would the tour take? And would she be spending the entire time with him?

Michael must have pressed the elevator button for them because the door opened as they were approaching. They stepped inside, and as the doors slid closed, her heart climbed up to lodge in her throat.

Would he stand too close again? Bring up what happened last night?

Thankfully his phone chose that moment to start ringing. He looked at the display and said apologetically, "I have to take this."

She breathed a quiet sigh of relief and silent thank-you for the caller's convenient timing. He talked during the entire ride down to the lobby and the walk to the limo that was waiting for them outside the front door. She got in first, sitting with her back to the driver, and he slid in across from her. He was still talking as the car pulled out of the lot and headed east.

She sat back and tried to relax, hating that she felt so awkward and inept around him. When she worked at her parents' practice her competence had never been in question. In fact, she usually felt as though she was butting her head against the ceiling, desperate to break from the confines of the position her parents kept her in. She knew she was damned good and she had wanted to prove it, but they were always holding her back. As an investigator she felt completely out of her element and was flying blind, but at least they were giving her a chance to prove herself.

She glanced at Jordan, thinking that she would kill to see a photo of what he'd looked like when he was still in his awkward, geeky phase. Probably not half as awkward and geeky as she had been. Despite being two years younger than her classmates she had been several inches taller than most of the other girls, and straight as a board from neck to knees, with no sense of fashion and a bad case of acne that weekly visits to a dermatologist couldn't even clear up. Not to mention a sister who took morbid satisfaction in reminding Jane on almost a daily basis just how pretty she *wasn't*. To say that she had self-esteem issues was a serious understatement.

She wondered what her life would have been like if instead of constantly tearing her down, her sister had tried to help her. If, when Jane complained to her mother that she wasn't as pretty as Mary, her mother had told her that she was pretty in her own way, instead of saying, "You have something better than beauty, Jane, you have brains."

If her own mother didn't think she was pretty, there was clearly no hope for her.

She looked out the window, watching the city pass by, feeling inexplicably sad. Maybe they were right. Maybe she was fooling herself into thinking anything had changed. Maybe the kind of pretty she had now, the kind that came from layers of overpriced cosmetics, didn't count anyway, because underneath it she was still the same Plain Jane. Maybe all she was doing was cheating the system.

"Penny for your thoughts."

She turned to find Jordan watching her. She was so lost in thought she hadn't even realized he was off the phone.

"It looks like it might rain again," she said.

"I've never known the threat of rain to make someone look so sad."

Did she really look that sad?

She shrugged. "I'm just ready for spring. I've never been much of a cold weather person."

"Do you have any special plans tonight?"

"Plans?"

"For your birthday."

Oh, that. "Not tonight. But I'm having dinner with my family on Friday."

"You have brothers and sisters?"

"Two brothers, one sister."

"Older or younger?"

Why the sudden interest in her family? And wasn't she supposed to be pumping *him* for information? "I'm the youngest."

He nodded sympathetically. "I know how that is."

"You just have the one brother?" she asked, even though she already knew the answer. But if she kept him talking, she might learn something valuable to the case.

"Just Nathan. Although why my mother had children at all is a mystery to me. She wasn't exactly maternal."

"Mine was Supermom. She had a full-time career and was home to help us with our schoolwork every night."

"There it is," he said, gesturing out the window as they approached the refinery.

She had driven by it hundreds of times but she'd never actually been there. The sheer size had always astounded her. With all its stacks and towers and maze of pipes and tubing that seemed to stretch for miles, it was a wonder they could make heads or tails of it. "So, you're in charge of all of this?"

He smiled and nodded. "Yep."

She could see that he took a tremendous amount of pride in that fact.

"But I don't do it alone. I have a stellar staff." He pointed to a building at the south end of the complex. "That's our research facility. We employ several of the leading scientists in the field of alternative fuel, and devote more money annually into biofuel development than any of our competitors. I'm particularly interested in the use of algae as an alternate energy source. We're even considering a company name change to reflect the changing industry."

She had no idea Western was so versatile. "It sounds as if you really love what you do."

"It's an exciting industry to be a part of right now."

"What made you get into the oil business?"

"My brother."

That was sort of sweet. "You wanted to follow in his footsteps?"

"Actually, I did it to piss him off."

She must have looked really surprised, because he laughed.

"Okay, that wasn't the only reason. I figured it would be a stepping stone to something bigger and better. Turns out I really liked it. And I'm damned good at it. So good that I'm going to be CEO."

"You sound pretty confident about that."

"That's because I am."

"It doesn't bother you, competing against your own brother?"

He locked his eyes on her, and something in his expression made her knees feel squishy. "I believe that when you want something, you should go after it, all pistons firing. Don't you agree?"

Normally a question like that, spoken with such a suggestive undertone, would have her scrambling back into her shell. Instead she heard herself say, "I guess it just depends on what you want."

A grin curled his lips, but before he could reply the limo came to a stop and the door opened. She breathed a sigh of relief, because with that single comment she had exhausted her arsenal of witty comebacks. This flirting business sure wasn't easy, but with a little practice she just might get the hang of it.

She had figured that while Jordan conducted his business there, he would assign someone to take her on a tour, but that wasn't the case. He took her on the tour himself. Not only was the refinery a fascinating and complicated operation, it was obvious that everyone—from the managers to the men on the line—liked and respected him, and the feeling was clearly mutual. Jordan greeted the workers warmly, shaking hands, addressing almost every one of them by name. And his vast knowledge of the inner workings of the plant completely blew her away. By the time they finished the tour she knew more about refining oil than she ever imagined possible. And after seeing Jordan there, interacting with the people, she simply could not imagine him willingly doing anything to cause damage or harm here.

"So, what did you think?" he asked when they were in the limo and on their way back to Western Oil headquarters.

"I actually had a really great time. I never imagined an oil refinery could be so interesting."

"There wasn't time today, but someday soon I'll take you to the research lab. That's where the real magic happens."

"Are you in charge of that too?"

"That's my brother's territory, but I love hanging out there. My second choice to majoring in business was science."

"What made you choose business?"

"There's more money in it. And I'm good at it." His cell phone rang and he pulled it out of his coat pocket. "Sorry, I have to take this."

She looked out the window while he talked, realizing,

after they got back into the heart of the city, the driver was taking them in the opposite direction of the corporate building. Either he was lost, or Jordan had a stop to make before they went back.

The limo pulled up in front of Café du Soleil, one of the priciest French restaurants in the city. He obviously had a lunch date. She imagined he would send her back to the building alone, then the limo would go back and get him when he was finished.

Jordan hung up his phone just as the attendant opened the door to let him out, but he didn't move. "Ladies first."

Confused, she said, "Excuse me?"

"Well, I suppose we could eat in the car, but it's much nicer inside."

Wait a minute. *She* was his lunch date?

"Earth to Jane."

"We're eating here? Together?"

His brows rose. "Are you embarrassed to be seen with me or something?"

"No!" she said, laughing at the utter ridiculousness of the question. What woman wouldn't want to be seen with a man like him? "Of course not, I just…"

"It's your birthday, and since you don't have plans for this evening, you get a nice lunch."

"That's really sweet of you, but you don't have to do that."

"I don't have to, but I want to."

And she wanted him to, too. But what if someone she knew was there, and her cover was blown? Not that this was a regular hangout for her. It was about two stars out of her price range. And other than the people at Edwin, no one knew where she was working.

"If you don't like French cuisine we could go somewhere else," he said.

She was being silly. Of course she wouldn't run into anyone she knew there. And she couldn't ask for a better opportunity to get to know him.

"Lunch here would be lovely. Thank you."

They got out of the limo and went inside, Jordan placing a hand on her back as they walked through the door.

"Mr. Everette," the pretty young hostess with an authentic-sounding accent said. "So nice to have you back."

She took their coats, handing them off to the other young woman standing nearby and said, "Right this way."

Jane glanced around as they walked through the restaurant, relieved when she didn't see anyone she knew. She did notice the appreciative looks women cast Jordan as he passed, though. Not that she blamed them. Had she she been dining there, and he walked in, she would have looked at him exactly the same way.

The hostess seated them near the window and said, "James will be right with you."

She was barely gone ten seconds when James appeared at the table. He addressed Jordan by name, listed the specials, then took their beverage orders. Jane ordered a Perrier.

"Are you sure you wouldn't like a glass of wine?" Jordan said. "Or better yet, champagne, since it is your birthday."

"I shouldn't while I'm working."

He grinned. "I promise not to tell your boss."

She was about to decline, and had to remind herself that this was not about her "job" at Western Oil. This was about the investigation, and pumping Jordan for information. For that, she could be the type of woman who imbibed at lunch.

She smiled and said, "In that case, I'd love some."

He ordered an entire bottle and the waiter trotted off to fetch it.

"I take it you eat here often, Mr. Everette," she said.

"Often enough to know that the *boeuf bourguignon* is to die for."

She looked at the menu, which was written entirely in French. And since she couldn't read French, she set it aside and said, "Then I think I'll have that."

"I have an idea," he said. "How about, when we're not in the office, you call me Jordan?"

"Okay. Jordan." It was completely ridiculous, but using his first name seemed so…intimate. "Does Tiffany use your first name when you're not in the office?"

He grinned. "No. And in answer to your next question, no, I don't take her out to lunch either."

"That wasn't my next question."

"Well, I figure it was bound to spring up eventually."

James reappeared with their champagne and poured them each a glass, then he took their orders. When he was gone, Jordan held up his glass and said, "A toast, to your… twenty-third birthday?"

He definitely knew what to say to make a girl feel good. "Twenty-ninth," she said, lifting her glass.

"Get out. You don't look a day over twenty-five."

She clinked her glass against his and took a sip. Of course it was delicious.

Jordan took a sip, then set his glass back down. "So, what was your next question?"

She opened her mouth to answer him, glancing past him at the the man walking in her direction from the restrooms. Her breath caught and her heart dropped, and her first instinct was to slide out of her chair and hide under the table. This *could not* be happening.

Please don't let him see me, she begged silently, willing herself to be invisible.

"Jane?" Jordan said, his brow furrowed with concern. "Are you okay?"

The man passed by the table, glancing briefly at her, and she held her breath…then he did a double take and stopped in his tracks.

Her heart plummeted into the pit of her stomach.

"Jane? Is that you?"

Seven

Jane cursed silently, but pasted on what she hoped was a pleasant, yet slightly disinterested smile. "Oh, hello, Drake."

Her ex looked her up and down and laughed. "Oh my God, I hardly recognized you. You look… *Wow*. What happened to you?"

What he meant was, what happened to drab, Plain Jane at whom men never cast a second glance? Well, Drake wasn't exactly God's gift to women. He wasn't particularly tall, or well built, or even all that good-looking, and the hairline that had begun to recede in his early twenties was now a full-fledged bald spot.

She ignored his question and instead asked, "How have you been?"

"Great! I don't know if you heard, but Megan and I are engaged. We set a date for this spring."

"Oh, congratulations," she said, digging her acrylic nails into the meat of her palms. She knew she was better off without him, but the news still stung. She had been with him for five years, two of those living together, but they had never once talked marriage.

After only nine months with Megan they were already *engaged?*

Drake had always complained that Jane didn't love him enough, and that she put her career before him, and it was probably true. He was her first serious boyfriend, and she had just assumed that he was the best she was ever likely to do, which in hindsight wasn't fair to him or her. He needed someone who worshipped the ground he walked on. Someone he could lord over and take care of. A woman who didn't threaten his massive ego. Megan, who wasn't exactly blessed in the brains department, was the perfect mate for him.

Still, it had been humiliating to be dumped for a woman with the IQ of a pencil sharpener.

Drake shook his head and laughed. "I just can't get over this. I mean, look at you!"

He glanced over at Jordan, who was watching the exchange with a mildly amused expression. "I'm sorry, you must be Jane's…?"

"Jordan Everette," he said, accepting Drake's out-stretched hand.

"Drake Cunningham," Drake said. "I'm with Cruz, Whitford and Taylor. Junior partner."

Jordan clearly felt no need to validate his own ego by stating his occupation or position. He only nodded politely.

"I went to school with Jane," Drake said and Jane cringed inwardly. *Please don't say it*—"U of T Law."

Jordan flicked a look of surprise her way. "Is that so?"

She cursed silently. Now there were going to be questions, like why a law graduate would settle for a job as a secretarial temp. *Thanks a bunch, Drake.*

Drake turned back to Jane. "I heard you left the family practice, but there was no word as to who picked you up."

And thank God for that. He could have just completely blown her cover. If he hadn't already. "Actually, I've been taking a break from law," she said, and left it at that. She didn't owe him an explanation anyway.

Drake nodded somberly. "I totally get it. The law is cutthroat. Some people just can't take the pressure."

She gnashed her teeth and resisted the urge to kick him in the shin. It had always chapped his ass that Jane had a higher GPA, and graduated with higher honors.

He had to be loving this.

"Well," he said, glancing at his watch, "I have a meeting. But it was good to see you again. And I guess I'll be seeing you at the reunion."

"Reunion?" Jordan asked.

"Once a year a group of us from our law school graduating class get together and have a party," Drake told him.

Jane suddenly felt sick to her stomach. "I didn't see your name on the RSVP list." It was the only reason she had signed up to attend.

"I was supposed to be abroad but I rearranged my schedule." His face softened and he touched her shoulder, giving it a squeeze. "Hey, if it's still too hard for you—"

"Of course not," she said, resisting the urge to bat his hand away. Feeling him touch her turned her stomach, but she refused to give him the satisfaction of thinking she cared one way or the other.

"Great, then I guess we'll see you there."

We. Of course it was too much to hope that he wouldn't be bringing his fiancée.

Giving her shoulder a condescending pat, he walked away, and she grabbed her champagne glass and downed it in one swallow.

"Please tell me you didn't date that guy," Jordan said.

"Um…"

His brow lifted. "*Seriously?* Not only is he an arrogant jerk, but in the looks department you are *way* out of his league."

That was the first time anyone had accused her of that. "We were together for five years."

He looked so disappointed in her. "At least you came to your senses."

"Actually, he dumped me for Megan. About nine months ago."

"Tell me you're over him. Because you can do better, trust me."

"Of course I'm over him. He was never the love of my life. I'm just…I guess I'm still a little…bitter. And betrayed, since I'm the one who introduced him to Megan."

"She's a lawyer?"

"A dog groomer."

His brow popped up again.

"We owned a bichon frise and we took him to her for grooming. When Drake dumped me, my new apartment wouldn't allow pets, so she got my boyfriend *and* my dog."

"With the exception of the dog, I'd say you got the better end of the deal."

He was right of course. She never would have been happy married to Drake, even if he had asked. Her family thought he was the perfect man for her, which in retrospect should have been her first clue that the relationship would end in disaster. She should have taken it as a sign to run screaming in the opposite direction.

"So, you're a law graduate," Jordan said.

There was no denying it now. "My parents and my siblings, they're all lawyers, so it was just assumed I would be too."

"Let me guess, they're not too thrilled that you've abandoned the law."

"Actually, they don't know that I have. I lied and told them I've been working in the corporate law department of Andersen Technologies, a small corporation in El Paso. It's just easier that way."

The waiter appeared, depositing their salads at the table and refilling her glass.

She took a generous swallow. She should be thankful, that could have gone a lot worse.

Then why did she feel so lousy?

"So when is this reunion?" he asked.

"Next month. But I'm not going."

"Why not?"

"I can just see it," she said, breaking her roll and slathering butter on one half, even though she had pretty much lost her appetite the instant Drake appeared. "Me still single and alone while Drake struts around with his new fiancée on his arm. I don't think so. It would be too humiliating."

"So don't go alone."

"That's a great idea. The problem is, I'm not dating anyone right now."

"So take a friend."

"The thing about ending a long-term relationship is that friends pick sides, and since most of them were Drake's to begin with, I lost those in the split too."

He shrugged and said, "In that case, take me."

Eyes wide, Jane dropped her roll into her salad. Jordan stifled a grin as she swiftly fished it back out. "Take *you*?"

"Why not?" Jordan said. "I like parties."

She set her roll down and wiped her hand on her napkin. "Look, I appreciate the gesture, but I can't ask you to do that."

"You're not asking, I offered."

She shook her head. "I can't."

"Jane, that guy takes way too much pleasure from the fact that he thinks you're all alone pining for him. He needs a reality check."

"But that *is* reality. Except for the pining part. I *am* alone. And taking my boss to a party—"

"So I won't be your boss."

"But you *are* my boss."

"No one else needs to know that."

She nervously licked her lips. "What am I supposed to say? You're my…boyfriend?"

Her discomfort made him smile. She seriously had no clue how attractive she was. "Boyfriend, *lover*…whatever."

"But it would be a lie."

She didn't seem to have a problem with lying to him on a daily basis, and lying to her family about where she worked.

"Then you don't have to tell anyone anything." He slid his hand across the table and slipped his fingers around hers. They were ice cold, so he flashed her a smile that was sure to warm her from the inside out. "Besides, actions speak louder than words."

Her lips parted with a soft gasp and she tugged her hand free, eyes darting nervously to the people at the next table. "No. He would never buy that someone like you would date someone like me."

He sat back in his seat. "Why not?"

"Because…" She frowned and shook her head. "Never mind. I just…I think it would be a bad idea. I'm better off not going."

"Then he wins."

"So he wins, so what? It's not a competition. I don't care what he thinks any longer."

Another lie. For reasons that totally escaped him, she did care, which was why he'd offered in the first place. He saw the way she'd paled when Drake approached the table—although that could have had more to do with her fear of blowing her cover. But the pain in her eyes when he announced his engagement, that was real.

Rather than hide behind her morals—and her obvious insecurities—she needed to confront the situation. Confront Drake and Megan. Until she did, she would have a tough time moving on. Not that he had much experience with long-term romantic relationships. He'd never been with the same woman for five months, much less five years. Hell, five weeks was pushing the envelope. But he did know an awful lot about being let down by people he thought he could depend on.

And if that wasn't reason enough, he was pissed that the jerk had ruined her birthday lunch. And even worse, after five years together, he hadn't even remembered to wish her a happy birthday.

He wanted to push the issue, but he had the feeling that once Jane made up her mind, it would be hard to change it, so he let it drop. For now. Instead he tried to engage her in another round of witty banter, to lighten the mood, but she wasn't biting, and she only picked at her food. That guy had really done a number on her.

Honestly, he shouldn't have even cared. The problem was, he liked Jane. The fact that she genuinely seemed to have no clue how attractive she was fascinated him. And though he'd brought her here to screw with her, it didn't seem right to kick her while she was down. Besides, hurting her was never his intention. Hell, maybe he could help her.

There was definite chemistry there. Maybe what she needed was someone to pay attention to her, to make her see how beautiful and desirable she really was. To make her feel special. And while sleeping with her would of course be his ultimate goal, wherever this thing between them went, he would make certain that it was mutually beneficial.

The sort of woman he usually dated knew what she wanted, and wasn't shy about going after it. And what they usually wanted was his money, but since he had no intention whatsoever of getting tied down, that had never been a problem. Right about the time he began to get bored, they realized that they were wasting their efforts and the relationship fizzled out. No harm, no foul.

It might be an interesting change if, for once, he was the one doing the pursuing. And he was willing to bet, if she would give up what had most likely been a reasonably lucrative career as an attorney, for what he guessed was an entry-level position at an investigation firm, she wasn't hung up on status and wealth. Not to mention that she needed someone to show her that she could do better than that arrogant creep she had wasted five years with.

The more he thought about it, the more he liked the idea. Yes, she had been lying to him since the minute she met him, but that was her job, so technically there was no malicious intent. Besides, he wasn't exactly being honest either.

Jane was quiet on the ride back to the office, and other than thanking him for the tour and for lunch, didn't say more than a few words for the rest of the afternoon. She knocked on his office door at six to tell him she was leaving for the night.

"Is there anything you need before I go?" she asked. She just looked so…depressed.

"You know, he isn't worth it," Jordan said.

"I know. The truth is, I don't even know why I'm upset.

I didn't want to marry him. I don't even think I loved him."
She shrugged. "Maybe I'm just a sore loser."

"Try not to let it ruin your night. Call a friend. Go out
for drinks. Do something fun. It's your birthday."

She smiled, but it didn't quite reach her eyes. "I definitely will."

She was lying.

"Well, thanks again for the tour, and for the lunch."

"It was my pleasure."

"I'll see you tomorrow."

"See you tomorrow."

He had half a mind to walk her back down to her car,
but his cell rang. Since it was his mother, he was inclined
to let it go to voice mail, but he answered it. "Hey Mom,
what's up?"

"Well, did you talk to him?" his mother demanded.

Her brusque greeting didn't phase him. She always did
like to get right to the point. "Talk to whom?"

"Your brother."

Confused, he asked, "About what?"

"The invitation. To Nathan's graduation."

"You mean the wedding?"

"That's what I said," she snapped.

He saw no point in arguing with her. "You know I did.
I called you yesterday to tell you that he's inviting you.
Don't you remember?"

She was quiet for several seconds then said, "No, I'm
sure I would have remembered. I've been home all day."

He wasn't sure why her being home today had any
bearing on a call he made yesterday. "Well, I did."

"So, is he inviting me?"

Hadn't he just said he was? "Mom, are you okay?"

"I jush wish you would ansher me!" she slurred.

No wonder she wasn't making any sense; she was

hammered. He wondered if things had gone south with her latest man-friend, the filthy rich baron. Was she wallowing in self-pity?

"Yes, Mom, Nathan is inviting you. As I told you yesterday, you'll be getting an invitation any day. Probably tomorrow."

"And Mark will be there?"

Mark? "You mean Max? Nathan's son?"

"That's what I shed."

He sighed. There was no point continuing a conversation she wouldn't even remember in the morning. "Mom, I have to go. I'll call you tomorrow, okay?"

She mumbled something incoherent then hung up. He shook his head and dropped his phone on his desk. That was weird. His mother drank socially, but he'd never known her to get good and sauced. First time for everything, he supposed.

He turned back to his computer and tried to concentrate on his work, but his thoughts kept drifting back to Jane. If he knew women—and he liked to believe that he did—she was probably sitting home alone, with a gallon of chocolate ice cream and a spoon, watching a chick flick and having a pity party.

Well, that wasn't his problem. He couldn't force her to have a good time. Of course, if he hadn't insisted that they go to lunch, she wouldn't have seen her ex and she might actually be enjoying her birthday. So in essence, it was his fault.

He cursed and tossed down his pen. She was miserable and he was to blame, so of course there was only one thing he could do.

Make it right.

Eight

Jane wasn't expecting anyone to stop by, so she was surprised when, at seven-thirty, someone knocked on her door. She dropped the spoon into the ice cream container, set it on the coffee table and paused the movie she'd been watching. It was probably one of her siblings stopping by to say happy birthday. And while normally it annoyed her when they stopped by unannounced, she could use a bit of cheering up tonight.

Clad in a U of T sweatshirt, fleece pajama bottoms and fuzzy slippers, she shuffled to the door and pulled it open—and for an instant she thought her eyes must be playing tricks on her. Or maybe she'd fallen asleep on the couch and she was only dreaming that Jordan was standing in the hall outside her apartment door.

He was still dressed in his work clothes, and carrying a small square bakery box. It never ceased to amaze her how truly beautiful he was, although for the life of her she couldn't imagine what he was doing here.

He took in her shabby clothes, his gaze settling on her feet, and said, "Nice slippers."

Thank goodness she hadn't washed off her makeup yet. He probably would have taken one look at her, turned and run. "I wasn't expecting company."

"Despite promising me that you would go out and have fun, I kept having this mental picture of you sacked out in front of the television watching a chick flick, drowning your sorrows in a gallon of chocolate ice cream."

And he cared enough to stop by and make sure she was okay? First the tour, then lunch, now a visit to her apartment? Maybe she *was* dreaming.

"Am I right?" he asked.

Not exactly, but freakishly close. "It's a pint of caramel nut swirl and I wouldn't exactly call *The Terminator* a chick flick."

"The point is, you're here, and not out celebrating."

Yeah, and how did he even know where "here" was? Probably the same way he knew it was her birthday. The HR office had all of her personal information.

"You know," he said. "I dropped everything to race over here and save you from an evening of self-pity. The least you could do is invite me in."

Right, that would be the polite thing to do, even though the idea of Jordan in her apartment made her pulse skip.

"Sorry, of course." She pulled the door open and stepped out of the way, doing a quick mental inventory of her living room and kitchen, but any incriminating evidence was on her desk in the spare bedroom. There was nothing else in the apartment linking her to Edwin Associates. Not even in her bedroom. Not that he would be going in there. "Please, come in."

He stepped into her living room, and she closed the door behind him. He handed her the box. "This is for you."

"Oh, thank you."

Jordan took off his coat and hung it on the coat tree by the door. Then he did the same with his suit jacket. She stood watching, unsure of what to say or do. The whole point of the investigation was to catch his interest, and clearly she had. Now she didn't have a clue what to do about it, how to take control of the situation. He was too much man for a woman like her.

He loosened his tie, undid the top button on his shirt and rolled the sleeves to his elbows. He was making himself right at home, and she was a jumble of nerves. Her apartment wasn't what anyone would consider spacious, but with him there it felt downright tiny.

He nodded to the box that she was still clutching. "Aren't you going to open it?"

Of course, where were her manners? She slid the top open, and inside was a mini cake. "A birthday cake?"

"I figured you probably didn't have one, and everyone should have a cake on their birthday."

That was the sweetest thing anyone had done for her in a very long time. She hadn't heard word one from her own family—the people who were *supposed* to care about her—and this man who she barely knew had gone above and beyond to make the day special. "Thank you, Jordan."

"I'll bet that would go really well with a cup of coffee."

A cup of coffee was the least she could do. "Is French pressed coffee okay?"

"Of course."

She carried the box to the kitchen and set it on the counter, then she put the kettle on to boil and got out the coffee press and beans.

"Did you just move in here?" Jordan asked, gazing around her sparsely decorated living room.

"Nine months ago. I just haven't gotten around to doing much with it. I sold most of my furniture when I moved in with Drake, so I didn't have much of my own stuff when I moved out." She measured out the beans and set the grinder on Coarse, and when it was finished poured the ground coffee into the press. When the water started boiling she poured it in and set the timer on the oven for four minutes.

"This is good," he said.

She turned to find him leaning in the kitchen doorway eating what was left of her caramel swirl ice cream.

"It's my favorite," she said.

He took another bite and licked the spoon. "I hope you don't mind sharing."

"I have three more pints in the freezer." He could eat her ice cream anytime. And watching him, the way his tongue swept over the spoon, was giving her a hot flash, so she busied herself cutting them each a slice of cake.

"So, have you thought anymore about the reunion?" he asked.

"I haven't changed my mind, if that's what you mean." The timer beeped and she pulled two cups down from the cupboard.

"It doesn't seem fair that you should have to miss it just because your ex is there."

"Maybe I'll go next year." She pressed the plunger down then poured the coffee, adding a dash of creamer to his and leaving hers black. Picking up both cups, she swiveled around to hand him one, unaware that he was standing right behind her. She stopped so abruptly that the coffee sloshed over the brim of both cups and landed—of course—on him.

"Oh my God, I am *so* sorry."

He looked down at the stain spreading across the front of his shirt. "I'm beginning to think you're doing this on purpose."

She set the cups down and grabbed the towel hanging from the oven door handle. She ran it under the faucet, wrung out the excess water, and handed it to him. At least this time she hadn't lobbed an entire cup at him. "I didn't know you were right behind me."

"Don't worry about it." He dabbed at the stain, but it was already setting in. That was another of his shirts she had probably ruined. A few more days with her and he was going to need a new wardrobe.

"Maybe if we throw it in the washing machine right now it won't stain," she said.

His mouth tilted into one of those adorable grins. "You know, if you wanted to get me out of my clothes, all you had to do was ask."

Did he really think she was trying to get him naked? "I wasn't... I didn't mean—"

"Jane, I'm *kidding*." He tossed the towel onto the counter. "I came here to cheer you up and instead you're a nervous wreck."

He was right. He had been nothing but nice to her, and she was a bundle of nerves. What did she think he was going to do? Attack her? Why couldn't she relax when she was with him?

"I'm sorry," she said, feeling like a complete dope.

"Maybe I should just go."

"No!" She said it so forcefully he flinched. Was there no end to her making a complete ass of herself? She took a deep breath. "Of course you can go if you want to, but you don't have to."

"What is it about me that makes you so edgy?"

"I don't know. I guess I just suck at this."

"At what?"

"This...this..." she gestured absently "...flirting thing. That is what we're doing, right? I mean, I'm not imagining things, am I?"

That made him smile. "You're not imagining anything. And for the record, you're damned good at the flirting thing. When you're not acting like you're afraid of me."

"I'm sorry." There was no point in trying to pretend she was a sexy temptress when clearly she wasn't fooling anyone. "I just...I'm not used to being around men like you."

"Jane, you were around me all day and you were fine."

"Yes, but there were other people around."

"So, being *alone* with me makes you nervous."

She nodded.

"Because we have chemistry?"

"You're my boss."

"I told you last night, not after we leave work."

No, but he was still the subject of the investigation, and already she was having a tough time remaining impartial. "I could lose my job."

"I won't let that happen."

Maybe the makeover had been a bad idea. Of course, then he wouldn't have noticed her at all. Maybe the truth was, she wasn't cut out to be an undercover investigator. She wasn't cunning and clever. And she wasn't a manipulator. She wasn't even a very good liar. This was just too hard.

"Jane, do you like me?"

Why did he have to make this so difficult? "Yes, I like you, but—"

"And I like you too."

She almost asked him why. Why would someone like him like someone like her? Was it because of what he saw on the outside? Because she obviously didn't have the insides to match. "You barely know me."

"Is it too much to ask for the chance to *get* to know you?"

She chewed her lip, unsure of what to do, how to move forward. Though it defied logic, for some reason he seemed to be interested in her. There had to be a way to use that to her advantage. Could she use her ineptitude as a tool to string him along, to keep things from moving too quickly? To keep herself from getting into a situation that crossed the lines of morality?

It might actually work.

"Okay," she said.

He narrowed his eyes as if he didn't quite believe her. "Are you *sure?*"

"Yes, but under one condition. No one can know. When we're at work, I'm your secretary, nothing more. And that goes for the parking lot as well."

"Fine, but I have a condition too. You have to stop being afraid of me."

It's not as if she could shut it off like a switch. "I'll try."

"Maybe it would help if we break the ice."

"Break it how?"

"I think I should kiss you."

He thought *that* was going to make her less nervous? Just the idea had her heart racing. Not only because the thought of kissing him thrilled her, but she wasn't *supposed* to be kissing him. "Jordan—"

"Just one little kiss. It'll work. Trust me." He held out his hands. "Come here."

She looked at them nervously.

"I'm not going to bite," he said, then added with a grin, "unless you want me to."

At her wary look, he said, "Sorry, no more joking around." He wiggled his fingers. "Come here."

She really shouldn't be doing this, but honestly, what was the harm in one little kiss? Maybe it would eliminate that element of uncertainty. Besides, who would know?

She took a deep breath. *Okay, here we go. You can do this.*

She stepped toward him and took his hands, aware that hers were trembling. He held them loosely, very nonthreateningly. Without her high heels she was considerably shorter than him. At least six inches. She found herself focusing on the loosened knot of his tie.

"Jane, look at me."

She raised her eyes to his and just like last night in the parking lot, she was riveted. His irises were clear and bright; a mottled collage of brown and green flecks that were light at the outer edges, but grew darker and more intense as they reached the pupil. His eyes were just as extraordinary as the rest of him, and she couldn't stop herself from wondering again, what was he doing *here?* With *her?* Wasn't there an heiress or a supermodel he'd rather be kissing?

He tugged gently on her hands, drawing her closer. Her heart was beating so fast and hard it was becoming difficult to breathe. She hoped she didn't make an even bigger fool out of herself by dropping in a dead faint.

He lowered his head, leaning in, and she lifted her chin to meet him halfway, her eyes drifting closed. Then his lips brushed across hers.

Holy cow, she was kissing Jordan Everette. Or, he was kissing her. And it was…*perfect.*

If a soft peck felt this nice, she could just imagine how

a real kiss would feel. But she didn't want to imagine, she wanted to *know*.

He was right about one thing, she was feeling a whole mess of emotions right now, but the one she didn't feel was nervous.

He pulled back and looked down at her, searching her face, his voice a little rough when he said, "I know we agreed to one kiss, but you still look a little edgy to me."

One kiss, two. Who was counting, anyway?

He let go of her hands and reached up to cup her face in his palms, and the thrill of feeling him touch her made her knees go weak. This time when he kissed her, it wasn't a peck. This was deeper and hotter.

It wasn't as if she had never been kissed before, but she had never been kissed quite like this.

In what she considered a bold and daring move for someone like her, she reached up and laid her hands on his chest, feeling hard muscle and heat beneath his shirt. And he must have liked it because he made a gravelly sound in his throat. Then one of his hands dropped down to settle on her lower back, easing her in a little bit closer, against all that warmth and sinew. Probably too close, but at the same time not close enough.

One of his hands slipped under her sweatshirt, his palm settling against her bare skin, and in the same instant her leg buzzed where it was pressed against his thigh, as if he had a bee in his pants. She gasped with surprise at the unusual sensation and Jordan jerked his hand from beneath her shirt.

"Sorry. I'm supposed to be kissing you, not copping a feel."

"It's not that. Your leg is buzzing. It just startled me."

"It's my phone." He pulled it out of his pants pocket and

set it on the counter. "I have it on vibrate but it's rung four times since I've been here."

"Maybe you should answer it. It could be important."

"Being here with you is important too."

How was it that he always managed to say exactly the right thing? And as much as she wanted to keep kissing him, it was probably better that they take a break.

She stepped back, out of his reach. "You should at least look and see who it is."

He sighed and grabbed the phone from the counter, frowning as he thumbed through his recent calls. "There are three calls from Nathan, and two from Memorial Hospital."

"Call your brother, Jordan."

This time he didn't argue.

He dialed his phone and his brother must have answered on the first ring. "Why am I getting calls from Memorial Hospital?" Jordan asked him.

He listened for a minute, and she could tell by his deepening frown that something was wrong. Calls from hospitals were rarely ever favorable.

"But she's only fifty-four," he said. "Isn't she too young for that?" He listened for another minute, then said, "We can talk about it when I get there. I'm leaving right now."

He hung up his phone looking confused and a bit shell-shocked. "My mother had a stroke."

She gasped softly. "Is she okay?"

"They're not sure the extent of it yet, but they said she's not in any imminent danger. They have to run more tests."

Jane's maternal grandfather died from a massive stroke, so she knew from experience that it could be much worse. "Is there anything I can do?"

"I have the feeling this is going to be a long night, so I

probably won't be at work tomorrow. You'll have to hold down the fort."

"I can do that."

"I hate to bail on you, but I have to get to the hospital."

She touched his arm. "Of course. You should be with your family."

She followed him to the door where he put on his suit jacket, then his coat. "I'll call you tomorrow."

"If there's anything you need, just say the word."

"How about dinner Friday night?"

"I have dinner with my family Friday. But I'm free Saturday."

"You pick the place," he said, then he leaned down and kissed her, a soft brush of his lips that left her weak all over. "I'll see you later."

When he was gone, she closed the door, leaned against it and sighed. Oh, man, she was in trouble. If his phone hadn't rung, she could just imagine what they would be doing right now. And it would have nothing to do with drinking coffee and eating cake.

She wasn't supposed to like Jordan, but she did. Way too much for her own good. At least she was smart enough to realize that it wouldn't last. She was just a passing phase. She had to keep that in mind when he was kissing her, and touching her.

She couldn't deny that she was attracted to him, and being around him was a bit of a thrill, but it wouldn't last. If she wanted to come through this with her career intact, she needed to keep her perspective.

Next time they were alone, she wouldn't be giving in quite so easily.

Nine

Jordan didn't appreciate the severity of his mother's condition until he walked into her hospital room twenty minutes later. For some reason he expected her to be sitting up, her usual primped self, demanding and difficult and making a general nuisance of herself. He figured it was some sort of volley for attention. To see her lying in bed, pale and weak and hooked to a maze of tubes and wires was a shock. And though he had never seen her so much as flinch in the face of adversity, she was scared.

Nathan sat in a chair across the room. He stood when Jordan came in.

"Hey, Mom," Jordan said, walking to her bedside and taking her hand. She squeezed his weakly. "How are you feeling?"

She blinked rapidly and patted her throat.

"She can't talk," Nathan said.

He was about to ask why, but a nurse walked in.

"Time to change your IV, Ms. Everette," she said cheerfully.

Nathan nodded his head toward the door. Jordan tried to let go of his mother's hand to follow him, but she tightened her grip, looking panicked.

"Mom, I need to talk to Nathan for a minute. I promise I'll be right back."

She reluctantly let go of his hand. He followed his brother out into the hall. "She looks bad, Nathan."

"I know. But the doctor assured me that she's stable."

"Why can't she talk?"

"They think the stroke affected the speech center of her brain. She also has some weakness on her left side."

"But it's not permanent."

"He said that with physical therapy the weakness will improve, but she'll probably never be able to talk normally, even with speech therapy."

For a woman so hung up on appearances, that was going to be difficult for her to accept. "How did this happen? Isn't she too young?"

"Apparently not. The doctor did say that it would have been a lot worse if she'd waited any longer to come in."

"How did she get here?"

"A gentleman friend. I guess she called him and she wasn't making any sense. He suspected something was wrong and called 911."

Jordan's heart bottomed out. He leaned against the wall beside the door, shaking his head at the depth of his stupidity. "Son of a bitch."

"What?"

"She called me too. She was slurring her words and asking about things we already talked about. I thought she was drunk. I should have realized something was really wrong."

"Jordan, there's no way you could have known. Like you said, she's not that old. A stroke was the last thing we would have expected. If she had called me I probably would have assumed the same thing."

But she hadn't. She'd called him. She'd needed his help and he had completely failed her. If she hadn't called her "man friend" who knows how much worse off she could be? She could have *died*.

"I should have at least gone and checked on her," he said.

"You know that if it were one of us with a problem, she probably wouldn't even be bothered to show up at the hospital."

That didn't make him feel any less guilty. If he had realized there was a problem and called 911 immediately, maybe the damage would have been less severe.

When they walked back into the room she was waiting anxiously. After that, any time he and Nathan even got close to the door she would get a panicked look, but when she tried to speak, the words came out garbled and slurred.

She drifted in and out of sleep all night while the brothers took turns sitting at her bedside. Nathan had called their father as a courtesy, even though he and their mother hadn't spoken a civilized word in years, so both Nathan and Jordan were shocked when he came to visit Wednesday afternoon. Even more shocking was that she looked happy to see him.

It gave Jordan and his brother a chance to sneak off to the cafeteria to grab a cup of coffee and a bite to eat.

"She's not going to be able to stay by herself for at least a couple of weeks," Nathan said. "Maybe even longer. We'll have to hire a full-time nurse. And both speech and physical therapists."

"Or she could stay with you," Jordan said, grinning at the look his brother shot him.

"I would never do that to Ana. Although, the fact that she can't talk will make her a lot less annoying."

"That's a horrible thing to say," Jordan said, but he was trying not to smile.

"It's pretty ironic, don't you think? She couldn't be bothered to be there for us, but we're expected to take care of her."

"She's really scared. I've never seen her like this. It's hard not to feel sorry for her."

"I give her a month before she's back to her demanding and manipulative old self."

Jordan wasn't so sure about that. Maybe this would be a wake-up call for her. A chance to become a decent mother—a decent human being—before it was too late. Or maybe he was just fooling himself.

"I sure was surprised when Dad showed up," Nathan said. "Or maybe it isn't such a surprise, all things considered."

"What do you mean?"

"I think he still loves her."

"Still? I didn't know he ever did. I thought they had to get married because she was pregnant."

"I thought so too, but Dad says no. He told me, and I quote, 'He loved her more than life itself, and all she wanted from him was his name and as much of his money as she could get her greedy hands on.'"

"I guess that explains why he was always so unhappy."

"He told me that he was bitter and heartbroken and instead of taking it out on the person who deserved it, he took it out on us. The same way Grandma Everette took it out on him."

Jordan laughed. "Get out. Frail little Grandma Everette used to knock Dad around?"

"That's what he said. And she probably wasn't so frail back then."

Damn. It was tough to imagine their father letting anyone push him around. And Jordan had just assumed that their parents hated each other. He never understood why they had stayed together for twenty years. Maybe their father had held on to the hope that she would grow to love him. Clearly that had never happened.

When they finished their lunch and got back to their mother's room their dad was still there. He was sitting on the edge of the bed holding her hand. As far as Jordan could recall it was the first time he'd ever seen them touch.

He just hoped she wasn't afraid and clinging to the past. He hoped she wasn't using their father, and as soon as she was well would cast him aside yet again. He hoped, but given her behavior since…well, as long as Jordan could recall, the odds weren't very good.

Though she felt more than a little devious for taking advantage of the situation, Jordan's absence had given Jane unlimited access to his office for two days. She had to keep reminding herself that it was her job, and really, she was doing him a favor. If she wasn't able to prove he was guilty, that could only mean that he was innocent. His career would be safe, and he would be none the wiser.

That was what she hoped anyway.

She searched through his files but there was nothing incriminating, so, using the jump drive, she downloaded his emails—which weren't password protected—and spend most of the afternoon at her computer reading them. She also uploaded a spyware program that would make it possible for the tech guys at Edwin Associates to monitor any future emails.

Most of his current emails were of a professional nature, and the handful that were personal had nothing to do with the sabotage, nor were they the least bit suspicious. What she needed to see were his personal financial files, but he obviously didn't keep those at work, meaning she needed to get on to his personal computer at home. When she reported her findings, or lack thereof, to her superiors, they reached the same conclusion. She was to continue to monitor his phone calls and take the steps necessary to infiltrate his home. She also wanted to get a look at his incoming and outgoing calls on his cell phone. Until there were grounds for a warrant, they couldn't get a hold of the call records from his provider.

Her bosses seemed pleased, and maybe a little surprised, to learn that Mr. Everette was actually pursuing her, and if they were concerned about her crossing any lines, they didn't mention it. If it meant getting the information they needed, maybe they would forgive a few minor transgressions. The question was, could she? Could she sell herself out that way?

Between the investigation and her regular duties, Jane was swamped, so she stayed late Thursday to keep on top of things. She didn't get home until after ten. She grabbed her mail on her way into the building and rifled through it as she walked up the stairs to the second floor—her Visa bill, a few pieces of junk and something that looked like a wedding invitation. Curious, she started to rip it open as she walked down the hall to her apartment.

"I was beginning to think you weren't coming home," someone said. She squeaked with surprise, stumbling to a stop and dropping the mail.

Jordan grinned up at her from where he sat on the floor outside her apartment door. "Late night at work?"

Her heart lifted at the sight of him, then took a sharp dive. "Did something happen? Is your mom okay?"

"She's fine," he said as he pushed himself to his feet. He was dressed in black slacks and a black leather jacket. "In fact, they're cutting her loose tomorrow."

She crouched down to collect her mail. "What are you doing here?"

He shrugged, looking physically and emotionally drained. "All I know is, I was on my way home from the hospital to get some sleep, and somehow I ended up here. I guess I just wanted to see you."

She didn't even know what to say. Of all the people he could have gone to, he chose her?

"I know I shouldn't keep dropping in on you un-announced."

"No, it's okay." She walked past him to unlock the door.

"I can leave if it's a bad time."

She pushed the door open and switched on the light. "It's not a bad time. Come in."

He walked inside, and she stepped in behind him, closing and locking the door. She turned to tell him to take off his jacket, but before she could get the words out his arms were around her, pulling her close, hugging her fiercely. She dropped her purse and wrapped her arms around him, hugging him just as hard.

He buried his face against the side of her neck, his breath warm on her skin. "You cannot even imagine how long and stressful the past two days have been."

"Do you want to talk about it?"

"Right now, I think I'd just like to hold you."

That was okay too.

Since it was what he seemed to need, she held him close,

rubbing his back, until she could feel the tension begin to leak out of him. Seeing this vulnerable side of him, knowing that he even had one, changed her perception of him somehow. Yes, he was rich and powerful and gorgeous, but underneath it all, he was just a man. An extraordinary one, unquestionably, but nothing to feel threatened or intimidated by. In fact, it was a kind of a turn-on.

"Have I ever told you how good you smell?" he asked.

Something in his voice, in the way he nuzzled her neck, made her heart beat a little faster.

He lifted his head and pressed his forehead to hers, eyelids heavy as he looked down at her. "Okay, I lied."

"About what?"

"I want to kiss you. I've been thinking about it almost constantly for the past two days."

The thrill she felt knowing he wanted her seemed to cancel out any shred of her common sense. "So, kiss me."

She didn't have to tell him twice. And, oh, could he kiss. If she never kissed another man as long as she lived, she would go to her grave knowing she could never find anyone who did it better. And something told her that this time it wouldn't end there.

She didn't want it to.

He let go of her to take his jacket off, then he pushed her coat off her shoulders to the floor. When he started to unfasten the buttons on her jacket, she knew in the back of her mind there was a reason this was wrong, why she should tell him to stop, but for the life of her she couldn't remember why. She didn't *want* to remember.

He pulled her jacket open but he didn't take it off. Instead he gazed down at her, tracing a finger along her skin just above the silk shell she was wearing. "You are so beautiful, Jane."

He made her *feel* beautiful. As if she deserved this.

He dipped his finger below the shell to caress the uppermost swell of her breasts. First the left, then the right, and her breath started coming faster.

"If you're going to tell me to stop, do it now," he said, his voice rough. "Because I'm about two minutes from taking you into your bedroom and making love to you."

She fisted his shirt and tugged it from the waist of his pants. "It's the second door on the right."

With a look that could melt snow, he scooped her off her feet and carried her—actually *carried* her—down the hall to her bedroom. A little voice asked her what the heck she thought she was doing. She wasn't actually going to sleep with him, was she? Because that was against the rules. But for the first time in her entire life she didn't care about the rules. She wanted to do something totally illogical and completely spontaneous. She didn't care if it was bad for her, as long as it felt good.

Jordan set her on her feet beside the bed and she kicked off her shoes. "We need light," he said.

She switched the lamp on, hoping, as she tugged her jacket off, then pulled her top over her head, he wasn't disappointed by what he saw. Did she look as good as he made her feel?

"Don't stop there," he said, unbuttoning his shirt as he watched her. "Keep going."

She had never done a striptease for anyone, but he filled her with a confidence she'd never felt before. And maybe it was wrong, but she would do just about anything right now to make him happy.

She reached back to unzip her skirt, thankful, as she wiggled out of it, that she'd worn her matching black lace bra and panties. His low growl as his gaze slipped down to her legs said he was a man who appreciated thigh-high stockings.

"The bra too," he said, watching her intently. If she didn't know any better, she might think he was challenging her, seeing just how far he could push. Maybe he was.

She undid the clasp and slipped it off, then hooked her thumbs in the waist of her panties and eased them down, but when she reached for the elastic edge of the thigh-high he shook his head. "Those can stay. My turn now."

She waited for him to start undressing, and when he didn't, when he grinned and said, "What are you waiting for?" she realized that he wanted *her* to undress him.

He'd probably been with dozens of women, most more experienced or well-versed in making love than she was, but she didn't care. She was here now. And she knew somewhere deep down that this was special. He had picked *her*.

His shirt was already unbuttoned, so she pushed it off his shoulders. He was so beautiful, so *perfect*.

He fished his wallet from his back pocket and tossed it on the bedside table. Probably because that was where he kept the condoms, and they were going to be needing one. The thought made her knees go weak. She was really going to do it, she was going to sleep with him.

"Keep going," he said.

She unhooked his belt then unfastened his pants, pushing them down. He kicked them, and his shoes out of the way, then bent over to pull his socks off. All that was left was his boxers, and if the tent in the front was any indiction, she was going to like what she found underneath.

"On or off," he said. "Your call."

Why did she get the feeling he thought she wouldn't do it? The old Jane would probably be afraid. She would be worried that she would do something wrong and disappoint him. But this was the new Jane, and she was no longer afraid of anything.

She grasped the elastic waistband and pulled them down, then she circled his erection in her hand and squeezed. He groaned and heat pulsed against her palm. She smiled up at him and said, "Off."

She felt like she would go crazy if he didn't touch her soon, and he didn't make her wait. He sat back on the bed and pulled her down with him, rolling her over so that she was on her back and he was looking down at her. Then he kissed her, and she felt so hot with lust, if not for her skin holding her together, she would have melted into the sheets.

He didn't hedge or fumble. He knew exactly what to do to drive her crazy without her ever having to utter a word. His solitary goal, as far as she could tell, was to give her as much pleasure as possible, as many times as possible, before he would even think about himself.

She'd heard that men like him existed, but she honestly believed it was a myth, that those women who bragged about their generous lovers were all lying through their teeth and really had the same boring and pathetically unsatisfying sex lives as she did.

Boy, had she been wrong.

It seemed like forever before he finally grabbed his wallet and pulled out a condom. He pushed her thighs apart and knelt between them, dangling the package in front of her. "Care to do the honors?"

She'd never actually "done the honors" before but if that was what he wanted she would try. She didn't even care if she fumbled a bit. And somehow she didn't think he would either.

She took the packet from him and tore it open with her teeth. As she rolled it down the length of him he closed his eyes and sucked in a breath, digging his fingers into the meat of her calves. She probably took a little longer than necessary, but he wasn't complaining.

When she was finished she asked, "Is that right?"

He opened his eyes and gazed down at her handiwork. "Looks good to me." He grinned and added, "Felt good too."

He lowered himself over her. "Are you ready?"

She was ready the minute he walked through the door.

She wrapped her legs around his waist, pulling him closer, and with his eyes locked on hers, he slowly thrust inside of her. She had some random, fleeting thought about how this wasn't supposed to be happening, but as he groaned and thrust again, the last remnants of doubt fizzled away. And as he rolled over on to his back, pulling her on top of him, all that she cared about was making him feel good.

It was no-holds-barred, pulse-pounding, headboard-banging, twisted-in-the-sheets, rolling-all-over-the-bed sex. And it was *fun*. She had no idea that sex was supposed to be fun.

Afterward, they both lay flat on their backs, side by side, limp and satisfied. And only then did the possible repercussions of her lack of good sense hit her square between the eyes.

What had his brother Nathan told her? Jordan had a short attention span when it came to women. He liked the chase, but once he got what he was after, he lost interest. So of course, genius that she was, she'd gone and given him exactly what he wanted with practically no effort on his part whatsoever.

Brilliant.

In one act of pure idiocy she had compromised her

principles, crossed the lines of morality and put the investigation in the toilet.

Way to go, Jane.

There had to be a way to begin repairing the damage she'd done. A good start would be to get him the heck out of her bed, back into his clothes and out the door. That was when she realized how quiet he'd become. She pushed herself up on her elbows to look at him. His eyes were closed.

"Jordan?"

He didn't answer. She gave his arm a gentle nudge, and when that got no response, she gave it a shake. Nothing. He was out cold. He had actually rolled over and gone to sleep.

How was that for a cliché?

Of course, considering he'd barely slept for two days, and then had a vigorous workout, she could hardly fault him; besides, that was the least of her worries. The sad fact was, she wouldn't be sleeping with him again.

She shook him again. "Jordan, wake up."

He mumbled something incoherent and rolled onto his side.

It looked as though she had no choice but to let him stay the night, since nothing short of a dousing with ice water was going to wake him. And though she doubted he would rouse anytime soon, just in case, she would have to leave her makeup on, so he didn't see how she actually looked. Then he would *really* lose interest.

He didn't budge when she untangled his feet from the blankets and covered them both, nor when she leaned over him to switch off the light. She lay there wide awake beside him, listening to his slow, deep breaths, plotting her next move.

She sighed. It was going to be a really long night.

Ten

The smell of coffee woke Jordan from a dead sleep. He opened his eyes, confused for a second by the unfamiliar room, then he remembered last night and smiled. He rolled over and reached for Jane, but her side of the bed was empty and cold.

Rubbing the sleep from his eyes, and some moisture into his contacts, he grabbed his watch from the bedside table and squinted to read it. Seven-thirty. He should have been up over an hour ago. But he was having a tough time caring, considering how freaking incredible last night had been.

He'd come here with the expectation of some harmless necking, and thought—or hoped—that if he played his cards right he might cop a feel or two. Well, so much for her so-called lack of confidence with men. He'd been with supermodels who were nowhere close to as comfortable in their own skin as Jane had seemed to be last night. She had completely blown him away, surpassing by leaps and bounds every preconceived notion he had drawn since she stumbled into his life Monday morning.

The idea of the timid and apprehensive Jane had intrigued him, but the real Jane fascinated and bewitched him.

He shoved himself up out of bed, grabbed his clothes from the floor and got dressed, then followed the scent of coffee to the kitchen.

Jane was sitting at the table, already primped and dressed for work, drinking coffee and working on her laptop.

"Good morning."

She looked up and smiled. "Good morning. There's coffee. Can I get you a cup?"

"I'll get it," he said, pressing a kiss to the top of her head as he walked past. There was already a cup and the creamer waiting on the counter beside the coffee press. "Sorry I conked out like that last night. I don't even remember falling asleep."

"I figured you were pretty tired."

"So tired I didn't even take my contacts out," he said as he fixed his coffee.

"You wear contacts?"

"Since college when I finally ditched the glasses. Without them I'm blind as a bat." He carried his coffee to the table and sat across from her. Maybe it was his imagination, but there was a weird vibe. Not the typical "morning after" glow. At least not what he would expect after an evening of sex that was, if he was being totally honest, about as good as it ever got.

Jane closed her laptop and pushed it aside. "I wear the kind you can leave in, so I don't have to take them out."

"Me too, but it feels good to take them out every few

days. Especially when I haven't gotten much sleep." He sipped his coffee, then set the cup down and asked, "So, is there a reason we're discussing contact lenses and not what happened last night?"

She cradled her cup in her palms, running her thumbs along the brim. "Last night was...*wow*."

"Yes it was."

"It meant more to me than you could possibly imagine."

Oh boy. If she was about to tell him that she loved him he would have a serious problem.

He must have looked uneasy, because she smiled and said, "Don't worry, I'm not picking out china patterns or anything. It's completely the opposite. I feel as if I've been walking around with my eyes closed, and being with you has finally opened them."

"I'm not sure I follow you."

"This is a little embarrassing, but, Drake was my first serious boyfriend."

"Serious, as in..."

"He's the only man I ever slept with. And it was never... Well, let's just say it was *nothing* like last night. I had no idea it could be so...so..."

"Remarkable?"

"*Yes!* All this time I had no idea what I was missing. And if I had married Drake, I never would have known." She reached across the table and put her hand over his. "For a long time I've just been drifting. I didn't know that there was more to life, so I didn't even bother trying to find something better. Now I feel as if I'm actually ready to move on. Meet new people and take chances. I feel like there's someone out there who can actually make me happy."

Someone other than him, she meant.

That was harsh. Especially for her, who didn't seem

to have a vindictive or mean bone in her body. Every time he thought he had her pegged, she did something to completely blow his perception. Or was this an act? A part of her cover. Or did she really feel that way? Either way, it worked just fine for him, because he didn't do forever. He didn't even do long-term.

"So what you're saying is you're dumping me. After one night?"

"Come on, Jordan, you can't dump someone that you aren't technically with. I like you. I could probably love you. But there's just no future for us. It's not what you want. You're not a forever kind of guy, and that's what I'm looking for. What I need."

This was the part when he should be relieved that she was giving him an out, so he wouldn't have to break her heart later. So why instead did he feel...slighted?

"I'm almost thirty. If I'm going to have a family I have to start thinking about settling down. Oh, and speaking of settling down..." she let go of his hand "...look what came in yesterday's mail."

He took the white card she held out. It was an invitation. For Drake and Megan's wedding. "Wow. How totally inappropriate."

"I know. What moron thinks it's okay to invite the woman he dumped for his fiancée to the wedding? It defies logic."

"Not if you're an arrogant ass."

"I keep thinking about how it must have made Megan feel that he even wanted to invite me. I actually feel sorry for her. Granted, she's not the sharpest tool in the shed, but she's a sweet person."

"Should I assume you won't be attending?"

"Are you kidding? I won't even justify it with a response. But you're right, I do need to go to the reunion. To show him that I really don't care about him anymore, because honestly, I don't."

"I'd still be happy to go as your date."

"I think this is something I need to do on my own. And under the circumstances, I don't think it would be a good idea. But that doesn't mean I wouldn't like us to be friends."

How many women had he used a variation of that exact line on? Probably too many to count. To date, he was friends with none of them.

What if he didn't want to be "friends"? What if he wanted more?

As far as he could tell, he had two choices. He could honor her wishes and back off, or he could agree with her, tell her they could be friends, then seduce her anyway.

Jane sat at her desk, finishing up a few last minute things so she could meet her family for dinner. She glanced over at Jordan's office. Other than a short lunch meeting, he'd been in there all day with the door shut.

She had been stressing all day, worried that she'd overdone it with her let's-just-be-friends speech that morning. She hoped that by turning him down, she would actually make him want her more. That he would see it as a challenge. Telling him that she was looking for a serious relationship had been a risky move, but she had given it a lot of thought and she was confident it would do the trick.

At least, she was *trying* to be confident. Deep down she was terrified that she had completely blown it. All she could do now was wait for his next move. The ball was in his court.

At six-thirty she shut down her computer, grabbed her coat and purse, then rapped on Jordan's door.

"Come in," he called, so she opened it. He was at his desk, engrossed in whatever was on his computer screen.

"I just wanted to let you know that I'm leaving for the night," she said.

"Okay," he said, glancing up at her. "I'll see you Monday."

"See you Monday." She closed the door, frowning. She had half expected him to mention the date that they were supposed to go on Saturday night, and maybe suggest that they go as friends.

He was taking her brush-off a little too well.

She walked to her car, a knot in the pit of her belly. In her attempt to fix this, had she only made matters worse?

It wasn't until she was at the restaurant, and caught a glimpse of her reflection in the glass door, that she remembered her family hadn't yet seen her new look. The suit and high heels she couldn't do much about, but she could probably slip into the ladies room and remove her makeup before going to the table.

Take off her makeup? What was she, a *child?*

No, she was an adult woman who had just as much right to wear makeup as anyone else, and wear whatever clothes she wanted. Whatever weird hold her family still had over her, it needed to stop.

Besides, knowing them, they probably wouldn't even notice.

The hostess took her coat and she walked to the table, where everyone was already seated and had been served drinks. And contrary to what she had anticipated, there were no birthday balloons or banners. No gifts in sight.

Well, that didn't mean they weren't going to celebrate. "Hi everyone. Sorry I'm late."

Everyone looked up to greet her, and seven jaws dropped in perfect unison.

Okay, so maybe they would notice.

Mary was the first to find her voice. "Oh my God, are you wearing *makeup?*" she asked, as if Jane had just committed some unforgivable crime. Both Mary and her mother were wearing makeup and no one seemed to have a problem with that.

"Yeah, so what?" she said, sliding into the empty chair beside her sister and setting her purse on the floor by her feet.

"What did you do to your hair?" her oldest brother Richard asked.

"I had it styled." She opened her menu. "Have we decided what we're ordering?"

"What's with the suit?" her brother Will asked. "Did you come from a costume party or something? And where are your glasses?"

A costume party. Nice.

She glared at him. "I traded my glasses in for contacts, and the suit is new."

"Is this about Drake?" her father asked. "I heard that he's engaged."

He would have to bring that up. "This has nothing to do with Drake or anyone else. I just felt like I needed a change. And I don't appreciate getting the third degree."

"Can you blame us for being curious, sweetheart?" her mom said. "We hardly see you, then you come in looking so…different. Sometimes I feel as if I don't even know you anymore."

Was it too much to expect her family to be happy for her, or at least support her decisions? Why did everything have to be a fight with them? It seemed as though whatever she did lately they saw as a further departure from the fold.

"I think she looks fabulous," Richard's wife, Cyan, announced, and Jane sent her a grateful smile. "That suit is super-chic and I love the new hairstyle. The cut and color really complement your complexion and the shape of your face. And the shade of shadow you're wearing really makes your eyes pop."

Cyan was the owner of a fashion consulting firm that catered to the uber-wealthy and chic, so the compliment really meant something coming from her.

"I think she does too," Sara piped in. A quiet and unassuming first grade teacher, Will's wife tended to fade into the background during family functions. Sort of like an adorable potted plant. It wasn't easy competing for attention with a bunch of outspoken, power-hungry professionals. Jane knew. She had been trying most of her life, but she lacked the killer instinct. Which is probably why she'd let her family roll over her and make her decisions for her for so many years, and why they felt so threatened now that she was finally gaining her independence.

"I don't think anyone is suggesting that Jane doesn't look good," her dad said, shooting Sara a look that made her shrink low in her chair. Always pick on the weakest, that was her family's motto. "We're just concerned."

"Are you having some sort of premidlife crisis?" Richard asked.

"Can we just drop this?" Jane asked.

"You don't have to be such a bitch about it," Mary mumbled and Jane had the very immature inclination to pull her hair. It was her freaking birthday for God's sake, or at least it had been Tuesday, and not a single one of them had even acknowledged it.

The waiter appeared to take their food orders and along with the lasagna she doubted she would even eat, she ordered a pomegranate martini. After he left, the conversation turned to the family practice, which under normal circumstances would irritate her, but she was just relieved they were no longer focused on her. She ordered a second martini when the salad was served, then another when the main course arrived. At the rate she was going, she'd have to take a cab home.

She picked at her dinner, trying not to let it depress her that despite what she'd believed, they really didn't plan to celebrate her birthday. Her entire family had forgotten. The minute they had gotten over the initial shock of her new appearance, she was back to being invisible. They didn't even ask her about work, or what she'd been up to.

Jane decided that she would duck out before everyone ordered an after-dinner drink. She opened her mouth to tell them she was going, when behind her someone said, "Jane?"

At the sound of the familiar voice, her heart plummeted. In an instant this dinner went from sad and depressing to her worst nightmare.

She turned in her seat, hoping it just sounded like him, but was actually someone else, and for a second she thought maybe it was. In faded jeans, cowboy boots and a black, untucked shirt with the sleeves rolled up, Jordan looked like a regular guy—albeit a breathtakingly gorgeous one.

"I thought that was you," he said.

She shot up from her chair. "Jordan...hi."

This could not be happening. Her undercover assignment did not just walk in on dinner with her *entire* family! "What are you doing here?"

"I was in the bar, having drinks with a friend. I was just getting ready to leave when I thought I saw you sitting there." He flashed her a grin that made her stomach flop. "Small world, huh?"

One hell of a lot smaller than she'd ever imagined.

Although she had the sneaking suspicion that their bumping into one another was no accident.

Yes, she had hoped he would pursue her, but not in the middle of a family dinner!

"Honey," her father said. "Aren't you going to introduce us to your friend?"

Jane realized everyone at the table was watching them. Figures that *now* they would notice her. Although it was Jordan they were focused on.

She had no choice but to introduce him.

"This is Jordan Everette. Jordan, this is my family."

He shook hands with everyone, and she hoped that once the introductions were out of the way, he would leave.

"Jordan, why don't you pull up a chair, have a drink," her father said.

"I don't want to intrude."

"Don't be silly," her mother said, in her sweet, Southern-belle tone. "We would love it if you'd join us."

"In that case I'd be happy to."

Crap.

He pulled up a chair from a neighboring table and sat beside Jane, lounging casually, so close their thighs were practically touching. She wished he would back off a little. She didn't want her parents to get the impression that they were involved.

Her father signaled the waiter and everyone ordered drinks. Jordan asked for a Chivas on the rocks. Jane ordered another martini.

"So, do you and Jane work together?" Rick asked Jordan.

Jane's pulse started to hammer. She had told Jordan about how she was deceiving her family about her job, but if he slipped up and said something about them working together at Western Oil, she was dead meat.

"No, I'm in the oil business," Jordan told him.

She was so relieved that if she hadn't been sitting, her legs would have given out.

"What do you do?" Will asked.

"I'm in management."

Jane could see everyone digesting that information. Her family could smell money and power a mile away, and though Jordan wasn't dressed like an executive, and he was young, the platinum Rolex on his left wrist said he was either old money, or at least upper middle management. They probably figured he pulled in a salary in the low to middle six figures. And she wasn't about to set them straight.

"So, are you two dating?" Mary asked.

"Mary!" Jane snapped.

"I've asked her out," Jordan said, grinning adorably, draping his arm over the back of her chair and pinning her with that judgment-wrecking gaze. "But she turned me down."

He was obviously teasing her. She just wished he would do it from a little farther away. The scent of his aftershave was shorting out her brain. His looks he couldn't really help, but he could at least have the decency not to smell so darned good.

She tore her gaze from Jordan's and turned to her sister. "We're just friends."

The waiter brought their drinks, then Jordan asked about the law practice, and that became the focus of the conversation. Though her defection from the fold was mentioned, thankfully no one dwelled on it. In fact, her name didn't come up much at all. But of course her parents didn't hesitate to sing the praises of her sister and brothers and their many legal accomplishments. But what else was new? Jane may have had more of her own accomplishments if they hadn't continually held her back. She was hands down a better attorney than her sister, yet Mary had been allowed to build an impressive client base while Jane had been given the grunt work.

She was sure they were all curious as to why someone so charming and personable and devastatingly attractive would have any interest in being friends with someone like her. Maybe that was why Mary flirted shamelessly the entire time. Maybe she thought that because he and Jane were just friends, it was okay. Or maybe she was doing it to show her up. It wouldn't be the first time.

Jane had skipped two grades, so she was only one grade behind her sister in high school, and it never failed, if she showed any interest in a boy, Mary would go after him with all pistons firing. And if Jane complained, Mary's answer was always the same. "What's the big deal? It's not as if he would ever go out with *you*."

And she was right. But that didn't make it hurt any less, or make Jane feel any less betrayed.

After a second round of drinks, Jordan said he had to go.

"It's early," her mother said. "There's no need to rush off."

"Yes, you should stay," her father said.

"I really need to go." He pushed up from his chair. "It was a pleasure meeting everyone."

"The pleasure was ours," her father said, shaking his hand.

"I hope we'll see you again," her mother said, shooting Jane a look that said she was out of her mind for not snapping him up and marrying him at the first possible opportunity.

"It was really nice meeting you," Mary said, shaking his hand and holding it several seconds longer than Jane considered appropriate. Would it be totally immature to give her a good hard knock in the head?

When she finally let go, Jordan turned to Jane. "I guess I'll see you around."

Jane knew that if she stayed after he left, she would be subjected to the third degree all over again. She didn't like being ignored, but being grilled wasn't a whole lot of fun either. There was no happy medium with her family. Leaving with Jordan was her only chance for escape, so she hopped to her feet and said, "I should get going too. I'll walk out with you."

Eleven

"Are you sure?" Jordan asked.

She was *so* sure. "Yeah, I should get home. It's been a busy week and I'm exhausted."

She said a quick goodbye to her family, who didn't even implore her to stay. Nice. It was great to know that they cared.

Only as she walked away from the table did she realize just how tipsy she was feeling. When she and Jordan got to the lobby, and were waiting for the hostess to fetch their coats, she leaned up against the wall for stability.

"Your family seems nice," Jordan said.

"Yeah. They do *seem* nice."

His brow rose. "Are you suggesting that they aren't?"

"They're a family of extremes. Either they're demanding and bossy and trying to run my life, or they ignore me completely."

"You know that your sister is jealous of you."

She laughed. "Jealous of what? She's pretty and successful."

"And she obviously doesn't like you having something that she can't."

"What do you mean?"

He reached into his jeans pocket and handed her a business card. *Mary's* business card. "She stuck it in my hand when I was saying goodbye."

Jane shook her head. Un-freaking-believable. Clearly nothing had changed.

She tried to hand the card back to him and he said, "You keep it. I won't be needing it."

That made her smile.

The hostess appeared with their coats and when Jordan helped her into hers, she nearly lost her balance.

"You okay?" he asked, grabbing her arm to steady her.

"Yeah, I think I had two or three martinis too many. My family often has that effect on me."

"Then you shouldn't be driving."

"I would never drive impaired. I'll call a cab."

"Why would you pay for a cab when I can give you a lift home? I'll even arrange to have your car delivered to you so you don't have to come back and get it."

It would be silly to turn down the ride. Now that she knew she still had his interest, she had to be sure to keep it. Without overplaying her hand this time. "That would be great, thanks."

He ushered her outside and handed his valet slip to the attendant, who dashed off and pulled up a minute later in a shiny silver sports car that looked a little like the Batmobile. And very expensive. It was exactly the sort of car she pictured Jordan driving.

He helped her in, then walked around and got in the driver's side. The interior was dark gray leather and smelled like a mix of new car and Jordan's cologne. A country station was playing on the radio, which surprised her a little. He struck her as more of the classic rock type.

"So, what kind of car is this?" she asked as he pulled out of the lot and zipped into traffic.

"A Porsche Spyder Coupe."

"It's nice."

"Thanks."

"How much does a car like this cost, if you don't mind my asking."

"Six hundred and some change," he said, downshifting to turn a corner.

"Six hundred *thousand?* That's... Wow."

He looked over at her and grinned. "Yeah, but it makes me look good."

It sure did. And it was a testament to just how loaded he was. He was so easygoing and unpretentious, she sometimes forgot the magnitude of his wealth and power. And for whatever reason, he wanted *her*.

The thought made her smile.

"So, I figured you would be celebrating your birthday with your family tonight."

The smile slipped from her face. "Yeah, me too."

He glanced over at her. "Are you saying that they *forgot?*"

She shrugged and said, "It's not a big deal." And if she kept telling herself that, maybe she would start believing it.

"Have you ever forgotten one of their birthdays?"

Of course not. She was reliable Jane. "I think it's my punishment for leaving the practice, for going against their wishes. Sometimes they act like I'm not even a part of the family any longer."

He reached over and brushed her hair back from her

face. It was such a sweet gesture, for some stupid reason it made her feel like crying. But she was not the crying type, so it must have been the alcohol.

"Families suck," he said.

Wasn't that the truth. She was so tired of feeling as if she wasn't good enough, as though what she wanted, and her happiness, didn't matter. She sighed and laid her head back, letting her eyes drift closed. She listened to the melody playing softly on the radio, and Jordan's voice singing slightly off-key with Keith Urban.

She must have drifted off, because the next thing she knew, Jordan was calling her name and nudging her awake.

Jane's eyes fluttered open and she bolted upright. "I'm sorry. Did I fall asleep?"

"It's okay," Jordan said, rubbing her shoulder. "We're here."

She looked out the windshield, a frown creasing her brow. "Um…where is *here?*"

He cut the engine. "The parking garage of my building."

"I thought you were taking me home."

"I did. To my home."

She shot him an exasperated look.

He grinned. "I'm sorry, did you want me to take you to *your* home?"

She shook her head and laughed, as if she thought he was hopeless. "Yeah, that was the idea."

He liked making her smile, making her happy. "Well, in my defense, you never actually specified. But since you're already here, you may as well come up and have a look around." After all, that was probably part of her plan to get information. She must have figured out by now that there was nothing in his office to suggest he had anything to do with the sabotage. Logically the next place to look would be his home. Not that she would find anything there either, but she could try. He wanted her to know that he would never do anything to hurt anyone. He didn't even know why he cared. He just did.

"Jordan—"

"Listen, it's nine o'clock on a Friday night and you're clearly upset. What kind of friend would I be if I let you spend the evening alone watching Arnold Schwarzenegger, scarfing caramel nut swirl ice cream."

He could tell by her expression, that was exactly what she would have done.

"You must think I'm an idiot for even caring what they think," she said.

He draped his arm over the back of her seat, leaning in. "Jane, I just spent two days at the bedside of a mother who missed my high school graduation because she had a hair appointment."

"Seriously?"

"Seriously. So who do you think is the bigger idiot?"

For a long moment she just looked at him, searching his face. "How do you do it?"

"Do what?"

"Always manage to say exactly the right thing," she said, then she slipped her hand behind his neck, pulled him closer and kissed him. It was the last thing he expected. He thought he was going to have to work for it, seduce her into seeing things his way. He wasn't sure *what* he'd done but obviously it had worked.

She broke the kiss and gazed up at him. "Take me upstairs, Jordan, right now, before I change my mind."

"Let's go."

They got out of the car and crossed the garage to the elevator. The second they were inside, and the doors slid closed, her arms were around him and her lips were on his.

He had kissed a lot of women, but no one put more heart and soul into it. More honesty. If he were a better man, he would take into consideration the fact that she was slightly compromised by the drinks, and maybe not thinking one hundred percent clearly, but as she rubbed her hand over the crotch of his jeans she seemed to know exactly what she wanted. And there was no question for him either.

The doors opened at the top floor. He grabbed her hand and pulled her into the foyer of his penthouse.

"You own the entire top floor?" she asked.

"I own the building. I live on the top floor." He punched his code into the pad and opened the door, pulling her inside. It was dark, but for the lamp next to the couch.

"Wow," Jane said, taking in the open-concept space, tugging her jacket off and draping it across the back of an overstuffed chair. "This is nice. It's not at all what I expected."

He did the same with his jacket. "What did you expect?"

"Something more modern. Glass and steel and black leather. And I like the dark wood and the earth tones, and the furniture looks so soft and comfortable" She unbuttoned the jacket of her suit and tossed that on the chair too. She wore another one of those sleeveless, silky numbers underneath. "It's so…homey and warm."

"Thanks," he said, unbuttoning his shirt. "I've always believed a house should be a home. Although I can't really take credit. I hired a decorator."

She nodded to the bank of windows across the room, clearly dazzled by the panoramic view of the city. "The view is amazing."

"It's the main reason I bought the building."

She pulled her top over her head and dropped it on the growing pile. She wore a sheer white bra underneath. Her breasts were on the small side, but what she had was so beautiful, he didn't care. He had always been more of a leg man, and hers were long and lean and perfect, especially when they were wrapped around his waist. Or his shoulders, or pretty much any part of his body.

She unzipped her skirt and pushed it down her legs. Under it she wore a matching thong and, hot damn, those thigh-high stockings.

She grabbed the front of his shirt, backed herself against the wall beside the door and pulled him in for a kiss. And damn could she kiss. She pushed the shirt off his shoulders and he tugged it down his arms. She arched her back, rubbing her lace-covered breasts against his chest, devouring his mouth. He slipped a hand inside her panties and she moaned, biting down on his lower lip. He dipped into her wet heat, teasing her with feather-light strokes.

Her breath was coming harder and faster. He yanked the cup of her bra down and licked the tip of her breast, then he sucked it into his mouth. She gasped and her head fell back. Since she seemed to like it, he did the same thing to the other side. She moaned and started to shake all over, then her body clamped down hard around his fingers. He'd been with women it took forever to satisfy, until it was more of a chore than actual fun. Jane was not one of those women.

"Maybe we should move this to my bedroom," he said.

She gazed up at him with lust glazed eyes and tugged his pants open. "No, right here. Against the wall."

"Condoms are in the bedroom."

She shoved his pants down and he kicked them off. "I've got it covered."

"You're on the pill?"

"IUD."

Good enough for him. He slid her panties down and she stepped out of them, then he lifted her off her feet, pinning her hard against the wall. She gasped and clamped her legs around his waist, wrapped her arms around his neck. He was afraid he might have hurt her, but her smile said she liked it. Despite her willowy physique, she was no delicate flower. She liked it a little rough; she wasn't afraid to experiment either.

His eyes locked on hers. He thrust inside of her, and without the condom to dull the sensation, the pleasure was so intense he nearly lost it. He tried to keep a slow, steady pace, but that just didn't seem to be cutting it. Jane clawed her fingers through his hair, bumping her hips in time with his thrusts, moaning, *"Harder."* He had no choice but to give her what she wanted, and when her muscles clamped around him and she moaned with release again, he tried to hold back, but seeing her look of utter bliss did him in.

"Just when I think it can't get any better, it does," she said breathlessly, still clinging to him.

He dropped his head on her shoulder, breathing hard. "Have I mentioned how good you are for my ego?"

She laughed. "I seriously doubt your ego needs any help from me. I think you're probably the most confident man I've ever met in my life."

"And I'm more irresistible than I thought. I brought you here with every intention of seducing you, but you beat me to it."

"I guess after five years of mediocre sex, then nine months of no sex at all, maybe I feel as if I deserve a little fun."

His knees were close to buckling, so he carried Jane the five feet to the couch and sat down with her in his lap. "Is that all this is? Fun?"

She loosened her arms from around his neck, gazing at him with a puzzled look. "Where else do you see this going?"

He shrugged. "I don't know. All I do know is that one night with you wasn't enough. Call me selfish, but I wanted more."

"How much more?"

"I don't know."

"A day, a week?"

A lifetime? The way he was feeling tonight, he couldn't imagine ever *not* wanting her. He barely knew her, yet he felt more connected to her than he'd ever felt to a woman. He didn't even care that every so often she had to lie to him. That had to mean something, right?

"I don't know how long." He reached up, stroked her cheek. "All I know is that everything in me is telling me that *right now,* this is what I need."

"The same rules apply. No one can know. Not our families or our friends. And especially not the people at work."

"Why?"

She sighed. "Because that's what *I* need."

Did he honestly think she was going to tell him the truth? That sleeping with a man she was investigating would get her fired. And who was he to judge her? By not telling her he knew who she really was, wasn't he being just as dishonest? But the truth was going to come out eventually. He could only hope that when it did, they would have grown tired of each other. They could move on with their lives and no one would be hurt.

"That means no more following me to dinners with my family."

He opened his mouth to deny it, and she held up a hand to shush him. "Don't insult my intelligence. That was a little too coincidental. And trust me when I say that getting to know my family is a headache that you don't want. If they think we're dating, and they find out who you are, once they get past the shock of someone like you dating someone like me, they're going to be planning our wedding."

"What do you mean, someone like me dating someone like you? Do you really think I'm that shallow?"

"Isn't that what you like people to think?"

She had him there. It was just easier that way. And hell, maybe he was a little shallow.

"I'll stay away from your family," he said.

"Thank you."

His stomach rumbled loudly, and Jane grinned. "Hungry?"

"I skipped dinner."

"The truth is, I didn't do much more than pick at mine. Being with my family has a way of killing my appetite."

"We could order in."

"And eat naked in bed? I've always wanted to do that."

Her honest enthusiasm made him smile. "Anywhere you want."

And when they were finished eating, he was going to spend the rest of the evening making love to her.

Twelve

Despite being up half the night making love, Jane woke at her usual six-thirty the next morning—with a very naked, very warm, and very aroused male form curled up behind her.

Tempted as she was to roll over and wake Jordan in a very pleasurable way—of which she could imagine several—this would be the perfect opportunity to do some snooping. Other than the living area and his bedroom, she hadn't seen much of the apartment. The one room she was most interested in finding was his office.

Her heart thumping with adrenaline, she slipped out of bed. Jordan mumbled in his sleep and rolled onto his back. Her clothes were still in a pile by the front door, so she tiptoed across the cool wood floor to his closet to look for something to wear. It was pitch-black, so she stepped inside and switched on the light, and when she saw her reflection in the floor-to-ceiling mirror across the room she actually gasped.

Her hair was a tangled mess, the mineral foundation had completely worn off, leaving her horrible freckles exposed, and what little was left of her eyeliner and mascara was smeared below her eyes. Thank God she'd woken before Jordan. If he had seen her like this, for who she really was—boring Plain Jane—he wouldn't be so eager to continue their affair.

She grabbed a button-down shirt off a hanger and slipped it on, then she switched off the light and peeked out into the bedroom. Jordan was still sound asleep. She crept back to the bed where she'd left her purse and snatched it up off the floor. Thank goodness she kept her makeup with her at all times. She made her way quietly to the bathroom and stepped inside, leaving the door open just a crack, so the snap of it closing didn't wake him.

She switched on the light and dug through her purse for her hairbrush, using it to tug the tangles from her hair, which of course left it limp and lifeless. She flipped her head over and gave it a firm brushing in the hopes that she could beat at least a little bit of body into it. Then she fluffed it into place. Not great, but not awful either. But she really had to do something with her face.

She found a rag and a hand towel in the closet and began to scrub off the remnants of last night's makeup. *One should always begin with a clean canvas,* the makeup artist had told her. She dried off and scowled at her reflection. A couple of weeks ago she wouldn't have thought twice about going to work this way, but now she could barely stand the sight of her naked face.

She pulled her makeup bag out and fished through it for her mineral foundation and applicator brush. She opened the jar and dipped the brush in, tapping the excess off, then raised it to her cheek—

"Good morning."

She jerked in surprise at the sound of Jordan's voice and the brush slipped from her fingers. It dropped to the granite countertop, leaving a poof of mineral powder, then bounced over the side, hit the toilet seat and rolled into the bowl with a soft sploosh.

Crap. What was she supposed to do now?

"What are you doing?" Jordan asked, leaning in the doorway looking rumpled and sexy, wearing nothing but silk boxers and a smile.

She cupped her hands over her naked face, since there wasn't much else she could do. "Could I have a minute, please?"

He looked at the brush in the toilet, then the makeup bag. "Are you putting on makeup?"

"Yes," she mumbled through her fingers.

"It's six-forty on a Saturday morning."

"I know what time it is."

"So come back to bed."

"Just let me fix my face."

"Why?"

"Take my word, you don't want to see me this way."

His expression went from amused to puzzled. "You're serious."

"Very. So please, get lost and let me finish."

He folded his arms over that ridiculously toned chest. "No."

"I'm not kidding, Jordan, leave."

"You've piqued my interest. Now I *have* to see."

He was blocking the doorway so running wasn't an option, and he outweighed her by at least sixty pounds, the majority of it muscle, so forcing her way past him wasn't going to work either.

"Jordan, *please,*" she said, feeling desperate.

"I'm not leaving," he said, "so you may as well drop your hands."

This was it, she thought. The end of her career at the agency. He was going to see how she really looked and realize the woman he'd been having an affair with was a fraud.

Feeling resigned and defeated, she dropped her hands to her sides. Jordan's eyes searched her face and she steeled herself for the look of disappointment. The indignation of a man who was known for dating supermodels and beauty queens realizing that he'd been tricked into bed with Plain Jane Monroe.

Instead, a grin curled his mouth and he said, "You have freckles."

Her hands flew back up to cover her face, and mortified, she turned away from him. "I hate them."

"That wasn't an insult," he said with a laugh. "I think they're adorable."

"They're awful. *I* look awful."

"What are you talking about? You're beautiful, Jane."

"You don't have to lie to me to save my feelings. I know what I look like."

He stepped behind her and wrapped his hands around her wrists, forcing her to face the mirror, then he tugged her hands away from her face and held them at her sides. She averted her eyes, but he said, "Look at yourself."

Reluctantly she gazed at her reflection.

"Tell me what you see."

"Nobody. Without the makeup I'm so plain, so boring, I might as well not exist."

"Is that what you really think, or is that your family talking?"

Not just her family. Everyone.

"It isn't makeup that makes a person beautiful, Jane. It's what's on the inside." He let go of her wrists and turned her to face him. "And you are the sweetest, most passionate, and most *beautiful* woman I have ever met." He laid his hand on her chest. "Because of what's in here."

Did he really see her that way? Did he really appreciate her for who she was on the inside?

"In school they called me Plain Jane."

"Shame on you for believing them."

She smiled and laid her head against his chest and he wrapped his arms around her. She may not have been completely honest with him, but one thing that she told him she meant with all her heart. She could love him. In fact, maybe she already did a little. And it had nothing to do with his wealth and power. In fact, she wanted him in spite of those things. He made her feel good about herself. No one had ever done that before.

"I know how tough it can be, ignoring the hurtful things people say," he said.

"What could anyone say to you that you couldn't refute by looking in a mirror?"

"I want to show you something," he said. He took her hand and led her out of the bedroom and into the next room. He switched on the light and her heart picked up speed when she realized they were in his office. It was the size of the entire living space of her apartment and decorated in rich colors and dark polished wood. Very masculine and surprisingly homey. And considering the clutter, he clearly spent a lot of time there.

If she was going to find anything incriminating, this is where it would be. Or where she would find proof to exonerate him. Because really, that was what she wanted now. She didn't believe for an instant that he was capable of putting anyone's life in danger, much less a whole group of people. He just wasn't that kind of man.

She glanced around the room, taking a mental photo for future reference. Getting the job done might require getting in and out quickly.

She knew that when he found out who she really was he would be furious, and he would probably never forgive her for betraying him, or be able to trust her, but she would at least be able to live with herself knowing that she had helped clear his name.

He pulled a framed eight-by-ten photo off the bookshelf and handed it to her. "It's the ninth grade science fair winners. Guess which one is me."

There were five winners, none of whose faces she could see very clearly. One was a girl, whom she could eliminate because if Jordan had once been a female, Jane would have heard about it by now. That left four boys, who all wore glasses. But one had black hair, so he was out too. The final three had lighter hair and ranged from tall for their age to downright puny. The one in the middle looked pretty average, but with the potential to be cute as an adult, and he'd won first place. She pointed to him. "This one."

"Wrong," Jordan said. "I'm the geek midget who came in third."

Wow. She knew he'd been small for his age, but she never imagined he was *that* small. And yes, he looked pretty geeky, but who didn't at that age? "This is ninth grade," she said. "Everyone goes through an awkward stage."

"Except I looked like that until I was eighteen. Not to mention that I was painfully shy and withdrawn. Which my father thought he could cure by *toughening* me up."

"Toughening you up how?"

"Calling me a sissy, pushing me around. Basically bullying me. And who knows, maybe it would have worked if Nathan hadn't always stepped in to defend me. Even if I had wanted to stand up for myself, he never let me. He would get between me and my dad, get in his face, and it inevitably got physical. Which made me feel guilty."

"Physical?"

"Shoving, punching, backhanding. I can't even tell you how many times Nathan and I got cracked across the mouth when we were kids. My old man was a real bastard back then."

"Where was your mother when this was happening?"

He shrugged. "Somewhere else. She was never much of a mother. It took me years to figure out that her ignoring me was nothing that I'd done. She's just selfish and cold. Well, up until Tuesday anyway. The stroke changed her. But for all I know, once she recovers, she may go back to being her old self."

"It makes my family seem not so bad," she said. "And I have a really hard time trying to imagine you as shy."

"I changed in college. My first year I grew nine inches, and since tall and scrawny was even worse than short and scrawny, I started working out. Girls actually started to notice me, and ask *me* out. It boosted my confidence and drew me out of my shell. I swore I would never be that awkward, insecure kid again."

She handed the photo back to him. "I guess the difference is, I never came out of my shell. At least, not until recently. I never figured out how to be confident. No one ever took me seriously. They still don't."

He set the photo back on the shelf. "But you left the family practice, that took guts."

She wished she could tell him about working at Edwin

Associates, how she had followed her dream. She didn't like that he thought she was nothing more than an office temp, that she was wasting her potential.

"I don't plan to be an office temp forever," she told him. "I'm going to do something big."

"I don't doubt it." He slipped his arms around her, under the shirt, drawing her against him so they were skin to skin. He was so big and warm and strong. She laid her head against his chest, hugging herself close.

"Did I mention how sexy you look wearing my shirt?" he asked. He eased it back off her shoulders, pressing kisses to her neck, and she started to get that electric, tingly-all-over feeling. He slid his hand down to cup her behind, drawing her against him and she could feel that he was getting aroused too.

"I have an idea," he said. "I have to go into work for a while to catch up on a few things, but I don't have to be to there for a couple hours. Why don't we go back to bed for a while?"

That sounded perfect to her. She took his hand and led him back to the bedroom. They would make love, and then afterward, while he got ready for work, she would start searching his office. She wouldn't feel guilty either, because she wasn't trying to find evidence of his guilt. She was going to find the source of the two hundred thousand dollar deposit, and to whom he had wired the thirty thousand dollar payment. Because she was sure there was a reasonable explanation.

She knew deep in her heart that Jordan hadn't done anything wrong, and she was going to prove it.

Jordan sat at his desk later that morning, and though he was supposed to be working, he couldn't keep his mind off Jane. She was really getting under his skin. So much so that when he dropped her at home on his way to work, he told her he wanted to see her again that evening. They made plans to get together at his place again. He would pick her up at five and they would order in dinner and watch a movie—if he could manage to keep his hands off her for longer that ten minutes.

He tried to recall the last time he'd been so into a woman that he'd wanted to see her two nights in a row. It had been so long ago that he couldn't even remember. Nathan had lectured him about finding the right woman, and how, when he had met Ana, he just *knew*. Of course Jordan had scoffed at the idea. He told Nathan that there were so many "right women" he wouldn't know which one to choose. But after spending time with Jane, getting to know her, the idea of being with anyone else just felt...wrong.

He used to think that if he ever did decide it was time to settle down, it would take months and months for the relationship to develop. But when he kissed Jane for the first time, it felt as if something significant had happened, as though a critical part of him that he hadn't even realized was missing had shifted into place.

He shook his head and laughed at himself. A week ago if someone had even suggested such a thing were possible he would have called them crazy. And the fact that she was deceiving him and he still felt this way defied logic. But when was love ever logical? Or easy?

His phone started to ring and he found himself hoping it was Jane, but it was Nathan.

"Hey, I need a favor," Nathan said.

His first reaction was to automatically say no, because that was the way it had always been between him and Nathan. Nathan, no matter how many times Jordan had dissed him, continued to make an effort, and Jordan cut him off at every pass. But frankly, Jordan was a little

tired of that game. Yeah, Nathan's meddling had made his
life less than ideal, but he thought he was helping Jordan.
Maybe it was time he let the past go.

Really let it go this time.

"What do you need?" he asked.

"Ana and I are supposed to go to a fundraiser tonight
and our babysitter just called to say she has the flu. We
called everyone else we could think of—"

"I'll watch Max," he said.

There was a pause, then he said. "Jordan?"

"Yeah."

"I was just making sure. For a second I thought I had
the wrong number. I figured I would have to beg or bribe
you or something."

"I love seeing Max. It sounds like fun." He was
supposed to see Jane tonight, but there was no reason why
she couldn't babysit with him. She could come by after
Nathan and Ana left, and leave before they got home.

"You're sure?" Nathan asked.

"I'm sure."

"Because I know you're not a much of a kid person."

"What are you talking about? I love kids, and they love
me."

"When was the last time you changed a diaper?"

Never, but how hard could it be? "I'm sure I can figure
it out. Besides, I'll have reinforcements."

"Reinforcements?"

"I'm going to invite a friend to come by and help out."

"You're bringing a *date* to babysit?" Nathan asked.
"You're joking, right?"

"She's more than just a date. She's…special."

"Special how?"

"I've been seeing this woman, and it's getting pretty

serious. And I think…" He laughed and shook his head. "I can hardly believe I'm about to say this out loud."

"You think what?"

"I think I'm falling in love with her."

For several seconds Nathan was silent, as if he was waiting for Jordan to yell *psyche!*, then he said, "Damn, you're serious."

"It's weird, I know."

"When did this happen? Is it someone I know?"

"We met a couple of months ago," he said, in part so Nathan wouldn't suspect the woman in question was Jane, and because the idea that he could fall in love with a woman after a week—especially after he'd been so adamant that he would never fall in love—seemed far-fetched even to him.

"So, when do I get to meet her?"

"Soon, I think. Maybe she'll be here tonight when you get back," he said, even though he knew she wouldn't. "So, what time do you need me there?"

"We have to be there at seven, so how about six-thirty. That will give Ana time to drill you and show you where everything is."

"Sounds good. I'll be there at six-thirty."

"See you then," he said, and before he hung up added, "And thanks, Jordan."

Jordan hung up the phone with a smile on his face. Next he dialed Jane's number. She didn't answer her home line, so he tried her cell. She answered on the first ring.

"I was just thinking about you," she said, which made him smile again. "I'm at the market and I just passed the whipped cream. I was thinking maybe we need to have another picnic in bed."

That sounded good to him, but the food play would have to wait until later.

"Slight change of plans tonight," he said, and told her about agreeing to babysit. And his plan to get her in and out undetected.

"Are you sure that's a good idea?" she asked. "What if they come home early?"

"Then we'll sneak you out the back."

"I don't know…"

"Jane, I want to see you tonight." And the night after that, and the one after that.

"Okay, but whatever time they're supposed to be home, I'm leaving an hour early."

"Fine, I'll give you the code for my front door and we can meet there after I'm done at Nathan's."

"That would work," she said, and he knew exactly what she was thinking. Being alone at his place would give her time to search for evidence, which he was sure she would have done this morning while he got ready for work, if he hadn't pulled her into the shower with him. But he had a few things he needed to take care of before he was ready to let her rifle through his personal files. Things that could be taken out of context if someone happened to stumble upon them.

He would stop home before he went to Nathan's and deal with that, then she would be free to investigate. He only hoped that she would find, or not find, what she was looking for soon, so they could start to have a normal relationship.

"I'll text you the address for Ana's condo," he said. "Be there at seven."

They hung up and Jordan forced himself to focus on work for the rest of the afternoon. He packed it in at five and went home to take care of his personal files. He gathered all the hard copies, then backed up the computer files onto a removable drive and locked it all in his office safe. Then he deleted the questionable material from his hard drive, including any emails he may have exchanged that could be misinterpreted. The idea was to give the impression that there was nothing to find, not encourage her to dig deeper.

When he was finished, it was nearly time to leave. He gave his mom a quick call to check up on her, expecting the nurse to answer, more than a little surprised when it was his dad who picked up. At first he thought he'd hit the wrong number on speed dial, but it was definitely hers.

"I was just calling to check on Mom," he said.

"She's having a really good day. She's napping now, but both the speech and physical therapists were here this morning and they say she's already making remarkable progress. She always was strong-willed."

Sure, if strong-willed was code for selfish and cold-hearted. "Dad, what's going on? What are you even doing there?"

"I'm helping."

"What happened to the baron she was so fond of?"

"I guess he showed his true colors. She needs a friend right now."

"What did she ever do to earn your friendship? I know she seems different now, but there's no guarantee she's going to stay that way."

"I'll be here for her as long as she needs me," he said.

Jordan wondered how the future Mrs. Everette number five felt about that, but he didn't ask. He just hoped his dad knew what he was doing. He may have been a real bastard when Jordan was a kid, but he'd really made an effort to change, to be not only be a better father, but a better man. Jordan hoped it didn't come back to bite him in the ass.

Thirteen

Jane hadn't been convinced that spending the evening at Nathan's place was wise, but she was glad that she'd put aside her doubts and come by. Not only was it a chance to spend time with Jordan—and get some alone time in his apartment later—watching him play with his nephew was probably one of the cutest things she'd ever seen.

Max was just under a year old with dark curly hair, big brown soulful eyes and a heart-melting dimpled grin. And he clearly adored his uncle Jordan. After a pizza dinner, which Max scarfed quite enthusiastically for someone with so few teeth, he and Jordan roughhoused on a blanket on the family room floor until eight when it was time for a diaper change and pajamas. But this time instead of wanting his uncle, he climbed into Jane's lap on the couch and snuggled up with his bottle.

"I guess he likes you," Jordan said with a grin.

She had never been much into kids. She'd never babysat

as a teen, and neither of her brothers had started families yet, so she had zero experience with them. And that line she fed Jordan about being ready to start a family was only meant to scare him away. But when Max gazed up at her with his big brown eyes she found herself thinking, *I want one of these.*

Halfway through the bottle his lids began to droop, and shortly after that he was out cold.

"Looks like he's ready for bed," Jordan said, gathering his limp little body from Jane's arms and carrying him to his crib.

While she waited Jane spread a blanket out in front of the fireplace and sat down, gazing into the fire. She hadn't expected to have this much fun tonight, nor had she expected Jordan to be such a natural with his nephew. She couldn't help wondering if he had plans to start a family someday.

Playboy that he was, she seriously doubted it, and if he did, she doubted it would be any time soon.

"Have I mentioned how sexy you look tonight?" Jordan asked from behind her.

She looked up at him and smiled. "Only about ten times."

He sat on the blanket beside her. "And I'll probably tell you ten more times."

She couldn't deny that she did look pretty good. She had taken a trip to the mall today and splurged on some new clothes. She had updated her professional wardrobe, so why not her casual clothes too? She had always assumed that skinny jeans would only accentuate her lack of figure, but the sales girl had insisted she try a pair on. They looked so good that she'd bought herself three pairs. She'd also purchased two peasant-style blouses and an emerald cashmere sweater that she was wearing now.

She looked young and hip and absolutely nothing like the drab woman she'd been the week before. She only wished she'd given herself a makeover years ago. She wished she'd had the confidence.

"So, we've got a couple of hours before you have to leave," he said. "What would you like to do now?"

"We could watch a movie."

"Or we could play a game."

"A board game?"

He grinned. "I was thinking more of a role playing game. Like, you're the teenage babysitter, and I'm your boyfriend, and you snuck me in."

She stifled a smile. "Why would I do something like that? I could get in a lot of trouble. If we got caught, they would tell my parents, and I would get grounded."

He grinned. "Because you find me completely charming and totally irresistible." He leaned close and nibbled her neck. "Besides, the element of danger is what makes it so exciting."

"Maybe I'm not that kind of girl."

"Maybe…" he said, lying back against the blanket and pulling her down beside him "…we could just make out."

It was tough to turn down an offer like that, especially when he was giving her that devilish grin. And God knows she did love kissing him.

"Just for a little while," she said, "and only kissing."

"Scout's honor," he said, but either he wasn't a very loyal scout or he wasn't a scout at all, because he had a serious case of wandering hands. At least initially, he didn't try to reach beneath her clothes, and because it felt so nice she didn't stop him. And when he slipped his hand under her sweater she figured it was above the waist, so it was okay. But when he undid the button on her jeans she put her hand over his.

"Jordan, we really shouldn't be doing this here."

"Trust me," he murmured against her lips, and when he slid the zipper down she let him. He eased his hand inside, touching her on top of her panties. In no time he had her breathing hard and arching against his hand.

"Not such a good girl anymore, are we?" he said with a wicked smile. Then he slipped his fingers past the delicate fabric. She moaned and clawed her fingers though his hair, kissing him hard as pleasure rippled through her. When it got to be too much, she grabbed his wrist to stop him. "Enough."

"Uh-uh. I want to do that again," he said, but she wanted to make him feel good too. She got up on her knees and pushed him down on to his back, then she unfastened his jeans.

He grinned and said, "Maybe I'm not that kind of boy."

Apparently he was though, because when she freed his erection from his boxers he didn't try to stop her, and when she leaned over and took him in her mouth he moaned and sank his fingers through her hair. He pushed his jeans down his hips to give her better access and within minutes she could feel him tensing. He had a special sensitive spot just below the family jewels, and when she touched him there he lost it.

"I think I like this game," he said, grinning up at her.

Her too, but it was time they act like responsible babysitters and behaved themselves.

Nathan and his fiancée weren't due back for several hours, so they straightened themselves up, laid down together on the couch and switched on the television. But apparently there had been some sort of change of plans because less than half an hour later the door opened and Nathan and Ana walked in.

* * *

Jane sat at her desk Monday morning, one eye on her computer screen, the other on the phone. She wasn't sure why she was so worried, since technically she hadn't done anything wrong. Nathan knew that the investigation would necessitate her getting close to Jordan. Hell, hadn't he been the one to call her into his office and give her advice on how to keep Jordan *interested*? Well, he was, so she shouldn't feel guilty for doing exactly what Nathan had told her to. Right?

The problem was, when she and Jordan were putting on their coats that night, and Jordan's back was turned, Nathan had given her this *look*. She couldn't help feeling that in his eyes, she had done something immoral. Which technically she had, but as far as she could tell, he didn't know that she'd slept with Jordan. Unless Jordan had confided in him, not realizing that this information would be enough to get her fired on the spot. But Jordan didn't seem the type to kiss and tell.

The fact that Jordan had left for the refinery at least a half an hour ago, and Nathan hadn't summoned her to his office was a good sign, right?

Someone walked into the office and she looked up from her screen to find the Mr. Everette in question looming over her, looking none too happy.

Oh hell.

"Is he here?"

She shook her head, hoping he came to talk to his brother and not her. "He'll be at the refinery most of the day."

"In his office," Nathan said, jerking his head in that direction. "Now."

Oh, this was not good. She got up and walked into

Jordan's office and Nathan followed her in, closing the door behind them.

"This has got to end," he said. "You need to get the information you came here for and get out before this thing you have going with my brother goes any further."

Okay, so he clearly knew something was going on, and he believed that if it wasn't sexual, it would be soon.

"I know how that probably looked the other night, but as I told you before, the investigation would necessitate a certain level of intima—"

"He's falling in love with you."

She blinked. "What? No, he's not…that's ridiculous. Jordan doesn't do love. He doesn't even get tied down."

"Apparently he does now."

She shook her head. "No, that's not possible. You've got it all wrong. It probably just looks—"

"Jane, he *told* me."

No way. "He actually told you that he's in love with *me?*"

"He told me that he's been seeing a woman, and that he's falling in love with her, and he was going to have her come over while he babysat. So unless there was some other woman with you guys at my place, he had to be talking about you."

Suddenly her heart was beating so fast she could hardly breathe. Could it be possible that Jordan really did love her?

"You're sleeping with him," Nathan said.

Jane bit her lip. She could deny it, but hadn't she lied enough? And when he learned the truth, wouldn't it just make things worse?

He sighed and shook his head. "Look, I know how persuasive my brother can be, but seriously, I thought you would have the professional ethics, not to mention the good sense, to know when to draw the line."

He was right. There was no excusing her behavior. But in her own defense, never in her wildest dreams had she imagined that Jordan would fall for her. And the fact that she was falling for him too was beside the point, because the minute he found out that she'd been lying to him all this time, that would be the end of it. She knew that for a fact because if the tables were turned, she didn't think she could ever forgive that kind of deception. "I take full responsibility for my actions," she said.

"I could have you fired for this," he said.

Yes, he could, and she would deserve it. But she was so close to wrapping up this investigation. "I have access to his home office. To his files and his computer. I just need a little more time."

"Find what you need and end this thing."

"I will." Phew, that was a close one.

He pulled the door open and started to leave.

"Nathan, wait."

Hand on the knob, he turned back to her.

"For what it's worth, I really care about Jordan. I could love him." Could? Hell, who was she kidding? She already did.

"But?"

"But I know that once he learns the truth..." She shrugged, not even sure why she was telling Nathan this. "It's going to be over. He would never be able to trust me again."

"For good reason," Nathan said, twisting the knife a little deeper. But she deserved it.

Nathan left and Jane tried to concentrate on work, but her mind kept wandering. Nathan was right. She needed to get this investigation wrapped up. The twenty minutes she'd spent in his home office after he'd gone to sleep Saturday night, and while he was in the shower Sunday morning, hadn't been close to adequate. There were just too many papers to go through, and she needed more time to copy the files off his hard drive, even though she was convinced she wouldn't find anything. She knew Jordan hadn't done anything wrong.

Her cell phone rang and though she half expected it to be Jordan, it was her sister, Mary.

"We need to talk," she said. "Are you busy tonight?"

"Actually, I am." She was meeting Jordan at his place after work for another "picnic" in bed.

"This really can't wait," she said, sounding almost desperate. And Mary didn't do desperate.

"We could meet for a drink at twelve-thirty," Jane said.

"That'll work."

They agreed on a place, and when Jane arrived her sister was already there, nursing an apple martini.

She stood and hugged Jane when she reached the table, which in itself was sort of weird, but when she said, "Oh my gosh, you look fantastic!" Jane knew something was up.

She took off her coat and sat down. "Okay, what do you want?"

Mary feigned an innocent look. "What do you mean?"

"The only time you're nice to me is when you want something from me."

"That's not true."

Jane glared at her.

"Okay, maybe it is a *little* true."

The waiter stopped by the table and Jane ordered a Manhattan. When he was gone she pulled Mary's business card from her purse where she'd stuffed it Friday night. "You can have this back."

Mary actually blushed as she took it. "I take it you guys aren't just *friends*."

"It doesn't matter. It was a rotten thing to do."

She stuck the card in her purse. "You're right. I just thought…" she shrugged. "I don't know what I thought. But his name sounded really familiar, so I looked him up on Google."

Uh oh.

"COO of an oil company, huh? The guy is a *billionaire*. How'd you swing that one?"

She folded her arms. "Because clearly a man like him would never go for a dog like me."

Mary blinked. "That isn't what I meant. I've always thought you were pretty, you just never seemed to try very hard to look…nicer."

Years of resentment suddenly welled up and threatened to choke her. "Maybe because every time I tried, I was shut down. Everyone made me believe I was destined to be Plain Jane forever."

Mary looked genuinely confused. "When did anyone ever do that?"

"It was constant. Like when I tried your makeup and you laughed at me."

"Of course I laughed at you. You looked like a cheap hooker."

"Did you ever think to show me the right way to do it?"

"Why? So you could be smarter *and* prettier than me?"

Jane drew back in her chair, feeling as if she'd been slapped. *"What?"*

"You don't like the way you've been treated, Jane? Well, boo hoo. Do you have any clue how hard I've had to work to keep up with you? How many times I had to listen to Mom and Dad bragging about your vast accomplishments to people. And 'Mary, oh, she's the *pretty* one,' like I was some idiot they kept around because they felt sorry for me."

Jane had no idea her sister felt that way. Mary always seemed so confident in the fact that she was better than everyone else.

The waiter deposited Jane's drink and the bill at the table. She took a sip then told her sister, "You aren't an idiot. Idiots are not accepted into law school."

"No, but do you think I like knowing that you're always going to be a better lawyer than me, even though you've never applied yourself?"

"Never *applied* myself?" Was she kidding? "I was never given the chance. I got stuck in the back doing everyone else's grunt work."

"Oh, poor Jane. I am so *sick* of that self-righteous bull. When did you show even an ounce of motivation to do more? Do you think the rest of us built a client base by just sitting back and letting cases fall in our laps? We've all worked damned hard building our careers. What makes you think you deserve special treatment? A higher GPA? Well, I hate to break it to you, baby sister, but that's not the way it works in the real world."

Jane didn't know what to say. Maybe she could have been more aggressive. Maybe, because school had come so easy to her, she expected the same in her career? And now that she thought about it, was it any different at Edwin Associates? If the undercover position hadn't literally fallen into her lap, would she have spent years feeling unappreciated, and passed over when it was no one's fault but her own? "I guess I've just always felt that you guys were trying to hold me back."

"The only one holding you back is *you*. Not that I'm complaining. It worked out great for me. All your hard work made me look good."

"And now that I'm gone?"

Mary leaned forward, imploring her, "Please come back."

The sudden plea surprised her. She'd been taunted and badgered about leaving the practice, she'd been made to feel she was an outcast, but never once had anyone asked her to come back.

"Mom and Dad are too proud to say so, but they miss you, and they *need* you there. We all do."

She scoffed. "I seriously doubt that."

Mary shook her head. "See, there you go underestimating yourself again."

She was right.

"If this was some sort of protest against the family, hasn't it gone on long enough?"

"It wasn't like that. I just wanted to try something… different. I felt underappreciated."

"They appreciate you. Believe me. Even if they don't know how to express it. And they're driving *me* crazy!"

"Better you than me."

"You should come back. Unless you're really happy in your *new* job," Mary said. "Which, by the way, I know for a fact is *not* at Anderson Tech. I have a friend from college who works there."

Damn. If she had known that, she would have picked a different company. "You didn't tell anyone?"

She shrugged. "I figured if you were going to lie, you had a pretty good reason."

"I would have told Mom and Dad the truth, but I knew they would be upset, and it wouldn't be worth the hassle. They would just tell me I'm wasting my law degree."

"What are you doing?"

"Something they definitely wouldn't approve of."

Mary gasped and said in a hushed voice, "Are you a *stripper?*"

Jane laughed. "Of course not! Why would even you think that?"

"Well, there's your new *look* and you definitely have the body for it."

"Are you forgetting that I'm slightly lacking in the breast department?"

"You're proportional. Besides, a lot of men go for that look."

"Well, I'm not a stripper. It's nothing that racy."

Mary leaned in closer. "So what is it?"

She wondered if she could trust her sister with the truth. "You have to swear not to tell anyone. Not Mom and Dad, or the boys. And especially not Jordan."

She looked puzzled. "He doesn't know where you work?"

"You have to *promise*."

"*Okay,* I won't tell a soul, I promise."

She told Mary about Edwin Associates, and that she was on her first undercover assignment.

"Not racy! Oh my God, are you kidding? That is so cool." She laughed and shook her head. "I am, like, so completely impressed right now. It must be so exciting."

Exciting? Maybe it should have been, but in reality the lying made her stomach knot and the sneaking around gave her anxiety. Yes, it was only her first assignment, but she was beginning to believe that she just didn't possess the killer instinct.

If she was being totally honest with herself, the only thing she really enjoyed about the job was spending time with Jordan.

"Mary, I hate it."

"What? Why?"

"I was going crazy cooped up in that dinky little cubicle

they put me in. I wanted to be out in the field, where the excitement is, but the truth is, I'm not any good at it."

"I find that really hard to believe. You excel at everything you do. You always have."

"I fell in love with the man I'm supposed to be investigating."

Her mouth fell open. "Oh my God, are you investigating *Jordan Everette?*"

"Shh! Keep your voice down."

Mary slapped a hand over her mouth. "Sorry!"

Jane leaned in closer and said quietly, "I've been working as a temp secretary in his office."

"And things got hot and steamy? Sounds like a porno movie."

Jane laughed and kicked her under the table. "We've never done anything at work. And it wasn't like I went after him. He pursued me."

"I'm not surprised. Clearly the man has it bad for you. The way he was looking at you the other night...*wow.* I can't even remember the last time a man looked at me that way. I always knew you could do better than Drake the snake."

"Drake the *what?*"

"Drake the snake. That's what the family has been calling him since he left you for Megan."

"He did me a favor."

"Obviously, because now you're in love with a man who's rich and powerful and *gorgeous,* who seems to worship the ground you walk on."

"And who is going to hate my guts when he learns who I really am."

"Hmm, that could be a problem. Not to mention that you're still investigating him, right? For all you know he may be guilty."

She shook her head. "No, if you knew him, you would know he isn't capable of hurting anyone."

"Because after a week you know him that well? Sounds like maybe you're not being objective."

Mary was right. Without a shred of proof she already had him exonerated. "As I said, I suck at this."

"So quit."

"I can't."

"If you don't like it, why not?"

Because the minute she did, it was going to be over for her and Jordan. He would learn the truth. "I'm just not ready to give up yet."

"What you mean is, you're not ready to give *him* up."

Exactly. The longer she dragged this out, the longer she could be with Jordan.

And the more it would hurt when it was over.

Fourteen

Despite the doctor's warning that she might never talk normally again, in the three weeks since her stroke, Jordan's mom had been defying the odds. Though he and Nathan had both feared that the embarrassment of having an impediment would hamper her recovery, and maybe cause her to hide herself away, they couldn't have been more wrong. She had welcomed visits from her friends and held her head high when her speech necessitated her repeating things to be understood. Only ten days after her discharge she returned to her bridge club and even attended a charity luncheon.

Even more remarkable was the way the stroke had changed her. Jordan didn't know if it was the damage to her brain, or simply the realization that she wasn't invincible, and life was precious, but she suddenly seemed to realize how important her family was to her. She welcomed visits from her sons and Nathan had even begun bringing Ana and Max to see her. For someone who had no interest in her own children, she was turning out to be a doting grandmother.

But the weirdest thing by far was her relationship with Jordan's dad. He'd been spending an excessive amount of time at her place. So excessive that his fiancée packed her things and moved back to Seattle. Jordan had never heard his parents utter so much as a single kind word to each other, but now it seemed that they had finally connected. Jordan wasn't sure if it would last, but for his father's sake he hoped so.

And then there was Jane. Despite nearing the three week mark, when normally he would begin to get bored with a woman—especially one he was spending nearly every waking moment with, he found her more intriguing and more desirable every day.

He wished her part of the investigation would finally close so that they could have a normal relationship. He wanted to take her out in public, do the normal things that couples do. A nice dinner and a trip to the theater or even just burgers and a movie. She was fanatical about them not being seen together in anything other than a professional capacity. He was getting tired of the sneaking around.

What he didn't get was, what was taking so long? He knew for a fact that she'd had more than adequate opportunity to search both his office at work and at home. He made sure that she had access to his computer and all but a select few of his financial files. There wasn't much about him that she didn't know, or have access to, yet they were still playing this game and there seemed to be no end in sight.

There was one thing he was going to miss when she was done though. Jane was an awesome secretary. In some ways even better than Tiffany. And God knows he'd kept her busy. With an equipment upgrade happening in just two days, followed by a vigorous safety inspection, Jordan had been spending more and more time at the refinery. It was during the last upgrade that the sabotage occurred, and tensions were high both at the refinery and the corporate office. As COO, the responsibility of keeping the men safe fell almost entirely on Jordan. This time before they brought the equipment back online, he planned to personally inspect every inch of the line.

The Friday before the scheduled maintenance, he was going over a few last minute changes to the schedule when Jane buzzed him.

"You have a call on line one from a Peter Burke."

Jordan tensed. Peter Burke was a manager at the refinery. However, Jordan suspected that his call had nothing to do with a work matter. They had discussed this and Peter knew better than to call Jordan at the office regarding personal matters.

"I've got it," he told Jane. "And could you please close my door?"

"Of course." She disconnected and appeared in his office doorway. She flashed him a smile, then closed the door.

He took a deep breath, then picked up line one. "Peter, what the hell are you doing calling me here?"

"I've tried you at home and on your cell. I've left you messages. I can't talk to you at the refinery."

"I would have gotten back to you when I had the time."

"Jordan, I'm desperate."

"I told you that I would get you the money and I will."

"But if I don't get it soon—"

"Now just isn't a good time. With the upgrade next week *everyone* is under scrutiny. Especially the refinery workers."

He cursed under his breath. "I'm sorry, Jordan. Maybe I should just come clean, tell everyone the truth."

"And risk losing your job, and your family?"

"Considering what I've done, maybe they would be better off without me. If I don't get the money soon, it might be out of my hands."

He closed his eyes and sighed. It was emotional blackmail. He never should have let himself get pulled into this mess. "Look, I have about half in cash in my safe at home. Will that be enough to hold you until I can get my hands on the rest?"

"That would be great," he said sounding relieved.

"This time, I want you to get some help, Peter."

"I will. I promise. I won't screw this up again."

"I'll get the money together and call you with a meeting place."

"Thanks, Jordan. I owe you."

He certainly did. But this was the last time.

He grabbed his coat and headed out of his office, wondering for a fleeting moment if Jane could have been listening in on his phone conversation, but she was at her desk, talking on her cell phone. She looked up at him and smiled. "Mary, I have to let you go. I'll call you later." She hung up and said, "Sorry about that."

"Your sister?"

"Yeah, she was giving me another lecture on the virtues of coming back to work for my parents."

She had been weighing the pros and cons of going back to the family practice for a couple of weeks now. Personally, he thought it was an excellent idea. "Still haven't made up your mind?"

"I'll probably do it, if for no other reason than I'm running out of money." She grinned. "I guess I sort of like making her beg."

He laughed. She was starting to sound more and more like him all the time. But he was glad she was patching things up with her family. It seemed they were both doing a bit of that lately.

"You're leaving for the refinery already?" she asked.

"Yeah, I have a stop to make on the way there. Do you have that equipment list I asked for?"

"Right here," she said, grabbing the folder from the corner of her desk and handing it to him. "Are we still on for tonight?"

"Absolutely. Do you want to cook or pick something up?"

"I doubt I'll be done here before six, then I have to go home and change, and I would have to stop at the market—"

"Takeout it is. Unless you want to go to a restaurant somewhere." At her exasperated look he shrugged and said, "It was just an idea."

"I'll see you tonight." She smiled up at him. She looked like her normal self, but when he looked deeper there was something in her eyes...what if she had been listening? She could have taken what he said completely out of context. But she knew him, and she had to know by now that he was one of the good guys, that he wouldn't deliberately do anything to hurt anyone. She had to care about him as much as he cared for her.

He had this burning need, this sudden desire to hear her say the words.

"Come here." He took her hand and pulled her up out of her chair, leading her into his office and shutting the door.

"Jordan, what are you—" She let out a soft gasp as he pulled her into his arms, and when he kissed her, she melted against him.

He gazed down at her, cupping her face in his hands. "I love you, Jane. I've never said that to a woman. But I need you to know how much you mean to me."

She smiled up at him. "I love you too, Jordan."

He closed his eyes and pressed his forehead to hers. He never imagined that hearing those words would feel so good. So why, as he kissed her goodbye and walked out, did he have the sinking feeling that something just wasn't right?

Maybe his guilty conscience was finally getting the best of him.

Jane sat at her desk, replaying Jordan's conversation on the mini digital recorder, trying to come up with some logical explanation for what was said, feeling sick all the way down to her soul because she knew what she had to do.

She had been so certain that he was innocent, that he would never do anything to hurt anyone. She still couldn't wrap her head around it, couldn't make herself believe it. Whether or not he was actually paying this Peter Burke person a bribe to tamper with equipment, she couldn't sit back and do nothing. If she didn't report this, and there was another explosion, if people were hurt because she had proof but did nothing, she would never be able to live with herself.

Jordan's sudden declaration of love wasn't making this any easier. It was almost as if he knew who she was, knew she was listening, and suspected that she would turn him in. Maybe he thought that telling her he loved her would change her mind.

But how could he know? Wouldn't he have said something?

Though she had strict instructions to take all new

information directly to her boss at Edwin Associates, she just couldn't do it. She palmed the mini recorder and walked down the hall to Mr. Blair's office, hands trembling, heart beating so hard her chest ached.

She must have looked as bad as she felt. When Bren saw her, she frowned and said, "Honey are you okay?"

Come on Jane, pull it together, be a professional.

"I need to see him," she told Bren. "It's urgent."

She picked up the phone and buzzed her boss, relaying the message, then she told Jane, "Go on in."

Swallowing back her distress, and squaring her shoulders, she walked into Adam Blaire's office.

He rose from his seat, "Miss Monroe."

"I have something I need you to listen to." She pressed Play and handed him the digital recorder.

He sat back down, stone-faced as he listened to the entire conversation. When it was over he hit Stop, then muttered a curse that she didn't think men as polished as him uttered in mixed company. Then he looked up at her and said, "Sorry."

"It's okay."

"Has anyone else heard this?"

She shook her head. "I thought it would be best if I gave it to you first."

"You did the right thing. Where is he now?"

"On his way to the refinery."

He picked up the phone and dialed his secretary. "Get Jordan back here immediately. Tell him to come straight to my office. It's urgent." He hung up and gestured to the chair across from his desk. "Have a seat, Miss Monroe."

He wanted her to *stay?* The information she'd gathered was quite possibly about to ruin Jordan's career, *his life,* and Mr. Blair wanted her to watch? She knew there were people who relished this moment, took personal and professional pride in bringing down the bad guys, but she felt like garbage.

Jordan had told her he loved her, and she had betrayed him.

God, she hated this job, and the second she was out of here, she was going back to the office and submitting her resignation. After that she was going to see her parents, and she would *beg* for her old job back if she had to. She would rather work in a fast-food burger joint earning minimum wage than put herself through this again.

"Miss Monroe?"

She looked up and realized Mr. Blair was watching her. "Huh?"

"Are you okay?"

Other than the fact that she felt like she might be sick? "I'm fine. I just…"

"You like him."

Was she that transparent? She bit her lip and nodded. "He's just so…so…"

"Charming? Personable?"

Not to mention sweet and sexy and generous and kind. "I didn't expect to find evidence against him."

"There's still a chance that there's a reasonable explanation."

He didn't believe that, and neither did she.

"You two have become…close?" he asked.

She no longer had to worry about her career as an investigator. It was over. She didn't see any point in lying to him. Besides, when Jordan walked in and saw her there, he was going to be furious. Adam would have to be a moron not to realize that something had happened. And he was no moron.

She nodded. "I didn't mean for it to happen."

He smiled, which he didn't seem to do very often. "We never do, do we?"

"I can't do this again. I'm going back to the law."

His brows rose. "You're a lawyer?"

She nodded. "I left our family practice and started working at Edwin Associates six months ago. This was my first undercover assignment."

"For what it's worth, I never would have guessed. You gave the impression of being a seasoned professional. And if you're looking for a job, I'm sure we can find a place for you in our law department."

"I appreciate that," she said, but once she left today, she would never set foot in the Western Oil corporate headquarters ever again. It would be too awkward.

The door opened and Jordan walked in, still wearing his coat, and Jane's heart sank to her toes.

"You wanted to see me," he said.

Mr. Blair stood, and motioned Jane to come stand to the side of him. "That was awfully quick."

"I hadn't left yet. I was grabbing a sandwich in the coffee shop to eat on the way."

Jane waited for him to ask what she was doing there, for surprise or confusion. For *something*. But he didn't even look at her.

Why didn't he look at her?

"Why don't you have a seat."

He folded his arms. "I get the feeling I'm about to face the firing squad, so I think I'd rather stand."

Mr. Blair pressed Play on the recorder and set it on his desk. After about three seconds, Jordan said, "I recall the conversation, considering it took place, oh, about twenty minutes ago."

Adam stopped the recording. "If you haven't already

figured it out, Miss Monroe isn't a temp. She's an undercover investigator for Edwin Associates."

Jane waited for the anger, for the disdain, but still, nothing. Didn't he care that she'd been lying to him? That he'd told her he loved her not twenty minutes ago and she had ratted him out?

There was only one logical explanation, one that made her blood go cold. He already knew. He had known from the start, and all this time he had just been screwing with her. To what? Throw her off the scent, so she wouldn't learn the truth?

Some investigator she'd turned out to be. She'd been played and she hadn't had a clue.

"I know how the conversation sounds," Jordan told Mr. Blair. "But it isn't what you think."

"So tell me what it is."

Jordan nodded in her direction. "She has to go."

She. That's all she was now? One minute he was telling her he loved her, now they weren't even on a first name basis?

Humiliation burned her cheeks, drove a spike through her heart. How could she have been so stupid? How could she have believed that someone like him would truly care about someone like her? It was all a game to him.

"She brought this recording directly to me instead of reporting to her boss," Mr. Blair said. "And there's nothing stopping her from doing it now, so I think you owe her an explanation too."

"What I'm going to tell you can't leave this room."

"I'll make that determination after I hear what you have to say."

He stepped forward, putting his hands on Adam's desk and leaning in. "No, you have to swear. Or I turn and walk, the consequences be damned."

That surprised her, and Mr. Blair too. He nodded and said, "Okay, it doesn't leave this room."

Jordan backed away from Adam's desk. "Peter Burke is a manager at the refinery."

"I know. He's the one who lost his wife last year."

Jordan nodded. "Ovarian cancer. He's raising their four kids alone. Even with health insurance the medical bills wiped him out. He was on the brink of bankruptcy, about to lose his home. He's a good guy, a loyal employee. I felt sorry for him and I offered to help. And for obvious reasons I wanted it kept confidential."

"Or every employee with a down-on-his-luck story would be hounding you," Adam said.

"Exactly. I figured I would give him the money, he would get back on his feet and everything would be cool. But it wasn't. His wife's death hit him harder than anyone realized. He started drinking, and gambling, then he started missing work, screwing up on the job. We tried to cut him slack, tried to get him help. Then he came to me a few months ago, just before the explosion. He got himself in deep with a loan shark and they were threatening him, threatening to hurt his kids. He was desperate."

"Let me guess, he owed them thirty thousand dollars," Adam said.

Jordan narrowed his eyes at him. "You knew?"

"Only that you received a wire from an offshore account for two hundred thousand, and wired thirty back out."

"From *my* offshore account," Jordan said. "Most of my money is tied up in investments. When I need cash I dip into my other accounts."

"So I assume he's asking for money again?" Mr. Blair said.

"He's in bad shape. He was supposed to join Alcoholics Anonymous. I even found him a sponsor, but he stopped going after a couple of meetings. He's back in deep with the loan sharks and now his sister-in-law is trying to take his children. Those kids are all he has left. I don't know what he'll do if he loses them."

"So why the secrecy?"

"The fewer people who know about this, the better. His sister-in-law has already filed to get custody."

"And her lawyer will be talking to all his coworkers," Jane said. If the sister-in-law had a good lawyer, and she probably did, his work would be the first place they would look for dirt.

"People are already being subpoenaed," Jordan told her, then he turned back to Adam. "And there's another reason I wanted to keep this from you. A selfish reason."

"I'm listening."

He took a deep breath and blew it out, as if what he was about to say was a struggle for him. "Though I didn't tamper with the equipment, or directly cause the explosion, I'm responsible."

Fifteen

Jordan had been holding that in for so long, carrying the guilt, it was a relief to finally let it out. And he could thank Jane for that. At first he'd been pissed that she'd ratted him out, especially after claiming to love him. But she had done him a favor. She had stopped this before it completely spiraled out of control.

"How are you responsible?" Adam asked.

"I knew Peter was having a rough time. He'd just quit drinking and the pressure was high. Whoever tampered with the equipment clearly knew it too, because it happened in Peter's section."

Adam sat back in his chair. "You think he missed something."

Jordan nodded. "I do. Knowing what a mess he was, I never should have allowed him to be a part of the safety inspection. I should have called someone else in, but he insisted he could handle it."

"Jordan, had you considered that he could be the one who tampered with the equipment?"

"Considered and dismissed it. He's a good guy. Besides, what reason could he have had to do it? I was giving him the money he needed."

Adam got a thoughtful expression on his face. "Maybe you did cut him too much slack, but you had no way of knowing that someone was planning to tamper with the equipment. Had it not been for that, things could have gone smoothly."

"But it happened, and it's about time I take responsibility for my part."

"It was a judgment call. A bad one maybe, but there was no malicious intent. But something is going to have to be done about Peter."

"I know. Anyone else would have fired him months ago. Maybe I should have."

"I don't want to tell you what to do, but sometimes you have to let a person hit rock bottom before they can learn to help themselves."

He honestly thought he could help Peter, that he would listen. Up until now, Jordan had always considered his arrogance an asset, but he had screwed up this time. Thought he was above reproach.

He glanced up at Jane. She stood there taking it all in. He could only imagine what she was thinking. And he knew he couldn't keep lying to her. He owed her and Adam the entire truth.

"There's something else I have to tell you," Jordan told Adam. "I knew Jane was an investigator."

"How long?" Adam asked.

He looked at Jane. "From the first day."

Adam shook his head. "Christ, Jordan. Why? Why

didn't you say something? Why go along with it, wasting everyone's time?"

He had a whole list of excuses, but there was really one reason. "Because I was pissed, and stupid. And arrogant enough to think that I could have a little fun at everyone else's expense."

"Excuse me," Jane said, her face pale, looking like she might be sick, walking past him to the door.

"Jane!" he called after her, but she slammed it shut behind her. He cursed. If she would have just let him finish. "Are we through here?" he asked Adam.

Adam's laugh was a wry one. "Not even close, but what I have to say can wait. From the looks of it, you have bigger problems."

He was right about that, because at this moment, the only thing in his life that really mattered was Jane.

By the time he caught up with her she was gathering the few personal items she had on her desk and shoving them into her purse.

"We need to talk," he told her. "You didn't let me finish."

She didn't even look at him. "What's left to say? You played me. You were just having fun at my expense."

"Only at first."

"You know. I should have realized. I mean, someone like you being attracted to someone like me? How ridiculous is that?"

"Not ridiculous at all."

"I've got to hand it to you though, you had me snowed. And everyone else apparently."

"I never once lied about the way I feel about you, Jane." She turned to him. "Forgive me if I don't believe you."

"You weren't exactly honest either."

"I'm sorry that I lied to you, Jordan, but I was doing my

job. And not very well apparently, because not a day went by that I wasn't sick with guilt for not telling you the truth. I fell hard for you, knowing that the minute you learned my real identity you would probably never want to see me again."

"And you thought you would improve your chances by turning me in?"

"What if I didn't and something had happened? What if more people had been hurt?"

"You didn't trust me."

"You will never know how hard it was for me to give him that recording. But you're right, I guess I didn't trust you. Which is why I think we should end this right now."

"Jane." He reached for her and she jerked her arm away.

"Just tell me this," she said. "If it hadn't been for what happened today, would you have ever told me the truth?"

"The point is that I *did* tell you."

She looked so…disappointed. "No, that's not the point, not at all." She grabbed her purse and her coat, turned to him and said, "Goodbye, Jordan."

And idiot that he was, he didn't even try to go after her.

"We found him."

Jordan looked up from his monitor to find Adam leaning in his office doorway later that evening, looking smug.

"Found who?"

"The saboteur."

His heart dropped. "Are you serious?"

"Only he isn't."

Yeah, it had been a really long day, but Jordan was coherent enough to realize that Adam wasn't making sense. "I'm not following you."

He crossed the room. "After our talk today, I got to

thinking. Call it a hunch, but I called Edwin Associates and told them to bring Peter Burke in for questioning."

"Adam, you promised—"

"I told them to tell Peter that we'd caught the man responsible for the sabotage, and that it was you."

"Me?"

"He cracked in ten seconds flat."

Jordan suddenly felt sick to his stomach. "It was Peter?"

"Peter caused the explosion, but it wasn't sabotage."

"Are you saying it was an *accident*?"

"It was a few minutes before that section was supposed to come back online and he noticed a faulty gauge. Instead of calling in a maintenance crew and delaying things another day, he thought he could adjust it himself. And maybe he could have if he hadn't been half in the bag at the time."

"So, all this time we thought it was deliberate, and it was really just an accident?" He shook his head. "Unbelievable."

"I think the guilt was getting to him. He was ready to confess."

"How did you even know to question him?"

He shrugged. "Like I said, it was a hunch."

Everyone had been so convinced it had been deliberate, no one had even considered that it was just a stupid mistake. "This is my fault," Jordan said. "In my attempt to help Peter, I only made things worse."

"Yes, you did."

"And you should be asking for my resignation."

"I should, yes."

"But…?"

"When I consider all the good that you've done for the company, it only seems fair to give you another chance. But I will be watching you."

He didn't have to ask to know that he'd lost any chance at the CEO position. He'd been so sure he was infallible, he'd gotten cocky. He had done this to himself.

"So, what happens to Peter now?" Jordan asked.

"Suspension. Only after he completes a rehab program will he even be considered for reassignment."

"You didn't have to do that. You could have just fired him."

"I could have, but you vouched for his character, and I trust you. If you say he's a good guy, I believe you."

"And if he screws this up?"

He shrugged. "At least we tried."

"So, with the mystery solved, I guess that means you can retire now."

"That's the plan. With any luck I'll be out of here by the end of the month, which will give me a full month and a half with Katy before the baby is due."

"Then what? Stay-at-home dad?"

Adam grinned. "Actually, Katy's family owns a ranch, and since we own the adjacent land, I was thinking I may just give ranching a try."

"I guess that means your replacement will be announced soon."

"The board meets Monday to appoint my successor."

Jordan already knew that it wasn't going to be him, not after today. Which seriously sucked, but he'd done this to himself. He thought he was invincible. That the rules didn't apply to him.

"I noticed that Miss Monroe is gone," Adam said.

"HR is putting in for a replacement. Someone should be here tomorrow morning."

"Did you and she work things out?"

"If by working it out you mean her saying it's over and leaving in a huff, then, yeah."

"Maybe this is a stupid question, but did you say you were sorry?"

"Of course I did." Hadn't he? "She seems to be pretty clear about what she wants. Or doesn't want. Besides, it's better this way," he said, knowing the second the words left his mouth that they weren't true. But it was out of his hands. He couldn't force her to love him, to forgive him. "When it comes to relationships the only thing I'm really good at is keeping them superficial and short."

"Well, if you change your mind, there's always groveling."

That wasn't going to happen. He had tried to reason with her, tried to work it out. The ball was in her court now.

The board's choice was announced Monday afternoon. As of March 1, Emilio Suarez would be appointed CEO of Western Oil. Nathan's relationship with Ana killed his chances, and Jordan didn't have to ask why he was passed over. Emilio had worked hard to become who he was, and he deserved the position. And though Jordan was disappointed, he was okay with it. Odd considering just a week ago he had been wholly convinced the spot was his. A lot had changed since then.

He had changed.

After Jordan returned from the refinery, Nathan stopped by his office. "Got a minute?"

"Come on in." It was only six, but he felt as if he'd worked a twenty-hour day.

"I heard that the update at the refinery went off without a hitch."

"Yep. We're running at full capacity."

"So…I guess you heard that Emilio got the job."

Jordan nodded. "Yep."

"I thought you should know that I turned in my

resignation. I'm leaving Western Oil. Word is going to get around quickly and I wanted to be the one to tell you."

He should have seen this coming. "Just because you didn't make CEO, you're going to quit?"

"That's only part of the reason. You and I both know, now that I'm connected to the Birch family, it's only a matter of time before they push me out. Ana's father wants me to come work for him. He made me an offer I just couldn't refuse."

Jordan didn't have the energy to be angry. Nor did he know why he should be. He should be happy for Nathan, yet in a way he felt as if he was being abandoned. He didn't like change, and with both Adam and Nathan leaving, and Emilio as CEO, Jordan had the feeling that things would be very different. But he forced a smile and said, "That's great. You deserve it."

"I was afraid you might be upset."

"Because I'm that much of an arrogant jerk?"

"Sometimes."

Yeah, he deserved that.

"You know, if you ever decide you want to leave Western, I'm sure I can pull some strings…"

Jordan's main motivation for working at Western had been the need to prove that he was better than Nathan. To get out from under his brother's shadow. In hindsight the whole thing seemed childish. And the real pisser was that despite what a jerk Jordan had been, and continued to be, Nathan was still looking out for him. He was a good brother. And clearly the better man. And though it might be easier to start over somewhere new, he needed to face what he'd done and make amends.

"I appreciate the offer," he told Nathan. "But I'm content where I am. I like my job, and the people I work with."

"Well, if you ever change your mind…"

"You'll be the first to know."

"By the way, the wedding is next weekend and you still haven't RSVP'd. Will you be bringing a date or going stag?"

Why did he get the feeling that Nathan wasn't asking just to confirm his attendance at the wedding. "It's over."

"I thought you loved her."

"I can't make her love me."

"I was under the impression that she already does."

"She lied to me."

"And you lied to her." At Jordan's surprised look, he added, "Adam told me that you knew who she was all along and didn't say anything. Dumb-ass move."

"There's a first for everything."

Nathan laughed and shook his head. "Well, at least you still have your ego."

"I apologized, she walked out the door. The ball is in her court now."

Nathan shot him a disbelieving look. "*You* apologized. You actually said, 'Jane, I'm sorry.'"

Well, he thought he had, but when he replayed the conversation back in his head, he realized he hadn't actually said the words. "There was an implied apology."

"How's the view from up there, Jordan?"

He frowned. "Up where?"

"Your moral high horse."

Jordan rubbed his hands over his face. Nathan was right of course. He was being an idiot. But only because he didn't know what else to do. "My longest relationship before now was less than six months. Even if I wanted to make this work, I don't have a clue how."

"You'll figure it out."

"How?"

"You could start by telling her how you feel. And I suggest a real apology this time."

"And if that doesn't work?"

He shrugged. "You beg?"

"And if she still says no?"

A slow smile crept across his face. "You're scared. You're afraid of being rejected."

Damn right he was. He was Jordan Everette, billionaire. Ladies' man. Women chased him, not the other way around. But Jane, she was playing by an entirely different set of rules. She didn't want Jordan the billionaire, she wanted the man who, until recently, he'd kept locked up inside. She was the only woman who had ever really seen him.

"I don't have to tell you that this sort of thing doesn't happen every day," Nathan said. "You take the risk."

That was Nathan, still looking out for him. But this time Jordan didn't mind. Because Nathan was right.

Jordan pushed himself up from his chair and told his brother, "You've got a point."

"I do?"

Jordan laughed. "Yeah, and I have to go."

Sixteen

Jane was still at work Monday evening when her sister stopped by her new office.

"It's after eight. What are you still doing here?"

"I was just going over a few of our active cases, bringing myself up to date."

"So, how does it feel to be back?"

Last Friday after she'd left Western Oil, Jane swallowed her pride and went to see her parents. When she told them she'd just quit her job, they all but begged her to come back. She had insisted that this time things would have to be different. She wouldn't let herself fall back into the rut of doing everyone's grunt work. She planned to take charge of her career, build a client base. They promised to help make that happen. And on top of everything else, she even managed to negotiate a better salary. Then the family took her out to dinner to celebrate. They were happy to have her back, and it was good to be back, to feel as if she were in charge of her life again.

"Good," she told her sister. "It's nice to be doing a job I know I don't suck at."

"So…have you talked to him?"

Jane didn't have to ask who she meant. Jordan was all she had been able to think about. And she missed him. She missed their dinners in bed and the way he teased her. She missed the way she felt when she was with him, as if she were the most beautiful and desirable woman in the world. She felt as if a chunk of her soul had been ripped away, and she wasn't sure how she would ever feel whole again.

"Not a word," she said.

"He'll call."

"If he was going to, he would have done it by now." It's not as if she hadn't expected this. She knew that when the truth came out, it was going to end. She just hadn't expected it to hurt this much.

"You're probably right," Mary said in that deadpan tone of hers. "I'm sure he's completely forgotten you by now."

Jane shook her head. "I really hate you sometimes."

"Don't tell me you're still mad at him."

"No." Mostly just heartbroken. Because after obsessing over it the entire weekend, she couldn't honestly say that his lie was really any worse than hers. Yes, she had been doing her job, but if she had done it properly, she never would have slept with him. She would have drawn the line. She was just as guilty as he was.

But if he wanted to try to make it work, wouldn't he have called by now?

Maybe the sad truth was that when he had time away from her to think about it, he decided that he didn't love her as much as he thought he did. Maybe she had just been a novelty. Because she may as well face it, men like him didn't love women like her. Only in fairy tales.

"You want to go out and get a drink?" Mary asked. "Or ten?"

Jane smiled. "Maybe some other time."

"If you need to talk, just call. I don't care if it's 3:00 a.m."

"Thanks, Mary."

After another hour, Jane packed up her things and walked out to her car. She considered stopping to pick up dinner, but she wasn't hungry. She hadn't been for days. She drove straight home instead, grabbing her mail and sorting through it as she walked up the stairs. Mostly junk, and a few bills, the usual—

"I was afraid you weren't coming home."

She squeaked with surprise at the unexpected voice and dropped her mail all over the hallway floor.

Next to her door sat Jordan, on the floor, waiting for her.

Her heart instantly jumped up into her throat. He wore jeans and cowboy boots and his black leather jacket.

He pushed himself up to his feet. Then he looked down at the mess she'd made. "Aren't you going to pick that up?"

She crouched down and quickly gathered her mail. Then walked cautiously to her door and pulled out her keys. This didn't necessarily mean anything. Maybe he was just here to return her toothbrush, or to pick up the tie he'd lost under her bed last week.

"Can we talk?" he asked, and maybe it was her imagination, but he seemed nervous. She didn't think he got nervous about anything.

She opened her door and gestured him inside. She closed the door behind them and took off her coat. Normally he wouldn't hesitate to make himself comfortable, but this time he just stood there. She couldn't decide if that was a good or a bad thing.

"You can take off your coat," she said.

He shrugged out of it and hung it on the coat tree beside

hers. He wore an emerald-green shirt that brought out the color in his eyes. He looked so good she wanted to cry. And she wanted so badly to throw her arms around him. She had to force herself to remain rooted to that spot.

"Jane, I screwed up," he said. "I am so sorry for lying to you. And I don't care that you ratted me out. I deserved it. And the only reason I didn't want to tell you that I knew who you were is that I was so afraid of losing you. I just... I can't live without you and I'll do anything—"

Before she even knew what happened her arms were around him and she was holding him, and he was holding her, and she had never felt anything so wonderful in her life. She buried her face in the crook of his neck. "You're forgiven."

He was quiet for a second, then he said, "That was a lot easier than I thought it would be. I really expected to have to grovel."

She laughed and hugged him harder. "Honestly, you had me the second I saw you sitting outside my door. I missed you so much. I *love* you so much."

He caught her face in his hands and kissed her. "Not half as much as I love you. Whether you like it or not, you are stuck with me."

She was so completely okay with that.

"But if this is going to work," he said, "we're going to have to make some changes."

"Changes?"

"Well, first, your car."

"My car?"

"It doesn't suit you."

"It was a gift."

"*Six* years ago. I think you've pushed this polite thing a little too far."

He was probably right.

"We're both going to take Friday off to shop for a new one. And this apartment…" He shook his head. "Either decorate it and get some furniture, or give it up."

"And go where?" Another apartment that she wouldn't furnish or decorate?

"Move in with me. You're there most of the time anyway."

He had a point. She basically only came home to change her clothes and do her laundry. But that was a pretty huge step. "You're sure you want that?"

"Do you think I'm the type of guy to ask a woman to move in with me on a whim? I mean, considering you're the only woman that I ever have asked."

She smiled. "I guess not."

"And the final, most important thing, I want us to be a *real* couple. I want to go on dates—in public. I want to show you off to my friends. And I don't care how obnoxious or overbearing they are, I want to be a part of your family. And I want you to be a part of mine. And if your bosses at Edwin Associates don't like that they can—"

"I quit."

"You did?"

She nodded. "Friday right after I left Western Oil. I'm back at the family practice."

"Is that what you really want?"

"I think so. I definitely want to be practicing law. If not with my family, then at some other firm. But for now I think this is where I need to be."

"I don't know if you heard, but they announced the new CEO."

She held her breath. "And?"

"Emilio Suarez."

"Oh Jordan, I'm so sorry."

"You know, I was so convinced I was in, you would think I'd be really upset, but honestly, I'm okay with it. Emilio is a good guy, and he worked really hard for it. Yeah, I wanted to be CEO, but I'm happy with what I'm doing right now."

"By the way, I didn't get to tell you how amazing it was, what you did for Peter Burke."

"And it almost cost me my job. He was responsible for the explosion."

She touched his cheek. "I heard. I'm sorry he let you down. You deserve better."

He smiled and kissed her softly. "What I deserve, what I *need,* I've got right here."

She hugged him, wondering if this was really real, if maybe she was dreaming.

"Now that we're officially together, you know what this means."

"What?"

He grinned down at her. "I can be your date for the reunion."

She laughed. "Are we back to that again?"

"Come on, I *really* want to go. I even got you something special to wear."

"Like a dress?"

"Nope. Even better. It's in my coat pocket."

What could he have possibly gotten her that would fit in his coat pocket? She reached in and felt something small and hard, and as she wrapped her hand around it she realized it was a ring box. He got her a ring? The question was, what kind of ring?

She pulled it out and looked at it. It was white with the name of a local jeweler in gold on the top, the kind of jeweler only men like Jordan could afford.

This is not what it looked like. As much as she wanted

it to be, it wasn't even possible. It was just too soon, especially for someone like him. Yes, he wanted her to move in with him, but that was a far cry from a marriage proposal. They would probably have to live together for years before he was ready for that kind of commitment. It was probably just a friendship ring. Or maybe even earrings in a very small box.

"Aren't you going to open it?"

She turned to him, gasping when she realized he was down on one knee. "Jordan?"

He grinned. "Open it."

This could not be happening. She opened it with trembling hands, and inside was the most beautiful and the *biggest* diamond engagement ring she had ever laid eyes on. "Oh my God."

"I know it's fast," he said. "But I also know that you're it for me. I think I knew it that first day when you tripped and dumped coffee all over me."

She smiled.

"I love you, Jane, and that isn't ever going to change."

She didn't need years, or even months to know that he was it for her, too. They were supposed to be together. She didn't even know how she knew it. She just knew.

"So ask me," she said.

He gazed up at her with one of those adorable grins. The kind that made her knees go weak. "Jane Monroe, would you marry me?"

"Yes," she said. "Absolutely."

With the promise of everything she could ever want from a husband shining bright in his eyes, he took the box from her, plucked the ring from its satin bed and slipped it on her finger.

* * * * *

INNOCENT 'TIL
PROVEN OTHERWISE

AMY ANDREWS

Amy Andrews has always loved writing, and still can't quite believe that she gets to do it for a living. Creating wonderful heroines and gorgeous heroes and telling their stories is an amazing way to pass the day. Sometimes they don't always act as she'd like them to—but then neither do her kids, so she's kind of used to it. Amy lives in the very beautiful Samford Valley, with her husband and aforementioned children, along with six brown chooks and two black dogs. She loves to hear from her readers. Drop her a line at www.amyandrews.com.au

For Kelly Hunter and Anna Cleary,
two fabulous writers who encouraged me to
stretch my wings.

CHAPTER ONE

'Two shots of tequila and keep them coming.'

Aleisha Gregory groaned at Kat's choice of Friday-night poison as she reluctantly plonked herself on the bar seat next to the leggy blonde. Saturday night was usually tequila night and she knew from experience that the Mexican liquor had a nasty habit of making her friend's clothes fall off, usually with wildly inappropriate men.

Which was fine. Kat was a grown woman after all. Until the panicked phone call she always received at the crack of dawn the next day asking to be picked up from a strange address and the ensuing couple of days of vocal self-loathing.

'Think I'd rather have something with an umbrella.'

After years of drinking sessions with Kat, Aleisha had learned that cocktails went down slower. Besides, it was still Happy Hour and eight-dollar cocktails could not be sneezed at.

Kat glanced at her friend and tisked. 'Ali, Ali, Ali. You city girls, no stamina.' She turned back to the boy/man behind the bar. 'Make it two daiquiris instead. And if you could make them all pretty and pink you will hold a special place in my heart for ever.'

Ali watched as Kat batted her eyes at the bartender. His pronounced Adam's apple bobbed convulsively once, twice, before he practically fell over himself to fill Kat's orders.

Ali wouldn't mind betting he could make a daiquiri with polka dots if Kat had requested it.

She rolled her eyes at her friend. 'He's a child, Katarina.'

Kat ignored her. 'Right,' she said, looking around the dimly lit, half-full bar, her keen eyesight scanning the offerings, probing into corners, assessing tonight's selection of possibles. 'Let's get you hooked up.'

Ali shook her head. 'Kitty Kat, since when have I ever hooked up?'

'Precisely!' Kat poked Ali in the shoulder. 'Maybe if you'd hooked up a little more often you might not have ended up with Terrible Tom.'

Ali winced. Kat's insights could be a little brutal from time to time. 'Well, I didn't end up with him, did I?'

'That's only because Two-Timing Tom is a jerk. Trust me, you had a lucky escape.'

Ali blew a persistent curl out of her eye. Funny, she didn't feel lucky. Tonight she was surprised to realise she still felt a little raw. Even a year down the track.

Admittedly, it has been a particularly heinous year.

The bartender placed their cocktails before them with a flourish and Ali watched him blush as Kat bestowed him with her you're-such-a-big-clever-man smile and then totally ignored him.

'What happened to your hand?' Ali asked the besotted bartender.

He looked down at the small red laceration gracing the back of his hand. 'I was trying to break up a dog fight this arvo.' He smiled at Kat. 'One of them took exception.'

Ali rolled her eyes at the lame attempt to impress. 'Did you get a tetanus shot?'

The bartender dragged his gaze to Ali. 'Er...no. Should I?'

Ali gave a brisk nod. 'Absolutely.'

He glanced at Kat, who shrugged. 'Okay, I will... thanks,' he said, before withdrawing to take another order.

Kat shook her head at her friend. 'You're hopeless.'

Ali sighed. 'Sorry, can't help it.'

Kat grinned, then lifted her glass and clinked it against Ali's. 'Here's to getting lucky.'

Ali clinked automatically but knew in her heart she'd settle for just getting through. Getting through this night without completely breaking down and ending up curled in a foetal position on her bed. Mostly she'd been able to put the hurt aside and get on with things. But knowing what was going on over on the other side of town brought it all back into sharp focus.

She looked into the creamy pink swirl of alcohol and figured that a few of these might just do the trick. She matched her friend's giant-sized swig with one of her own and felt the almost immediate slug as the alcohol hit her square between the eyes.

Ali placed the glass back on the bar. 'I can do this,' she said.

Kat nodded. 'Of course you can.' And she took another swig. Then she nudged Ali's shoulder. 'Guy over the other side of the bar, he's checking you out.'

Ali thought it highly unlikely anyone would be checking her out when she was sitting next to God's-gift-to-mankind. Seriously, why would a guy settle for Ms Average when he could take a shot at Ms Holy-Cow? But, used to humouring her friend, she followed Kat's line of vision anyway.

Okay-looking man. Nice suit. Nice eyes. Nice smile.

Nice. Nice. Nice.

Tom had been nice. In the beginning.

Ali sucked in a breath. Tom's betrayal with a sultry twenty-year-old redhead had shaken her perennial self-confidence and left her feeling old—at the advanced age of almost thirty—and ugly.

Before that particularly awful experience she'd known, the way a woman did, that she was attractive. Sure, not in Kat's league, but she hadn't been blind to the fact that men checked her out. She had good hair, nice skin, a size-twelve figure and a set of D cups.

But this last year, for the first time ever—thanks to Tom—she'd felt downright unattractive. His infidelity had hit her right in the libido.

The guy pushed off the bar and headed towards them. 'Oh, no,' Ali groaned, having another swig of cocktail. 'He's coming over.'

Kat laughed. 'Okay now,' she said hurriedly, reinforcing the ground rules. 'Tonight is about hooking up. About moving on. It's not about falling in love or happily-ever-afters. It's about you getting back up on the horse. About getting out there again.'

Ali sighed. 'I hated being out there.' And she had. She'd never been more content than when she'd been part of a couple. 'I loved being off the horse.'

'And how'd that work out for you?'

Kat saw her friend's face fall and was instantly contrite. She squeezed Ali's hand and dropped her voice lower.

'I'm sorry, babe, but you have to get past this. Terrible Tom is—' Kat checked her watch '—right at this moment, saying I do to the woman slash child he cheated with while he was engaged to you and you were pregnant with his baby. The very same Tom who broke up with you the day you miscarried, when you were lying in a hospital bed bleeding and sobbing, telling you he never wanted *it* anyway.'

Ali played with the frosty stem of her glass, barricading her heart from the emotional tumult threatening to consume

it. She had to admit, as the guy moved closer, Kat made a
very good argument.

'So I'd say you're well past due for a little moving-on sex.
It's time, Ali. Tom cut you off at the knees. But it's been a
year—stop letting him win.'

Stop letting him win.

Kat's advice, brutal as ever, ricocheted around her head.
Did she really want to spend the night bumping bits with a
stranger? No. But she really didn't want to spend the night
thinking about Tom doing it with his brand-new wife either.

'Okay,' she sighed. 'Okay.'

Kat grinned and nudged her with her shoulder. 'Just try,
Ali, okay? That's all I ask. And do not, I repeat, do not, di-
agnose some obscure medical problem the second he sits
down.'

'Okay, okay. I'll try. I promise.'

Just try. Just try. It chanted in Ali's brain as Mr Nice
plonked down on the bar stool beside her.

'Hello, ladies, how are we doing tonight?'

Kat squeezed Ali's hand and plastered a bright smile on
her face. 'Fabulous,' she beamed. 'Even better now you're
here.'

'And what are two gorgeous women such as yourselves
doing sitting all alone at a bar?'

Ali shuddered at the easy patter. The guy was obviously
well versed in pick-up lines. She braced herself for the inevitable where-have-you-been-all-my-life and studiously
ignored his deviated septum and associated nasally inflec-
tion.

Just try.

And she did. For five minutes it was all going well. He'd
even bought them another daiquiri each. And then he asked
the fateful question.

'So, Ali, what do you do?'

Ali spoke before even thinking the answer through. 'I'm a brain surgeon.' She felt Kat tense beside her as Mr Nice threw back his head and laughed. 'No, really, I *am* a brain surgeon.'

Or at least she had been until recently.

'You know, a neurosurgeon?' she clarified for the grinning man, irritated by his obvious disbelief.

Mr Nice's smile wavered and then fell and she sensed rather than saw Kat's shoulders droop.

'Oh, right, really?' he said, checking his watch and downing his drink in one swallow. 'Well, um…nice meeting you ladies but I gotta…uh, rush.'

Ali watched Mr Nice retreat as if she'd just confessed to having Ebola. Kat gave her an exasperated look. 'What?' She spread her hands. 'I never mentioned his obvious sinus problems, not once.'

Kat raised an eyebrow. 'Neurosurgeon?'

'I *am* a neurosurgeon. Why does no one believe me when I say that?'

Kat sighed. 'Because it's a cliché, babe.'

'Being a neurosurgeon is a cliché?'

Good to know that a decade of study and killer shifts had been reduced to a cliché. Well, wasn't that par for the course for the way her life had been running lately?

Not that it mattered because she was never going back. Ever.

'No, babe. The line's a cliché.' Kat looked at her friend and sighed again. 'Ali, you gotta know that intimidates men.'

Ali rolled her eyes. 'I don't have time in my life for cavemen, Kitty Kat.'

'Tonight you do, babe. Tonight you do.'

Ali shook her head. 'Oh, I don't know Kat…I've never been very good at this.'

Kat grinned. 'Well, lucky for you, I am. Now trust me

on this, let's just stick with your current occupation, okay? Remember, the coffee shop?'

Ali hesitated pulling her bottom lip between her teeth. *How could she forget?*

'You promised you'd try,' Kat implored.

'Okay, fine.'

Max Sherrington reluctantly followed his best friend, Pete, into the bar. God knew he'd rather not be drowning his sorrows in a public place. He had a nice bottle of aged Scotch at home a client had given him that he'd been saving specifically for this day.

The day of the yellow legal envelope.

There was nothing like twenty-year-old whisky to soothe the tension in a man's shoulders and dull the ache in his chest.

But Pete had insisted. And Max knew that when Pete insisted he rarely took no for an answer. He also knew his friend only had his best interests at heart. Pete had been worried about Max and his antisocial behaviour for the last eighteen months.

Max figured, on this day especially, he could give Pete a little of his time.

He had no doubt his friend, a chick magnet if ever there was one, would pick up within the hour and then he would be free to go home to an empty house and a full bottle.

'Right, I'll get the first round,' Pete said, his eyes swivelling the length and breadth of the bar, his gaze coming to rest on a blonde in a red dress whose legs went all the way up to her armpits.

And look at that—she had a friend.

He smiled and tapped Max on the chest. 'I think I see the answer to all your problems.'

Max followed Pete's gaze and almost groaned out loud.

'Why on earth would I want a Tori clone? I thought I was here to exorcise my wife.'

'Ex-wife, bud. Ex,' Pete pointed out.

Ex. That was right. The papers today made it official. He really was going to have to start thinking of her in the past tense.

'Ex,' he said grimly.

Pete slapped him on the back. 'Relax, the blonde's mine. The cute friend is yours.'

Max looked at the other woman. She had a nice face, large eyes, a little snub nose and a bow mouth. Compared to the artfully made-up blonde, she was quite understated. No make-up save some glossy stuff on her lips, no jewellery, no fuss.

But then there was the hair. A riot of short corkscrew curls, the kind that you couldn't get at the hairdresser, sprung from her head. They spiralled like spun sugar and reminded him of butterscotch. An errant one flopped down to brush her eyelashes, which she absently blew away as she swished a straw in her glass.

It was difficult not to notice she also had a great rack.

And looked about as impressed to be here as he did.

'Cute? What the hell am I going to do with cute?' he demanded as an image of peeling her bra aside slid unbidden into his brain. It annoyed him further. 'I don't need cute,' he grouched.

'If you ask me—' Pete grinned '—cute is exactly what you need.'

'I'm doing fine,' he insisted.

Pete gave his friend an exasperated look. 'No. You're not. You've been like a bear with a sore head for the last year and a half. You work twelve- and fifteen-hour days, you've been through five PAs and the only thing you have to break your killer work schedule is a punishing training regime for your next bloody marathon. Oh, and you haven't had sex since Tori left.'

Max grimaced. 'I should never have told you that.'

Pete looked into his best friend's shut-off gaze. He shook his head. 'You really need to get laid.'

Max felt his neck muscles tighten further. If he never got involved with another woman, it would be too soon. Celibacy had been working just fine for him.

He shot his friend a grim look. 'You do know that going without doesn't *actually* kill you, right?'

Pete looked at the shell of a man before him. He'd never met a zombie but Max was doing a fairly good impression. 'I would dispute that.'

Pete glanced back at the blonde, pleased to see she'd spotted him. He smiled at her and she flashed him a dazzler of her own. He turned back to Max. 'Go and find us somewhere to sit, and remember—when I bring these women over do not tell them you're a lawyer. People don't like lawyers.'

Max gave his friend a belligerent stare. That was easy to say when you had them on tap. 'They do if they ever get in trouble with the law.'

Pete sighed. 'Not so much then either, buddy.'

Half an hour had passed since Ali had sent Mr Nice packing and things hadn't got any better. No matter how hard she tried to be cool about picking up men in a bar or going home with a stranger—it just wasn't her.

'Oh my God, hottie approaching ten o'clock,' Kat murmured. 'He has a friend too.'

Ali glanced in the indicated direction. Yep. He was a hottie. If you were into overt good looks. Having learned the hard way that there was often not a lot of substance behind a pretty face, she wasn't as thrilled as Kat.

She couldn't see his friend. Not that it mattered. She downed the dregs of her third daiquiri. 'Sorry, Kitty Kat, but I'm done. This just isn't working for me.'

'No, wait,' Kat said, grabbing Ali's hand as it reached for her bag. 'Okay, fine, don't have moving-on sex, go home to the apartment and wallow if you want. Just give me another half an hour.'

Kat glanced up at the rapidly approaching man and Ali followed suit. 'I want that guy,' she said. 'So help a girl out. Just stay for a while, occupy his friend for a bit. I don't want him to feel like a third wheel. This guy could be *the one*. I don't want to put his friends offside from the get-go.'

Ali rolled her eyes. For as long as she'd known Katarina she'd been searching for *the one*. God knew she'd been through enough men in this crazy pursuit. She looked at the pleading in her friend's ridiculously blue eyes. She guessed it wouldn't kill her to stay a little longer...

Especially if Kat's focus was on seducing herself a man rather than finding one for Ali to seduce. She knew how this game went—she'd certainly played it often enough. She knew her role and she knew when to get lost.

'Okay. Thirty minutes.'

Kat winked. 'That's all I need.'

Pete ushered Ali and Kat over to the low table Max had scored. Four padded seats that looked remarkably like footstools were placed evenly around the table.

'This is Kat and Ali,' Pete announced to Max, holding Kat's hand as she lowered herself onto a stool.

Ali rolled her eyes as she sat herself down unaided.

'And this is Max.'

'Hi, Max,' Kat said brightly.

Ali gave an uninterested nod as she stared into her glass

and rode the buzz from her fourth daiquiri. It was probably time to stop now.

Max inclined his head politely. 'Ladies.'

The smooth deep baritone of his voice washed over her like a slow sexy saxophone note and pulled Ali out of the buzz even as it added more bubbles to her blood. She looked up despite herself.

Into two very compelling grey eyes heavily fringed by dark brown lashes. She blinked, surprised by their intensity. By the sadness that lurked in them. By the time she'd widened her gaze to take in all of him a few seconds later, those eyes had totally sucked her in.

She knew all about eyes like that. Had seen them in the mirror every morning for the last year.

'So,' Pete said, indicating the daiquiri glasses. 'Are you ladies celebrating something tonight?'

'More like commiserating.' Kat grinned and put her arm around Ali's shoulder. 'Ali's ratfink ex married his trollop an hour ago and I brought her here to get resoundingly drunk.'

'Ah, well done.' Pete smiled, holding up his beer bottle and clinking it with Ali's glass. 'It's the Australian way, after all. Our forefathers would be very proud.'

'Well,' Kat said, crossing her legs and circling her ankle, 'she ruled out my first option.'

'Oh?' Pete asked, mesmerised by the slow rotation of a fire-engine-red stiletto. 'What was that?'

'Voodoo doll.'

Max almost choked on his beer as Pete threw back his head and laughed. Max raised an eyebrow at the woman who had been thrust upon him. Pete had been right—she was cute with her little snub nose and that persistently floppy curl.

It was a shame her olive gaze was so damn serious—it

counteracted the cute very effectively. Max would have to be blind not to see the *keep out* signs.

'Voodoo doll?' Max queried.

Ali temporarily lost her train of thought with the combination of his sad eyes and jazz-band voice. Add to that his classic bone structure—pronounced cheekbones, wide jaw—and full mouth bracketed by interesting indents that she guessed were probably dimples were he ever to exercise them, it was hard to find again.

An interesting three-day growth peppered his jaw. It would have looked designer on Pete but the way Max rubbed at it, a little absently, a little harried, added to his jaded appeal.

'Kat enjoys being dramatic.' She shrugged, picking up the thread.

'What a coincidence,' Max said dryly as he glanced at Pete. He looked back at Ali and rolled his eyes. Her mouth twitched into a small smile and he found himself intrigued despite himself.

Pete ignored his friend. 'I like it. Maybe we could have done the same for you, Max?' Pete leaned in close to Kat. 'Max's divorce was final today.'

Ali watched as Max's gaze, which had glinted with humour just seconds ago, grew suddenly bleak again and it stopped the breath in her lungs. He looked as if he'd had his soul sucked out.

And didn't she know how that felt?

'I'm sorry,' she murmured.

Max looked directly at her. For a moment he felt a bizarre connection with her, a recognition of a fellow human being in misery. Ali had obviously had it rough too.

He shrugged. *'C'est la vie.'*

Silence fell between the four of them for a moment or two before Pete dived back in. 'So, Ali, what do you do?'

Ali dragged her gaze from Max to Pete. Not that Pete was even looking at her. She fought the urge to smile. She had to give the man his due—Pete was doing his damnedest to play the charming host. But she didn't for one moment think Pete gave a rat's arse what she did.

She slid a sidelong glance at Kat who had tensed. 'I'm a b—

'Barista,' Kat finished.

Ali blinked, not comfortable with her promotion from humble coffee-shop girl to barista. And certainly still not comfortable with the chain of events that had led to her current state of employment.

Even though she loved the simplicity, the freedom of it. Even though it appealed immensely as an alternate career path.

'Oh, whereabouts? Max and I are often looking for good coffee.'

Ali cleared the emotion from her throat. 'The River Breeze, at Southbank. It's Kat's place.'

A five-minute conversation followed on the merits of different coffees. It required very little input from Ali and Max.

'That's excellent,' Pete murmured. 'We'll have to drop by, won't we, Max?'

Max slid his friend a patient look. 'Why yes, Pete, we will.'

Ali suppressed a smile. It was obvious Max wanted to be a party to this as much as she did. He looked as if he'd come straight from work, his teal and grey striped tie loosened, his top button undone.

Well, why didn't they just speed it up? Pete and Kat could barely keep their eyes off each other—why drag it out? Get the regulation chit chat out of the way so she and Max could both leave and tomorrow their friends could justify jumping into bed together at such short acquaintance.

'And what do you do, Max?' she asked politely.

Pete, who was smiling at Kat, jumped in quickly. *Too quickly.* 'He's an accountant.'

Ali looked from Max to Pete and back to Max again. 'You're not an accountant, are you?'

Max felt himself smile. It wasn't something he'd done a lot of lately. It felt foreign so he stopped. 'No,' he said dryly, ignoring Pete's eye roll.

Ali felt the full impact of that brief smile. His dimples became defined and deepened. His grey eyes seemed less bleak. She had to wonder how he'd look in full blown belly laughter. 'So, what do you really do?'

'I'm a lawyer.'

Ali's first instinct was to flee. After all, Tom was a lawyer. Not to mention she was going to spend the next who knew how long—months probably—with a lawyer. A very, very good one apparently.

The best.

Still…

The desire to flee was overwhelming and she pushed up off her chair reflexively. Kat caught her wrist and held tight before Ali even had the chance to lift her backside.

Max ran the back of his knuckles along his jaw, taking time to process Ali's surprising reaction. 'You either don't like lawyers or you're a fugitive.'

Kat laughed. 'And they say I'm dramatic. Ratfink ex is a lawyer,' she explained.

It was an explanation that seemed to satisfy Pete, Max noted. But then Pete had ceased thinking with his head the second he'd laid eyes on Kat.

Max, on the other hand, wasn't so sure.

'I'll get us some more drinks,' Pete said.

Kat jumped up. 'I'll come with you.'

Before either Max or Ali could say no to another the love-birds were halfway to the bar, Pete's arm firmly wrapped around Kat's waist.

And then they were two.

CHAPTER TWO

MAX returned his gaze to Ali, who was looking ready to bolt again. 'You're not really a barista, are you?'

Ali huffed out a breath. 'No. I just work in Kat's coffee shop.'

Which was the truth. Or a semblance of it anyway. She did work at the River Breeze.

Now.

Come Monday she was going to spend an awful lot of time talking to her *very, very* good lawyer about what she'd done before that and she had no desire for a preview.

And besides, that part of her life was over.

Max watched Ali fiddle with her straw. She seemed tense and drawn. There was obviously more of a story there. But even more obviously she didn't want to talk about it.

Which suited him just fine.

He glanced over at the bar where Pete was charming Kat. He looked back at Ali. 'So,' he said, trying to lighten the mood. 'I'm a little out of practice with this. Should I be asking you your star sign or something?' He even forced a smile to his lips.

Ali glanced at him, startled to think he might actually be serious. His self-deprecating grin allayed that fear immediately even as it did funny things to her pulse. She gave a half-laugh. It was a relief to talk to him without Kat hovering. Without expectations. Knowing that he was also no longer trying to appease his friend.

'Something like that, I suppose. I think if you really wanted to impress me, though, you'd try and guess.'

Max liked the sound of her voice. It was evenly modulated. A voice for radio. Or for soothing frightened animals. He smiled and played along. 'Hmm, let me see,' he said, rubbing at his jaw. 'Virgo.'

Ali raised an eyebrow. She knew zip about the zodiac but she could play along. 'Interesting,' she murmured. 'And what makes you think that?'

Now he was stuck. Max didn't have the faintest idea. He'd obviously been out of the game too long. He shrugged and then grinned. Hadn't he seen the Virgo symbol often depicted as a curly-haired chick? With large breasts?

'Because you're a woman?'

Ali held her breath as his dimples lit up. It didn't hurt that he'd noticed she was a woman either. 'Is that an answer or a question?'

Max frowned. 'I'm sorry?'

'You don't seem too sure about me being a woman.'

'Oh no, sorry.' Max let his gaze drop briefly to the barest hint of cleavage he'd been ignoring since she'd sat opposite. She had some kind of a silky blouse on, which glided interestingly across her chest with the slightest movement.

He returned his eyes to her face. 'I'm very sure about that.'

Ali blushed. Actually blushed. She could feel her nipples tighten in blatant response to his appraisal and she blushed some more.

Max laughed as her cheeks grew a very cute shade of pink. 'So did I guess right?'

Ali struggled to clear her head and act cool, as if good-looking men bantered with her every day. She shook her head. 'Libran, I'm afraid.'

Max snapped his fingers. 'That was my next guess.'

Ali laughed. 'Right.'

Max took a swig of his beer, watching her as he tilted his head back. She'd relaxed a little. They both had. 'Your turn.'

Ali cleared her throat, her gaze fixed on the tanned column of his neck as she absently swished her straw through her drink. Then, when she realised she was staring, she narrowed her eyes and fixed him with a speculative glance.

She knew already of course—it was a no brainer. It had to be Sagittarius. She could picture him stripped to the waist, all planes and muscles, a bow pulled taut, his torso powerful but leashed, ready for action.

Ali swallowed. Was it legal to have such indecent thoughts about a total stranger? Maybe she could ask him for his legal opinion?

Right—as if she could pull off such an obvious flirt.

The sad fact was she just hadn't been born with the flirt gene. 'Pisces.'

Max sucked in a breath. Something had been going on behind those serious eyes. Her pupils had dilated and they'd gone almost khaki they'd darkened so much. It took a moment for her words to sink in. Then he laughed.

Ali frowned. 'What?'

Max grinned. 'A fish? You think I'm a fish?'

Ali smiled back. Those dimples were really something. And when that smile went all the way to his eyes, it was truly something as well. 'Fish are...cute,' she said.

'They're cold and slimy and scaly. Seriously,' he mocked, 'do I seem any of those?'

No, he didn't. She'd bet his skin was warm and smooth and that his mouth was hot and sweet. Ali felt her smile shorten as her brain wandered into dangerous territory. They held each other's gaze and his shortened too as if they'd both remembered simultaneously that this was just pretend flirting.

For show. For the sake of their friends.

Some music started up loudly behind them and Max was pleased for the interruption. He looked at his watch then leaned in closer to be heard. A whiff of rum and strawberries made him want to move closer. 'How much longer do you think we need to stick around for?' He indicated the approaching lovebirds. 'I think we're just in the way now, don't you?'

Ali concurred. 'Most definitely.'

Pete and Kat arrived back to the table carrying more drinks. 'Here we are,' Kat announced, placing them on the table as she sat.

Ali looked at the fifth daiquiri and her stomach rebelled. The four previous ones had well and truly hit their mark and she knew another would not be kind to her head in the morning.

'Ah, no, thanks,' she said, pushing the offered drink aside. She risked a brief glance at Max, who nodded slightly and she stood. 'I'm done in. I'm going to go home.'

'Oh no!' Kat implored, standing also. 'Just a little longer.'

'It's okay, you stay. I'll get a taxi home.'

'No, Ali, I can't let you get a cab home by yourself.'

Max, taking his cue, rose to his feet as well. 'It's okay, I'll see she gets home safely. We can share a cab.'

Ali looked at him, surprised. This, she hadn't expected. Didn't need. 'No, really, it's okay. I'm a big girl—I can get a taxi all by myself.'

Max smiled. 'I don't mind. Really.'

His dimples, appearing suddenly again, were her undoing. She knew he wanted out of this mating ritual as much as she did and she felt like a co-conspirator. She just hoped they weren't being too obvious in their rush to get away.

'Okay...sure.' They could always part ways once they were out of sight.

'Well, I suppose, if you really think it would be all right...' Kat murmured, looking at Pete and then back at her friend, hope and gratitude blazing in her eyes.

Ali nodded. 'Can I have a word first?'

Kat grinned, knowing what was coming. 'Yes, Mother.'

Ali dragged her friend to the side slightly. It was pointless telling Kat not to sleep with Pete. Blind Freddy could see that was where the night was heading. But she couldn't walk away without knowing that her best friend was going to be safe.

'Have you got condoms?' she asked Kat.

'Yes. Would you like some?' Kat teased.

'Some? Bloody hell, how many have you got?'

Kat shrugged. 'It's a big bag. I like to be prepared. I can spare a few.'

A few? Ali blinked. Of course. Regular Girl Scout was her Kat. 'I'm catching a taxi with him, Katarina.' Or pretending to anyway. 'I am not sleeping with him.'

Kat shook her head in dismay. 'He really is very attractive, you know.'

Ali didn't need her friend to tell her that. Everyone in the bar could see that. But even worse than his good looks was his wounded air. Somehow that appealed even more. She knew, without it ever being spoken, he understood how deeply relationships could wound. And that was way more dangerous.

She pursed her lips about to say something then Kat whispered, 'Moving-on sex,' before squeezing Ali's hand and walking back to Pete.

'Are you ready?' Max asked.

Ali flicked her gaze to Kat who winked at her. 'Sure.'

A minute later they were heading out of the doors.

'They didn't exactly protest too much,' Max said, his hand still at her elbow. She was wearing a floaty black skirt and he liked how it swung around her legs and seemed to skim in all the right places.

Ali laughed, feeling lighter now her escape was at hand. Or maybe it was the way her whole arm was warm from his touch or that her side tingled from the accidental contact of their bodies as the crowded confines of the bar had forced them closer.

He released her arm once they were outside in the comparably empty street. Ali stuck out her hand. 'It was nice meeting you, Max. Thanks for making that whole friend set-up thing less awkward.'

Max shrugged and ignored her hand. 'There's a taxi rank just around the corner?'

'Oh no,' she said quickly, dropping her hand. 'You don't have to do that. It's okay, really. They can't see us now,' she joked.

He shrugged again. 'I have to get a taxi home. You have to get a taxi home. It makes sense.'

Their gazes caught and locked for a moment. His was all serious again, grey and solemn, his brow furrowed. She longed to see his dimples one more time and was surprised by the urge to lift her finger and trace the indentations either side of his mouth.

'Okay,' she acquiesced before she did something really dumb like follow through on that impulse.

Unfortunately the queue was staggeringly long for so early in the night and Ali almost groaned. Yes, they'd had a bit of banter going at the bar, but now, with their friends nowhere in sight and no real need to talk to each other, would it be horrendously awkward?

They joined the queue and stood silently for the first minute. Ali felt each second tick by like a bloody great dooms-
day clock. The movement of the crowd jostled her against
him and her nose brushed against a cotton clad pectoral. She
apologised and pulled away. But not before she'd inhaled a
goodly dose of him.

Boy, oh, boy! He smelled like pheromone-laced chocolate. 'Sorry about the fish thing,' she said, her scrambled
brain snatching at the first disjointed thought that passed
by.

Max bestowed her with a half-smile as he cupped her
elbow to steady her. 'I'm sure my ego can stand it.'

Ali returned his smile. He didn't look like a man whose
ego was easily dented. 'So what *is* your sign? Really?'

He rolled his eyes. 'Sagittarius.'

Ali bit her lip as the image from earlier returned with full
force, enhanced further by his intoxicating scent. Despite
the suit she had no trouble imagining him as the famed ar-
cher. Half beast, half man.

All animal.

Max watched her eyes darken again and his gaze was
drawn to where her teeth dug into the fullness of her lip.
His stomach clenched and his hand tightened on her arm a
fraction. 'What?'

Ali shook her head, trying to dispel the image. 'Nothing…
it's nothing,' she said and dropped her gaze to the hollow in
his throat.

Hair sprung from her head as he looked down on her
crown but she hadn't been fast enough to hide the rise of
colour in her cheeks. 'You blush easily,' he murmured.

Ali clamped her eyes shut as more heat suffused her face.
'Yes,' she said, then risked a glance at him. 'Sorry.'

Max shook his head. It was refreshing to meet anyone

who could still blush these days. It didn't happen often in his line of work and it did tend to colour his world view.

'Don't be,' he said. 'It's...' he made a show of searching for the right word, then smiled at her '...cute.'

Cute? She was never going to hear the end of that one, was she?

She opened her mouth to say so but he was looking at her with those solemn, sad eyes, his smile not quite reaching them. And the heat at her elbow was radiating to her fingers. And the jostle of the line kept pressing them together, creating more heat wherever they touched. And his scent filled her nostrils. Invaded her brain.

And she felt more like a woman right now than she'd felt for an entire year. *Maybe ever felt.*

Ali could feel herself melting on the inside.

And she totally lost her train of thought.

It was crazy. She'd known the man for two seconds. Yet here she was liquefying into a puddle at his feet because he had sad eyes and looked at her as if she was a woman.

She shook her head as Kat's treacherous voice murmured *moving-on sex* in her head.

Ali cleared her throat, determined to pick up the thread of her last coherent thought. 'You're not going to let me forget the Pisces thing, are you?'

Max chuckled. 'Not a chance.'

The queue moved forward and it seemed only gentlemanly to Max to slide his hand to the small of her back and usher her along. Still his fingers tingled and he rubbed them absently against her blouse to erase it.

'Nearly there,' he murmured as the front of the queue came into sight.

Ali swallowed as Max's fingertips seared through the fabric of her shirt and set fire to every cell in their vicinity.

She shut her eyes briefly as her nipples beaded against her bra and long forgotten muscles deep inside her trembled.

God, this was insane!

Was it possible to orgasm through a completely non-sexual touch to an area far away from the usual erogenous zones?

With a stranger?

In public?

She squeezed her thighs together, shifting back slightly, and was thankful when his hand dropped away.

Ten minutes later they were about five groups away from the head of the queue when they were given the chance to jump it to complete the numbers for a share cab. Max raised an eyebrow at her and Ali leapt at the chance to shorten the agonising experience of constantly being bumped against him.

His warmth was way too compelling.

His voice way too smooth.

And he smelled way too male.

It was not her intention to do anything other than go home but her libido seemed to have roared to life tonight and she wanted to get out of his orbit pronto.

Just in case.

Her life was complicated enough.

Max grimaced as Ali's body was jammed against him by the third person climbing into the back seat. He could smell the alcohol on the other passenger and he turned slightly, his arm along the back of the bench seat shielding Ali from the worst of it.

It did however push them even closer together and he was excruciatingly aware of her breast squashed against his ribcage, her thigh pressed along the length of his, her curls springing against his jaw, tickling his neck.

It won't be long. It probably won't kill me.

And then she shifted, her fingernails accidentally scraping against his thigh, and the sensation travelled all the way to his groin and inside his underpants. He went very still as his arousal intensified.

What the hell was happening to him tonight? He hadn't thought about being with another woman for over a year and now he was acting like a teenager on a first date. Every move, every breath, every whiff of her perfume headed directly south.

Maybe it was as Pete said. Maybe he did need to get laid.

But not her. Definitely not her. He had enough baggage of his own without picking up hers too. Maybe when he got home he'd go find his little black book.

Dust off the cobwebs...

Because he definitely *was not* going to ask her to come up for a coffee. He *was not* going to kiss her. And he *was not* going to sleep with her.

Ali had complicated written all over her.

And then she turned her olive-green eyes on him and gave him a small smile. 'Thanks so much, for tonight,' she murmured. 'For rescuing me from the Kat-and-Pete show and distracting me from a day I didn't want to have to think about.'

Max swallowed. Her mouth was so close, it would be too easy to move his in closer...

'I think we rescued each other,' he said, returning her small smile. 'We both needed a laugh. I had a good night too. Better than I'd expected.'

Ali nodded. It was nice to know she'd helped him too. It gave her something else to ponder other than the trip of her pulse and the scorching heat of his body against hers.

Despite that, however, Ali also felt overwhelmingly tired. How she could be in such a heightened state of awareness and simultaneously sleepy wasn't a conundrum her brain cells were up to. She could only assume four daiquiris had something to do with it. It was certainly their usual effect.

She yawned loudly. 'Sorry,' she apologised.

Max smiled. She blinked at him slowly through heavy-lidded eyes and he felt another fiery dart to his groin.

'It's fine,' he dismissed. 'Lay your head on my shoulder. Go to sleep.'

At least then she wouldn't wiggle so much.

Hopefully.

Ali opened her mouth to protest but the very small part of her that wasn't utterly turned on was so very tired and somehow she felt safe here next to him with his heat and the daiquiris and the rock of the cab lulling her.

What could it hurt to drop her head against his very inviting shoulder? To sigh as he shifted to make her more comfortable? Place her hand across his chest, burrow it beneath his jacket lapel, feel the scrape of cool satin lining as she snuggled in closer?

'Ali? Ali?'

Ali murmured as the low sexy notes of a saxophone disturbed her pleasant slumber. The smell of man surrounded her and it had been long—so long—since she'd been held that she pushed her face closer to the source. The warm cushion beneath her cheek was fragrant, a steady boom soothing her into a state of bliss.

'Ali?'

The voice was more insistent this time and she fluttered her eyes open, shifting to look up towards the source of the rumbling beneath her ear. It took a few seconds for the world to come into focus. For the steady grey gaze to register, the purr of an engine, the glare of an internal light.

Max smiled as the woman he barely knew bathed him with her sleepy olive gaze. He hadn't felt remotely like moving away from her when they'd got rid of their other back seat passenger and had decided it wasn't right to disturb her.

Besides she'd been warm and soft and smelled like woman and as agonising as it had been he'd forgotten how good it felt to have curves and perfume pressed against him.

'Hey, sleepy head. This is my stop.'

'Sorry.' She smiled back but didn't move. She couldn't. She was utterly reluctant to leave this strange cocoon that balanced on a precipice between platonic and promise.

There was something about his smile. Ali had got the impression from the beginning that he didn't smile much. Or certainly hadn't had much reason to since his marriage had crashed and burned. And God knew she got that. The slightly wounded air about him had loaned him a tragic edge that had tugged at her heartstrings back in the bar.

But right now his smile was tugging in other places and she couldn't deny they'd made a connection tonight, no matter how reluctantly.

Their proximity and the glow from the internal light gave her a close-up she hadn't had as yet. She noticed for the first time his brown hair was lightly streaked with grey. It gave him a bucketload more virility and in that hazy half-world between sleep and arousal it seemed only natural to move her hand up to stroke his matching stubble.

And natural too, to follow with her mouth, pressing it briefly against his. And even though his lips didn't react she felt the thunder in his chest beneath her hand and saw his pupils dilate.

Max shut his eyes and felt all his earlier resolve disappear. 'Do you want to come up?'

Ali nodded.

Hell, yes!

CHAPTER THREE

BETWEEN the taxi, the lift and his apartment door, Ali was having second thoughts. 'I don't usually do this.'

Max paused, the key in his hand hovering near the lock. He could hear the tremor in her voice, see the way she wasn't quite meeting his eye. It was curiously touching.

He dropped his hand. 'If it's any consolation, I don't either.'

Ali glanced at him, surprised at the genuine note of sincerity in his voice.

'There's been no one since my wife left.' He grimaced and corrected himself. 'My ex-wife.'

Their eyes locked and held. She caught a glimpse of his unhappiness again, a swirl of misery in his open honest gaze.

'We don't have to do this,' he murmured. 'We can get in my car and I can take you home.'

His voice stroked her skin in all the right places and she could feel her nipples tighten. She could go home—he was obviously a gentleman. Or she could go through his door.

And feel like a woman again. Attractive, wanted, desired.

She pulled her bottom lip between her teeth. 'Does it make me a bad person if I want to stay?'

Max smiled. She *was* very, very cute—all puzzled and indecisive. Wanting to and yet not. They were close, so close and the mix of her perfume and almost maidenly hesitancy was a potent combination.

She was staring at his top button. He placed a finger beneath her chin and lifted her face until she was looking straight at him.

'It makes you even more desirable,' he said, his voice husky. And he followed it up with a swift hard kiss, catching her sigh as he pulled away.

Ali stumbled against him slightly, reaching for him as she reeled from his cataclysmic five-second, closed-mouthed lip-lock. How on earth would she survive anything more lingering?

Desirable. He'd said desirable.

She looked up at him shyly, heart hammering, aware suddenly that her hand had bunched up his shirt. She smoothed it automatically as he looked at her expectantly.

Waiting.

She cleared her throat, afraid he might well have kissed her voice away. 'Wow.'

Max gave a half-smile. 'Indeed.' Her bow mouth was parted and she had a kind of stunned look on her face and he had to admit to wanting to see that look again.

Preferably with her clothes off.

'There's more where that came from,' he murmured.

Ali responded to the gentle tease in his tone and his weary smile. It made her want to soothe his brow and let him get lost in her body at the same time.

She held her breath and jumped in. 'Better open the door then.'

It might be crazy but maybe, tonight, crazy was just what she needed.

Max inclined his head before turning to put the key in the lock. He twisted it and shoved the door open. He glanced back at her and gestured for her to precede him.

Oh God, oh God, oh God.

This was really going to happen. Her pulse thrummed a little faster, her breath hitched a little higher. She took a step and faltered, her mind racing ahead, mentally preparing.

'Wait.'

Max dropped his hand and raised an eyebrow. 'Yes?'

'What about…do you have condoms?'

She might be practically vibrating with sexual need but having already interrogated Kat it would be hypocritical to not take charge of her own situation. The doctor in her had seen too many women duped into having unprotected sex by men who were prepared to lie to them to get it.

She knew it was a lot harder to say no when you were almost at the point of no return.

Max blinked at the unexpected question. *Did he?* They hadn't used condoms in their marriage… Wait, yes, he did. Pete had bought him a box shortly after Tori had left and shoved it in Max's bedside-table drawer but not before he'd slipped two into Max's wallet.

Neither supply had been touched.

Max leaned against the doorjamb and grinned at her suddenly fierce-looking face. 'Yes. An entire box.'

Ali ignored the light teasing note in his voice. 'Sexual health is no laughing matter.'

Max attempted a sombre nod. 'I agree.'

Ali couldn't stop the smile that tugged at her mouth. 'I suppose you think I'm being ridiculous?'

Max shook his head. He pushed away from the doorjamb and held out his hand. 'I think you're cute. Very cute.'

'Great, more with the cute,' she grumbled.

But her pulse skipped madly and she didn't hesitate a moment longer. The tingle as his fingers folded over hers streaked heat up her arm, confirming the rightness of it all.

Max stepped backwards, tugging her gently forward, over the threshold of his apartment. Then inside. Shutting the door with a careless shove, he shrugged out of his jacket and pulled off his tie, his gaze firmly fixed to her softly parted lips.

He crowded in close to her, backing her up until she bumped against the door. Her perfume seemed to thicken as the heat between them intensified. He could hear her breath shorten and knew his had followed suit. His whole body had tightened in anticipation.

Everything was tense.

Everything was hard.

Everywhere.

He placed a hand either side of her head and watched her watch him. Watched her olive eyes darken a shade or two as he picked up that errant curl, stretched it out and let it go.

It sprang back, flopping once again across her eye.

'Cute curl,' he said, dropping a kiss on her eyebrow, the curl brushing his lips.

He ran his index finger down the straight neat line of her nose to where it tilted up slightly at the end. 'Cute nose.' And he dropped a kiss there too.

He moved his palm down to cup her jaw, tracing the outline of her lips, feeling it right down to his groin as they parted on a soft whimper. 'Very. Cute. Mouth,' he whispered.

Ali waited for the inevitable kiss, practically drowning in a fog of desire. She felt as if he'd been stroking her insides instead of dropping chaste kisses, nibbling around her edges. And she needed more. It was as if he'd drugged her and she was craving that next hit.

Max took his time stroking her lips, sweeping his thumb across the glossy cushions. Her breath was warm against the pad of his thumb, the beat of her pulse was wild beneath his palm and her throat moved convulsively as she swallowed. Each sweep intensified his longing but he was determined to hold back.

He knew when he let go and kissed her, really kissed her, there would be no holding back.

No more gentle.

No more slowly.

No more easy.

It had been a long time. And his appetite was back.

Ali had reached screaming point. How could a simple brush to her mouth be felt everywhere? How could it bead her nipples to unbearable hardness? How could it undulate through muscles so deep inside she didn't even know she had them until now? How could it pool liquid heat in places that it hadn't even touched?

'Cute, cute, cute,' Max whispered.

Ali groaned. 'Shut up and kiss me properly.'

And then she took matters into her own hands, standing on tippy-toes and dragging his face towards her, closing the maddening distance.

Max inhaled as their lips met, sucking in her heat and her breath and her sweet, sweet perfume and it was like rocket fuel through his already charged bloodstream.

He exploded.

He ground her against the door, pinning her with his mouth and his hands and his hard, hard body. Demanding entrance into her mouth with his tongue and sweeping inside like a conquering general. She tasted like rum and strawberries and his hunger intensified. Angling her head back, he plundered every moist morsel of it.

She moaned beneath his onslaught, clutched his shoulders, pulled him in deeper and he gave her more. His hands slid to her hips, gripping them hard then releasing only to grip them again, pulling her harder, closer, nearer each time.

His erection strained against the maddening friction, getting harder, more demanding.

His lips left hers to explore all the soft, sweet places of her neck and she moaned again. He'd forgotten how soft women were. How they fitted to a man's body, how they yielded against all the hard angles and planes and moulded just right.

Her fingernails dug into his back and she gasped, 'Max,' as he laved the frantic pulse in the hollow of her throat.

He claimed her mouth again revelling in her noises. He'd missed those mysterious womanly noises. The gasps and the whimpers. The little sighs and moans and the desperate, unintelligible urgings that came from deep inside when you hit a sweet spot and they *did-not-want-you-to-stop*.

She opened for him wide, matching the fervour of his mouth with her own and it was a very potent mix. Heady and sexual and dirty.

Good, dirty.

It had been a long, long time since he'd felt this good. Since he'd last kissed a woman he didn't really know. And he'd been more than fine with that. He'd been happily married, perfectly content. But that was then and this was now and Ali was shifting against him with reckless abandon that felt good everywhere.

For the first time in a long time he felt good.

Everywhere.

And he was going to damn well take what was on offer.

Pete had been right. He did need this.

Ali could barely breathe from the lust slugging her system, thickening in her veins like molten lava, beading like liquid mercury. She was dizzy and light-headed but strangely heavy-limbed all at once.

His tongue was stroking against hers—prodding and probing and lapping against her mouth as if it had been crafted especially for him from the world's sweetest chocolate. She could taste beer and opened to him to taste some more.

His hands were clamped on her hips, scorching his palm prints into her flesh like a brand and his groin was pressed so intimately against her she already knew what it was going to feel like to have him inside her.

She'd forgotten how great this was. How kisses could last for hours. How the taste of someone new could be so endlessly fascinating you just couldn't stop. How the need to touch them, taste them, became an overriding imperative. How being intimate with a man could make you feel loose and yet tight in all the right spots.

She realised it was probably the first time in a year she'd gone this long without thinking about Tom.

If this was moving-on sex then she was a convert.

She thrust her hips against his hard belly again and rubbed herself against the even harder ridge that was driving her mad. She wanted to touch it. Feel its steel and its heat and its purpose. Wanted to touch all of him. To see him naked. To press her lips to every inch of his flesh.

To make him moan.

To make him come.

To make him beg for more.

'I need to see you,' Max groaned into her neck as he pulled her blouse out of the waistband of her skirt.

And she knew exactly how he felt. She wanted more. Needed more. More than passionate kisses and fully-clothed fumblings. She needed to see his flesh. Familiarise herself with his skin. Surround herself with the aroma of pure male animal. Inhale the very essence of him.

She followed suit, pulling his shirt-tails out of his trousers and fumbling like a two-year-old with his buttons as he licked heat along her collarbone. It rendered her fingers totally useless and her eyes rolled back as his tongue dipped lower, tracing the full curve of one breast.

How long had it been since a man had taken the time to seduce her so thoroughly? Tom had certainly never been this thorough. And those few teenage fumblings had been exciting at the time but had most definitely lacked the finesse that oozed from Max's fingertips like some kind of sexual magician.

Or was that genius?

A fingertip whispered against her nipple and she almost fainted from the pleasure. She gripped his shirt for fear of falling and moaned her pleasure—again.

His half-opened shirt brought her back to her original mission and she tried again to divest him of it. But as his fingers continued to lightly tease her nipples, stoking her pleasure higher, she gave up the battle, grasped both sides of his shirt and ripped.

A button pinged on the door near their heads and it momentarily shocked them out of their haze. Ali, breathing hard, stared at his bare chest, stunned by both her handiwork and his pure male magnificence.

She blinked. 'I'm…I'm sorry,' she murmured.

Max, breathing even harder, looked down at his tattered shirt. 'I have a dozen more,' he said.

And reclaimed her mouth.

She speared the fingers of one hand into his hair, dragging his head closer as her other hand stroked his chest, his back, his belly. She felt his muscles contract in her wake and broke off the kiss to follow with her mouth. To put her lips where her fingers had been.

She kissed down his neck. Nibbled at his collarbone. Ran her nose across the rounded heat of a perfectly formed pectoral. And swiped her hot tongue across his disc-like nipple.

Ali was sure it sizzled but his loud groan obliterated the soft hiss.

Max could feel his control unravelling as she laved his chest with her tongue. It made him harder and hotter and hungrier than he'd ever been. He didn't want her to stop but he needed more.

He pushed her back. Her face was flushed, her mouth moist from its ministrations and his breath hissed out. 'I want to look at you,' he half groaned, half growled.

Ali sucked in a breath at his guttural command. She was incapable of thinking never mind denying him. Everything felt good and him looking at her could only feel better.

She smiled at him through lust-laden lids. 'Be my guest.'

Max made short work of the buttons on her blouse. Two glorious mounds of soft female flesh greeted him and he just stared for a few moments. She was wearing a see-through bra and he could clearly see her nipples scrunched like perfectly edible berries.

'Max,' she whispered, uncaring of the plea in her voice as she wantonly arched her back. Didn't he know he couldn't look at her as if he wanted to eat her without following through?

He ran both thumbs down the centre point of each breast, grazing the nipples as he went. Her breath hitched loudly and his erection surged at the strangled whimper that slid from her lips. He reached down into the deep valley between and unsnapped the front clasp. They sprang free— round and full, falling softly into a natural pendulum, the aroused nipples precisely centred.

He filled his hands with her and they spilled over his large palms. He squeezed, brushing his thumbs over the taut buds teasing him with their perfection.

'Max,' she moaned, clutching his head as he bent over them and created exquisite havoc with his tongue.

When he tugged a nipple deep into the heat of his mouth she bucked and cried out, her heel kicking at the door. And he got harder. He slid a hand behind her, between her shoulder blades, pressing her closer still, wanting to taste all of her, to devour all of her.

Her moans, her murmurs, her little strangled sobs were a powerful turn on and he wouldn't stop teasing her until he'd wrung every single one from deep inside her. Tonight was about forgetting but it was also about remembering. He'd been good at this. And he wanted to be one man that Ali never forgot.

Ali was sure she was drooling. She certainly felt as if she was babbling incoherently. Her breasts had been an erogenous zone that Tom had never really paid attention to. Sure, he'd liked that she had them, that they looked good, that he was the envy of his friends. But he'd virtually ignored them when they'd been making love.

It was a revelation to be with a man who treated them with such reverence. Who was content to worship them as if they were the most perfect set of breasts that ever existed.

She could have been perfectly happily have him do this all night. In fact as his teeth grazed a sensitive peak and her belly contracted she was damn sure after a year of abstinence she could get off on this alone.

But she also needed to explore him. Was hungry to feel the hot, hard length of him. In her hand. Against her belly. Deep inside her.

Summoning the few functioning brain cells she had left, she reached for him. Her hand found her target instantly, thick and straining against the fabric of his trousers. She scraped her nails against him and he lifted his head from her breasts on a groan.

Max looked Ali in the eye as she squeezed him hard. 'Oh, God,' he panted, shutting his eyes at the erotic torture. Ali smiled at him, her face flushed, her olive eyes khaki with undiluted lust.

'Don't stop,' he whispered and lowered his mouth to a peaked nipple and sucked on it hard.

Ali clutched harder, fumbling for the zipper, not wanting to stop but needing more access. Needing to feel the warm silky flesh covering all that hardness. Needing to feel all of him.

Max reared back bellowing loudly when her hand made its first contact. She palmed the length of him and his breath hissed out like a steam engine. She did it again and he moaned deep and low. And when she rolled her thumb across the spongy firmness of his head he cried out.

And then he kissed her. Deep and hard, his tongue thrusting in sync with the motion of his hips as her hands continued to grip him, encircle him.

'I want you in me,' she whispered against his mouth. 'Now!'

Max needed no further encouragement. He reached for her skirt and rucked it up both sides, his hands sliding around to the cheeks of her backside, squeezing tight, urging her closer to him. His hands found the narrow strip of fabric sitting on each hip and figured she was wearing some kind of G-string.

He grabbed one side and yanked, snapping it as if it were dental floss. 'Sorry,' he murmured against her mouth with not one ounce of contrition.

Ali smiled. 'I have a dozen more.'

And then his fingers were stroking her and Ali couldn't have cared less if they were made out of spun gold and were the rarest knickers in the world.

'Condom,' Max said to her as he slid first one finger and then another into her tight moist heat.

'Wallet,' he directed and then claimed her nipple.

Ali's knees buckled and she was grateful when he braced his legs against hers for support. Reluctant to let go of all his magnificent male hardness, she fumbled in his trouser pocket with her other hand. Locating his wallet was easy but getting it out and open while his fingers filled her and rubbed in just the right spot was a task almost beyond her. She could already feel a delicious tightening.

Max lifted his head. 'Hurry,' he growled and turned his attention to the other nipple.

There was no choice. She had to let him go. Still, her hands shook as she located the foil packet and then opened it. The steady rhythm of his fingers moving her inexorably closer to orgasm caused her to fumble as she attempted to roll it on.

'Ali, for God's sake,' Max groaned into her neck.

'I can't…concentrate,' she panted as a ripple undulated through her. 'You…oh…dear God…' she drew in a ragged breath '…that feels so good.'

Max smiled at her lust-drunk expression. It felt good to see that look, to know he'd put it there. 'What, this?' he asked, circling his fingers.

Ali gasped. 'God, yes, please…stop. I'm never going to be able to put this damn thing on otherwise.'

Max acquiesced but kept his hand firmly in place. 'That better?'

Ali shut her eyes as the ripples petered off. 'Marginally.' It was enough to accomplish her goal anyway and it was Max's turn to pale as she created her own brand of havoc sheathing him slowly and thoroughly.

'Ali,' he warned, squeezing his eyes shut, ruthlessly suppressing the urge to rear like a rutting stallion.

It was Ali's turn to smile but she heeded his warning nonetheless, completing the job post-haste. 'Go,' she said,

leaning forward and kissing him full and hot and open.
'Now!'

Max didn't have to be asked twice. He slid his hand down
her thigh and urged her leg up. He bent it at the knee and
held it close to his waist as he pushed inside her in one easy
movement.

Ali gasped, digging her fingers into his shoulder blade.
'Yes.'

Max repeated the movement, sliding higher this time,
her gasp mingling with his groan somewhere inside their
heated kiss.

Max pushed again and again. The movement rocked her
against the door and jiggled her breasts most enticingly. Too
enticingly as he switched his attention from her mouth to
her still-taut nipples.

Ali whimpered. The delicious push and pull of Max and
the erotic swipe of his tongue were all-consuming. She
burned, throbbed, ached, yearned. The pressure built and
built, the ripples returned and her breathing grew shorter,
harder, faster.

Max could feel the ripples too. The sensation started at
his belly button and radiated down. Ali's desperate little
gasps and the thrum of his own blood strengthened it. His
biceps trembled, his shoulders quivered as the sensation
raced like a rogue electrical storm through every muscle
group.

It finally came to rest down deep and low and grew, ex-
panded, intensified.

'Max!' Ali gasped as her orgasm hit, clutching him close.
'Max, Max, Max!'

He felt her tighten around him, her muscles undulating
along his length, milking him, demanding his surrender.
His blood tingled. His nerve endings tightened. And when
she threw her head back against the door in a silent scream

he yielded to the demands of both their bodies, joining her somewhere in the stratosphere, holding tight as starlight rained down on them.

Ali felt heavy as she bumped back down to earth. But curiously weightless. She shifted in Max's arms, aware that he was essentially holding her up.

Max gripped her thigh, not wanting to move, not wanting to spoil a moment that would be with him until the day he died. 'You okay?' he asked.

Ali shook her head. She never knew sex could be completely mind-bending. How had she got to twenty-nine and not known that sex could be this good?

'I doubt I'll ever be okay again. I think I just touched the stars.'

Max smiled. It *had* been pretty incredible. He lifted his head from the hollow of her neck. 'Pretty good for a fish, huh?'

Ali laughed as she traced her fingers through his stubble. 'Please tell me you can do that again.'

Max chuckled. 'I may need a moment.'

She laughed again, feeling light and loose and free of a year full of baggage—even if only for tonight. 'It'd be such a shame not to put a few more of those condoms to good use. Don't you think?'

Max kissed her neck. 'Absolutely.'

CHAPTER FOUR

ALI was going to throw up.

She couldn't remember ever being this nervous. Not even that time when one of the world's top neurosurgeons with a reputation for being an arrogant jerk had peered over her shoulder during her first ever solo op and demanded she explain the rationale for every single scalpel movement and instrument choice.

Sure, she'd had butterflies—her career had been at stake. But she'd known her stuff. Had been confident in her ability. Surgery she knew. Surgery she could do.

But this?

This was a complete unknown. This was utterly terrifying!

The nervous squall lashing her insides was not helped by the pitch and roll of the taxi. The driver was riding the accelerator like a yo-yo and it took all her skill to keep the cardboard tray with the two take-away coffee cups balanced and upright.

The aroma of Arabica beans infused her nostrils as the liquid sloshed in the cups, intensifying her nausea. Ali was glad she'd made the decision not to put anything into her stomach today. Adding food to this volatile mix of shredded nerves and perpetual motion wouldn't have been pretty on the floor of the cab.

She was never more grateful than when the taxi pulled up in front of the exclusive riverside high-rise. She paid the driver and gingerly stepped out of the cab, her thigh muscles wobbling as she regained her land legs. She craned her neck upwards. The mirrored blue glass cast a mighty shadow over the Brisbane River somehow looking cold and clinical even in the sunshine.

More cold and clinical than an operating theatre ever had!

She forced her legs to move towards the glass sliding doors, her fingers gripping the tray of hot beverages. She entered the building and headed towards the steel and frosted-glass directory, her heels tapping on the glossy Italian-looking marble.

She perused the directory, searching for Messrs Sherrington, Watkins, Appleby and Dawson finding them on the forty-sixth floor. Ali's stomach dipped at the thought.

She entered the lift, pleased to be alone as she juggled the tray and her bag to push the button. Her nerves ratcheted up another ten notches as the lift launched effortlessly to the lofty heights of the penthouse floor. Of course it glided silently, in tip-top shape as she expected everything was in this state-of-the-art building.

She noticed she was biting her bottom lip again as she checked out her reflection in the mirrored back wall and she released the swollen piece of flesh that had been under constant attack all weekend and was now quite tender.

It was hard to believe the terrified looking woman staring back at her was her.

Aleisha Gregory.

Dr Aleisha Gregory she reminded herself.

But not for much longer.

She flicked the usual curl from her eye and fiddled with a lapel to distract her from such defeatist thoughts. She felt strange all suited up like this. The black jacket with a fine burgundy pin-stripe felt odd, as did the matching tailored trousers. The soft burgundy silk of her blouse fell lightly against her skin caressing the fullness of her breasts, not all starched and abrasive like her baggy scrubs when she'd first put them on in the morning.

She'd give anything for those scrubs right now. Or her regulation jeans and T-shirt, but her mother was a great believer that one should *dress* for appointments and, after their phone call this morning, she just couldn't override Cynthia Gregory's voice.

The elevator pinged and the fist that had been shoved up under her diaphragm ground a little deeper. Ali took a deep breath and stepped out into the plush pile of expensive carpet. A gleaming glass door opposite the lift pronounced that she had indeed reached the offices of one Godfrey Sherrington.

She entered the foyer area dominated by a large reception desk constructed from a slab of timber that was heavy, dark and glossy. The rest was fairly regulation—if watching every television law show ever made was any indication. Muted lighting, leather accessories, expensive greenery and even more expensive art.

'Can I help you?'

Ali dragged her gaze off a painting that could easily have hung in the National Gallery and focused on the not-too-young, not-too-old receptionist who somehow blended with the understated elegance of the surroundings.

'Yes, I'm here…' Her voice wobbled and she cleared it. 'I have an appointment with Godfrey Sherrington.'

Her name was enquired after and a phone call was made and then she was directed to the very masculine-looking lounge. 'Mr Sherrington will be with you in a moment.'

Ali sat, the reality of it all suddenly hitting her. Her legs felt as if she were back in the taxi and she was grateful for the soft leather of the lounge even if it did look as if it belonged in an exclusive men's club.

Or an expensive brothel.

Her gaze fell on a portrait of a kindly-looking grey-haired gent. A plaque at the bottom announced him to be Godfrey Sherrington. Ali felt her spirits rise. He looked just the ticket. Aged. Wise. Scholarly. Experienced with the law.

Hell, even the name Godfrey inspired confidence. It conjured images of several generations of legal men. Well-known and respected barristers, QCs, maybe even a judge or two.

She'd been told by the hospital's CEO he was the best damn medical defence lawyer in the country and looking at this portrait she could believe it.

Godfrey Sherrington looked like a man who could melt an opposing team's argument with a few blistering words and then sit down, pat her hand and assure her everything was going to be okay.

She really hoped so. Because she was going to need a lot of hand patting through this whole ordeal. And it really did help settle her churning stomach to think that Godfrey Sherrington's hand would be soft and wrinkled. Like her grandfather's.

'Mr Sherrington will see you now.'

Ali started, the tray tilting perilously. She stood and followed the efficient receptionist down a hallway to the end door. The woman knocked and opened in one smooth movement. She indicated another set of leather lounge chairs clustered around a low table and said, 'Mr Sherrington won't be a moment.'

Ali, whose heart now beat so loudly she was sure seismologists all over the world were wondering what the hell was going on in Brisbane, watched the woman disappear.

She stood in the middle of the palatial room looking the proverbial fish out of water.

Massive glass windows afforded her a million-dollar view of the city skyline and down the river. So this was how the other half lived. Her office at work was a two-by-two shared affair just large enough for a desk, two chairs and a skinny examining table.

She moved towards the windows, feeling less and less comforted by the prospect of a lawyer called Godfrey. This was the big league!

She looked down spying a RiverCat speeding from Eagle St Pier across to Southbank. Her gaze tracked the boat and watched as it disgorged its human cargo. She followed the antlike movements of the disembarked passengers as they enjoyed a sunny Brisbane morning and would have given anything to be down there with them—not a care in the world.

She followed the meandering path of the riverside walk and suddenly realised she could see the River Breeze. Kat's pride and joy. And her current refuge from a world gone crazy.

Max washed his hands at the vanity and inspected his face. He'd gone with the whole shaggy look when his life had gone pear-shaped and though the style was frowned upon in the ultra-conservative world of law, being one of the principals in a respected law firm, not to mention a top-notch lawyer with a fearsome reputation, gave him a whole lot of latitude.

Certainly his great-great-grandfather Godfrey Sherrington the first would not have approved. But at thirty-five he'd long ago stopped giving a damn what people thought. This last eighteen months particularly.

He dried his hands, then checked his tie was straight. The

same tie he'd worn to the bar on Friday night. Henceforth to be for ever known as his lucky tie. He smiled at his reflection. He'd been doing that a lot since Friday.

Pete had called around Saturday night to watch the game with him and had known something was up within minutes.

'Okay,' he'd said. 'What's the matter?'

Max had taken a swig of his beer, his gaze firmly fixed on the television. 'What do you mean?'

Pete's eyes had narrowed. 'You're smiling.'

Max had chuckled. 'Jeez, sorry.'

Pete's eyes had narrowed even further. 'And now you're laughing?' He'd processed it for a second or two. 'Oh my God,' he'd said. 'You got laid, didn't you?'

Max had hidden his next smile by taking another swig from his bottle. 'Are we watching this game or not?'

Pete had tried in vain to dig out the details but Max had always abhorred locker-room talk and had seen the consequences of it played out too many times in courtrooms. He'd refused to confirm or deny anything and Pete had eventually given up.

But even now Friday night was still bringing a smile to his face. It had been incredible. She had been incredible. Generous. Playful. Adventurous. And even if he never saw her again, he knew their night together would go down as one of life's best memories.

Although, he had to admit, seeing her again was a very attractive proposition. Not that he knew anything about her other than her first name. No numbers were exchanged, no promises were given. But he could find her if he wanted to. He had no doubt that Pete was in touch with Kat so finding Ali would be very easy.

But.

They'd both known the score on Friday night. They'd

both known they were convenient bodies to get lost in for a little while. To forget for the night.

Still, he couldn't deny the strength of the urge to see her again if only to thank her for helping him to see that there was life and laughter after a decree absolute.

Nah. Who was he kidding? He had a whole box of condoms and he'd like nothing more than using them all up with her.

He shook his head as an image of her lying naked on his bed flashed before him, that damn curl falling in her eye, a Mona Lisa smile playing on her very kissable mouth.

He really needed to stop.

He couldn't be thinking about Ali when another woman waited for him outside. One who was no doubt scared and nervous and worried sick. One who deserved his full, undivided attention.

Dr Aleisha Gregory needed him to have his head in the game. She was relying on him. As was Brisbane Memorial Hospital—one of his, and the firm's, biggest clients.

'Get it together, bud,' he told his reflection before pushing off the sink.

Striding out into his office a moment later, he located the figure by the windows and announced, 'I'm so sorry to have kept you waiting.'

Her back was to him and she was obviously enthralled by the views from the forty-sixth floor. And then her curly butterscotch hair registered and a sudden sense of foreboding descended.

Ali frowned as a familiar voice invaded her turbulent thoughts. She turned. 'Max?'

Max blinked. What the—? His eyes raked her from top to bottom, not quite trusting that he hadn't just conjured her up. Errant curl, sexy mouth, blush spreading across high cheekbones.

It was her all right.

He glanced at the tray in her hands with the two coffee mugs boasting a River Breeze logo. He relaxed. She'd found out through Kat where he worked and decided she'd drop by. Bring some of that coffee Kat had boasted about on Friday night.

Hell, he was all for spontaneity. Especially if it came in such a delectable package. And hadn't he just been thinking he'd like to see her again?

He might not be in the market for a relationship but a little bit more of Friday night he could definitely handle.

He smiled. 'Well, this is a nice surprise,' he murmured, moving forward.

When he stopped in front of her he had absolutely no intention of kissing her. But then her mouth parted slightly and he grasped her lapels, yanked her forward and kissed her with a hunger that he hadn't realised still existed until their lips met.

Ali's gasp was smothered by the ferocity of his expert mouth and for a few seconds she was too stunned to do anything. But a flood of memories from Friday night returned on a rush of hormones.

He smelled better than she remembered. Felt better. If possible, even kissed better.

Ali wasn't sure what was going on and at the moment she didn't care because for the first time all morning she didn't feel in imminent danger of throwing up. For the first time all morning she'd forgotten about the whole stupid mess she was in.

So she melted against his mouth and hung on for dear life. Which was just as well because when he released her just as abruptly a good minute later, she staggered slightly.

Hell, she even whimpered.

'For me?' he asked, taking one of the cups and parking his butt on the deep window sill behind him.

'Er...' she said, straightening and trying to order rather scattered thoughts. Actually she'd bought it for Godfrey Sherrington but she guessed he could have hers. It probably seemed a silly gesture to a legal god, but Ali had wanted to break the ice, endear herself.

She wanted Godfrey Sherrington to like her. To believe her. Not just because he was defending her and he had to, but because she knew deep in her heart that this mess wasn't her fault and she wanted him to know it too.

'It should be hot enough still,' she said absently. 'I made them scalding just as the taxi pulled up so they should be a good temperature right now.'

She was babbling. She knew that. She needed to stop. But he was so near, his broad shoulders blocking her view, the knot of his tie at her eye level. She'd kissed what lay beneath that knot. Knew what he smelled like there. Had felt that pulse push against her lips.

She dropped her gaze to rid herself of the image only to be mesmerised by his swinging leg. The movement pulled the fabric of his trousers taut across his thigh. A thigh she knew. She'd touched. She'd gripped. Licked.

Gnawed.

She shut her eyes briefly. *Stop it!*

'So,' she said, taking a step back and clearing her voice. She would concentrate on the matter at hand if it killed her. 'I'm sorry, do you work for Godfrey Sherrington? Are you his...understudy?'

She massaged her forehead as she groped for the right terminology. 'Or article clerk? Second chair? I don't know... whatever the hell they call it in legal circles?'

Max frowned. What on earth was she babbling about?

'Because, no offence, but I've heard he's the best and,

apart from the obvious conflict of interest here, I really need the best. And, not to put too fine a point on it but I think the hospital expects it too. I really don't want to be palmed off to his…assistant.'

Max straightened, pushing off the window sill, that feeling of foreboding returning.

The hospital expects?

I really need?

Don't want to be palmed off?

He looked straight at her, the woman he'd spent hours and hours in bed with three days before, exploring every inch of her body. The woman whose lip gloss he'd just thoroughly kissed off.

'Ali,' he said quietly. '*I* am Godfrey Sherrington.'

She stared at him blankly. 'But you're Max.' Max whose taste was still on her tongue, whose smell was still on her skin.

Max stalked past her, cramming a hand through his hair. He stopped at his desk, placed his knuckles on the side and bowed his head. 'You're Aleisha Gregory, aren't you?'

Ali stared at his back as the implication slowly sank in. 'Oh, my, God.'

Max turned and sat on the edge of his desk. 'Indeed.'

The nausea that had threatened all morning suddenly rose and Ali placed a hand over her mouth. 'I'm going to be sick.'

Max knew exactly how she felt. This was a complete disaster! 'Yes,' he replied miserably.

'No,' Ali said urgently, dropping her bag with a thunk and travelling towards him, 'I'm *really* going to be sick.'

Max started at the urgency of her tone and the sudden pallor that had turned her golden complexion white as paper. 'Bathroom through that door.' He pointed.

Ali made it just in time. Not that she had anything to

bring up but it didn't stop the waves of retching or the hot tears that spilled over her lids and coursed down her cheeks.

This. Could. Not. Be. Happening.

Had she really spent several sweaty hours rolling around in bed with her lawyer the other night? Her kick-arse, top-notch, take-no-prisoners, best-in-town lawyer?

She groaned. Was nothing ever going to go right for her ever again? Was she cursed? Had she broken a mirror? Walked under a ladder?

She'd been a good person, hadn't she? She gave to charity. Never cheated on her taxes. Always told checkout staff if she'd been given too much change.

She operated on people's brains, for crying out loud!

Ali dragged herself up to the basin. She looked awful. Her nose was running, she had red eyes, a blotchy neck and two wet tracks running down her cheeks.

It was the only time in her life she wished she wore make-up so she could do a quick repair job. But seriously what would have been the point when she spent eighty per cent of her day behind a surgical mask?

Maybe after all this was over she'd get a job at a department store where she could put on a face every day and do something frivolous like sell handbags.

She loved handbags.

A knock sounded on the door, followed by, 'Ali? Are you okay in there?'

Okay? Did he have any idea how *not* okay her life was? How the one person she'd pinned her hopes on to make it all okay again—her lawyer—turned out to be a man she'd had hot, sweaty, best-sex-of-her-life with not even seventy-two hours ago.

She'd told him then she was never going to be okay again but this was a whole other twist.

'Ali?' Louder this time.

'I…I'm fine,' she called. 'I'll be right out.' There was no point hiding away in here—it wasn't going to make the problem go away.

Ali jerked the tap on and threw water over her face, scrubbing at it with her hands. Then she pulled off some paper towel and dabbed at the moisture, patting herself dry. She gave herself a quick once over in the mirror.

Still awful. But less soggy.

Just as well she hadn't gone and done something really foolish on Friday night like thinking there was something more to their time together other than a sexual tryst. Because the face that stared back at her now was not the face a woman wanted a man to see.

Ali took a deep breath and used an unsteady hand to push the door open. Max, who was standing at the windows, turned when he heard the click.

They looked at each other for a moment or two. 'So,' she said. 'Is Max a name you give to women in bars so they won't laugh at you when you tell them your real name?'

Max would have had to have been deaf to miss the sarcasm. He raised an eyebrow. 'People who live in glass houses shouldn't throw stones, *Ali*.'

She held his gaze, refusing to waver. 'Ali is short for Aleisha,' she snapped.

'And the coffee-shop-girl routine?'

'I *am* a coffee-shop girl. Right now, coffee-shop girl is me.'

Right now coffee-shop girl was looking pretty damn good all round.

Max regarded her silently for a brief moment before wandering back to his desk and throwing himself in his chair. He speared his fingers through his hair again and leaned back into the plush leather.

'My full name is Godfrey Maxwell Sherrington. My

father apparently insisted, family tradition et cetera. My mother, who, thank goodness, was a little more sensitive to modern conventions, realised it was an unfortunate name to lumber a seventies child with, acquiesced to this demand only under the proviso that I would be called Max. I've never been called anything other than Max.'

Ali watched the weariness that had so affected her on Friday night cloud his grey eyes again. Damn Max and those eyes. So, he hadn't deliberately misled her—it still didn't erase the fact that two cases of mistaken identity had landed them in a bit of a pickle.

And while her sappy heart, the part of it that sympathised with human misery, wanted her to go easy, the part fighting for her very existence tended to be more bitchy.

'It says Godfrey on the board downstairs, on the glass sliding doors in the foyer and on the door to this office,' she pointed out, ticking each point off on her fingers. 'And I bet if I find a piece of paper,' she said, marching over to his desk and whisking up a blank piece, 'it'll say Godfrey on your personalised stationery.'

She turned it around and pointed to the offending letterhead.

Max leaned forward, elbows on his desk, massaging his temples. 'It's my legal name. It's on all documents and signage. Just like Aleisha, no doubt.'

Ali glared down at him, annoyed that he was right and they both knew it. 'Doctors who work in the public health care system don't have stationery,' she said waspishly.

Max looked up at her, olive eyes going that stormy shade of khaki again. He sighed and indicated the chair opposite him. 'Sit down, Ali.'

Ali stood frowning at him for a few more moments. He returned her stare without wavering and she rolled her eyes.

'Fine,' she said, sinking into the plush leather of the most comfortable chair she'd ever had the pleasure of sitting in.

Well didn't that figure?

Her office chair gave her lumbar pain within a minute of sitting on its hard plastic seat.

In her next job she'd make sure a comfortable chair was written into her contract. An office job with an ergonomically designed chair—now that she could do.

'This is a disaster, isn't it?'

She looked exactly as she had the other night, big olive eyes uncertain, teeth pulling at her bottom lip as she'd asked if wanting to go to bed with him made her a bad person.

He remembered how that mouth had felt against his. How it had trailed all over his body. Stroked down his belly. Stroked lower...

'It figures, really. Pretty much par for the course for my life lately.'

Her words dragged him back from Friday night. Back to the present. For crying out loud—she was right there, in front of him! *Looking like hell.* As if her entire world had just been tipped upside down. And shaken for good measure.

Thinking about Friday night was *not* appropriate.

'Where do we go from here?'

There was finality in her tone that was heartbreaking and he rushed to assure her but she wasn't done with the one-sided conversation.

'Perhaps you can recommend someone else in the firm that could deal with the case?'

Max frowned, not quite keeping up with the leaps she was taking. 'I'm sorry?'

'I assume you'll have to recuse yourself?'

And then to his utter horror her face crumpled and she burst into tears.

CHAPTER FIVE

ALI wanted a hole to open up in Max's very expensive-looking Persian rug and swallow her up. Her heart thunked against her ribs as if a large piece of space junk had just landed smack in the middle of her chest.

This could not be happening.

Was it not bad enough to have slept with him? Did she have to go and add public humiliation to her sins?

'I'm s-sorry,' she snivelled, her nose and eyes streaming as she desperately tried to stem the tears that she'd held at bay for so long now.

Since her suspension.

Since before that—her ex, the baby.

'I don't know what's wrong with me, I n-n-never cry.'

Max knew. He'd read her case file several times. He knew her state of mind was shot. He knew she'd been through a roller-coaster ride of emotion. Of suspension and enquiries and reinstatements and further suspension while the case went to court.

He also now knew her ex had left her for another woman.

And then, to cap it off, she'd gone and slept with her lawyer.

'That'll be why, then,' he said dryly, her kicked-puppy gaze breaking through his well-fortified barriers as he handed her a tissue from the box on his desk.

Ali looked at the snowy white Kleenex in surprise as he waved it at her. He shrugged. 'Occupational hazard.'

'Really?' she asked, taking it, dabbing at her eyes, then blowing her nose.

Well used to being confronted with highly emotional people and situations in her own work environment, she found it a surprise to realise that medicine didn't corner the market on Kleenex usage.

'Sure. Most people come to lawyers when they're in trouble. They're usually pretty emotional.'

She sniffed as the vice gripping her chest eased a little and the last hiccoughy breath died.

'I'm sorry. Please don't think I'm this weak, weepy woman who cries at the slightest hurdle. I've just had…a really bad year.'

'Not at all. If it makes you feel any better the last person who cried in this office was a hundred-and-fifty-kilo drug dealer who could bench press our combined weight and had spent half of his life in maximum security.'

She smiled despite herself but his calm acceptance of her breakdown depressed her further.

Great.

He was the best. *The* best. Everyone said so. Everyone had assured her that in medical defence law he was *the* lawyer to have.

And she'd screwed it up, royally.

Sure, the charges weren't against her personally, but it was her alleged actions that had caused this whole mess and put the hospital in hot water. It was bad enough Brisbane Memorial had to fight this wrongful death suit—the last thing they needed was to lose their best lawyer because of her too.

The hospital needed a good lawyer. Needed *the* best. And so did she. She had a lot to prove here too.

A lot at stake.

Even if she was never going to pick up a scalpel again, her reputation had been damaged. And that she couldn't live with.

She had to prove her innocence.

And for that she needed the best.

She needed Max.

But now the last few months were wasted. All that time and money the hospital had ploughed into prepping the case had been sabotaged because of one hot sweaty night between the sheets.

Max looked over at a much more composed Ali. She looked like hell.

He really, really shouldn't want her this bad.

'I don't have to recuse myself.'

Ali sniffled. 'What?'

Max looked at her patiently. 'Ali, we slept together.' Not that there'd been a whole lot of sleeping going on. 'We met for the first time three days ago and slept together with no knowledge of what our relationship was going to be today. There's no law against it.'

Ali felt a moment's hope at his assurance but, given how badly her life had sucked the last year, she wasn't about to dance a jig. Things just hadn't been going her way.

'So...legally, we're fine,' she clarified. 'But what about ethically? Where do we stand there?'

Ali made hard ethical decisions in her job all the time— ethics she understood.

'Ethically I can be disbarred from sleeping with a witness.'

'Oh, God.'

His calm bluntness made her want to throw up again and she gripped the desk to ground herself. It was hard enough living amidst the ruins of her own professional life without feeling responsible for his too.

'If—' he jabbed his index finger at the desk for emphasis '—if, I had prior knowledge. Which I didn't.'

He searched her face. She still looked utterly miserable.

'It's okay, Ali,' he assured her. 'Here are the facts.' He pointed to his index finger. 'We met for the first time as strangers on Friday night. Correct?'

Ali nodded. 'Correct.'

He pointed to his next finger. 'It was a brief one-night stand that meant nothing to either of us other than a fabulous way to forget a miserable day. Correct?'

Ali swallowed as a little part deep inside her mewed in protest. She quashed it ruthlessly. Of course that was all it was—she barely knew the guy!

Just because she'd had the best sex of her life which had possibly ruined her for all other men was immaterial.

'Correct.'

He stabbed at a third finger. 'Unless you're some kind of closet bunny-boiler, which I seriously doubt, we have no intention of pursuing this relationship either during or after the trial. Correct?'

She shook her head emphatically. After the trial she had to work out what she wanted to do with the rest of her life. Start a new career. There would be no room for all-night-long sexual feasts.

No matter how mind-blowing it had been.

'Correct. Absolutely correct.'

'If, however—' he steepled his fingers '—this is a deal breaker for you, you feel uncomfortable with my representation given…' *how I licked every inch of your body* '…what transpired on Friday night, then, of course, I can recommend several colleagues who can take the case.'

He could practically see the cogs turning in her brain as

she chewed on her bottom lip. A lip he'd ravaged more than a little himself...

'But I have to warn you that starting over again with another lead lawyer would necessitate a continuance from the court that could set things back several months. And you need to know that, not only am I fully up to speed with your case, I'm also the best medico-legal lawyer in this city.'

Ali swallowed at the sheer arrogance of his statement. But there wasn't even one brain cell that didn't believe him. He was breathtaking in his total assurance that he was *the* man for the job. Between that and the way he'd calmly and methodically reeled off his points before, she could see how magnificent he'd be in court.

He could certainly hold his own in the arrogance stakes with any consultant surgeon she knew.

And somehow—whether it was his supreme confidence or the connection they'd made the other night—she trusted him.

She certainly didn't want to hang on for another few months. She needed to put this behind her and get on with her life.

Whatever it might hold.

'Okay.' Her voice sounded shallow and breathy and she cleared it. Her mind was made up—she had no time to sound indecisive. 'Okay, then.'

She looked so damn cute trying to conquer her anxiety and be brave with that silly curl flopping in her eye. It reminded him of her anxiety at his door on Friday night, which was the last thing he needed. He quickly cut off that train of thought and clawed back a modicum of professionalism.

'I have to be clear, though, that there is a line drawn between us now that neither of us can cross. We had no control over what happened a few days ago. But we do over what happens from now on.'

Aleisha nodded at his brisk businesslike tone. 'Of course.'

Whatever he said, whatever he wanted. As long as he continued with the case, she'd follow his demands to the letter.

She rose on shaky feet. 'How about we start over?' She offered her hand. 'Hi. I'm Dr Aleisha Gregory, pleased to meet you.'

Max looked at her, then at her hand, then back to her. He smiled as he stood and took her hand firmly in his and shook. 'Hi. I'm Max Sherrington.'

Ali felt his smile and the warmth of his hand go straight to her belly and she pulled her bottom lip between her teeth.

Max felt it too as his gaze followed the indent of tiny white teeth torturing a lush lip. 'Your lawyer,' he added.

Because God knew the way he wanted to swipe his tongue across that mouth didn't feel remotely lawyerly.

Half an hour later they were ensconced at a window table at Cha Cha Char, one of the many restaurants dotting the river walk area around Eagle Street pier. Max appeared to be a regular and Ali let him order one of their famous Wagyu steaks for her as she was still too keyed up to concentrate.

Too keyed up to eat, really, but her empty stomach was growling in protest and she was starting to feel light-headed. It was time to put something in her belly or soon her hands would be trembling and she wouldn't be able to take in what he was saying.

And she really needed to keep her wits sharp until this ordeal was over.

'Maybe we should have gone to the River Breeze as I first suggested?' Max murmured as he watched Ali play with her cutlery.

Ali looked up sharply. 'What?'

Her curls bounced to the abrupt movement and he remembered how they had felt trailing against his chest. 'You don't seem very comfortable here.'

Ali frowned. 'Oh. No… Here is…fine.'

The very last thing she needed right now was Kat's perennial cheeriness. Plus, she hadn't told her friend about her and Max getting naked and doing the nasty and Kat was too savvy not to take one look at them together and guess.

And then she'd never hear the end of it.

Max suppressed a smile as Ali returned her attention to her nearby fork. 'Kat doesn't know, does she? About us?'

Ali's fingers froze on the tines of the fork. She peeked up at him through her fringe as she chewed on her lip again.

'That you're my lawyer?' she asked, feigning innocence.

Max quirked an eyebrow. 'That we slept together.'

Ali's cheeks grew warm as she shook her hair back and looked at him fully. 'No.' She sighed. 'Kat's a romantic. Truly, it's best she doesn't know. Especially with this new… development. She'll start talking about destiny and, trust me on this, that's one load of hippy mumbo-jumbo I've heard one too many times.'

Max chuckled. 'You don't believe in destiny?'

Ali looked him square in the eye. 'I believe in hard work and self-determination.'

He nodded. 'Me too.'

There was a pause and Ali realised she'd relaxed a little. She picked up the spoon and absently doodled a pattern on the white tablecloth. 'Does Pete know?'

Max shook his head abruptly. 'I don't kiss and tell.'

Ali blinked at the sudden starch in his voice. 'I didn't think you would.'

Frankly it hadn't occurred to her that Max would be indiscreet. He hadn't struck her as the type. In retrospect that had probably been naïve but it was good to know her instincts had been on the money.

Max relaxed and even managed a small smile. 'Pete thinks he knows. He has a vivid imagination.'

Ali smiled in response. 'I think he and Kat are going to get along famously.'

The waitress arrived with their drinks, interrupting the only sense of shared history they had, and Ali was reminded that they weren't here socially. She took a sip of her diet cola and looked at him.

'So, what do we do now? I suppose you want to talk about what happened that night…at the hospital…'

Max shook his head. She was too strung out at the moment to dive straight in. He needed to build a rapport with her—a professional one this time.

And for that they needed to start from scratch. The facts of the case would be discussed ad nauseam over the following weeks—he needed her to trust him. To know that he was on her side.

'No. Not right now. I want to talk about you.'

'Me?' Ali really hadn't meant it to be a squeak but she rather feared that was exactly how it came out.

Max nodded. 'You.'

Ali was confused. She'd been bracing herself to go over the whole horrible mess again. Had just about made herself sick over it. 'I don't understand…'

'I know about the case, Ali. I know it inside out and back to front. And, trust me, we're going to go over and over it again with a fine-tooth comb. For now, I want to know what a file won't tell me. I want to know your favourite colour and what books you read and whether you've travelled and if you've had chicken pox. To understand you, to understand how this predicament evolved, to help you, I need to know who you are. I need a sense of you.'

Ali sobered. This she hadn't expected. But he was so sincere, his gaze gentle and full of empathy.

And she trusted him.

'My favourite colour is yellow. Not a soft gentle yellow you'd find in a nursery but bold, like sunflowers. I don't get time to read unless you count journals but the times I do I like to read something with a happy ending. I've travelled a lot both here and overseas. Tuscany is my favourite place. Yes, I've had chicken pox. I was sixteen and it knocked me flat. I did nothing but sleep for a week and avoid looking in the mirror. It was hideous.'

She dropped her gaze briefly, embarrassed by the rush of words. She raised her eyes and blasted him with a direct stare. 'What else?'

Max blinked, a little taken a back for a moment, then laughed. 'Okay then. We're obviously going to need to work on your technique for court.'

It was Ali's turn to blink. 'My technique?'

He nodded. 'You only answer the question. There's no need to elaborate. The more information you give, the greater potential for trouble. You should have just said, yellow, fiction, yes and yes.'

Ali felt as if she'd just flunked court preparation 101. She stared glumly into her drink. 'Oh.'

'It's okay,' Max assured. 'I'll go through all this with you.'

Ali glanced at him. There was so much for her to learn before she even got to court. 'So you would have answered those questions how?'

'Orange, biographies, yes and no.'

The startling efficiency of his quick-fire response was mildly depressing. Would she ever be that cool, calm and collected under cross-examination?

'And the long answers are?'

Max smiled. 'Orange, that blood orange you see at sunset as all the colours start to bleed into each other. I too don't have a lot of time to read anything other than work-related things, but I love biographies because other people's choices fascinate me. I've travelled extensively and I also love Tuscany, although I have a soft spot for Prague. And, no, never had chicken pox.'

Ali much preferred his long answers. She was far more comfortable with Max the man, than Max the lawyer.

Even if he had seen her naked.

'I hope you've had the vaccination. Chicken pox can be pretty brutal as an adult. I had a patient my first year out, a fit twenty-three-year-old, muscle-bound footy player, who wound up in Intensive Care with it. Went to his lungs. He arrested twice.'

Max chuckled. 'I'm betting you have a medical anecdote for every occasion, right?'

Ali chewed on her bottom lip. She did have a habit of being a walking, talking heath alert. Something that had always annoyed her ex.

She shrugged. 'Sorry. Occupational hazard.'

Max shook his head. 'Not at all. It's good to know. I'll arrange to get the shot as soon as possible.'

Ali felt awkward beneath his calm grey gaze. After going to bed with him on a mere hour's acquaintance, then crying and throwing up in front of him today and now this, he probably thought she was a nutcase. And she suddenly couldn't bear the thought of it.

'You shouldn't take your health for granted.'

Ali cringed. God, she sounded waspish. *Shut up. Just shut up.*

Max nodded. 'I agree.'

Their meals chose that moment to arrive and Ali could have kissed the waiter. The aroma of perfectly charred beef hit her empty stomach and it growled.

'This smells divine.' Her mouth watered as she picked up her knife and fork.

Max drifted the conversation to film and television as they ate. Ali was more relaxed now, which was exactly where he wanted her for the more difficult questions to follow. Listening to her speak, her low husky laugh, took him back to Friday night, and for the duration of the main meal he conveniently forgot that it could never happen again.

'Okay, I'm stuffed full,' Ali said, pushing her empty plate away and slouching back against her chair. She rubbed her hand over her belly.

Max watched the action. She'd removed her jacket and the burgundy silk of her blouse slid over the skin beneath with seductive ease. Her hand stopped abruptly and he dragged his gaze upwards. Ali was watching him, her olive eyes darkening.

For a moment neither of them breathed.

'Would you like the dessert menu, sir?'

This time it was Max's turn to be grateful for the arrival of the waiter who, oblivious to the sudden electrification of the air currents, was efficiently clearing the table.

'Ah...' Max needed a second or two to get his thoughts back in order. 'Ali?'

Ali, her breath short in her chest, gratefully looked at the waiter and shook her head. 'I couldn't possibly fit another thing in.'

'Not even some double-chocolate-coated cherries?' the waiter enquired. 'They're a house speciality and absolutely delicious.'

'Oh, yes, I can vouch for that,' Max agreed, his head finally back in the game. 'In fact bring us a bowl—I'll eat them if she doesn't. And some coffee?' He raised an eyebrow at Ali.

She nodded. 'Flat white would be good.'

'Same for me,' Max said. The waiter nodded and left with the plates.

Max glanced back at Ali. That errant curl had flopped in her eye and he almost reached out to pluck it away.

Almost.

But that would be crossing any number of professional boundaries. And he'd already crossed one too many.

'So…' He ignored the curl. 'Why did you become a doctor?'

Ali's heart, still recovering from their incendiary stare of a few moments ago, thrummed nineteen to the dozen. She sucked in a breath and reached for something light to dampen the crackling atmosphere. She just hoped her voice didn't shake as much as her hands.

'Well, that's a long story.' She cocked an eyebrow. 'Do you want the court version or can I elaborate?'

He knew she didn't mean it to sound flirty but he felt the husky timbre of her voice deep inside his groin. He gave her a grudging smile. 'I've cleared my schedule.'

Ali nodded slowly. At least this was safer ground than where they'd just been.

'I didn't always want to be a doctor. Not like most of my colleagues. Growing up, I wanted to be anything from the prime minister to a fairy.'

Max chuckled. 'I would have liked to have seen that.'

Ali watched as Max's dimples came out to play and found herself grinning in response. 'Unfortunately there were no universities for fairies.'

'Very short-sighted,' Max murmured, absently rubbing at his jaw.

Ali smiled and nodded as the rasp of his stubble stirred memories from Friday night, almost obliterating the reason she'd become a doctor. But it encroached like a big black cloud anyway, wiping the smile from her face. She dropped her gaze to the table where she traced a pattern with her finger on the tablecloth.

'I had a cousin—her name was Zoe. We were the same age and incredibly close.'

A flash of Zoe's strawberry-blonde hair wafted elusively through her mind, bringing a sharp stab of unexpected grief. But grief was like that—just when you thought you'd cried the last tear another whammy hit you from out of the blue.

'We were both only children and she lived three doors down and, well…we were inseparable.'

Max watched her doodle patterns and waited silently for her to continue, a sharp sense of foreboding refusing to lift its heavy hands off his shoulders.

'She was diagnosed with a brain tumour when she was sixteen. She wanted to be a neurosurgeon from the moment they first saw that ugly white blob on her CT scan. She had a plan to rid the world of brain tumours.'

Max scanned the top of her downcast head. 'What happened?'

Ali looked up from the table cloth. 'The cancer killed her. She didn't even last a year.'

It had been a terrible time in their family.

Dark. Long. Bewildering.

'At the end…the day before she died…I promised her I'd take the baton from her and never let it go.'

Max saw the shadows in her gaze intensify. Was Zoe's fervour living on in Ali or had Ali been living a lie? Trying her best to keep a deathbed promise to someone she'd loved?

Had it been a cross too big to bear?

'Do you ever wonder what you would have been if Zoe was still alive? Do you regret making such a big life decision at sixteen?'

Ali shook her head without hesitation, her eyes glittered

with purpose. 'No. Never. I love my job. And I'm a damn good surgeon, too. I can't imagine doing anything else...'

Except she had to—now. It didn't matter how good she was, she doubted she could ever go back after the trauma of the last year.

After the court case.

'Although, I gotta say coffee-shop girl is pretty damn cushy. Compared to being a surgeon it's a picnic.' She favoured him with a weak smile. 'It's a hell of a lot less stressful.'

Max heard the rawness behind the words and wasn't fooled by the feeble smile. What Ali was going through emotionally was very familiar to him. Most of his medicolegal clients wanted to chuck it all in by the time they got to him.

'You'll feel differently. Eventually. I promise.'

Ali shook her head. 'No,' she said emphatically. 'There are two things I'm never doing again. Going back into medicine and falling for another man.'

Max regarded her serious face. He would have tried to dissuade her again except he understood how she felt about being emotionally vulnerable to another human being again. That he could definitely relate to.

'I always tell my clients to never make any decisions until after it's all over. And besides,' he said, lightening his tone to a tease, 'what else could you do? There are still no fairy universities.'

Ali managed a faint quirk to her lips. 'Who says I have to do anything, right? I could be a lady of leisure travelling all over the world. Or become a llama farmer. Or write a book.'

Max wasn't fooled for a moment. There was no excitement in Ali's voice for any of her suggestions. No passion.

Her tone was flat; her eyes lacked the sparkle he'd seen when she'd told him about Zoe.

'You did all you could, Ali. Nathaniel Cullen's death was not your fault.'

Ali flinched as she heard the name again. Just when she'd thought she was immune to it, it jabbed right into her soft, spongy, bruised middle.

'Well, you have to believe me, you're my lawyer.'

Max shook his head. 'An internal hospital review believed it. An independent review commissioned by us believed it. The coroner believed it. I've been through each and every one. You, the hospital, have no case to answer.'

Ali bit down hard on her lip. She would not cry in front of this man again. 'And yet here we are, being sued anyway.'

'I've been doing this a long time, Aleisha, and I've defended my fair share of guilty clients and, believe me, you are not one of them.' He shifted in his chair. 'His parents are grieving. They're angry. They want to blame somebody. And they want their day in court. They want to be able to tell their story to a judge.'

Ali nodded. 'I know.'

And she did know. Heck, she even understood their motivations. She remembered how she'd felt when she'd lost the baby. She'd wanted to blame someone.

Anyone.

She'd wanted a focus for the maelstrom of feelings. A distraction from the overwhelming distress of being pregnant one day, growing a tiny human being, and then suddenly…not.

She'd chosen Tom. But it hadn't helped.

'But we're going to win this,' Max murmured. 'I promise you.'

Ali gazed into the steady grey depths of his eyes, desperate to believe him. She didn't even register the waiter placing her coffee down or slipping a little white bowl of cherries between them.

After a moment she said, 'I'm going to hold you to that. We fairies-in-waiting take our promises seriously.'

Max's chuckle made her shiver all over and his smile oozed confidence as he popped a chocolate-covered cherry in his mouth and offered her the bowl.

CHAPTER SIX

A FEW days later Ali was sitting around the law firm's oval boardroom table surrounded by men in suits murmuring to each other as they waited for Max to make an appearance.

She wasn't sure if it was because she was the only female amidst seven men but the room seemed oppressively masculine. From the dark wood panelling to the polished mahogany table to the heavy brocade drapes obscuring the sunshine and river view, it was as testosterone charged as a football locker room.

Ali smiled to herself at the image of a jockstrap carelessly flung and snagged on the corner of the gilt-framed, dark-as-night oil painting hanging on the opposite wall.

It was that or scream.

'You okay, my dear?'

Ali turned to the man beside her who had already asked her the same thing twice. Dr Reginald Aimes, the hospital's CEO, had been a tower of strength during this last year and his grandfatherly concern had been most welcome.

But his fussing today was getting on her last nerve.

'I'm fine, Reg,' she said a little more testily than she should have. 'I just want it to be over.'

'As do we all, Aleisha.' He patted her hand. 'As do we all.'

The door opened abruptly and Ali flinched as her pulse

skyrocketed. She was pretty sure it was the accumulated tension. Her nerves were shot these days. A year ago she'd had cast-iron control of everything. All had been well and her surgeon's hands had been steady and sure.

Nowadays the earth always felt unsteady beneath her.

But she couldn't discount Max's enigmatic presence either. He strode into the room with a purpose that bordered on arrogant, ushering in a potent mix of sex and charisma.

It was as if, for a moment, all the oxygen had been sucked from her lungs and she were back in his bed, underneath him, letting him obliterate the stench of a harrowing year.

Had it been almost a week? It felt like an hour ago.

All the other suits faded to grey as he dominated the room.

'Good afternoon, gentleman,' Max said. He nodded at Ali. 'Aleisha.' Then he sat.

'Ali,' she corrected.

Reg calling her Aleisha was just his old-fashioned sense of propriety and she'd long ago given up correcting him, but Max…

Max said Aleisha in a way that put so much distance between them she almost winced. And the last thing she needed right now was a distant lawyer. As unfortunate as sleeping with him had turned out to be, she'd felt that it at least connected them.

As if he now had a personal stake in this case.

That somehow he'd go that extra yard.

Max, ignoring the shine of her mouth and the way her soft pink blouse outlined her breasts, dismissed the correction with a flick of his wrist. 'I think it's best to stick with Aleisha or Dr Gregory.'

Ali was the woman he'd slept with.

Aleisha was a part of his case and his client's star witness. And God knew, as she continued to look at him with those big olive eyes that were taking him right back to Friday night, he needed every professional boundary he owned firmly in place.

The door opened again and a matronly, middle-aged woman entered. She took a seat next to Max where a stenography machine had been positioned on the table.

'Everyone, this is Helen. She'll be taking notes.'

As naturally as she was breathing, Ali's astute medical gaze took in Helen's enlarged knuckles as she placed her fingers on the keys and she absently wondered if the stenographer had seen a doctor about the arthritis.

There was a general murmur of welcome and Max immediately felt more businesslike with Helen beside him. Now all he had to do was ignore the fact that he'd dreamt about eating chocolate-covered cherries off Ali's body for the past three nights.

'Welcome, everybody. Thank you for taking time out of your busy schedules so we could all meet as one. I will of course be talking to you all individually over the next few days as I do my final preparations for the court case that's scheduled week after next, but it's important to have at least one meeting with everyone present.'

There were more general murmurs of agreement around the table.

'For now though we're going to start with Dr Gregory's testimony and then we'll follow the chronology of the incident and talk to each of you in turn as the events unfolded.'

Max shuffled some papers in front of him then glanced up at his captive audience. 'Any objections?'

Ali swallowed. God, he already sounded like a lawyer. His voice even seemed different. It was still low and smooth but there was a briskness about it that ruined the languorous melody she'd instantly noticed at the bar the other night.

Max braced himself, fixing a calm neutral smile to his

face as he looked at Ali. 'Dr Gregory, why don't you go through what happened the night Nathaniel Cullen died?'

Ali searched his unwavering gaze for a sign of the man she'd slept with after knowing him for a mere hour. For the man who'd tempted her with chocolate-covered cherries.

But he wasn't there.

A cool professional had taken his place.

Her heart thudded painfully in her chest. She'd told this story a hundred times. Practically everyone in the room had heard it that many times too.

It should be getting easier.

But it wasn't.

She took an unsteady breath. 'Okay.'

Max heard the quiver in her voice and was surprised by the urge to reach across the table and give her hand a squeeze. Instead he settled for an encouraging nod and a low, 'No one is judging you here, Aleisha.'

Ali bit back the natural habit of correcting the use of her name. She could see some warmth creep back into his gaze and for that he could call her whatever he damn well pleased.

'It was bedlam that night...' Her voice didn't even sound as if it belonged to her as a familiar rush of emotion bloomed in her chest and threatened to close off her throat. Reg patted her hand again and she took a sip of water.

She hated appearing weak in front of these suited men— her superiors. Surgeons had to be tough, detached, uncompromising.

It was an art she'd never quite perfected.

She knew it made her a better surgeon, a better doctor, just as she knew some of these men thought it made her unsuitable for the rigours of the job.

No doubt Max also thought it made her a terrible witness.

And that was unacceptable.

Ali cleared her throat and looked Max directly in the eye. 'I had a fifty-seven-year-old male patient with an evolving neurological deficit at the same time Nathaniel arrived in the emergency department accompanied by his mother.'

'That was at—' Max consulted his notes 'two in the morning?'

Ali nodded. 'Yes.' She took another sip of water. 'He'd presented almost twenty-four hours post falling out of bed complaining of a headache. He was stable neurologically and both he and the aneurysm patient were scanned one after the other.'

'Nathaniel first?'

'Yes. I reviewed Nathaniel's results as Mr Todd was being scanned. They revealed a very small extra-dural haematoma, two mm wide with no midline shift. Given Nathaniel's excellent neurological condition I decided to manage him conservatively as per protocol by closely monitoring him in our HDU and repeating the CT scan the next day.'

'This is standard practice?'

'Yes.'

Max made a notation, then nodded at her to continue. He could see how weary she was of the story but he wanted to hear it in her own words from her own mouth.

'What next?'

'Mr Todd's CT revealed a large leaking cerebral aneurysm requiring emergency surgical intervention. We were knife to skin within half an hour.'

Max nodded as he consulted his notes again. 'Nathaniel deteriorated while you were operating on Mr Todd?'

'Yes,' Ali confirmed. 'I was phoned in Theatre approx three hours later by my surgical resident. Nathaniel had just had a grand mal seizure and blown a pupil. He was drowsy but it was hard to assess whether this was post-ictal or due to the evolving extra-dural.'

He frowned. 'That's not typical, right?' He consulted his notes. 'Such a late deterioration?'

Ali shrugged. 'There was nothing typical about this case. But it's certainly not unheard of. Typically if someone was going to have an acute deterioration it would usually happen within a few hours post the original injury. Extra-durals are arterial bleeds so they can rapidly accumulate and the patient can just as rapidly decompensate as happened with Nathaniel.'

'Okay' He nodded. 'What then?'

'I told Jonathon, the resident, to get him to Theatre stat. I was just about finished with the clipping procedure and I had a senior resident with me who was perfectly capable of closing. I left Theatre Four and went straight into Theatre Eight where I scrubbed up again as they got Nathaniel on the table.'

'How long until you got knife to skin this time?'

'From the phone call? About fifteen minutes. But there was so much blood…'

Ali dropped her gaze to her water glass. Even now she could see its bright rich colour spilling over the green drapes, flowing to the floor, pooling around her clogs.

She'd heard about such cases, hell, she'd been no stranger to massive loss of blood on more than one occasion in the ER, but she'd never expected to witness it coming from an eighteen-year-old's head.

She'd never forget the blood.

She returned her gaze to him. 'I couldn't stop the bleeding. He arrested on the table and we couldn't revive him.'

She willed herself not to beseech him. She hadn't done anything wrong. She hadn't been negligent. Nathaniel Cullen had sadly been just another horrifying statistic. Another patient that despite medical advances and a hospital full of whizz-bang technology they just hadn't been able to save.

Simply put—he'd been unlucky.

But she wanted Max to understand that there was nothing she could have done. That her treatment had been no different from that any other doctor would have given that night including her consultant, Neil Perry, who sat opposite her.

Tom had asked her continually what she'd done wrong, where she had erred. He hadn't understood that sometimes, no matter what you did, patients died.

Did Max?

Max gave her a moment or two. Her bald statement had been flat and emotionless but there was pain in the depth of her eyes glowing like a freshly minted coin.

He was used to this level of emotion. He dealt with people and situations that were highly charged and rarely black and white. And he'd always been able to separate himself from the emotion.

But Ali's pain reached deep inside his bones.

The need to vindicate her overwhelmed him.

'What happened next?' he asked while he battled with his keen legal mind for a modicum of professionalism. 'You told the parents?'

Ali nodded. 'Yes. By this stage both Deidre and Gordon were at the hospital.'

'And how did that go?'

Ali blinked. 'How do you think it went? I had to tell them their son was dead. It was awful.'

Max nodded, letting her derision wash past him. He'd done some pretty damn difficult things in his job but he couldn't even begin to imagine the enormity of having to tell someone their loved one had passed away.

How many times had she done that?

'Were they angry at you, at the hospital, at that stage? Did they threaten to sue that night?'

Ali shook her head. 'No, at that stage they were too... broken. They were blaming themselves, saying they should have brought him in the previous night.'

Interesting. Max scribbled a quick note. 'Would that have made a difference?'

'Most likely not. As I said earlier the size of his extra-dural on admission almost twenty-four hours post injury was only two mm. I suspect there may have been nothing to find for many hours. Had he presented immediately I would have treated him the same—CT scan and close observation.'

'Okay, good, thank you,' he said. He held her gaze as he smiled at her. 'I know it's something you've been over and over ad nauseam. I appreciate your patience, Aleisha.'

Ali's gaze tangled with his as his gentle words soothed the raw wound that he'd just prodded again. It was almost as if he'd whispered into her ear. Even the way he said her full name laid gentle fingers against her skin.

The room shrank; gooseflesh broke out on her arms.

Breaking eye contact, she reached for her glass. 'No worries,' she murmured.

Max, realising he was staring at the curve of her neck and remembering how'd she'd arched her back when he'd kissed her there, also dropped his gaze.

A tsunami of lust fogged his vision and he shuffled the papers in front of him, hoping it looked purposeful instead of erratic.

Was he going to want her every day of the coming weeks?

Maybe he should have followed Pete's advice after Tori had left and put himself out there.

Got it out of his system.

He was obviously suffering from an overdose of testosterone now he'd broken his very long dry run. He'd forgotten how great sex was and now he was going to have to sit next to the very woman who'd reminded him, day after day, and not be able to do a damn thing about it.

He looked up to find the entire table, including Helen, looking at him expectantly.

Get a grip, man!

'Dr Perry, I believe you were the next one involved chronologically, followed by Dr Aimes and then the police.'

Ali was grateful that the following three hours required very little input from her other than the odd clarification or two, even if it was disconcerting to realise that Max had barely looked at her since he'd had to during her testimony.

In fact he seemed to be avoiding it. Even when he'd sought to clarify a point with her.

Was that a good thing or a bad thing?

She spent every minute of the three hours wondering.

By the time the meeting broke up she was tired and tense just about everywhere, a headache forming. Max disappeared out of the door with Reg and the other suits leaving only her and Helen in the room. She was suddenly strangely reluctant to leave this oppressively masculine space. In here people seemed to know what they were doing—things were certain.

Out there, nothing seemed sure.

Ali was distracted from her thoughts as Helen, whose fingers had tapped away for hours, rubbed absently at her disfigured knuckles as she packed up.

'How long has your arthritis been this bad?' Ali asked.

Helen looked up, surprised. 'Years…I just live with it now.'

'Stenography can't help,' Ali observed.

Helen shrugged. 'It's my job.'

'Are you under a specialist?'

Helen shook her head. 'Just my GP.'

Ali tutted at the older woman. 'Here,' she said, fishing around in her handbag for her purse. She located it and extracted the business card she was after. She stood and passed it to Helen as Max re-entered the room. 'He's a good guy. Tell him I referred you.'

'Trying to steal the best stenographer in the business?' Max joked.

Helen laughed and took the card. 'Thanks, Dr Gregory.'

Ali sat again as Max, who had relieved the arthritic stenographer of her load, departed the room with Helen. Her headache tightened its steely band across her forehead a little more and she propped her elbows on the table and cradled her face in her palms.

Listening to her professional life being discussed, her every action, every word being dissected, had been harrowing and Ali rubbed at her temples trying not to think about it.

'You should go home, put your feet up and relax.'

Ali didn't have to look up to know who it was but the deep husk in his voice ensnared her in its sticky trap, drawing her gaze in his direction regardless. He lounged in the doorway, one shoulder propped against the jamb, his jacket finally removed, his shirt cuffs turned up to his elbows, his hands stuffed deep into his pockets.

'Headache?'

Ali nodded. 'Harrowing session.'

He looked at his watch and pushed off the jamb. 'It's after six. Come with me—I've got some pills in my office.'

After six? It had been hard to tell the passage of time with the curtains closed. 'Isn't pill pushing illegal?' she said, forcing a light teasing note into her voice.

It had been so serious the last three hours, if she didn't get some relief from it she was going to crack up.

Max lazed back against the jamb again and gave a half-smile. 'I don't think paracetamol counts. And anyway, I'm giving them to you, not selling them.'

'Ah, but that's how you get me hooked. Give me a free taste and *bam*, suddenly I can't go without.'

Max felt the breath seize in his lungs. That was exactly what had happened to him. She'd given him a taste of her and now he couldn't think of anything else. He'd been thinking about those damn curls brushing his chest all afternoon. He'd barely taken anything in.

Thank God for Helen and her notes.

Ali watched as Max stilled and his grey eyes darkened to slate. She suddenly realised her words spoken in jest could be misconstrued and Max had most definitely misconstrued.

She too stilled as their gazes locked. Where the hell did she go from here?

Max recovered first. 'Well, I know a good lawyer if your habit ever gets you into trouble.'

God help her, she knew a good lawyer too. And he was leading her right into trouble.

He was trouble with a capital T.

It was another moment or two before Ali broke eye contact and rose from the chair. 'Thank you, some paracetamol would be much appreciated. I normally carry some with me but I appear to be out.'

Max breathed again as she made her way around the table. But it was only momentary. As she walked towards him he got his first glimpse of her fully clad body.

A skirt. She was wearing a skirt.

And not like the one she'd worn to the bar the other night, that was loose and floaty, that skimmed and hinted. No, this was one of those straight business skirts that moulded and clung and barely reached her knees.

Perhaps if he didn't already know in shocking intimate

detail what was under that skirt, it wouldn't have mattered so much. But he did—and now he was reminded of every inch.

Seriously? How was he supposed to think of her as Dr Aleisha Gregory, witness, when she was wearing that skirt?

The kind of skirt that was made to be slid up stockinged thighs...as she straddled him...in his car seat.

Ali felt her cheeks warm as Max's gaze lingered on her hips and legs. When he finally dragged his eyes back up to her face they'd darkened to graphite.

Their gazes locked for a moment. The heat from his sizzled along her nerve endings and Ali had the insane urge to pose for him. Rock one hip to the side, plant a hand on her waist, thrust her chest a little.

Max gave himself a stern mental shake and pushed off the doorjamb. 'Follow me.'

The gentleman in him should have gestured her to precede him but no way was he going to expose himself to every swing of her delectable hips outlined in a swathe of black cling wrap. It had been a long day and that skirt should come with a highly flammable warning.

Ali's legs were decidedly wobbly as she followed his long stride through the corridors to his office. Her heart beat a little too fast, her breath came a little too quick. And the hard points of her nipples rubbed painfully against the fabric of her bra with each step.

It was torture here in his jet stream as Max's sex-in-a-bottle cologne mixed with his arrogant masculinity. By the time she stepped into his office she was a nervous wreck.

Max, grateful for activity, sat in his chair and searched through a couple of drawers before he located his stash of paracetamol. He looked up.

Big mistake.

She was standing directly in front of his desk, her skirt

at eye level. And he suddenly realised she could straddle him just as easily in this chair as she could in his car.

No, no, no.

Annoyed at himself for the images he didn't seem to be able to erase, he thrust the blister pack at her. 'Bottled water over there.' He jerked his thumb over his shoulder to indicate the bar fridge behind him.

Ali blinked at his harsh tone but took the offering without comment. By the time she'd retrieved a bottle of water, swallowed two tablets and turned back to face him, he was standing at the door looking cranky and impatient.

He was holding his briefcase in one hand and his jacket in the other. 'Ready to go?'

Ali could feel her ire rise. 'You don't have to wait for me. I'm perfectly capable of finding my own way out of the building.'

'Don't be ridiculous,' he dismissed. 'I'm leaving, you're leaving. I'll see you out.'

He was pretty sure he could be trusted not to jump her in the lift.

Ali didn't know what had come over him but she didn't like this Max at all. She hoped it was courtroom Max because he sure as hell was surly.

'Fine.' She strode to the doorway, her chin up, and sailed right past him.

Too late Max realised as he fell in behind her he was about to get a close-up view of her backside whether he liked it or not. He gritted his teeth and deliberately fixed his gaze on a point in the centre of her back.

But then the bounce of her curls drew his gaze and he remembered anew how they had felt trailing over his skin as she had gone down on him.

They stepped into the lift in silence, each taking an opposite wall. Max pushed the G button and stared studiously at the floor. Silence grew large between them until Ali couldn't stand it any more.

'What do you think of a travel agent? They look like they lead a very glamorous life.'

Max frowned and lifted his gaze. 'What?'

'As a career choice, after the court case?'

'Well, I'm not sure how you're going to fit that in around being a neurosurgeon.'

'I told you, I'm not going to do that any more.'

He rejected the suggestion with one arrogant shrug. 'Of course you are.' Then he returned his gaze to the floor.

Ali bit back a retort and reached for calm. 'Is everything okay?' she asked. 'Did I not do good today?'

Max almost groaned out loud. 'You were fine,' he dismissed testily, glaring at her.

Ali blinked. 'You seem mad at me.'

He sighed. 'I'm not mad at you, Aleisha.'

He was mad at himself.

Ali glared back at him as calm deserted her and the throb in her head intensified. She hated being called Aleisha and she'd just had three solid hours of it.

'For God's sake,' she snapped. 'We're not in the boardroom now—can you please just call me Ali?'

Max felt the waves of hostility rolling off her clash and duel with his. He jabbed his finger at the red stop button and the cab ground to a halt.

Ali gasped as she clutched the rail behind her. 'Are you crazy? What the hell are you doing?' she snapped.

Max switched his jacket to his other side and buried his free hand deep into his pocket lest he lunged for her. Which was exactly what he wanted to do. Grab her, lift her against the wall, slide his hands beneath that damn skirt and do her right here, right now.

'I can't call you Ali. Not now.' He glowered. 'Ali's the

woman I've seen naked. I kissed her toes and licked her all over. For God's sake, Aleisha, I was buried inside you most of last Friday night.'

He removed his hand from his pocket to rake it through his hair. 'Ali's the name I called out as I came.'

Ali watched the agitated rise and fall of his chest and knew hers had followed suit. She could hear her breath roughen at the images he evoked.

She could almost feel the heat of his whisper as he'd groaned *Ali* in her ear.

Her arms broke out in goose bumps.

He stuffed his hand back into his pocket. 'I need to call you Aleisha. And I need to start right now. Ali is a woman I had one of the best nights of my life with. Aleisha is a witness. My client's witness. If I slip in court, call you Ali, they'll know. The judge, the opposing team, *your* hospital board—they'll all know. Because it'll be in my voice.'

Ali was stunned by his diatribe. He hadn't moved any closer, he was sticking firmly to his side, but she felt skewered to the spot by the barely leashed desire she saw burning in his graphite eyes.

Deep inside, her muscles contracted.

Max watched her watch him. He was mesmerised by the way the buttons of her blouse strained as she sucked air in and out of her lungs. He pushed his butt against the lift wall a little harder.

'Look, the truth is I'm very attracted to you and I haven't been attracted to anyone for a long time. God knows that damn skirt's driving me nuts and I'd like nothing more than to pin you against that wall—' he jabbed his finger in the direction of the wall she was leaning against '—and have my way with you. And if it wasn't for this...'

Ali swallowed, her throat suddenly dryer than a fallen autumn leaf, her pulse roaring through her ears. She looked at him for a moment or two seeing the possibilities, the fun they could be having, if the court case weren't between them.

'Yeh.' She nodded. 'If it wasn't for this...'

Max regarded her for a moment. 'So please, for the love of God, can we just stick with Aleisha?'

'Okay...Godfrey.'

There was silence for a moment, then Ali watched as his frown slowly slipped, his dimples flashed and he laughed. It slid between them as it had on Friday night and dissipated the tension to a low sizzle. She found herself laughing too.

'Touché,' he murmured.

Then he punched the ground button again and the lift lurched back into working order. The doors were opening at their destination ten seconds later.

'Go home,' he said, striding out of the lift. 'Get a good night's sleep.' *One of them might as well.* 'Tomorrow is a full day of prep.'

Ali followed him at a slower pace. Home wasn't that appealing. Kat was on a date with Pete and she didn't feel like being alone. 'I don't suppose you fancy getting a drink. Maybe a bite to eat?'

Max stopped abruptly and turned. His eyes raked her up and down. 'In that skirt? I don't think so.'

Ali blushed. 'I didn't mean...it wasn't...I'm not coming on to you.' Surely they could temper their attraction for each other in a restaurant full of people?

Max gritted his teeth as her 'coming on to you' had a predictable effect in his underpants. The still-open lift doors beckoned.

'I just thought maybe we could talk about the case away from the formality of your office,' she clarified. 'Like we did at Cha's.'

'I know. But I don't trust myself around that skirt. Here,'

he said, reaching for his wallet and pulling out a business card. 'This is my mobile and home phone numbers. If you want to talk outside the office, I think we'd better stick to the telephone.'

She took the card from him and noted how studiously he avoided touching her. He looked so serious it was hard to imagine, despite the pulse of sexual awareness prickling between them, that they'd ever been intimate.

'Anything I need to know in particular for tomorrow?'

'Yes,' he grouched. 'For God's sake, don't wear that skirt. Ever again.'

And he turned on his heel and strode away.

CHAPTER SEVEN

As she had feared the apartment was lonely when she opened the door brushing raindrops off her hair.

Kat had marched in with her bags a month after Tom had moved out and completely taken over. Ali had protested at the time, had wanted to be left alone to lick her wounds, but now she couldn't imagine her two-bedroom flat without Kat filling it with chatter and laughter. Making it feel like a home.

Ali flicked on the television so the house didn't seem so silent. She poured herself a glass of wine to chase away the last of her headache and then forced herself to eat some of the leftover pasta that Kat had cooked the night before and she hadn't been able to eat because she'd been too wound up.

Another advantage to having Kat around—she was an amazing cook. Ali had never eaten so well.

Then she took a quick shower, dressed in her pyjamas, poured herself another glass of wine and slid a DVD into the player in her bedroom. She turned out the light and pulled back the covers of her bed and snuggled down to watch the action film Kat had borrowed from the video shop on the weekend.

Action films weren't necessarily her thing but there were

worse ways to take her mind off things than watching Bruce Willis running around all shirtless and macho.

By the time the film finished she was halfway through her third glass of wine and feeling really mellow. Rain was beating against the roof and window pane, occasional lightning streaks illuminated the darkened room and Bruce had saved the world.

She reached for the remote to turn the television down and her gaze fell on Max's business card she'd tossed on her bedside table when she'd dumped her handbag earlier.

Before a second thought could enter her head, she was dialling his home number.

Max frowned as his phone rang at ten o'clock at night. He reached across the various files he had strewn across his bed and snatched the receiver. 'Hello?'

'So, I'm thinking movie stunt man...woman...whatever... sounds pretty wild and exciting.'

Max gripped the phone as her voice murmured into his ear just as it had the night she'd spent right here in his bed. 'Aleisha.' *He really didn't need this.* 'It's ten o'clock.'

She squinted at the clock. 'Sorry, I may be a little tipsy.' He chuckled and her nipples tightened.

'So, stunt woman, huh? What on earth brought that on?'

'Just finished watching *Die Hard.*'

'Which one?'

'Four.'

'You know Bruce would be dead a hundred times over in real life, right?'

'Of course. So?'

He smiled. 'So it's not very realistic.'

'I don't care.' The wine was making her belligerent. 'Besides, I like it when the good guy wins.'

Yeh, so did he. It was why he'd become a lawyer.

His mind drifted back to their heated exchange in the lift,

which, despite the mountains of work surrounding him, he'd been reliving most of the night. 'Are you still wearing that skirt?

'No.'

Max nodded, relieved. Which lasted a beat until the possibilities of what she *was* wearing started to parade through his mind.

'Because you're wearing an old pair of tracky bottoms and a paint-stained T-shirt that hangs like a sack on you?' he asked hopefully.

Ali looked down at her matching hot-pink vest-top and boy-leg knickers that didn't quite meet, leaving a strip of bare flesh exposed. 'Er…okay.'

Max shut his eyes tight. 'Oh, God, you're not, are you? Please tell me you're not naked.'

His voice was husky in her ear and this time everything tightened. 'Did we just move into an ethically grey area?'

'Yes. Are you?'

Ali swallowed. 'No.' Although she might as well be given how aware she was of her body right at this moment.

Max's breath huffed out in relief.

'What are you wearing?' she asked.

'Aleisha.' No way was he about to tell her he was lying on his bed in nothing but his underpants. Or that this conversation was making them decidedly tight. 'I hope you didn't ring just to talk dirty to me.'

Ali heard the warning note in his voice. 'Grey again, huh?'

'You could say.' Although *blue* may have been more accurate.

She sighed. 'Sorry.' She sipped her wine. 'But it's all your fault.'

Max chuckled at the petulance in her voice. 'You rang me.'

Before she could stop them words tumbled out. 'You've

jump-started my libido,' she grumbled. 'Tom managed to kill it dead. And I was fine with that, do you hear? Fine. I was over and done with men. And relationships. And sex. But now...'

Now one night with him and sex had managed to sideline the nagging worry that constantly gnawed at the back of her brain.

That wasn't good. The worry kept her focused. She needed to stay focused.

'Now?' he prompted.

'I can't get it out of my head.'

Max heard the bewilderment in her voice but also the longing and felt his body respond. He too had thought of little else.

But he wasn't going to talk sex with her on the phone. Not with his nearly naked body hard and aching and her wearing what he suspected was also very little.

Not when he was as done with women and relationships as she was done with men.

Not when he'd drawn a line he couldn't cross.

Ali's room glowed blue-white as more lightning lit up the night sky. 'Is it raining at your place?' she asked.

Max frowned at the rapid change in subject. He glanced at his window as rain pattered and formed tiny tributaries down his pane. 'Yes.'

Ali yawned and snuggled down into the sheet a little more. 'I love a rainy night.'

The rain and her voice, low and sleepy in his ear, seemed to cocoon him in a cosy domesticity despite the fact they lived miles apart.

It was equal parts nice and terrifying.

'Was there a purpose to this phone call?'

'You don't love a rainy night?'

Max detected the slightest trace of reproach in her voice. 'Aleisha.'

Ali tried not to be disappointed at his obvious exasperation. 'No purpose…Kat's not here and…' She pushed herself up in the bed. 'I'm sorry, forgive me. Kat always says wine gives me alcohol-induced Tourette's.'

Max chuckled and felt the terrifying ebb.

'You should ask me whatever you want about the case now. I'll be scarily honest.'

'Oh,' he teased. 'You haven't been until now?'

Ali smiled, pleased to hear his tone lighten. 'Of course I have. It was just…carefully considered. Filtered. Tonight, apparently, I have no filter.'

Max smiled at her candour. A question came straight to mind; still he hesitated before he asked it. It was a question on his list but not one he'd been looking forward to asking. Maybe in her relaxed state she wouldn't freak out.

'What happened with your ex?'

Ali sucked in a breath. That was one she hadn't expected. 'Oh.' Her brain grappled with his blunt enquiry. 'Is that relevant?'

Max grimaced at the alertness to her voice. It sounded as if she'd sobered up in a second.

And he'd been enjoying sleepy Ali.

'From what I gleaned on Friday night, the break-up occurred a year ago. About the same time as the Cullen incident. I'm thinking maybe there were extenuating circumstances we can work into the case.'

Ali felt the weight of the events that had king-hit her a year ago press her into the bed. But she wouldn't blame her personal life for her professional issues.

'There weren't.'

'Why don't you let me be the judge of that?' he murmured.

Ali shook her head. 'Tom left after Nathaniel Cullen died. Not before.'

Max dragged Aleisha's file closer. 'How soon after?'

Ali braced herself as the answer hovered on her lips. She was sick of the platitudes that little piece of info usually engendered and she most certainly didn't want to hear one from him. 'A week.'

Max's finger stilled on his pen. *A week?* Jeez, he sure knew how to kick a girl when she was down. 'Well, now, he sounds like a real charmer.'

A bubble of laughter escaped her lips at his unexpected reaction and she felt the same connection she'd felt on Friday—the camaraderie of two people who'd been through soul-destroying break-ups.

'You want to know the worst part? I'd just miscarried his baby when he told me. I was lying in a hospital bed still attached to a drip.'

Max dropped his pen and sat forward. 'What?'

'I was pregnant. Eight weeks. I'd only just found out two weeks before.'

Max didn't know what to say. The callousness of her ex's actions was shocking and the enormity of what Aleisha had been through hit him.

'So what you're saying is…you find out you're pregnant, one week later Nathaniel Cullen dies and a week after that you have a miscarriage followed closely by your fiancé ditching you.'

Ali shut her eyes tight. The cataclysmic events of a year ago didn't sound any better in his saxophone tones. 'Pretty much.'

Max eased himself back against his pillows. 'You've been through a lot,' he murmured.

She kept her eyes shut. 'It's been a bit of an *annus horribilus*,' she agreed.

'I don't suppose you've had a lot of time to grieve either.'

Ali slowly opened her eyes. 'There'll be plenty of time for that when this is all over.'

Max stared at his rain-spattered window. 'So, I take it your ex wasn't as devastated by the miscarriage as you?'

Ali snorted. 'Tom didn't want the baby from the beginning. He wanted me to get a termination.'

'The pregnancy wasn't planned?'

Ali gave a harsh laugh. 'No. The baby was a complete shock to both of us. I mean, we had talked about kids for the future, after we'd been married for a while, after I'd become a consultant.'

'So what happened?'

'We were careless, I guess. We were busy, he worked long days, often times with my shift work I worked nights—we played tag with each other's voicemail more often than not. Our sex life was sketchy but, you know, we'd been together for five years and life was crazy between his job and mine and sex just got squeezed in around everything else.'

'That happens,' Max said. God knew he and Tori had led the same frenetic existence.

'I can't take the pill because of my family history of clots and from time to time we…took educated risks. Obviously that didn't work out so well.'

Max tutted. 'Didn't you lecture me just last week on the importance of sexual health?'

'Yeh, yeh, I know. I'm a doctor, I should have known better. But you know what? It may have only been a couple of short weeks but being pregnant was the most amazing thing that ever happened to me.'

The soft note of wonder in her voice lanced his abdomen with a white-hot bolt of longing and his own thwarted desire to have a child returned with a crippling vengeance.

He drew his knees up. 'So you were pleased?'

Ali shook her head and sighed. 'It was the most inconvenient thing. The timing was wrong. We weren't married yet, I still had a good few years of exams and study, so did Tom. But…yes, I loved my baby from the second that little pink plus sign appeared. I can't remember ever wanting anything more.'

Max nodded. 'But Tom didn't feel the same way. That must have been a source of friction?'

'You could say that…I think he'd been planning on leaving for a while. He'd been seeing the other…the other woman for six months, apparently, and this obviously threw a spanner in the works. So we argued about it—a lot. The miscarriage was his get-out-of-jail-free card.'

Max noted her stumble and the huskiness in her voice when she talked about the woman who had turned her world upside down. Also the bitter edge as she described her ex's relief.

He understood too well the overwhelming sense of betrayal she felt. When he'd found out about Tori's infidelity he'd wanted to break things.

The other guy's face had been at the top of the list.

'And you were facing all this—the pregnancy and the friction with Tom—the night that Nathaniel Cullen died?'

Ali let that sink in for a moment. 'It wasn't affecting my work,' she denied.

'Of course it was,' he said as he scribbled some notes in her file.

'No.'

Max sighed. 'Just because it wasn't overt doesn't mean it wasn't affecting you. You just didn't realise it.'

'It didn't affect my judgement.'

Max ignored her. 'It could be important in the case.'

'No.' Ali sat forward. 'I don't want to have my personal

life out there for the world to know. It was humiliating enough first time around.'

'How many people know?'

'Maybe a handful.'

Max hesitated for a second while he debated telling her anything more. But it was best she knew everything. 'We need to be prepared for when the other side bring it up.'

Ali flopped back against her pillow. 'What? How are they going to know?'

'They'll have had you investigated.'

She vaulted forward again. 'What?'

'That's what I'd do if I was them.'

'Isn't that…illegal?' she spluttered.

'No.'

'Well, it bloody should be,' she grouched.

Max nodded. 'It might not come up, Aleisha. But if it does…forewarned is forearmed.'

Ali rubbed her temples as the last vestiges of her headache intensified briefly. She could see he was right. 'I could be a hairdresser,' she murmured. 'I bet there aren't too many hairdressers sued for wrongful death.'

Max chuckled. 'Probably not.'

'It'd be nice to transform someone too, don't you think? Kind of like plastic surgery. Without the permanency.'

Max's grin faded. 'You're going to be fine, Aleisha. We're going to win this case and you're going to get back on the horse.'

Ali pressed the receiver hard against her ear. Getting back on the horse was terrifying.

'No, I'm not.' It simply wasn't an option. 'Are we done with the questions now?'

Max heard the strain in her voice and wished he could be there to reassure her in person.

And to hell with the ethics.

'I think that's enough for tonight.' The rain had stopped and he capped his pen. 'Goodnight, Aleisha.'

'No, wait, hold up.'

Ali didn't want to leave it on such a downer. No way was she going to be able to sleep with her problems magnified tenfold by their conversation. And spilling her guts to him had only made her more curious about his ex. The woman who'd been married to a sex god and then foolishly let him go.

Perhaps the best time to have asked was last Friday night but there hadn't been a whole lot of talking going on.

'What about you?'

Max frowned. 'Me?'

'Sure. Doesn't this work both ways? I've told you mine, it's your turn to tell me yours.'

Max laughed. *So not going to happen.* 'Ah, no.'

'Oh, come on,' Ali cajoled. 'Think of it as trust building.'

'It's not relevant to the case,' he dismissed.

'Yes, it is,' she insisted.

'How?'

Try as she might she couldn't come up with a plausible link. She sighed. 'It's relevant to me.'

'No.'

'I'm trusting you with my most personal information, Max. Don't you think a little reciprocation is warranted?'

He snorted. 'No. I don't discuss my personal life with clients.'

Ali bristled. 'We've slept together, for crying out loud. The first person you've slept with since your marriage broke down. I *am* your personal life.'

Max had to admit she made a good point. Still…

Sensing his hesitation, Ali pressed home the advantage. 'Please, the house is quiet and the second I get off this phone with you my brain's going to kick in again and I'm sick of overthinking things. Besides, we have some solidarity here.'

Max's brow scrunched into a cynical frown. 'We do?'

'Sure. My personal life's in the toilet. So is yours. It'd be really nice to hear about somebody else's woes for a change.'

Max blinked. Had she really just said that? He began to laugh. Another man might have been affronted but she was right—his personal life sucked.

At least he could still laugh.

'Thanks for pointing that out,' he said after his laughter had subsided.

'Any time.' She grinned.

There was a pause for a moment and he knew she was waiting for him to start. He brooded for a minute—where to begin?

'How long were you married for?'

Her husky question took him back to happier times when his marriage had been new and he'd felt bullet proof.

He sighed. It was as good a place as any for the whole sorry saga. 'Eight years.'

'That's a while,' she murmured.

'Yeh,' he said bitterly. 'Long enough to know someone, you'd think.'

'She wasn't who you thought she was or she changed?'

Max mentally dismissed the options. 'We wanted different things. I just didn't realise it until the end.'

Ali waited for him to say more. 'So what did you want?'

'A family. Babies.'

Ali's heart thunked in her chest. 'And she didn't?'

'Apparently not.'

Ali felt her empty aching womb contract. She understood that yearning. She hadn't before, but she did now.

Max thought back to his childhood. 'I was an only child. It was lonely.'

She understood that too. If it hadn't been for Zoe her younger years would have felt barren.

'So…' She tried to find an easy way into her question. But there wasn't really one. 'Did you guys not…talk about children before you got married?'

Max straightened his legs, displacing her file, and crossed them at the ankle. 'Of course we did.'

The question irked. He remembered all the conversations he and Tori had had about parenting and how he'd ignored the warning voice inside his gut that had known her enthusiasm for having children was not as strong as his.

It was easy to blame her. Harder to face the truth.

'Tori wanted them. As much as I did, I thought. Not as many as I did. Two, she wanted two. I was confident I could have talked her into three.'

Ali heard the nostalgia in his voice, as if he'd just remembered the ways he'd planned on talking her into another baby, and felt a stab of something deep in her chest.

Jealousy? Regret?

'But she'd just joined a new firm and wanted to establish her career and, well…we were young, there was no rush. We agreed to start talking about it in a few years, when she turned thirty.'

Ali guessed from his voice that thirty came and went and Tori had delayed but she remained silent, letting him tell it in his words.

'I mentioned it on her thirtieth birthday and she was none too pleased. Fair enough.' He shrugged. 'It was probably the wrong time to bring it up. Thirty's a milestone for a woman and I should have been focused on giving her the best day possible instead of pushing my own agenda.'

Max shook his head as he remembered that time. He'd been so one-eyed over the whole issue. He should have known then that she didn't want the same thing.

'I gave her a couple more weeks and brought it up again. She wanted more time. Six months. A year. So I waited. Six months. A year. Two years. Three years. Then the arguments started. That I was crowding her, pushing her, she needed more time.'

Ali waited for a long time for Max to continue. The silence stretched like a giant deserted highway between them. Eventually she asked, 'Did she...did she ever say she didn't want a baby?'

'No, she just kept saying, not yet, I'm not ready yet.'

And he'd bought it because he'd desperately wanted to believe that one day she would be ready.

'To be fair she was the least maternal person I knew. I don't think she ever even picked up any of her nieces and nephews. But, I don't know...I just thought that would all change when she was pregnant with our baby.'

He'd hoped anyway. He'd hoped like hell.

'That's understandable,' Ali murmured. 'I wasn't the most maternal female on the earth either but suddenly, overnight, I became this baby-obsessed nutcase.'

Max smiled. Somehow he could imagine that. Ali, her belly big with child, glowing with health and anticipation, poking her nose into every pram that passed her on the street.

He felt his abdominal muscles tighten as an image of them together, his child in her belly, wormed into his brain.

He pushed it firmly away.

'And then I came home one night and she'd gone. Her wardrobe was cleared out, her toiletries gone from the bathroom, her car missing from the garage. She left a note saying she'd met someone else and was leaving.'

Ali blinked at the neutrality of his voice. But he couldn't fool her. She knew how deep a betrayal like this cut. 'I'm so sorry, Max. That's awful.'

Max snorted at the understatement. He'd been gutted.

'We met a few days later to talk things through. She told me she'd fallen in love with another lawyer from her firm, a new guy, she'd already moved in with him. She said she'd… never wanted a baby.'

Ali felt the sudden rawness in his voice right down to her toes. She'd seen the damage in his eyes at the bar last week but his subdued voice murmuring straight into her ear was far more potent.

'Did she say why she hadn't come clean years before?' Ali asked, her voice soft, gentle.

'Because she'd loved me and she thought she'd grow to want what I wanted. To want a baby. But she hadn't and she couldn't live a lie any more.'

The irony was not lost on Ali. She'd wanted her man to want their baby and he'd wanted his woman to want his.

In a perfect world they'd be perfect for each other.

But there was a world of ache in his voice and she wasn't convinced that he wasn't still a little in love with his ex-wife.

She waited a beat or two before asking. 'Do you still love her?'

Max gripped the phone. Tori's betrayal had cut too deep to feel anything other than contempt. Surely she knew that? Or did she still love Tom despite all that he'd done to her? He was suddenly damn sure he didn't want to know the answer to that and he was just plain weary of talking about the past.

'I think that's enough with the questions for one night, Aleisha.'

Ali shivered as his low husky tones feathered down her neck. He sounded so close he could have been in bed beside her.

Was that a yes?
'Get some sleep. I'll see you at prep tomorrow.'
The phone clicked in her ear.

CHAPTER EIGHT

Two weeks later Max was chatting to Reginald Aimes in the cavernous atrium of the courthouse the opening morning of Cullen v Brisbane Memorial when the aroma of warmed baked goods enveloped him in a cloud of intoxicating sweetness.

Despite his hearty breakfast his belly rumbled and he turned his head to identify the source just as Reg said, 'Ah, Aleisha, how are you, my dear?'

Ali, pulling close to the two men, grabbed Reg's outstretched hand and presented her cheek for his fatherly peck. 'Ready,' she said.

And she was. This thing had been hanging over her head for so long now, like a cancer. She was ready to finally be able to do something about it. To fight.

'Good.' He patted her on the shoulder. 'It'll all be over in a couple of weeks and Max is confident we'll win, aren't you, Max?'

Max dragged his gaze back from his search and smiled at her. 'Absolutely.'

She looked good. Tired, but good. He was pleased to see she'd taken his advice and dressed conservatively in dark trousers and jacket, flat shoes and minimal make-up.

Her hair was still a wild array of butterscotch curls that

were utterly feminine and completely distracting but, short of asking her to cut them off, he was stuck with them.

Both in this world and the more elusive, erotic world of his dreams.

A mobile rang. Reg patted his pocket and withdrew the ringing gadget. 'Excuse me,' he said. 'I've got to take this.'

They watched Reg move away and Max indicated for her to follow him. Ali tagged after him, out of the main foyer area and along several carpeted corridors. She felt surprisingly calm as each step took them further into the bowels of the old, yet still imposing building.

She suspected it wouldn't last. No doubt the second she walked into the courtroom she'd be a blithering mess. But for now, Ali felt good.

'In here,' Max said.

Ali waited for him to unlock a door and preceded him into the room. It was nondescript and boxlike with cheap grey vertical blinds covering the only window. Six chairs surrounded a small oval table, a far cry from the monolith in Max's boardroom back at the firm, and she noted that Max's laptop and briefcase had already claimed a spot.

She turned to face him. He hadn't moved from the doorway and she quirked an eyebrow at him.

Max stood, statue-like, suspended in a cloud of sponge cake and warm croissants, unable to breathe for a moment.

It was her?

She smelled like a patisserie?

He gave an inward groan at the unfairness of it all as the overwhelming urge to nuzzle her neck surged like a symphony in his blood.

As if she weren't good enough to eat already.

Max gripped the knob hard. 'Sit.'

Ali frowned at his tense request. 'What's wrong?'

'Nothing,' he dismissed, stalking to the table and sitting down as the door clicked shut.

Ali pulled out one of the chairs and sat, aware of a small twist of tension bunching her neck muscles. 'So, should we go over the procedure for the day again?' she asked.

They'd already been over it several times, including just yesterday, but Max didn't think you could ever be too prepared.

'Good idea.' Max nodded, launching into his spiel as he tapped his pen against the desk.

Ali tried to take it all in but the set to his jaw was making her nervous and she wondered if he knew something, some development that she hadn't been privy to.

'Is everything okay, Max?' she interrupted.

Max nodded and ploughed on, still tapping his pen. Ali was first on the witness list and he fully expected her testimony to take two days. And although he'd warned her, he didn't think she fully appreciated how gruelling it was going to be.

The last thing he needed was for her delicious scent to be screwing with his concentration. Which it was—big time! It was stirring a hunger in him that had nothing to do with his belly.

He stopped mid-sentence as another waft of her actually made his mouth water.

He threw down the pen. 'What are you wearing?'

Ali stared at him nonplussed. She looked down at her clothes. 'You said conservative. You said no skirts.'

'No, damn it,' he growled. 'I mean your perfume.'

Ali blinked. 'Vanilla oil?'

Vanilla. That was what it was. That was what was making him want to lick her neck.

'Kat gave it to me. It's supposed to be good for relaxation.'

'Is it working?'

'Yes. Or at least it was until you got all tense and cranky.'

'I'm not cranky,' he denied, but one look at her incredulous expression made him reassess. Max rubbed his forehead. 'Sorry, I…'

I, what, big boy?

I want to bury my face in your neck? I want to see if you taste the same everywhere? I want to throw you on this table and nibble you all over?

'You…don't like the perfume?'

Max stifled a groan. He rested his chin on his palm and stared at her for a moment. 'I think the problem is I like it a little too much.'

'Oh,' Ali said, her frown building and then slowly slipping as realisation dawned. 'Oh-h-h. You *like* it.'

Max gave her a grudging smile. 'I find it very…distracting.'

'Oh-h-h,' she said again, but fainter this time as his gaze strayed to her mouth and her breath seized in her chest.

They'd done well the last couple of weeks putting their first inauspicious meeting behind them. They'd both worked hard to keep things strictly business, to hack off the persistent, cloying tentacles that had attached themselves after their explosive night in bed together.

Max had even reneged on his offer for her to ring him after that first phone call had strayed into dangerous territory. He'd thought further phone contact would be unwise. That it blurred that line the case had drawn between them. And she'd agreed.

But suddenly she was back in his bed, under him and her pulse seemed to pick up the rhythm they'd set that night. She sucked in a breath as the air between them seemed to vibrate.

Max watched as her olive eyes darkened and her glossy

lips parted slightly. He remembered every detail of that mouth. How it tasted, how it felt against his, where it had been.

Ali swallowed as his gaze fixed on her mouth. She vaguely heard the slow steady drum of his fingers against the table as if he was weighing up his options.

To kiss or not to kiss.

It would be easier if she knew herself which way she wanted him to jump. But she had the feeling if he pounced— ethics aside—they'd be late for court.

Very, very late.

She licked her suddenly parched lips and instantly wished she hadn't as his nostrils flared and his fingers stopped drumming. 'I could…not wear it again…'

Max pulled his hand back and tucked it safely under the desk. It was too close to temptation above it.

There was just too much temptation all round!

He considered her proposal. The case could conceivably run for two weeks—could he face that intoxicating aroma attached to her delectable skin knowing how badly he wanted to taste it, day after day, for potentially a fortnight?

Without going insane?

But if it was helping her to relax then he couldn't argue with that. It was going to be a stressful couple of weeks and if vanilla oil helped then he didn't have the right to ask her not to wear it.

'No, it's fine,' he dismissed, his tone gentler. 'I need you relaxed. Whatever it takes.'

Even if it was going to have the opposite effect on him.

The door opened abruptly then, admitting Reg and two other board members along with Max's co-counsel, Gemma Ward, and Don Walker, a representative from the hospital's insurer. Max quelled the urge to spring back from Ali. They weren't close and they hadn't been doing anything wrong.

Not really.

But he was grateful for the horde's timely arrival anyway.

Twenty minutes later Judge Veronica Davies swept into the courtroom and called the case to order. Max was pleased to have scored her. He'd been in her courtroom many times and her reputation for being tough but fair was well respected.

Max straightened his notes as the judge went through the preliminaries. Reg and Don sat on his right. Gemma sat on his left. Across the centre aisle sat Deidre and Gordon Cullen and their lawyers.

Aleisha sat on the first row of seats directly behind him but still her delicious vanilla essence reached out. It curled seductive fingers into his gut and squeezed tight. He gripped the edges of his notes harder and prayed for patience.

He concentrated instead on Aleisha's reaction to Nathaniel's mother's contemptuous look. It had devastated her and his drive to vindicate Aleisha trebled. Every day she'd come to the prep session proposing a new profession and it had become a standing joke. But Max knew that Aleisha was serious.

If things went badly in court she would never return to medicine. Hell, he was beginning to believe that she probably wouldn't even if they went well.

'Mr Sherrington?'

Max looked up from his deathlike grip on his papers. He smiled at the judge and rose. 'Yes, Your Honour.'

'Call your first witness.'

Max felt a moment's trepidation—unusual for him. He never felt anything but one hundred per cent in control in a courtroom.

But no case had ever felt this personal before.

'I'd like to call Dr Aleisha Gregory.'

And so began two punishing days of questions about that awful night. Every second was dissected—every movement examined, every decision scrutinised.

Nothing was off limits.

Not her thoughts or her notes or her state of mind or her personal life. As Max had predicted, her break-up was trotted out, her miscarriage tossed around by the opposing side. She was stripped bare before everyone until Aleisha felt like a skeleton sitting in the chair, all her flesh torn away, exposed right down to her bones.

And then after they were done taking pieces from her on the stand they spent the remainder of the week and three days into the next taking pieces from her through other people.

As if she weren't there.

I'm right here, she'd wanted to scream. *I'm sitting right here in the first row.*

The Cullens said she and the hospital were negligent.

Max argued they weren't.

And on it went. Days of hearing from endless witnesses involved in the incident that night, their view of the events put under a microscope.

An army of expert witnesses dissecting her every action, half supporting the claim of negligence, the other half refuting.

Going from home to court, from court to home utterly wrung out from doing nothing at all. Just listening to her life, her career, her hopes and dreams slowly being dismembered.

Max was her only sanity. Every morning he'd tell her she was doing well and she clung to that like a buoy in a storm-tossed ocean because the legal argument was too intense and too intimidating to believe for a moment that she might actually be winning.

And she had to win. She just had to.

'I'm thinking air hostess,' Ali said into the phone. The court case was expected to wrap up tomorrow and she knew she wasn't supposed to ring but she was feeling particularly edgy tonight.

Max, who had dozed off surrounded by paperwork, glanced at the clock. 'It's almost midnight.'

'Sorry. Can't sleep.'

Max heard the strain in her voice as several ways to get her to sleep very unhelpfully reared their ugly, suggestive heads. 'It'll all be over tomorrow,' he murmured. 'And we're going to win.'

Ali nodded, wishing she could feel more confident. 'Right.'

'So…a trolley dolly?'

Ali shrugged. 'Why not? I could indulge my love of travel.'

'We're going to win, Aleisha.'

'And I love their uniforms.'

Max shut his eyes as a picture of Ali in a tight skirt, stockings and high heels slithered into his mind. She was leaning over him, her cleavage on display, serving him a drink and calling him *sir*. And then he was following her down the aisle, into the staff amenities, shutting the door, sliding her skirt up…

God. This was torture.

'So do I.'

Ali heard the unspoken in the low saxophone timbre of his voice. A delicious tingle spread from the hand holding the phone all the way up her arm. 'You have a thing for skirts, don't you?'

'Not usually.'

Ali gripped the phone harder as his meaning hit home. This phone call had careened quickly out of control. Maybe it was the end result of being forced to spend day after platonic day in his company when her body was craving something else entirely. When it remembered in fine detail how good they'd been together.

'Maybe you should see a doctor about that?'

'I am.'

Ali swallowed against a surge of desire thickening in her throat. 'Is he good?'

'*She* is.'

Ali's breath became choppy. 'Doesn't sound like she's cured you yet.'

Max's body tightened as the magnified sound of her rough breath brushed over his belly like a siren's call. 'Maybe I don't want to be cured?'

Ali's toes curled. 'I guess there are worse things to be hung up on.' *Even if she couldn't for the life of her think of a single one.*

Max couldn't agree more. Like vanilla and butterscotch curls and big, beautiful breasts. But this conversation was heading in the wrong direction—fast. For God's sake, there was just one night to go—he'd nearly made it. He had to pull it back.

'I think it's time we said goodnight.'

Ali stilled for a moment, a stab of disappointment mingling with relief. She should be happy he was bringing them back from the edge. *It was a completely inappropriate conversation to be having with her lawyer.*

But with her body humming like a tuning fork it was hard to concentrate on anything else. 'Wait,' she said, dragging her body back from the edge. There had been a purpose to this phone call—sort of. 'How well do you know the judge?'

Max frowned at the phone. 'Why? Are you suggesting we bribe her?'

Ali laughed and felt some of the tension ooze from her pores. Kat, who had just come in from work, poked her head in the door and smiled at Ali. Ali waved her in and Kat flopped on the bed.

'No. It's her mole, actually.'

'Her mole?'

'Yes, the one near her top lip.'

Max rolled his eyes. He knew the one she was referring to, it was rather unmissable. 'Yes?'

'I've noticed the last few days that she's been scratching it a lot and I don't like its shape and she has such pale skin... Do you know her well enough to enquire as to whether she's seen anyone about it and perhaps suggest that she should if she hasn't? I'd do it but I'm not allowed to talk to the judge so...'

Max blinked. He'd spent the last fortnight listening to her wackier and wackier suggestions for a career change because she couldn't see what was right in front of her—she was a doctor right down to her very cute toes.

From lecturing him on getting a chicken-pox vaccination to helping Helen with her arthritis, to dishing out dermatological advice to one of the court reporters and now this. And that didn't even take into account the Band-Aid she'd produced from her handbag when a child had fallen and scraped her knee in front of them on the street the other day as they'd been walking to the car park. Or the medicated lozenge she'd dished out to Gemma, who'd come down with a hoarse throat on day three of the court case.

Whether she liked it or not—Aleisha Gregory was a born doctor.

'Says the woman who wants to be an air hostess...' he murmured.

Ali gripped the phone. Max was right—she really had to stop dishing out unsolicited medical advice. Right after the judge had her mole seen to. 'So that's a no?'

Max shook his head, resigned to his fate. 'I'll talk to her.'

Ali smiled and winked at Kat. 'Thank you.'

Max chuckled at the little note of triumph in her voice and tried not to think of her crammed into an aeroplane loo with him, her skirt around her waist. 'Say goodnight now,' he murmured, not sure he was strong enough any more to do it himself.

Ali grinned. 'Goodnight now.'

Kat watched Ali as she rang off. 'You guys seem to get along well.'

Ali fluffed the covers and avoided Kat's keen gaze. 'He's my lawyer, Kitty Kat. Nothing else.' *And it would be very foolish to think otherwise.*

'I'm just saying...'

'Don't.' Ali was pleased she'd decided to keep the one-night stand to herself. She didn't want Kat to be building castles in the air.

'We've both come out of terrible break-ups and, oh, news-flash, *he's my lawyer.*' She grinned down at her friend. 'Besides...I think he's still in love with his wife.'

It was the first time she'd said it out loud and she felt instantly depressed. Just because sex with Max had been mind-blowing for her and there was obviously a strong sexual undercurrent raging between them, didn't mean he was emotionally engaged.

Kat squeezed her hand. 'Right. So best not fall for him, then.'

She nodded. 'Right.'

* * *

Ali awoke the next morning with a mass of nerves knotted in her stomach.

She thought she was going to throw up.

Even Max's 'we're going to win' assurances from their phone call last night weren't enough to untwist the knot. She hadn't really believed him then and this morning, looking at her wan reflection, big black smudges under her eyes, she still didn't.

Not even a positive prophesy from a crystal ball would have been enough to keep the doubt demons at bay.

For some Dutch courage she uncapped the bottle of Kat's vanilla oil and extracted the glistening glass dauber. She dabbed a drop or two at the base of her throat where her pulse fluttered, and dragged the warm glass behind each ear, smearing more oil there.

Sensitive to Max's predicament, she hadn't worn it after that first day. Every time he'd looked at her she'd been able to see the hunger in his eyes and, worse, had felt the answering pangs inside her intensify.

On a visceral level Ali had sensed that first day that their situation was perilously close to getting lost in the abyss of grey that made the line between black and white wavery and indistinct.

And she'd known it was best not to feed the beast.

But if there was ever a day she needed vanilla oil it was today. If she didn't relax a little she was going to blow a blood vessel or give herself glaucoma.

Today, she'd take any crutch she could get.

She inhaled as the scent surrounded her in its sweet embrace. It reminded her of baking cakes with Zoe, of porridge with brown sugar sprinkled on top, of a little bakery in Rome down beneath street level.

Happy memories. She smiled at her reflection. She was relaxing already.

Then a set of grey eyes, as grey as that abyss, flashed through her mind. She could almost feel the flare of two very male nostrils as they whispered against the skin of her throat.

Her stomach growled.

Max was engrossed in some case notes on his laptop when the aroma of vanilla undulated into the room like an exotic dancer. He turned abruptly to see Ali hesitating in the doorway.

Lust arced between them as the aroma put him right back in the middle of their flirty phone call from last night. 'Oh, God, Aleisha, really?' he groaned.

'Sorry.' She grimaced. 'I'm pretty wound up. I needed something. I figured hitting the red wine this early probably wouldn't look good to the judge.'

'It's fine,' he said even as his mouth watered.

Ali could see restraint and desire swirling like grey mist in the depths of his gaze. She could feel it rippling towards her, shimmering like fog as seductive as the devil's whisper.

She took a step back. 'I'll wait for you inside.' And she fled.

Max turned back to his laptop and sucked in a breath. Just one more day. That was all he had to get through.

Being in close contact with her for the last few weeks had been difficult with a fully charged libido—for which she was responsible. Every cell in his body was begging to touch her.

But it was all going to be over today.

Over for good.

No more weekend prep. No more squeezing her hand, clasping her shoulder, day after day, assuring her it was all going to work out.

Which was good. All good.

He'd say goodbye later today after it was done and walk away. Because he'd already got too close to this case.

Too close to her.

He'd vowed after Tori left that he was done with relationships but he was pretty sure that somehow he'd landed himself right back in the middle of one. Hell, he knew more about Aleisha Gregory after a few weeks' acquaintance than he'd ever known about his own wife.

He certainly knew she wasn't interested in a relationship.

And neither was he—the ink was practically still wet on his decree absolute.

This…thing had to end. Today.

As it happened the case didn't finish up by the end of the day. Some unexpected power outages caused a security alert and the building was evacuated twice, wasting three precious hours. Closing arguments were delivered in the dying hours of the work day and the judge decided to deliberate overnight and convene again in the morning for her decision.

Ali wasn't sure whether she wanted to cry, vomit or stamp her foot as she stood for the judge's departure. She'd psyched herself up for the big decision and it had been snatched away.

It was a major anticlimax.

And meant she had to come back tomorrow and face this all again.

Max turned to her. 'I'm sorry,' he said as her vanilla essence drove another nail into the insanity coffin.

She shook her head and sank back down into her seat. 'Not your fault.' .

'It'll be quick tomorrow,' he assured. 'You don't even have to be here.'

She lifted her head and looked him in the eye. 'Yes. I do.'

Max nodded as his belly did a triple somersault with a double twist. She was one gutsy woman. Sitting in court day after day stoically listening as her life was pulled apart and not buckling under the pressure was an act of courage.

He couldn't remember admiring a woman more.

Just one more thing that scared the hell out of him.

Fifteen minutes later Ali and Max caught the lift together down to the ground floor. It was half full and they shuffled to one side, keeping a safe distance between them. The cab lurched as it began its sluggish descent and Max grabbed the rail to prevent bumping into Ali.

He was excruciatingly conscious of Ali's delicious aroma and tried not to inhale during the journey. But the lifts were as old as the building and universally acknowledged as being the slowest in Brisbane so Max doubted he'd be able to hold his breath for the duration.

Unfortunately the lift also managed to stop on every floor, admitting more and more people, pushing them closer and closer together. By the time a rowdy group of men got in on floor five they were squashed against the back wall like tinned sardines.

And Max couldn't hold his breath any longer.

His body was blocking hers from the mass of bodies around them and his nostrils flared as they filled with her sweet macaroon scent. He felt his body respond, tighten, to their proximity and the carnal essence of her.

Her curls brushed his face and he shut his eyes as they lightly caressed his cheek with their springiness. The lift lurched to a halt at the fourth floor and their bodies bumped against each other. He reached for her hip to steady her.

Ali's stomach clenched as a heat down low mushroomed into her belly and down her thighs. She kept her gaze firmly fixed on the knot of his tie but she was hyperaware of his hand branding her, the heat of his body, the husk of his breath.

Max dropped his head slightly so his mouth was level

with her ear. He shouldn't be this close—they were in a lift full of people, for crying out loud—but didn't seem to be able to stop. He nuzzled her hair for a moment then murmured, 'I want to kiss you. I know I shouldn't but I do.'

He'd been going to say that he'd talked to the judge, who had already made an appointment to see her GP, but it seemed his mouth had a mind of its own.

And the truth had a funny way of coming out.

As a lawyer, Max knew that better than anyone.

Ali, grateful for the loud buzz of conversation around her, shut her eyes as his voice whispered to every cell screaming for his touch.

'I've wanted to kiss you every day since that night.'

'Don't, Max…' she whispered, turning her head slightly towards his ear.

He groaned quietly into her neck where she smelled so, so sweet. Being with her every day and faking a professional façade while the air sizzled between them was impossible. 'I can't take much more of this.'

Ali's body swayed closer until they were touching from torso to hip. She wanted to get closer. To turn her head and mash her mouth to his, wind her arms around his neck, grind her pelvis into his.

'Tomorrow…' she whispered.

The lift bumped none-too-gently to the ground and brought Max firmly back to earth in more ways than one. But the crowd started to push forward and it was too late for Max to remember there wasn't going to be a tomorrow.

Not as she meant anyway.

Even though his body demanded it.

That when they left court tomorrow, it would be the last time they saw each other.

The triple somersault his stomach had performed earlier

had scared the hell out of him. The intensity of the way he'd wanted her just now in a crowded lift even more so.

It was better to chalk their one-night stand up to experience and move on.

Repeating it was something neither of them needed.

Max allowed himself to be propelled out of the lift, aware of Ali at his elbow. Their pace slowed as the crowd dispersed.

'So…I'll see you at nine tomorrow?' he asked.

Ali, her body still grappling with an infusion of lust that had hijacked her body, frowned at him. How could he be so together when her oestrogen receptors were shorting out?

'Ah…okay, sure…'

Her confused look made Max want to reach out and snatch her to him so he gripped his briefcase handle hard and stuffed his other hand deep in his pocket. He really had to get away from her.

And her damn vanilla essence.

He nodded. 'Bye.'

And then turned on his heel and walked away.

The phone rang at nine-thirty just as Max had finished drying himself off from his shower and he almost didn't answer it. After all he knew who it was going to be and he'd just spent two hours pounding the city pavements and the cliffs around Kangaroo Point trying to run her out of his system.

But he did anyway. Because he just didn't seem to have any self-control where Ali was concerned.

He secured the towel around his hips and snatched up the receiver on his bedside table.

'So I'm thinking lift designer.'

Max chuckled despite himself and his determination to keep the call impersonal and brief flew out of the window. He sat on the side of the bed.

'Seriously, those lifts at the courthouse are too damn slow.'

Max's smile slipped as he remembered those couple of electric minutes where he'd totally lost his mind and nuzzled her neck. He appreciated her attempt to dispel any awkwardness by making light of what happened but his body stirred beneath the towel regardless.

'Those lifts are too damn full,' he growled.

Ali, who had just speared a piece of veal tortellini, paused with it halfway to her mouth. What the hell would have happened if they'd been alone in the lift this afternoon?

'Probably just as well,' she murmured.

Max sighed as he swung his legs up on the bed and lounged against the pillows. 'Yes, I suppose you're right.'

There was a moment of silence during which the pasta stayed suspended on her fork halfway to her mouth before Ali slipped it in and forced herself to chew.

'So…' Max groped around for something to say that wouldn't get him disbarred. 'Is Kat home tonight?'

The existence of Ali's flatmate, even peripherally, was a good deterrent. God knew he was counting on Kat's omnipresent state tonight, both in the flat and his mind, to help him keep a tight rein on his libido.

'She was, of course, because we all thought today would be the day we'd know the outcome and she cooked my favourite pasta meal but her younger brother Damian, who is, shall we say, enjoying the freedoms of the city now he's at uni, rang to say he was in the lock-up for being drunk and disorderly—again—and could she come and bail him out and she was furious and told me he could just sweat it out for a few hours because I was more important but I told her not to be silly, that Damian was much too pretty to be sitting in the lock-up with pimps and drug addicts and she must go…'

Dear God, she was babbling.

'So she left reluctantly but, boy, oh, boy is she ever steamed. I think she's going to threaten to tell her parents this time if he doesn't clean up his act. She's promised not to tell the other two times but I think her goodwill has just run out…'

Max gripped the phone harder. *Great, so she was alone in the flat. Probably in her pyjamas. Lying on her bed.*

Ali cringed at the silence that followed. 'Sorry,' she apologised, poking at her pasta. 'I'm babbling…'

She speared another tortellini shell and brought it to her mouth. It dropped off before it made it to its final destination, landing on her hot-pink vest-top.

'Damn it,' she cursed, sitting up.

Max frowned. 'What?'

Ali leaned forward as she picked the food off her pyjama top, dismayed to see a huge red sauce stain on her top. 'I spilled some food on my pyjama top. Hang on,' she said, 'I'll just go and take it off.'

'Aleisha?'

There was no reply. Max stared at the receiver and then bashed it against his forehead three times as he heard rustling on the other end.

Was she trying to kill him?

Ali walked through to her en suite pulling the top over her head as she went. She threw it in the wicker hamper, then returned to the bed. She picked up the phone as she sat and pulled open her bedside drawer looking for something else to wear.

'Sorry,' she said, raising her shoulder to cradle the phone against her ear. 'Back again.'

Max shut his eyes. 'Please tell me you're not shirtless now.'

Ali's hands stilled in her drawer. The raw edge in his

voice streaked straight to a place deep inside her belly. She looked down at her bare breasts. The nipples scrunched instantly. The desire that had engulfed her in the lift swamped her body again.

She was suddenly aware of the cool air on her skin. The feel of the cotton sheet at the backs of her thighs. The slight tickle as her caramel curls brushed her shoulders. The prickle of every tiny hair on her body. The hum in her blood.

She was aware, too aware, she was a woman.

She withdrew her hand from the drawer.

Would it hurt to be semi naked talking to him? She was an adult and in the privacy of her own bedroom. The idea was alluring. Enticing. Naughty...

And very, very grey.

'I'm afraid so,' she murmured huskily, swallowing against her suddenly arid throat. 'Why, what are you wearing?'

Max shut his eyes as an image of her laid out on his bed, her naked breasts bare to his gaze, formed with startling clarity. Every muscle in his body was on high alert. 'A towel.'

Ali also shut her eyes. 'So we both seem to be rather... undressed.' The thought was as alluring as it was forbidding.

Max's eyes flew open as the possibilities paraded through his mind.

Oh, no, he wasn't going there.

He couldn't.

He groped for a way to get the conversation back from careening out of control and grabbed the first ill-formed thought that came along. 'Yep, all ready for bed.' Then he realised what he'd said and hurried to clarify.

'For sleep, I meant. To sleep...'

Ali smiled. She knew what he'd meant and she grabbed hold of the conversation redirect gladly.

'I wish.' Ali doubted sleep would be easy to achieve tonight. 'I don't think I'm going to be able to sleep very much. I've barely managed two or three hours a night since the case went to court.'

Max nodded. He'd known insomnia had plagued her throughout the court case. It had plagued him since Tori had left, hence his marathon training. He'd basically run until he was exhausted.

The only time he'd slept soundly in the last eighteen months that hadn't been fatigue induced had been the night they'd spent together.

The thoughts he'd had last night while talking to her on the phone returned. There was nothing quite like a good orgasm to induce a deep, satisfying slumber.

He shut his mind against the illicit suggestion that was forming. *Tried anyway. And failed.*

Damn it, he'd managed to shut the door on it last night, he could do it tonight.

But she hadn't been shirtless last night...

And while his mind was struggling with the door his mouth had other ideas.

'I know a good way to get you to sleep...'

CHAPTER NINE

ALI's heart tripped in her chest at Max's low husky words. The possibilities quickened her breath.

'Is it…appropriate?'

'No.' It was very, very inappropriate. But…it wasn't as if he were sleeping with her. He was just…bending the rules a little.

Walking that fuzzy grey line.

Ali swallowed. 'What did you…have in mind?'

'Are you wearing underwear?'

Ali's heart pounded so loudly through her ears it sounded as if a brass band were playing at the end of her bed. Surely he could hear it?

'Yes.'

Max felt the soft graze of terry towelling taunt his hardness as her husky response stroked fingers of desire up the backs of his thighs and deep into his buttocks.

'Take them off.'

Ali's breath stuttered out at his shocking suggestion. 'I don't think…I mean I'm not sure…'

Her almost maidenly hesitation inflamed his desire further. 'I want to stroke you all over. I need you naked.'

'But…' Ali groped for a modicum of sense in a brain quickly liquefying into a puddle of lust. *Was he suggesting what she thought he was?* 'You're not here.'

Max chuckled at her confusion, at her determination to hold onto sense despite the breathy quality to her voice that told him she was as titillated as he was.

'You're going to do it for me.'

Ali sucked in a breath. *Oh, God. He was! He was suggesting it.* The thought of phone sex with Max invaded and conquered every cell.

Dared she?

It was one thing to be topless and talking to him—it was naughty and he didn't have to know. It was another entirely to be naked, talking to him and…touching herself.

And him knowing.

Max could hear nothing but the tortured husky timbre of her breath. 'Take them off, Aleisha,' he murmured again.

Ali, her last skerrick of resistance obliterated by his illicit demand, whispered, 'Okay.'

She stood, holding the phone to her ear with her shoulder again as her shaking hands slipped her knickers down her thighs and past her knees. She stepped out of them and kicked them free.

Max, his own pulse loud in his ears, could just make out the rustling as Ali removed her underwear.

She'd done it. She'd actually done it.

He felt her low hoarse, 'What next?' right down to his toes.

'Lay on the bed.'

Ali, her legs suddenly as useless as boiled spaghetti, sank onto her pillow-topped mattress. The white cotton sheet felt as decadent as black satin. Her bed suddenly seemed to hover like a magic carpet.

The bedside lamp, which had always needed a brighter bulb, now bathed her body in a soft sexy light and Ali almost gasped as she watched her breasts swing and bounce seductively with every movement.

She put the phone on speaker and set it near her head. 'Okay.'

Max heard excitement and anticipation in the breathy roughness of her voice. His body ached but he ignored his own discomfort.

He shut his eyes and imagined he was lying in bed with her. 'You have the most amazing breasts,' he murmured. 'Soft but still firm. And big. I like how big your breasts are. I'm touching them, Aleisha. Can you feel it? They fill my palms. I like how my hands look on your breasts. They feel big and rough against all that softness.'

Ali felt her stomach twist deep inside at his words. Her eyes fluttered closed as his voice evoked the images he described. His hands on her breasts—caressing, stroking, kneading.

'Are you touching them? Touch them, Aleisha.'

Ali's hands seemed to move of their own volition in response to his rough command. 'Oh,' she cried out, biting down on her lip as her nipples tightened the second her fingers tentatively touched the swell of one breast.

'What?' he murmured.

Ali shivered. 'My hands are cold but my skin…my skin is hot. I have…goose bumps.'

Max almost groaned as he saw the aroused peaks of her breasts in his mind's eye. 'Your nipples are hard, yes?'

'Yes.'

'Like berries.'

'Yes.'

'Touch them,' he demanded in an urgent whisper.

Ali ran her finger lightly over a taut brown peak. She bit down on her lip as a streak of molten lust arrowed its way to her middle and oozed rivulets of sensation from her belly to her thighs.

'They feel good, don't they, Aleisha? I wish you could

taste them. They taste like you, all sweetness and spice and they feel ruched against my tongue. I'm swiping my tongue across one of those hard little buds right now. I like how you do that funny noise at the back of your throat when I suck one deep inside my mouth.'

Ali heard the moan escape from her lips and drift into the air somewhere above her head. She flattened the pad of her thumb against each nipple and pushed hard to ease the tingling his words had evoked.

Max gripped the phone. 'I love making you moan. I like watching your nipple when I let it go and watch how it gets all hard as the air hits it. Put your fingers in your mouth, Aleisha, make your nipples wet for me.'

Powerless to resist the low sexy commands coming from the phone, Ali did as she was bid, smearing warm saliva on her nipples. It cooled rapidly against the heated flesh and she gasped as her nipples tightened to an almost unbearable intensity.

'You like that, don't you, Aleisha?'

Ali shifted restlessly against the bed, eyes still closed, head tossed to the side. 'Yes,' she breathed heavily as she channelled Max's hands cupping and squeezing her breasts.

Max's breath hitched at the note of sexual abandonment in her voice. 'What else do you want, Aleisha? Tell me.'

Ali tossed her head to the side. She wanted to feel his mouth on hers, to feel him deep inside her. 'I want to…touch you…' she murmured.

Max's erection kicked hard against the confines of the towel. It would be so easy to loosen it, slip his hand down, touch himself as she was doing.

His body was all but demanding it.

But *that* he couldn't justify. In this strange new world of ethical ambiguity he seemed to be co-existing in with Ali, *that* would be taking it too, too far. That would be well and truly stepping over the line.

And this wasn't about him.

'No,' he murmured. 'This is for you. Only you.'

Ali opened her eyes, opened her mouth to protest. If he could play, why couldn't she? But then he said, 'Spread your legs, Aleisha,' and she lost her mind.

'Call me Ali,' she begged as the sheets rasped against the backs of her thighs adding to the sensual overload.

'No.' *Too, too far.*

'Please, Max,' she implored as her fingertips trailed lightly over her belly.

He ignored her. 'Are you ready for me down there? I can still remember how you taste. I dream about it.'

Ali felt her body flush with heat as she breathed heavily into the phone. There was an unbearable tingling between her legs and she pressed her bottom into the mattress to ease the deep-seated ache.

'Touch yourself,' he urged, remembering vividly how sweet she was. He gripped the sheet beside him to stop himself from ripping off the towel. 'Are you wet?' he asked, his voice so deep and rough he barely recognised it. 'Are you ready for me?'

Ali mindlessly followed his command. She quivered as her first tentative touch caused a pulse to throb to life deep inside.

'N-no,' she murmured as her light touch found her wanting.

'I don't believe you,' he murmured. 'I can hear it in your voice, Aleisha. You. Are. Ready.'

Ali hesitated. It had been many years since she'd done any kind of self-exploration and even with the devil himself whispering illicit instructions, urging her on, it felt… juvenile.

'Do it, Aleisha,' he growled, already picturing her pleasuring herself in his mind's eye. Already hearing her throaty cries as she orgasmed in his ear. 'You know you want to,' he added, dropping his voice another octave. 'You know you want to come. You know you want me to make you.'

Ali shivered. She did. God, help her, she did. She was going to hell, *no doubt about it*, but right now the dictates of her libido were drowning out all sense.

She slid her finger inside. Internal muscles contracted around her and an involuntary moan slipped from her mouth.

Ali shivered as her finger met the warm slick lubrication that Max craved. That she craved. 'Oh yes,' she half sighed, half moaned.

'I told you,' he whispered. 'I told you, you were ready for me. Now, touch your breasts again,' he ordered.

Ali mindlessly did his bidding, her still erect nipples flowering beneath her dewy touch.

'I want to taste them,' he half crooned, half groaned.

His admission, low and sweet, caused another deep contraction and Ali felt a surge of moisture at the apex of her thighs.

'I want you to taste them too,' she whispered. 'I want you to taste between my legs too.'

Max groaned into the phone as an image of him kneeling between her thighs paralysed him.

'Stroke yourself.' His husky command was urgent. 'I want to hear you come. I want to hear you call my name as you come.'

Ali slid her hands back down. She was ready. Eager for her touch. Throbbing for release.

'Ah-h-h,' she cried as her sensitised flesh leapt to life at her first exploratory stroke.

'Yes,' Max whispered as her whimper got him harder

still. 'Close your eyes. Pretend it's me. Me touching you, tasting you.'

Driven by his sexual rhetoric, Ali found the hard little nub she sought easily. She stroked it at his urging and it reared against her touch, painful in its sensitivity.

She almost orgasmed instantly. 'Ah-h-h,' she murmured.

'You like that? Can you feel me? I love how you taste.'

Ali cried out as the line between pleasure and pain blurred and the sensations overpowered her.

'Easy, Aleisha,' Max murmured, his voice low and steady. 'Take it easy. Don't rush. I like to go slow. I like to savour every little whimper, every little squirm.'

Ali instantly slowed the pace, eased back on the pressure. She sucked in a breath as the sensations dropped to a slow hum, a languorous buzz. A small whimper escaped as the maelstrom subsided and she could breathe.

Max heard the frantic edge to her indecipherable utterings lessen and the ratcheting tension in his neck and shoulders eased.

'That's good,' he crooned, desperately fighting to control the freight-train pace of his own breath. 'We have time, we have all night.'

Ali relaxed as he murmured sweet nothings in her ear. He told her how he wanted to kiss her all over. How he dreamt about her. How her vanilla scent drove him crazy and he'd fantasised about doing her on his desk in her skirt.

And soon the storm was on her again. But she was prepared for it now, had kept pace with its build and she welcomed the maelstrom with all its thunder and lightning.

'Oh, God, Max,' she moaned as she pushed away the first ripple.

'It's okay, Aleisha, you can let it go now.'

Ali shook her head, her eyes squeezed shut. No, she

needed him to say her name. Her real name. 'Ali,' she snapped as she pushed away another ripple. 'It's Ali.'

Max shook his head. *Was she trying to kill him?* 'Damn it, Max,' Ali panted. 'Say it.'

'No,' he insisted.

Ali refused to come without hearing it. 'I'm not...' She slowed the pace. 'I won't...'

Max set his jaw. 'Yes, you are. Yes, you will.'

Slowing the pace didn't work. Her body was already spiralling. 'Max!'

Max heard the growing desperation and knew she was close. 'It's too late, Aleisha, you're there,' he goaded, hanging onto his last skerrick of restraint.

'No...I won't,' she insisted as a pulse started to spread from her fingers out. She shook her head, ignoring the dark warning in his voice, fighting the pull.

'Come, Aleisha,'

'No.' *Damn it, no.*

Max could feel his chest pounding, his breath bursting in his lungs. She was fighting it. Fighting her own orgasm. Fighting the one thing he could give her—the only thing.

'Let go, Aleisha, let go.'

'Damn it, Max,' she cried out because she was almost there and she couldn't hold it back any longer, she wanted it too much and she simply wasn't strong enough to hold out against him.

Another thing she couldn't control.

Max recognised surrender when he heard it. 'Yes,' he breathed. 'Yes, *Ali*, yes.'

His rough, almost pained words reached her through the haze delivering what she'd craved on a broken whisper. 'Max,' she panted as she broke into a thousand pieces.

Max gripped the phone as Ali's cries reached an ear-shattering crescendo. They vibrated down the line directly into his brain, twisting like a tornado through every cell in his body.

Torturing, tormenting, teasing.

Even as they eased, dropping to low throaty whimpers, they taunted him with their passionate intensity. Right in his ear she seemed so close.

Touchable. Real. Concrete.

As if she were in bed beside him.

Ali slowly spun back to earth, sucking in frantic breaths, grappling to understand what she'd just allowed to happen as her hands fell uselessly on the bed beside her and her bones turned to liquid. 'Max...I...' she panted. 'That was...'

Max heard the confusion in her breathy voice. 'It's okay,' he murmured. 'I know.'

He knew? *Did he do this often?* 'But, I...'

She what? She couldn't think. *Hell, she could barely breathe!* 'You called me Ali,' she murmured, because it had whispered into her ear at just the right moment and ricocheted around her head echoing to the time of her orgasm.

He grimaced at his slip, annoyed at himself for succumbing. But her cries had pushed him to the edge and it had seemed like the most natural thing in the world to do.

'It's okay, Max,' she yawned as his silence stretched. 'It was just what I needed.'

Max should have been pleased that he'd given her what she needed but his body was aching, his honour was dented and her voice in his ear was just too damn much. 'Go to sleep, Aleisha. Sweet dreams.'

It took Ali a moment to realise the phone had gone dead and she stared at it for a while before she hit the end button.

She was asleep in under a minute.

Max, still awake at four a.m., finally admitted defeat and hit the pavements again.

* * *

Ali met up with Reginald Aimes the next morning on her way into court and they were chatting in the foyer waiting for the rest of the team when Max approached from behind. Ali blushed as he greeted her, their telephonic tryst from last night still making her hot all over.

She was nervous too in her deliberately provocative clothes. Last night she'd selfishly taken what was on offer from him. This morning she wanted to show him what was on offer from her.

Max studiously avoided looking at anything other than her eyes. The back view of that banned sexy skirt combined with sheer black stockings, stilettos and white clingy blouse he could definitely make out her bra strap through had been enough of a jolt.

His air-hostess fantasy given form and shape.

He wouldn't give her the satisfaction of checking out the front view in front of Reg. 'You look…well rested,' he commented politely as a cloud of vanilla enveloped him and his libido growled.

Ali kept her face neutral. 'Thanks, I had some…help.'

Max quirked an eyebrow. 'You took my advice about a sleeping pill?'

She shook her head. 'Apparently there are other more… alternative ways, to get off to sleep.'

Max's lips twitched. 'Massage, deep breathing…something like that?'

Ali pressed her lips together as his husky commanding whisper from last night revisited. Her skin goosed. She was acutely aware of Reg beside her ignorant to the subtext.

She nodded. 'Something like that.'

Reg's phone rang and he excused himself. Max glanced over his shoulder then back to her, allowing his gaze free rein. He shook his head. 'Seriously, Aleisha? That skirt? The vanilla.' He kept his voice low. 'Are you trying to drive me insane?'

'I think that's only fair after last night,' she murmured.

Max felt his resolve to make a clean break weaken. 'It's working.'

Aleisha smiled. 'I'm also not wearing any underwear.'

It had seemed a rather daring thing to do this morning as she was dressing but it had been sufficiently titillating to distract her from the day ahead and anything that could do that was a good thing as far as she was concerned.

Max narrowed his gaze as his resolve disappeared into the fires of damnation right along with his soul.

To hell with ending it—he could do that tomorrow.

'So, you're feeling better today?'

Ali quirked an eyebrow at the sudden gravelly quality of his tone. 'Rested. Very rested.'

And more than a little resigned. Yesterday had been nerve-wracking—today was a complete anticlimax.

'Good, because when we walk out of this courtroom in an hour or so—win or lose—you and I are going straight to bed. And don't expect to be getting out of it any time soon.'

Ali swallowed as lust rolled through her belly like a giant Mexican wave.

It took Judge Davies twenty minutes to sum up the case and hand down her finding that Brisbane Memorial and Dr Aleisha Gregory had no case to answer in the death of Nathaniel Cullen.

Ali, who had been holding herself erect in her chair for the entire time it took her to get there, suddenly sagged as everyone around her leapt to their feet and erupted in cheers and applause.

It was over. It was truly over.

Somebody grabbed her by the elbow and yanked her up

and hugged her, then someone else did the same and a third person pecked her on the cheek.

Max stood in front of her, the last to pass on his congratulations. 'We won.' He grinned.

Ali nodded, her heart filling with relief, vindication, gratitude, and something else that seemed too complex to even analyse right at that moment.

'Thank you.' She smiled. 'Thank you.'

She looked over at Nathaniel Cullen's parents. They were sobbing quietly, their lawyer talking to them in hushed tones, and her joy at being exonerated lost a little of its sparkle.

The bottom line was an eighteen-year-old boy was dead—there weren't any winners here.

But then people were chatting around her about an immediate lifting of her suspension and contacting the medical registration board to push along her start-back date and press releases and she was being swept out of the courtroom as everyone talked at once.

Max found her in the middle of the huddle five minutes later.

'Excuse me, gentlemen,' he said, grabbing her hand. 'Aleisha will be taking the weekend off to think about her next steps. Reg, she'll be in on Monday morning to talk to you—my secretary will set up an appointment.'

And then he pulled her out of the crowd, his fingers interwoven with hers, and stalked away with her. He let go of her hand a few moments later as he approached the lift and jabbed the down button. Then he fished in his pocket for his mobile and flipped it open.

'Valerie?' he said, his gaze capturing Ali's as he spoke. 'Tell Helen to cancel my appointments for today and re-schedule. I'm going to be unavailable.'

He paused, obviously listening to something Valerie was saying, and Ali's mouth went dry at his predatory gleam.

'Yes,' he said, his eyes holding hers. 'All day. And I *do not* wish to be disturbed.'

The ancient lift dinged as it arrived and Ali stepped in as Max ended the call. Max stepped in also. The lift was empty and he took up position beside her.

The second the doors shut he dropped his briefcase, turned to face her, then dragged her close until she was squashed against him. He swooped his head down and plundered her soft mouth just as he had fantasised about last night. Her tiny whimper inflamed him and he walked her backwards, pressing her against the wall.

Their ragged breathing was loud in the silence as the kiss careened out of control.

His fingers grasped the material of her skirt and hitched it up one thigh. His hand took over, pushing beneath the tight fabric feeling the curve of silk clad female thigh beneath. His hand hit lace and he changed direction, moving to the back of her thigh, skimming bare flesh now as his palm slid further north.

And then he hit pay dirt.

One naked buttock filled his hand and he groaned against her mouth. 'You really don't have any underwear on, do you?'

Ali sucked in a breath, her head spinning, her hands clasped to his jacket lapels as her body clamoured for his hand to go further. She gave a half laugh. 'Did you think I was lying?'

He squeezed the gloriously naked flesh in his hand. 'I was hoping you weren't,' he murmured as he nuzzled her neck, sucking in her vanilla essence.

The lift bumped to the ground and they pulled apart. Thankfully the lift took its usual extended time to open giving Max time to step back and pick up his briefcase and Ali time to yank down her skirt.

By the time the doors finally opened they were standing apart staring straight ahead, all business. Only a very close observer would have noticed the unevenness of their breath.

'My car,' Max said as he strode out of the lift. 'Follow me.'

Ten minutes later Ali had been deposited in Max's sporty car in the darkened surrounds of the underground car park, waiting for him to join her. The scent of worn leather, the feel of it—like her favourite pair of kid gloves—against the backs of her thighs and the aroma of man, of Max, surrounded her.

She felt her pulse slow as a heavy sensation she was fast coming to recognise as lust stirred in her belly. He opened his door and she watched as his thigh came into view and the sensation liquefied into a surge of molten heat.

And so when he said, 'I thought that was an excellent result,' she lunged at him before he even had the chance to start the car, just as he had done in the lift, opening her mouth against his, thrusting her tongue as she moaned against his lips.

Then suddenly he muttered an expletive and she was hauled onto his lap, straddling his thighs in her impossibly tight skirt, his hands ploughing beneath the fabric, past her lace-tops, pushing the skirt higher and higher until he was grasping both of her naked buttocks in his hands.

She reached for his tie as they devoured each other's mouths, sliding it out of his collar with a satisfying zip. His buttons were next and she managed to get a few undone before one of his hands wandered to the apex of her thighs and stroked.

Her breath hissed out and her back arched as his finger found just the right spot.

Max took advantage of her bared neck and latched on to the pulse that beat a frantic tattoo at the base of her throat. His arm hit the gear stick, his knee bashed against the centre console and anyone could come along at any minute and spot the great Max Sherrington making out in his car with a former witness, but cream puffs and macaroons infused his senses and he gorged like a starving man.

He laved her neck and she tasted every bit as sweet as she gasped and mewed in response.

Ali could barely think as his finger stroked deep inside her but she knew she wanted more. She'd been there done that last night, right now she wanted the real thing, so she reached for his zipper without conscious thought, satisfied to find him hard against her fingers, aroused as she was.

Max groaned against her neck as her fingers brushed his erection through his trousers. He couldn't ever remember being this hard—not even last night as every nuance of her orgasm had been delivered directly into his ear.

He heard his zip give, loud even amidst their combined frantic breath. Felt her fingers on him, questing for a way to be closer.

He cried out against her neck when she found it. Her palm clamping around him—squeezing, milking. Flesh on flesh.

He wanted that too. To be closer. Wanted to feel her tight around him. To touch every inch of her. One hand abandoned the slick heat of her, needing to touch her breasts. He'd lived vicariously last night but not any more.

He fumbled with her buttons as she stroked him, needing to feel them, see them, taste them.

Ali revelled in the feel of him in her hand, thick and strong. But she needed more. She needed him in her. Last night, as she had touched herself at his command, she had fantasised about him stroking deep inside her but she didn't have to imagine now.

She could have.

'Max,' she cried as he pushed her partially undone blouse as far down her arms as it would go and she ground down against him.

Max felt her glide along the length of him as he yanked a bra cup aside and sucked heavily on an engorged nipple.

Ali threw her head back, her cry reverberating around the car. She lifted herself slightly, positioning him for entry.

'No, Ali, wait…' Max panted, some skerrick of sanity rearing its head amidst the maelstrom at just the right moment. 'Condom,' he panted.

Ali almost wept at his words. She needed him inside her. They were a whisper away from it.

How could she have forgotten about condoms?

She bit her lip, forced herself to stop grinding against the hard, hard length of him.

'Have you got one?' she panted.

Max squeezed his eyes shut, his fingers stilling then dropping away from her, gripping the outside of her thighs instead. 'No. They're at home.'

Ali stared at him for a long moment, their heaving chests and erratic breathing in sync. She bit her lip.

'Bloody hell,' she panted before awkwardly easing off him to sit in her own seat, trying to pull her skirt down and return her bared breasts to the confines of her bra.

Max also fixed himself up with shaking fingers, giving his breathing a chance to return to normal.

'How far to your place?' she asked.

Max's gaze dropped to her still unbuttoned blouse. 'Fifteen minutes.'

Ali looked him square in the eye. 'How fast if I don't do this up?'

He feasted his eyes on the white lacy bra cups. 'Ten.'

She nodded. 'I'll let you do whatever you want with them if you can get us there faster.'

Max made it home in eight minutes flat.

CHAPTER TEN

THE sky was just starting to lighten when Max woke early Sunday morning. He glanced over to Ali. She was lying on her stomach with her head turned away. One thigh stuck out from the sheet that barely covered her bottom.

His lazy gaze followed the long stretch of naked skin from where the sheet ended to the graceful dip forming the small of her back and up the gentle rise of her ribcage to the flat expanse of her shoulder blades.

And he wanted her again.

It would be so easy to run his palm up the contours of her back, drop a kiss on her shoulder, whisper his intentions in her ear just as if he had the last two days and nights. He could picture her sleepy smile now as she rolled over and snuggled all her warm female curves against him.

He even lifted his hand to do just that.

But the longer she stayed in his bed, the more times he reached for her, the more he wanted her. And after eighteen months on his own, it was a trifle alarming to think how quickly she'd become part of his world.

Two days ago he'd planned to make a swift break.

Now his whole damn bedroom smelled of vanilla. He was never going to be able to get rid of it.

He dropped his hand.

The same had happened with Tori. She'd just always been there. And look how disastrously that had turned out.

Maybe it was time to practise a little restraint? Get a little perspective?

He eased out of bed, careful not to wake her as he padded to his en suite and changed into his jogging clothes. Nothing like a brisk morning jog for clarity.

Ali stirred the moment Max vacated the bed, as if some sixth sense had woken her. She rolled over, reaching for him. When her questing hands came up wanting she cracked open an eyelid.

She almost mewed her disappointment.

Noises from the en suite were reassuring however and she dragged the sheet up all the way up to her armpits to cover her cool skin. Her eyes fluttered closed. Her body ached in a good way and she smiled to herself at the things they'd done to cause it.

Ali heard Max re-enter the bedroom and she opened her eyes. 'Morning,' she murmured as he appeared in his exercise gear, joggers clasped in one hand.

He glanced at her and his groin tightened. 'Sorry, I didn't mean to wake you.'

Ali raised an eyebrow. 'Doesn't seem to have bothered you before now.'

Max chuckled as he sat on the side of the bed to put on his joggers.

'You're going for a run?' She glanced at the clock. 'At this hour?'

'You're not a morning person, are you?' he said as he pulled on a sock.

Ali shrugged. 'I'm a shift worker. When we get the chance to sleep in the dark we take it.'

But then of course she realised she wasn't any more. A

shift worker. She really needed to stop thinking of herself as one.

Max pulled his joggers on and tied them up, steadfastly ignoring her very tempting presence behind him. He stood and turned. 'I can bring back some croissants for breakfast if you like? And the Sunday papers?'

Ali let her gaze wander up and down the magnificent length of him as he looked down at her, hands on hips. His thighs were moulded perfectly in the skins he was wearing. His broad shoulders, flat abdomen and smooth tanned biceps were beautifully displayed in his white singlet shirt with last year's Gold Coast Marathon advertised upon it.

Her breasts grew heavy. Heat spiralled in her belly.

'Did you know,' she murmured, 'that you burn off the same amount of calories during sex as you do during a five-k run?'

Max felt his breath hitch as she all but licked her lips as she looked him up and down. He felt completely objectified. *He really, really shouldn't have been so turned on by it.* He dug his fingers into his hips. 'I do ten.'

Ali smiled as she peeled the sheet back. 'Okay, then. I'll let you do me twice.'

Max swallowed hard as she flashed him her naked reclined body in all its glory. He toed off his shoes and stripped his shirt off over his head in a matter of seconds. *Forget clarity.*

Several hours later they were on his deck drinking coffee and reading the Sunday papers. His penthouse suite overlooked the Brisbane River and the sun glittered on the surface below. A light breeze ruffled the edge of the newspapers.

Ali glanced up through her fringe at a bare-chested Max. She was wearing his gown and her feet were in his lap snuggled up against his cotton boxers. He was absently rubbing her arch as he perused the sports section of the paper.

Her heart did a little flop in her chest. It smacked of domesticity and Ali couldn't remember being this contented in a long time. With the stress of the case behind her and the shiny new possibilities ahead, it had been an excellent couple of days.

Tomorrow was Monday and everything would no doubt change. Max would go to work and she had to figure out what to do with the rest of her life. So she'd take this moment of domesticity for what it was and worry about tomorrow tomorrow.

Max looked up and caught her watching him and smiled at her. 'I checked my messages while you were in the shower,' he said, his hands straying from her ankle to her calf and then back down again.

He couldn't believe he'd gone nearly forty-eight hours without checking his messages. He never did that. But then he'd never been quite so thoroughly distracted.

'Helen rang on Friday to say she booked an eleven a.m. appointment for you with Reg tomorrow.'

Ali grimaced. *Tomorrow.* There was that word again.

Max waited for Ali to answer. When she said nothing he asked, 'Have you thought about how soon you'll return?'

Ali sighed. He just didn't get that she really wasn't going back.

'Let's not talk about it, Max, please. Thanks to you I'm having a fun couple of days away from the real world. Just you and me. And it's okay,' she hastened to add in case he thought she was already picking out china patterns, 'I know it's not what either of us need in our lives and it's nothing serious. I know it's nothing more than two adults having some fun. But, we've both had a terrible year, I think we've earned a little fun, don't you?'

Max nodded. He couldn't agree more. 'Absolutely.'

She smiled. 'Good. For a moment there I thought I might have to take this gown off and distract you again.'

He grinned. 'Don't let me stop you.'

Heat licked quick and intense between them and her nipples pebbled against the soft terry towelling. Ali dropped her hand to the knot and watched as Max's gaze followed her movements—undoing the tie, opening the lapels a little and then a little more until her naked breasts were bared to his gaze and the soft morning sunshine.

Max licked his lips as her large breasts with perfect nipples sat bare and exposed for his own private viewing.

Him and anyone else out on their balconies on a beautiful Sunday morning with a pair of binoculars.

He leaned closer to her. 'Perfect,' he murmured.

A loud knock on the door halted his progress and he muttered an expletive.

Ali grinned. 'Saved by the bell.'

He shook his head. 'Don't move a muscle,' he ordered as he stood. 'It's probably just a courier with some papers.' Another sharp rap came from the direction of the front door.

'Later,' she murmured, securing the robe.

He dropped a brief hard kiss on her mouth. 'Tease.'

Ali smiled at him as he strutted away, his black boxers clinging to him like a second skin. She sighed at the perfection of him and then returned her attention to the book-review section.

Max swaggered into the kitchen and headed towards the door with a smile on his face, his early morning doubts behind him. Ali seemed to be on the same page as him. A weekend of fun. No strings. No promises. No commitments.

A perfect weekend.

Except for Pete, who was standing on the doorstep when Max opened the door.

Pete took one look at his friend's state of dress and quirked an eyebrow. 'Well, well, well,' he murmured.

'Go away,' Max ordered, attempting to shut the door.

Pete chuckled. 'Not for a million bucks.' He grinned, his forearm blocking the door's closure as he angled his body inside the apartment.

'Well, what do we have here?' Pete asked as his gaze strayed to the partially obscured deck where he could just see a decidedly female hand cradled around a mug.

'Nothing.'

Max didn't know what this thing between him and Ali was. And he resented Pete's appearance, forcing him to define it. He felt the disquiet he'd woken with this morning revisit. What were they doing?

And was he ready for it?

'Pete,' Max warned as his friend headed for the deck.

But Pete did what he always did—exactly as he pleased—and he was standing in front of Ali in less than ten seconds.

'Hello, Pete,' Ali greeted, trying to keep it light but wishing the ground would swallow her. Wishing that the real world hadn't intruded into her weekend fantasy world.

Max sighed as he pulled up behind his friend. 'You remember Ali, Pete?'

'But of course.' Pete beamed. 'Ali, Ali, Ali…how are you? I see you won the court case.'

Ali nodded. 'With a little help from my…'

She glanced at Max. What was he exactly?

Her lawyer?

Standing beside her in his underwear?

Damn Pete for his intrusion, for forcing her to ask all those questions she was putting off for the weeks ahead. 'Friends.'

Max could see Ali disappearing into the shell she'd been

humping around when he first met her. 'Was there something you wanted…*mate*?'

Pete grinned, looking from one to the other, unperturbed.
'Ah, yep, but you're obviously…otherwise engaged so it can
wait.'

'Excellent,' Max said, clamping a hand on Pete's shoulder.

'No, no,' Ali said, standing. 'You guys hang out for a bit.
I'll make myself scarce.'

Max opened his mouth to protest but Ali was already
picking up dishes off the table and heading into the kitchen.
He turned to Pete with exasperation and noticed his friend
checking out Ali's very delectable sway.

He clenched his teeth. 'Don't even think about it.'

Pete was taken aback by the sinister tone in his friend's
voice. Max was using his court voice. And frankly it had
always scared the bejeebers out of him.

Ali must mean something.

Which was just as well given the news he had to impart.

'So…you and Ali,' Pete said as Ali stepped into the apartment and out of earshot.

'What do you want?' Max demanded.

'Oh, come on, Maxy, throw me a bone. What's she like?'

Max thought back to their sexual feast over the last couple of days with absolutely no intention of sharing any of it.

'She's hell on my training schedule,' he dismissed with
a cryptic smile. 'Now…What. Do. You. Want?'

Pete hesitated. 'I found something out this morning that
I think you're not going to like. So I wanted you to hear it
from me. I think you may need to sit down.'

Ali hadn't planned on eavesdropping. But the window
near the sink faced the deck and it was already open, the
men's voices carrying easily on the light morning breeze
as they sat at the table.

'Okay. I'm sitting. Now what?'

Pete fished his mobile out of his pocket. 'I was online this morning. Tori posted a status update.'

Max frowned. He didn't care about social media. Or Tori. 'I thought Tori unfriended you?'

Pete shook his head. 'No. Just you.'

Max sighed. 'What is it?'

Pete paused for a moment to decide if there was some way to soften the blow. He handed the phone over to Max, open on Tori's social network page. 'She's pregnant.'

Max stared at the gadget in his hands, not quite comprehending for a moment even after he read the gushing update.

It's official—I'm pregnant. It's amazing how it all falls into place when you meet the right man. I haven't been this happy in a very long time. I love you baby. Both of you.

'You okay?' Pete asked.

Max clenched his jaw. Tori was pregnant. Tori, who didn't want babies, was pregnant.

And apparently ecstatic about it.

He remembered back to their one and only pregnancy scare. How angry she'd been, how indignant. How certain she'd been that she didn't want the potential new life that might have been growing inside her.

Her threats to have an abortion.

His hand tightened on the phone as he glanced at Pete without saying a word.

Ali didn't dare breathe as she stood at the sink. Max's rigid profile sucked the marrow from her bones.

He *was* still in love with his wife.

It was as plain as the nose on her face.

But that wasn't the worst of it. The truly horrible thing was she loved him. She'd actually fallen for him.

And...*he was still in love with his wife.*

Pete watched as his friend's knuckles whitened around his expensive new phone and wondered for a moment if Max was going to shatter the screen.

'She was a bitch, Max. She didn't deserve you.'

'She wasn't, Pete,' Max said, his voice controlled as he handed back the phone.

Max knew that he'd spent a good chunk of the last eighteen months hating Tori—for the affair, for leaving, for denying him a shot at being a father. But he also knew she'd essentially been a good person. He wouldn't have fallen for her if she hadn't been. The truth was, they hadn't wanted the same things and he'd always known it deep down inside.

'She just...didn't want *my* babies.'

Ali felt as if she'd taken a hammer blow to the middle of her chest at the lament in Max's words. She'd expected anger. She remembered the pain of Tom's betrayal—how deep it had cut—and Max had been betrayed doubly.

Instead she detected regret and loneliness and resignation.

And her heart broke. For him. And for her. She'd already loved one man who had ditched her for another; she wasn't stupid enough to make that mistake again.

She had to get out of here!

Pete was heading back out of the door when he ran into a fully dressed Ali searching the lounge room for her handbag she vaguely remembered discarding somewhere between the door and the bedroom.

'You're leaving?' he said, taking in her change of clothes.

Ali looked down at the outfit she'd worn into court on Friday morning and tried not to look guilty. 'Yes.'

'You heard?'

Ali nodded. 'Yes.'

'Please don't. He's going to need you today. Can you be here for him?'

Ali shut her eyes to block out the painful truth. *Even Pete thought he was still in love with Tori.* Pete, his best friend, the man who knew Max probably better than anyone else.

She nodded. 'Sure.'

'Promise?'

Ali nodded.

Even though she knew it was a promise she had no intention of keeping. There was absolutely no way she could stay a second longer than was necessary. Her heart had had enough trampling this past year, she needed to guard it as best she could from any further damage. If she walked away now and never looked back maybe it was just possible.

A quick goodbye and she was out of here.

Max was still on the deck when Ali joined him a few minutes later. He was staring out over the river, a frown furrowing his forehead. He didn't even seem to notice the tap of her heels against the wooden decking that echoed loudly into the tranquil morning air.

'Max?'

Max dragged his gaze away from the river and his turbulent thoughts. Ali stood fully dressed before him in that skirt, her butterscotch curls brushing the see-through blouse, and a sudden fierce welling of desire crashed like a tsunami through his system.

It was totally unexpected in his current state of turmoil. And utterly welcome.

Twenty minutes ago he'd resented Pete for making him examine what the hell he and Ali were doing.

Now it was clear.

Ali was who he wanted. Ali was who mattered.

He stood abruptly, the scraping of his chair ringing across the river. He took three paces towards her and hauled her into his arms, swooping his head, crushing his mouth to hers.

Her instant response was gratifying and he groaned as he grabbed both her butt cheeks and jammed her up against his hard raging body. He pulled at her blouse, unzipped her skirt.

Ali held onto him for dear life as her head spun and her insides turned to liquid.

'Max,' she panted, pulling away, her eyes shutting as his mouth moved to devour her neck. She was pretty sure Pete hadn't meant to be there for Max like this. 'Do you want to talk about this?'

Max ran his tongue over her ear lobe. He didn't want to talk. He just wanted to feel. To bury himself in her. Get lost in her essence. Just be with her. He wished he didn't want it so much. But he did. 'No.'

Ali gripped his biceps as his hot, desperate kisses eroded her determination to flee. She reached for a modicum of common sense in a rapidly diminishing world. 'I know what it's like, Max. To want a baby. To have that taken from you.'

'No talking,' he muttered against her neck as he yanked a bra cup aside and claimed her breast with his palm.

A surge of lust pounded through Ali's veins as his thumb stroked her nipple and she cried out. It washed through her brain crippling everything but the imperative to kiss back.

Long, deep, wet and hard.

Open-mouthed.

As good as she was getting. Better.

Obliterating everything. Making her forget. About Tori and the baby. About her promise to Pete. About her deep-and-getting-deeper-every-second love for him.

About practically fornicating in full public view on his deck.

And then he was kissing her again and lifting her up and carrying her, not breaking their lip lock or his stride as he blindly navigated the inside of the apartment. Suddenly she was horizontal on his bed, sucking in much-needed air as she watched him strip off underwear that was barely concealing him.

She should stop him, have more pride. Was it even her he was making love to? But she wanted him too fiercely, was powerless to resist the thrum in her blood and the love in her heart.

Powerless to deny him this outlet.

And too selfish not to take whatever of himself was on offer.

Because after today, she'd only have the memories.

With no underwear and her skirt ruched up around her hips she was totally bare to his fiery gaze.

She spread her legs in silent invitation.

Max grabbed a condom from the very well used box and was sliding into her moist heat within seconds. He groaned into her neck and let the wild impulsive rhythm playing in his head take control.

Ali, her clothes still askew, slipped out of the bed half an hour later. Max had drifted to sleep almost immediately and she'd been content to cuddle up close and listen to his breath, mentally cataloguing every husky nuance.

But it was time to go. She'd given up being a victim in court on Friday and she wouldn't leave herself open to it again.

She was a survivor. She could do it.

Her breath caught on a sob as a sudden rush of loss stabbed like a hot knife between her ribs.

Could she? Could she really?

How much loss could a human being take? How much more could she bear? Max. Nathaniel Cullen. Tom. Her baby.

The knife twisted viciously. God, she'd been so caught up in winning and being with Max she'd forgotten she'd promised herself she'd grieve her baby's passing after the case.

Her tiny, defenceless baby. The small but potent life force that she'd known for only a few short weeks.

The pain and the anguish of that horrible day drove the knife a little deeper and Ali stifled a sob. She pressed her palm against her belly, where her baby had grown. It felt so empty and the ache inside that had been there for a year intensified.

She looked down at a sleeping Max and her vision blurred. He'd lost a baby too. It might not have been conceived yet but, if his devastated face earlier was any indication, he'd wanted a baby as badly as she had.

Her heart felt as if it were cracking wide open. How much loss could it stand? First her baby and now the man she'd foolishly fallen in love with.

The man she loved, loved another.

Ali felt herself crumpling from the inside. She had to get out of here. She whirled away, strode out of his door and didn't look back.

CHAPTER ELEVEN

A WEEK passed, two, since Max had woken to an empty bed and a note on his kitchen bench. Ali had thanked him for the weekend and then left him in no doubt that it was all it was ever going to be. They were both still too raw from their previous relationships to be anything more than transient distractions, she'd written. And she had a life to get back on track. She didn't need any diversions while she was doing it.

Which was fine. Perfectly fine.

He just hadn't expected to miss her this much.

In the middle of a court case he'd suddenly realise he was thinking about her instead of listening to the proceedings. Or at home each night he realised he was waiting for the phone to ring. Itching to pick it up himself, hear her voice as she rattled off her next hare-brained career scheme.

And then there was the bedroom. Vanilla permeated his sheets and haunted his macaroon dreams. His towels carried the scent, even his shower.

She was everywhere and he missed her.

It wasn't the same as the way he'd missed Tori, either. In fact he'd been too angry to miss her and, if he was being honest, somewhere deep down there had been a small sense of relief.

But all there was now was a constant heavy feeling inside his chest.

He kept hoping an excuse would come up to ring her or see her. Anything…

And then in the third week his prayers were answered and he wished like hell he could take them back.

Notification of the lodgment of an appeal against the findings in the wrongful death suit against Brisbane Memorial Hospital and Dr Aleisha Gregory landed in his in-tray.

His heart sank as he read the documentation.

Anything but this.

It had always been a possibility, they'd known that, but he hadn't thought the Cullens would go through with it.

He stared at the papers for hours wishing it weren't his way back to Ali. But she had to be told.

And he didn't want it to come from anyone else.

Max jogged along the darkened Southbank pathway later that night on his way to the River Breeze café. At almost ten on a Tuesday night the place was nearly deserted as restaurants and outdoor eateries wound up their trade.

He didn't even know what he was doing here. He hadn't planned on telling her tonight at all. But the longer he sat with the news alone in his apartment, the more it felt like a ticking bomb.

In the end, he couldn't stand keeping it to himself any longer. He rang her home number and got no answer. He rang the River Breeze and got Kat who—thankfully—informed him that Ali was working until close. He'd left his apartment immediately, deciding an extra run would be good for his training schedule.

Thirty minutes later he was almost there and he slowed his pace as the lights of the River Breeze came into view. Unfortunately, despite grappling with the words all the way here, he wasn't any closer to finding the right ones.

Some lawyer he was if he couldn't even articulate a very simple concept without tying himself in a knot.

He paused outside, stretching out his legs on the bottom of four steps that led into the café, catching his breath, wanting to go in, desperate to see her and yet not under these circumstances.

Not wanting to be the portent of doom.

He almost changed his mind. Turned around and ran all the way back home. He could get Helen to ring her tomorrow during business hours, set up an appointment. But then the glass doors opened and he caught a glimpse of her and her butterscotch curls bouncing by and he knew he couldn't put it off any longer.

Ali was wiping down a table when the hairs on the back of her neck prickled and she turned to identify the cause even though, deep inside somewhere, she already knew.

He stood before her in his jogging gear looking warm and male and vital and her gaze devoured him. He looked as he had that morning she'd persuaded him to use her for his morning workout and it had been two weeks since she'd kissed him and every cell in her body was screaming.

'Max,' she said, hating the breathiness of her voice.

'Hi.'

It was another moment or two before Ali realised they were standing like statues staring at each other. His gaze felt like a white-hot laser as it grazed her breasts and her thighs and her belly and her body bloomed with heat.

Kat bustled by and Ali gained some cerebral function. 'Would you like a table?' she asked.

Max shook his head. She was all business in her tight black T-shirt, black trousers and long maroon apron emblazoned with a River Breeze logo. 'I'd like to talk to you.'

Ali felt her silly heart leap in her chest before she ruthlessly crushed it. The man was still in love with his ex-wife—what else was there to talk about?

'I'm busy,' she said stiffly because she couldn't bear to be this near to him and yet feel so far away.

Max looked around at the half-full café seemingly oblivious to their exchange. He shrugged. 'I can wait.'

Ali felt suddenly churlish as he stood there calmly looking at her. She'd meant what she'd said in her note—why didn't he just let her get on with it?

'Suit yourself,' she said and left him standing as she returned to the kitchen. To her job. Her very simple, non-stress, non-critical job.

Over the next half-hour Max sat and watched Ali as she flitted between tables. She laughed and joked, chatted, cleared away, took orders and generally seemed to fulfil the role of waitress very efficiently. But when he watched her examine a customer's leg and then go away and come back with some kind of cream in a tube he couldn't help but roll his eyes.

It was plain to all but her, apparently, that she had a true calling and being a waitress was never going to be a fulfilling career choice.

Finally, with all but two tables empty, she approached him with a couple of steaming coffee cups in hand. She plonked one in front of him and took the seat opposite. The aroma of Arabica beans enveloped him and Max watched as she stirred sugar into her coffee, waiting for her to say something.

Ali placed the spoon on the saucer and finally lifted her gaze to his. 'What do you want, Max?'

Max opened his mouth to tell her, to say *they're appealing,* but he shied away from the directness of it all. His gaze searched her face. She seemed weary and he wondered if she was getting as little sleep as him.

'I've missed you,' he murmured.

Ali's pulse kicked up a notch, her heart threatening to fly at the encouraging comment, but her head remained stubbornly level. 'Is that what you came to tell me?'

He paused. No, it wasn't, but it didn't make it any less true. 'I—'

A sudden commotion—a plate smashing, a woman crying out—interrupted what he'd been about to say and both he and Ali turned to identify the source of the intrusion. A group of people were huddled around a man on the ground who appeared to be having a seizure.

'Ali!' Kat called as she rushed from behind the cash register towards the table of uni students who'd been celebrating a birthday.

But Ali was already on her feet, moving towards the emergency, Max hot on her heels.

'What's happening?' a woman wailed.

'He'll swallow his tongue—here, put this spoon in his mouth,' someone else said.

'It's okay,' Ali said, her voice permeating the panic that had erupted as people at the table all reacted at once. 'Step aside,' she urged, a natural authority in her voice as she removed the spoon from the offending hand and pushed her way into the huddle. 'I'm a doctor.'

She got down on the floor beside the flailing young man and turned his head to the side while lifting his jaw a little to prevent his tongue from blocking his airway.

'Max, can you time the duration of the fit, please?' she asked. 'Kat, get my bag.' She smiled at the nearest girl, who was crying. 'It's okay—he's having a seizure but it shouldn't last too long. Clear some space for him so he doesn't hurt himself. Does he have epilepsy?' she asked.

There was a collective no. 'He did play football earlier

today and got crunched pretty bad in a tackle,' one of the party admitted. 'He was out of it for a few seconds.'

Ali kept her smile firmly in place despite the alarming news. 'Max, call an ambulance please.'

Max flipped out his phone and dialled. By the time he got through to triple zero the seizure had stopped and Ali was putting the young man into the recovery position. She calmly soothed everyone's frazzled nerves and explained that Josh, as he was called, would be very sleepy for a while as she shone a penlight she'd extracted from her bag into Josh's eyes.

Fortunately it was only minutes before the sound of a siren rent the air and two paramedics arrived on the scene. Max watched Ali as she worked in tandem with the paramedics, inserting a drip and getting a drowsy Josh onto the gurney while rattling off a lot of medical jargon.

It was now, right in this moment, watching her work methodically and efficiently, utterly engaged with the situation, that he finally got how devastating the Cullen case must have been to her.

How devastating the news of an appeal would be.

Working with medico-legal cases had blinded him to the emotional impact on the individuals working at the coalface. For him it was simple—in this big, bad, litigious world, doctors got sued. It was just the way it was now. And should be something every doctor prepared for.

But if Ali gave her all to every patient as she was right now, to Josh, a complete stranger—and watching her, how could he believe anything else?—then Nathaniel Cullen's death would have been a personal tragedy to her too.

Dr Aleisha Gregory was one hell of a doctor and he finally understood how much it must have damaged her to have had it snatched away.

How scary it would be to return after being ripped to shreds.

How gutting the appeal was going to be.

The ambulance departed in a screaming hurry fifteen minutes later and Ali watched from the bottom step of the café entrance as the red strobing became more distant. She rubbed at her arms as the adrenaline that had kept her sharp and focused dissipated, leaving her cold and shaky.

Still she hadn't felt this alive, this engaged, this…right… in a long time.

Max watched her from the café's open glass doors staring at the disappearing ambulance. After a moment he joined her, coming to a halt on the step behind. He placed his hands on her shoulders, then tentatively took over the rubbing action.

He expected her to protest, but when her hands fell to her sides he became bolder, rubbing briskly. They didn't say anything for a while, just watched the diminishing lights.

'Will he be okay?' Max asked when the lights finally faded.

She shrugged. 'Depends…if it's just concussion, sure, if it's something more serious… It's too hard to tell without looking at CT scans.'

Max applied gentle pressure to her arms and turned her around until he was looking down into her face. 'Are you okay?'

Ali felt a rush of love at his gentle enquiry. It bloomed in her chest like a mushroom cloud. 'Sure,' she said, swallowing hard against the block of emotion threatening to clog her throat.

As okay as she was ever going to be.

Max felt the raw, husky timbre of her voice reach right inside him. He pushed back that unruly curl flopping in her eye, lightly brushing her forehead as he went. It was gratifying to see her sway slightly towards him as she shut her eyes.

'You were awesome tonight,' he murmured.

Ali's eyes fluttered open. 'I did what anyone would have done,' she dismissed.

Max shook his head. 'No, Ali. You did what a doctor would do.'

Ali knew he was right. Knew that she was a doctor right down to her DNA. Knew that nothing she ever did would beat saving people's lives.

And it scared her witless.

To her complete and utter horror, she burst into tears.

'Hey, hey.' Max frowned as Ali's face crumpled and a primal mewing sob escaped her mouth like an injured kitten. He pulled her against him, rocking and crooning, dropping kisses on her hair as she cried as if the end of the world were nigh.

Love, pure and simple, rose up in his chest and rippled through every cell in his body and he held her tighter as the thought terrified and tantalised in equal measure.

He wasn't ready for something like this. God alone knew he didn't need it. His heart was still battered from his divorce and he wanted to protect it from the slings and arrows of another love.

But somehow, she made it feel whole again.

The fact was undisputable—he loved Dr Aleisha Gregory. *With everything he had.*

'She okay?' Kat asked, interrupting Max's staggering revelation.

Max startled. *He wasn't sure about Ali but he knew he was far from okay!*

Ali pulled away from his chest with great reluctance. 'Sorry,' she murmured, avoiding his gaze as she patted at her damp cheeks. 'I'm fine.'

'Why don't you both come inside?' Kat suggested. 'You look like you need a good stiff drink.'

Ali would have liked nothing more. But even after a few minutes back in Max's arms her heart was already bleeding—she didn't want to sit opposite him and make small talk when all she'd want to do was drag him into the River Breeze storeroom and have her way with him.

She just had to get away from him.

'No.' She shook her head. 'I'm going to go home to bed if the boss will allow it. I forgot how exhausting an emergency can be.'

And going home was much safer than drinking under the influence of her sex-starved libido.

Max watched the bounce of her butterscotch curls and wished he could go home with her, but the mention of the emergency brought his reason for being here back into sharp focus. In all the excitement of the last half an hour, and particularly the last few minutes, he'd forgotten it entirely.

And he doubted very much she was going to welcome him into her bed after that particular piece of news.

But it still had to be done.

'Could I bum a lift back to my apartment?'

Ali shot him an alarmed look. *For crying out loud, why didn't he just leave her to suffer this one-sided love alone?*

'Don't you need the exercise?' she enquired stiffly.

The question seemed to require that she check him out for proof, which she did. But all she found was a vest top that sat snug against a broad chest and a flat male belly and solid masculine quads outlined to perfection in thigh-hugging skins.

None of them appeared to require exercise.

She dragged her gaze back to his face to find one eyebrow quirked at her.

Max smiled, encouraged by her interest. 'No.'

Ali fought a surge of desire at his staggering self-assurance and a wicked whisper urging her to push him into the dark clump of trees she could see in the background and kiss that smug smile right off his face.

Why? Why did she fall for emotionally unavailable men?

'Fine,' she huffed.

It was impossible to deny the man who had fought for her innocence such a simple request. But she didn't have to like it.

'Shall we go?' he asked as she continued to glare at him.

His lazy smile and deep voice swept over her like the long low note of a saxophone and went straight to her pelvic floor. 'Fine,' she muttered again.

Max waited until they'd been driving for a few minutes before he brought up the incident at the River Breeze again. He'd run through the whole situation in detail and was still blown away by her skill.

It was that or think about the other thing that had blown him away tonight and he couldn't do that with her sitting beside him as if she were made from concrete.

'It felt good, didn't it?' he said into the silence. 'Josh?'

Ali flinched internally at his insight and contemplated lying. The last thing she wanted to do was talk about her future with the one man who wasn't going to be part of it—it just hurt too damn much. But the glow from helping out with Josh still warmed her.

She nodded. 'I felt…normal again.' She lifted a hand off the steering wheel and pressed it to her chest as her heart beat a little faster at the memory of it all. 'Like a doctor again. I was nervous but…I knew…I just knew it was me.'

Max smiled at her profile. 'You never stopped being a doctor, Ali.'

She shook her head. 'I did in my heart.'

'No, you didn't. Your head maybe, but not your heart. Every day you were dishing out some piece of medical advice or other. A Band-Aid here, a mole check there. You've lived and breathed it, Ali. It's what you are. And you're too good at it to throw it all in and become a waitress or whatever the hell else takes your fancy for twenty-four hours.'

Ali felt tears at the backs of her eyes. She knew he was right. 'I know,' she whispered.

Max lifted a hand to her shoulder. 'Thank goodness,' he murmured.

She gave him a watery smile as she pulled up in front of his apartment complex and turned the ignition off. The glow from her foray back into medicine had dissipated with the knowledge that she had to go back and face her demons but another glow had taken over.

A very unwelcome one at that.

His hand on her shoulder was warm and heavy and causing havoc everywhere. His heady male scent filled her little car and she had to grip the steering wheel hard to stop her doing something crazy like leaning over and gnawing on his bare bicep.

It would be easy if it were just sexual attraction. But she needed more. She needed him to love her with the same soul-deep, wrenching agony she loved him. She needed his all.

Max, who had fought the urge to touch her, to drop his hand on her knee, run it up the length of her thigh, for the entire ten-minute car journey broke the growing silence. 'I've missed you, Ali.'

Ali shut her eyes. 'Don't.'

'Come up with me,' he murmured.

Ali shook her head against the illicit image of them making love one more time. 'No.'

'I know you said in your note that you think we were

just distractions for each other but the truth is…I really like you, Ali.'

It was a complete understatement and an outright lie but he sensed she was poised to flee and he didn't want to frighten her away with the other L word.

Why would she believe him? She'd been hurt and scarred and was trying to get her life back on track. It was too much to dump on her tonight, especially following the huge revelation that medicine was her calling.

He needed to go slow with her. Woo her. Give her the time and space and support she needed. And hope that out of the attraction she felt for him, something stronger would grow.

Ali gripped the steering wheel tighter. She wanted to feel his mouth against hers again. Feel his weight on her, his hardness buried inside her. But she had her pride. She wouldn't accept crumbs from him.

Not when some other woman was getting the cake.

Max lifted his hand slowly and pushed a floppy curl out of her eye. He wanted to be able to erase the frown from her forehead. Love her with his body if that was all she allowed.

'Ali,' he whispered. He cupped her cheek and stroked the pad of his thumb along her cheekbone. 'Please, Ali.'

Sensing that she wanted it as much as he did, he moved in towards her, no longer able to resist the heady female smell of her that teased his nostrils and stoked his libido. He nuzzled her neck, inhaling deeply, dizzy with her scent. He licked up her neck, stroked his tongue over the lobe of her ear.

'I want to kiss you, Ali,' he murmured. 'I want to kiss you all night. Everywhere.'

Ali, hands still gripping the steering wheel, shut her eyes

and her mind to his serpent-like treachery. She couldn't succumb. If she did, it was a slippery slope to oblivion.

'Let me love you, Ali.'

CHAPTER TWELVE

ALI whimpered at his choice of words. Not fair, not fair, she wanted to cry as all her resistance melted to liquid.

Yes, she knew he didn't mean *love*. But he was just too near, too irresistible, too damn Max.

Max heard the noise at the back of her throat and felt Ali tense. He cursed the slip of his tongue but it had seemed the most natural thing in the world to say.

For a second, he thought he'd lost her.

But then her hands dropped from the wheel and she turned her head and her lips were seeking his and then they were on him and she was opening to him, leaning closer, clutching at his shirt, moaning as his tongue duelled with hers.

The kiss ignited and in seconds they were pawing at each other like horny teenagers. The temperature rose a degree or two as their noisy ragged breathing fogged up the windows.

Max pulled away as Ali's fingers stroked him through his shorts. He grabbed her hand, stopping the torture, but pressing it close, his head spinning from the delicious friction. 'My apartment,' he gasped. 'Now.'

Ali, her brain jumbled, her resistance melted, didn't even think of denying him. Of denying herself. She'd missed him. Missed this. She groped blindly for the door handle and stumbled out of the car.

Max was beside her, reaching for her hand, then hurrying her into the building. The lift was waiting for them and he dragged her in, not even waiting for the doors to close before he started kissing her again.

Ali hung on as he hiked her up the wall, balancing her on the cold metal hand rail. She locked her legs around his waist as the lift zoomed to the top floor and his kisses completely shorted out any rational thoughts. He kissed down her neck as his hands pushed under her T-shirt and boldly sought her breasts.

The lift arrived just as he freed one to his gaze and sucked hard on the puckered nipple. Ali threw back her head and cried out.

Then he was yanking her shirt down and lifting her off the hand rail and pulling her along behind him until they were at his door and then inside his door and then inside his bedroom.

'Take your clothes off,' he demanded, kissing her hard and deep as he pulled at his own.

His husky command and soul-drugging kiss made her legs go weak and she fumbled ineffectually with them. All that mattered was his mouth and the delicious havoc it was creating. Everything else was paralysed.

When Max finished with his clothes he worked on hers until she was finally naked, finally exposed to his greedy eyes, his greedy hands, his greedy mouth.

He pushed her back on his bed and watched as everything bounced and shifted just the way he liked it. 'God, I've missed you,' he whispered.

And then Ali reached for him and there were no more words, no more thoughts. Just moans and licks and gasps and whimpers. Delicious sensations sprinkling down on them like fairy dust. Holding on tight as their bodies moved to a rhythm uniquely theirs.

Building and building and building until they could no longer stay earthbound but flew up into the cosmos and floated amongst the stars.

Ali held onto Max, onto the stars, as long as she could. Even when he went to move off her she tightened her arms around him. 'No,' she protested. 'Not yet.'

She didn't want to ever let go. She wanted to imprint this moment on her brain for ever. Remember his weight and the warmth of his breath on her neck and the delicious sensation of him still being inside her.

Max held on tight trying to absorb her into his cells. He wanted to remember this moment too. Remember how his love was so overwhelming it felt as if it were spilling out of his pores, being released on his breath.

He bit down hard on the desire to tell her. It was too soon. She wasn't ready to hear it.

She shifted under him and he eased off, this time ignoring her protests. 'Shh,' he murmured, scooping her close, his hand automatically spearing into her hair, then running down the length of her spine and back up to her hair again.

Ali sighed as her orgasm and Max's magic touch lulled her doubts into oblivion. Her eyelids fluttered closed. And it was in this drowsy state her subconscious threw up a nagging question.

She opened her eyes. 'Why were you there, tonight?' she murmured. 'At the River Breeze? You said you wanted to talk to me?'

Max's hand stilled on her shoulder blade for a moment before continuing its lazy path.

'Yes,' he murmured.

Ali felt him tense a little and held her breath as her own

lethargy dissipated in response. What had he wanted to talk to her about? Something personal maybe? Her silly heart tapped crazily in her chest.

She released her breath on a husky note. 'Oh?' she said, keeping her voice light. She shivered as his fingers stroked like feathers over her skin.

Max waited a few moments before he spoke. 'I got notice today from Palmerston and McGarrick.'

Ali frowned. Why was that name familiar? 'Who?'

Max kept stroking, wishing it were going to be enough to stop Ali from flipping out. 'The Cullens' lawyers. They've lodged an appeal.'

It took a moment for the words to register in Ali's brain, sluggish from Max's petting. Then they roared in her head like a trombone. She half sat up, using his chest as leverage. Her heart boomed in her ears. 'Seriously?'

Max nodded. 'An appeal was always on the cards if we won,' he said as he brushed her curls back off her shoulder.

Ali flinched at his touch as she stared down at him. *How could he be so calm?*

Because he was a man and the last time she'd depended on a man for emotional support when she'd needed it most, he'd walked out of her life and hadn't looked back. How could she have been so foolish to have expected Max to be any different?

She should have learned a year ago that she could only depend on herself. That she had to deal with these things on her own.

The thought was so depressing an uncharacteristic rage welled in her chest. *This wasn't fair—it just wasn't fair.* She'd been put through the wringer and every time she was vindicated another hearing, another court case reared its ugly head.

She swung her legs over the side of the bed and buried

her face in her hands. 'This is never going to end, is it?' she despaired.

Max rolled up on his elbow, the defeated line of her back, the slump to her shoulders punching him hard in the gut. 'It won't be granted, Ali. It's going to be thrown out of court before it even gets that far.'

She turned her head to face him. 'How do you know?' she demanded.

He stroked a hand down her back. 'They have no grounds.'

Ali shrugged him away. 'That doesn't seem to have stopped them so far,' she shot back.

She looked back at the floor. Her undies and shirt were nearby and she reached for them. She stood, keeping her back to him, and stepped into her pants, then pulled her T-shirt down over her head.

Max watched her with dismay, ignoring the dictates of his body, which were urging him to drag her back down to the bed and pull her close. She'd just had her world yanked out from under her again. It was etched all over her face. Sex wasn't the answer.

'The appeal process is different, Ali. They don't have the grounds.'

Ali shook her head as she turned to face him. 'How do you know?' she demanded.

'It's my job, Ali. Just like you knew exactly what that boy needed tonight, how to help him, I know stuff to do with the law. You're a brilliant doctor. I'm a brilliant lawyer. Trust me.'

Except she was never going to get the chance to be a brilliant doctor, was she? Tears welled in her eyes and she dashed them away. This was all Max's fault. For telling her she was awesome, for insisting she shouldn't give up on medicine, for encouraging her to follow her calling, for shooting down every career choice she'd floated.

She'd bought into his fantasy only to have it crumble before she even got a chance to live it.

She'd worked on Josh tonight and had finally felt alive again. Finally known that medicine was in her marrow. Only to have it snatched away once more.

Max couldn't bear the sadness on her face. 'It won't get up,' he murmured.

She searched his face. 'What if it does?'

'It won't.'

Ali shook her head. She couldn't stay here, she had to get out. All she wanted was to have him hold her and tell her that he loved her. She couldn't bear that he didn't. Not now, not in her hour of need.

It was just like Tom all over again. She'd deal with the sickening prospect of the appeal by herself. At least she wouldn't feel let down. Betrayed.

And if she stayed, she might not be responsible for what she blurted out. She might even beg him to love her.

'I have to go.'

Max frowned. 'What?' He reached out a hand to her. 'Don't go. Not like this.'

Ali shrank from it. She couldn't bear for him to touch her, not without love. 'I'm fine,' she said tersely as the walls of her world crashed around her.

'Ali...don't. Let me help you.'

And that was when Ali lost it. He couldn't help her. In fact he'd just made things worse. So very much worse. He'd made her fall in love with him and made her want to be a doctor again.

She placed her hands on her hips and glared down at him. 'Help me? Help me?' she snorted. 'All you've done is made things worse,' she yelled.

She marched around his bed then, kicking aside discarded clothes looking for her bra and trousers.

Max sat up watching her stalk around the room, her curls bouncing, magnificent in her rage. She couldn't leave. Not like this. Not so angry.

Not at all if he had his way.

'It's going to be okay, Ali,' he said gently as she bent over to retrieve her trousers. She was angry and irrational—if he could just make her see it was going to be okay...

Ali's blood pressure hit the roof as she righted herself. She saw red with his Pollyanna views and his 'don't frighten the horses' voice.

'It's not going to be okay,' she snapped. 'It's never going to be okay again.'

Everything from the last year, all the upheaval and disappointments and losses—her baby, her poor darling baby—welled up in her at once. A lump of what felt like molten rock seemed lodged in under her ribcage and was growing larger with each breath.

'There are two things at the very beginning I told you I wasn't going to do,' she yelled, shaking her trousers at him. 'Get back into medicine and fall for another man. And you've made me break both those.'

Ali watched as Max's grey eyes widened. *Crap!* Now she'd completely humiliated herself. She rubbed at her chest. It was tight, impossibly tight; she could barely breathe.

Max stilled. 'What did you say?'

A tear escaped and she couldn't even be bothered to dash it away. She might as well make the humiliation complete.

'And then,' she yelled, ignoring him, 'when you get me excited about medicine again and you make me fall in love with you, you snatch them both back!'

Max frowned. *She loved him?* Did she just say she loved him? 'What?' He shook his head. 'How?'

'By telling me about the appeal,' she cried. 'And by still being in love with your wife.'

Max blinked. *What the—?* He raised himself to his haunches and held out his hand in a stopping motion. 'What on earth are you talking about?'

Ali could feel the hot tears flowing out of her eyes thick and fast now as she attempted to step into her trousers. 'I saw you,' she accused as she missed the leg hole and made a second attempt. 'With Pete on the deck that morning. Remember? I could hear everything from the sink. About Tori. The baby.'

Her own womb contracted at the thought. She wanted a baby, damn it. She wanted it with a ferocity that almost winded her.

She wanted Max's baby.

She sucked in a shaky breath. 'I saw how devastated you were.' Both legs were in now and she yanked the trousers up to her waist. 'I heard it in your voice. Only a man who's still in love with a woman would be so gutted.'

Max shook his head. 'You're wrong.'

'Am I?' she demanded, dashing away the tears. 'Are you sure it wasn't really her you were making love to after Pete left while you were having sex with me?'

Ali glared at him. She wanted to hurt him as much as she was hurting. She yanked her zipper up with a vicious tug.

The noise was as loud as a slap in the silence and Max reared back as if it had been. Her ugly suggestion made him want to cross the floor and shake her.

'I am not still in love with my *ex*-wife.'

Max's voice dropped to a low growl and Ali felt the hairs on the back of her neck rise. But she was damned if she was going to back down. Everything was a mess and it felt good to have someone else to blame for a change instead of herself.

'Well, you could have fooled me,' she snapped.

Max threw back the sheet and stepped out of bed. He picked up his underwear off the floor and put it on. His heart was pounding. *She loved him.* She'd said she loved him. It was his turn to be honest.

To hell with waiting. To hell with her not being ready.

He shoved his hands on his hips and glared at her. 'I'm in love with you.'

It was Ali's turn to rear back. She gasped. Her silly, silly heart leapt at his words. But her brain was in control. Her heart had got her into too much trouble in the past.

'No.' She shook her head wildly. She wouldn't open up her heart again. She wouldn't be fooled. 'I saw it—I saw your face. You're still in love with Tori.'

Max stood his ground. 'I was in shock, Ali. That's all. I was stunned…bewildered. But not because I still love her or have any lingering feelings for her—believe me, I fell out of love with Tori a long time ago. Because it was unexpected. Totally out of left-field. Because she'd so vehemently not wanted a baby. Finding out she was pregnant was a shock. And, yes, it hurt. But not my heart, Ali. It hurt my ego, my pride.'

Ali's heart lifted again. She so wanted to believe him. But she quashed it ruthlessly. 'So you're telling me if she waltzed back through that door, right now, wanting to try again, you wouldn't take her back?'

Max put his hand on his heart. 'That's right.'

'Even if she wanted to have babies with you?'

Max kept his hand firmly in place. 'That's right.'

'Even if she got on her knees and begged.'

Max nodded his head. 'I wish her well. I hope she's very happy. But the only woman I'm interested in having babies with is you.'

Ali's breath caught in her throat. The sincerity blazing

in his steady grey eyes was humbling. 'You want babies with me?'

Ali heard her voice crack a little as another hot tear welled up and spilled down her cheek. The deep empty place inside her filled up with a wonderful warm glow.

Max dropped his hand and took a step towards her. 'In time, sure. Lots of babies. Lots and lots.'

She halted him with a wave of her hand. A part of her wanted to leap in his arms, to rejoice in this startling turn of events. To believe him. But the saner part, the part that had taken too many knocks this past year, that had been unbearably hurt, couldn't believe that something was going right for once.

The thought of opening up her heart again was utterly terrifying. 'I don't understand,' she said suspiciously. 'When did this big revelation occur?'

Max looked at his watch. 'About six hours ago.'

Tonight? He'd only just realised tonight. Ali took a step back. 'That was rather convenient,' she said, her voice full of starch.

Max pushed a hand through his hair. She was scared, he understood that. Frankly he was pretty damn terrified himself. He knew how much it took when you'd already been hurt to put yourself out there and love someone else again. But love didn't let you choose.

He had to convince her. Because as terrifying as it was to love her, it was more terrifying not to.

'I was watching you with that boy and you were so incredible, so...amazing and then you burst into tears and I was holding you and I knew, I just suddenly knew that you were the most precious thing in the whole world to me. It was truly one of those biblical kind of things.'

Ali smiled for the first time since she'd leapt out of bed. Here they were in a state of undress yelling at each other after having just had hot sweaty sex and he was going all biblical.

'Biblical huh?'

Max smiled too. 'I saw the light.' He took a step towards her. 'Although in retrospect I think it was probably that first night. When you said fish were cute. I think I started falling right then and there.'

Ali grinned. It seemed like a hundred years ago now.

Max moved closer again. When she didn't object he took another step. 'How about you?' he asked.

Ali's smile faded as she remembered her own particularly horrible revelation that awful day Pete had come to visit. 'In your apartment that morning. When Pete was talking to you about Tori and you looked so gutted. That's when I realised.'

'Ouch.' Max took another step closer. *Nearly there.* 'So that's why you left.'

Ali nodded. 'I couldn't bear being with you knowing that you loved someone else. I'd already been down that road, Max. I couldn't do it again.'

Max nodded as he slid his hand around her waist tentatively. When she didn't protest he tugged her gently to him.

'You won't have to, Ali. I'm your guy. Your one-woman guy.'

Ali placed her hands on his biceps, her body already melting against the heat of him. She looked into his grey eyes, still trying to keep a hold of the door to her heart. 'Isn't that what we all think when we first get together, Max? Isn't that what you thought with Tori? It's what I thought with Tom. How do we know that we're not doomed to failure?'

Max smiled as he fingered that persistent floppy curl out of her eye. 'I guess we don't, ultimately. That's what makes love such a leap of faith. But I've never felt this deeply about anyone, not even Tori. And I know I want to be with your for ever. So what do you say? I'm ready to jump. Jump with me?'

Ali felt her throat clog with emotion. He was right. Love was a leap of faith. The door crashed open and she let the love flow out.

'Oh, Max. I love you so much. I'll jump with you anywhere.'

Max stared into the eyes of the woman he loved and felt whole for the first time in a long time. He dropped a kiss on her forehead, her nose, her cheek and a long lingering one on her mouth.

When he drew back they were both breathing hard. 'Come back to bed,' he whispered. 'Let's make love.'

Ali smiled at him. 'Mmm, I like the sound of that.'

'Good,' he said, nuzzling her neck. 'Because I'm going to spend a lifetime making love to you.'

Ali laughed. 'In that case, I'm going to spend a lifetime letting you.'

* * * * *